PILGRIMS OF THE
UPPER WORLD

Cover design by Alex Dimeff. Cover images:
Credit: Astronomy: a star map of the night sky. Coloured engraving by G. Zu-
liani after Castellan, with lettering by G. Pitteri, 1777. Wellcome Collection.
Public Domain Mark. https://wellcomecollection.org/works/jy2kyhu6. Image
has been modified.

Credit: Ana Atqenit (Worms Mahzor) f.149 verso., 1272. https://opensiddur.
org/prayers/lunisolar/pilgrimage/shavuot/ana-atqenit-i-am-the-one-an-ara-
maic-piyyut-for-introducing-the-first-commandment-as-read-in-the-targum/.
Image has been modified.

Library of Congress Cataloging-in-Publication Data

Names: Findlay, Jamieson, author.
Title: Pilgrims of the upper world : a novel / Jamieson Findlay.
Description: First edition. | New Orleans, Louisiana : University of New
    Orleans Press, [2023]
Identifiers: LCCN 2023024422 (print) | LCCN 2023024423 (ebook) | ISBN
    9781608012510 (paperback ; acid-free paper) | ISBN 9781608012589
(ebook)

Subjects: LCGFT: Thrillers (Fiction) | Novels.
Classification: LCC PR9199.4.F5486 P55 2023 (print) | LCC
PR9199.4.F5486
    (ebook) | DDC 813/.6--dc23/eng/20230523
LC record available at https://lccn.loc.gov/2023024422
LC ebook record available at https://lccn.loc.gov/2023024423

Printed in the United States of America on FSC certified paper.
First edition.

University of New Orleans Press
2000 Lakeshore Drive
New Orleans, Lousiana 70148
unopress.org

PILGRIMS OF THE UPPER WORLD

a novel

JAMIESON FINDLAY

Permission is gratefully acknowledged for use of an excerpt from *Quantum Information Theory* by Mark M. Wilde (Cambridge University Press, Second Edition, © 2013 and 2017). Reproduced with permission of the Licensor through PLSclear.

To Scott, brother and friend

ONE

He was a tiny faded man of splintered grain and unsettled gaze, spare as a cornstalk in winter, with the narrow face of an elf and teeth done in shades of ash. His big ears made him look like a wizened child. He could have been Kafka if that storm-lashed spirit had lived to be a shrunken fifty, or sixty, or seventy, or whatever this guy was. First he asked if I was discreet and then if I was Jewish.

"No and no," I said warily. "Why do you ask?"

He wore a threadbare gray suit that was too large for him and an off-white shirt with an open, soiled collar. A battered leather briefcase sat in his lap.

"I must know," he said. "Who I make business with." He spoke laboriously, in squeezed-out shards, his breath smelling of tobacco.

"You read Aramaic," he said, studying me.

"I used to."

"Only few people know Aramaic language. In this world."

That accent . . . Eastern European, maybe? He hunched like a pale crow in front of my desk, glancing nervously out the big picture window. A life spent largely without sunlight, I judged.

"How can I help you?" I asked briskly.

Through the window, the street was just waking up to the April morning. The light of Geneva always seemed to be a photographer's light; today it was rain-washed and drinkably clear. Across the way, a woman—back straight, dark hair in a braid—rode by on a metallic blue European-style bike, the kind with the curving step-through frame and wire handlebar basket. I'd seen her before. Serious face, far-horizon gaze, glasses . . . and today she seemed to be carrying something in her basket. I wanted to go to the window, but now the little man placed his briefcase on the desk between us.

"I have a book," he said.

"Yes?"

"An Aramaic manuscript. I need help."

I'd come early to the store, hoping to get some work done before opening, but this man had been waiting for me, watching the storefront.

"You want to sell this book?" I said.

"I want to translate it."

"Can I see it?"

"I did not bring it." He kept his eyes on his briefcase. "I must be careful."

Every now and then, I had somebody come into my store to tell me they had made a valuable literary discovery. The first edition of Stanley's *How I Met Livingstone*. A manuscript version of Huysmans's *À rebours*. A lost book of erotica by Sir Richard Francis Burton. Occasionally they had a blurred photo of the supposed title page, though never the actual manuscript. But if I were willing to advance them a small sum. . . .

"I'm a book dealer, not a translator," I said.

"But you did translation. And you are a man. Of books." He leaned forward, prompting a wheeze. "I want a man of books. Who is discreet."

"And not Jewish."

"Yes."

"Tell me, why is that so important?"

"A Jew cannot be discreet. I know. I am a Jew." He shifted his chair closer. "I can pay. Some money."

"That'll make a nice change for me. However . . ."

I wanted to tell him to come back with the book, but he was so spare, so childlike in his oversized suit. I said, "Describe this book for me."

He seemed to be sizing me up again—me and my operation, if I could call it that. His eyes took in the old brass cash register, the paint-spattered rolling ladder that lay broken against the back wall, and the hand-lettered sign that said in three languages, "Please leave all bags at the cash desk." He picked up a mauve cash register key from my desk—I had a bunch of spare keys, variously colored. It said, "NO SALE."

"The book is written by hand," he said, setting the key down. "Brown-black ink. Old. Five, six hundred year."

"How do you know?"

"I know."

I leaned forward. "How?"

He drew in his breath impatiently. "It has stains. And *vandalisme* . . . by worms. A watermark, too."

"A watermark?"

"A crown. I make researches. The book was wrote before the seventeenth century. Must be."

A bibliographic detail calculated to whet my interest, but too vague to mean anything. Crown watermarks were a dime a dozen.

"And the binding?" I asked.

"Old leather. Degrading. Like you."

"I beg your pardon?"

"Degrading. Like all humans. Like this." He touched my chipped mahogany desk, with its coffee-mug rings and scratches and scatter of Post-it notes. "And smelling," he added. I half-expected him to say "smelling like you," but he concluded: "Smelling like smoke of wood. And sweet . . . very strange. Like *vanille*."

"How did you get this manuscript?"

"I apologize. I cannot tell you."

I pushed my chair back. "I apologize, too. I can't help you until I see the book."

He blinked at me. The dusty sunlight around him had a fine granularity, like the stained-glass light of an old church, and showed every blemish and abrasion in his small face. For a moment he breathed hard and then turned spasmodically, his leg bumping against my desk.

"Shut this," he commanded, gesturing to the storefront blinds.

"M'sieur, as I say—"

"Please."

Moving to the window, I reached over the book displays to the blinds. I could hear him breathing impatiently behind me. When I returned to my desk, he was staring straight in front of him; I got the impression he was going through some kind of internal struggle. Opening his briefcase with nicotine-stained fingers, he drew out a single piece of paper. I switched on my desk lamp and removed from my bare forearm a stray post-it note I had picked up.

"I do not have the book," he whispered. "But I have a

fragment." He handed the page to me.

It was Aramaic, all right. He had drawn in the watermark first, in very light pencil; I could make out the faint spectral lines of a crown behind the text. The Hebrew characters had been written over it in a firm, dark hand. Jewish Aramaic script, and very accurately done.

"You copied this out by hand?" I asked wonderingly.

He leaned forward. "You can read it?"

I ran my eye across the first line.

"What does it say?" he demanded.

"Something about . . . worlds." I raised my eyes. "This looks like a Kabbalistic text."

His small body was taut now, as if he had been restrung from within. "Kabbalah, yes."

The Kabbalists had once been my passion. Nowadays I had no taste for mysticism, Jewish or otherwise.

"I want to know. . . ." He pointed to a word in the second line, רבי. "This is 'rabbi'?"

"Rabbi, teacher, master. But I thought you said you didn't know Aramaic."

He thrust out his chin, minutely bristled with silver hairs. "I know Hebrew, a little. But it is not enough." He pointed to a word in the middle of the page. "And this?"

I happened to know that one just because it was a favorite of the Kabbalists.

"'Names,'" I said.

"Yes!" He sat back, gratified. "The Holy Names. I knew that."

"For a guy who doesn't know Aramaic, you seem to be doing okay."

"No! I need someone. To help. I need someone."

He was certainly right that a knowledge of Hebrew would only get him so far with Aramaic. Same alphabet, yes, but they were linguistic sisters, not twins.

"What's this?" I asked, pointing.

Toward the bottom of the page, set off by blank spaces, was a mathematical formula.

His hand twitched slightly; for a moment I thought he was going to snatch the paper away.

"An equation," he said in a low voice.

"I can see that. What's it doing in an old religious book?"

"It is not a religious book. It is religious *and* scientific and. . . ." He looked flustered now, as if he had revealed too much. "I tell you, the book is real. If you are a Jew or not, no matter—please help me, please."

"Look," I said, "I studied Aramaic years ago, but I've lost a lot of it. I am not your man."

Snatching the paper away, he stood up and moved agitatedly to the window blinds, where he raised a slat to peer outside. His gray pinstripe pants, puckered at the waist by his child-sized belt, had been trodden upon at the heels, so that the cuffs were torn and dirty. What was it that somebody said about the writer James Agee—that wind, rain and mockery were his tailors? I got a lot of people like that in my bookstore.

After watching the street for a long moment, he returned and sat down stiffly.

"It is my life," he said, squeezing the phrase out from his diaphragm.

I opened a desk drawer and scrabbled around. "The Clerne Foundation," I said, drawing out a business card. "They know old books. They can help you."

He ignored the card and sat clutching the paper. Again I got the impression he was debating with himself. Suddenly he laid the paper on my desk and, turning it around, pointed to the equation.

"You asked me about this," he whispered. "I will tell you. But I beg, be discreet."

"As I say, m'sieur, I am *not* discreet. My ex-wife says—"

"This is the wave equation of Erwin Schrödinger."

Something told me that this conversation was about to go off the rails.

"You know it?" he said.

"I've heard of it."

"The heart of quantum mechanics. Schrödinger published it in 1926."

"Yes?"

He waved his hand impatiently at my obtuseness. "Why do we find this equation in a book that is five, six hundred years old?"

He was breathing audibly, glaring at me. Now I was wondering how on earth I was going to get rid of him.

"Talk," he said curtly.

"Pardon?"

"Talk. Argue. You move, I counter you, and so we reach the truth."

"No, let's not do that," I said wearily. "So this equation has been around longer than everybody thinks. Is that a big deal?"

He shook his head fiercely. "You do not understand. The Kabbalists lived in the old world. Demons, angels, golem. How could they know about quantum mechanics?"

"Listen, m'sieur . . . I'm sorry, I don't know your name."

"I am—" He looked as if he had just saved himself from giving too much away. "Zarandok."

"There is a simple explanation, M'sieur Zarandok. This book is not five or six hundred years old."

He gave a grimace-smile. "You think it is fake. You think I fake you."

"No, I think somebody has faked *you*. It may be Aramaic but it can't be very old."

He nodded grimly. "You think the author is modern. He writes this equation for a cheat. Yes?"

"That's what I think, yes."

"Then I say this man knows very much. For a cheat. Many pages have equations."

"Well, of course, he wanted to appear very learned, very—"

"Even me, I do not understand the equations. I know they are real. They mean something. But they are . . . outside my universe." He leaned forward. "I think they are outside the universe of Erwin Schrödinger."

No, pal, you just wrote that equation in. You lifted a bit of Aramaic text from somewhere and then plunked in that formula.

"Before, I was *sceptique* like you," he said. "But now I must have the truth."

"I want the truth too, but—"

"Do you?" He stood up suddenly, briefcase in hand. "Do you, M'sieur McCaskill?" The syllables of my name came out like three hatchet strokes: *Mack-ack-skeel*. He glared for a moment. "I leave this page. Tomorrow I come back at this hour." He hesitated at the door, turning. "Do not tell anyone. No wife and no man. Do not show the page. It is my life."

He was gone. Why did they always come to *me*, these lost ones?

*   *   *

With my laptop open on the kitchen table and my two long-neglected Aramaic dictionaries close at hand, I sat down to discover how much I had forgotten. I figured this guy Zarandok had just lifted his text from the canonical Kabbalistic work, the thirteenth-century Zohar, the Book of Radiance. I could have gone online to search the Aramaic version of the Zohar—things were easier now than in my time—but with the working day over, I was keen to try my hand at the text.

I was back in that world that had so captured me in my twenties.

Why Aramaic? my ex-wife Julie had asked me once, seeking to plumb the depths of my various oddities. I'll give you a little taste, I said, and wrote on a napkin:

אשא אוכמא כתיבא על אשא חיוורא

That's like the best old cheese you will ever try, I told her. Three thousand years went into that cheese. You've got the ancient Middle East in there: Aramaic was one of the main languages of the region from about 1100 BCE onward. You've got old Europe in there: Aramaic was the primary written language of the Kabbalah, the Jewish mystical tradition that emerged in medieval Spain and France. And you've got a world of biblical poetry in there: the line translates as "black fire written on white fire"—the

Kabbalists' favourite description of divine law.

I never knew (Julie had said) that a person could get an entire degree in cheese.

And this cheese of Zarandok's was one strange concoction. Like the Aramaic of the Old Testament, it had no punctuation, which meant that sometimes I wasn't sure if a phrase was a question or answer. But after a few minutes of thrashing around, I had the first couple of lines, more or less.

> . . . for Creation is many-gestured [?], and all worlds
> are governed by the names of the Blessed Holy One.
>   All worlds, master?
>   Know that there are countless worlds beyond the
> sky-blue house of Man.

After that, I got myself into a knot—there was something about Torah, and about the "remembered dead," and then somebody said (apropos of nothing, apparently):

> I think much of the beauty I have lost.

For a long moment I sat listening to the heart-silence of the night, but then the page drew me back.

Two speakers, clearly. A master and a student. Talking of first and last things, as Kabbalists loved to do. The master refers early on to Torah, the body of divine law as revealed in the first five books of the Bible. So far, typically Kabbalistic.

But it sure didn't sound like the Zohar.

As the night wore on, the text began to take shape, like

a Kodachrome photo developing before my eyes. A "many-gestured" Creation (if I'd translated that right); an abundance of worlds; this mysterious equation; the end of time.

> . . . all worlds will become one, all circumstances and kingdoms will be woven together, and the garment of Torah will be whole. And those we have lost will

The page ended there.

I went to the window and stood looking south at the vast limned shadow of the Salève, the French mountain that Frankenstein's monster scaled in Mary Shelley's story—the monster that asked himself, as we all do sometimes, "Why was I made this way?" I didn't want to go to bed; sleep had been no refuge for years.

Those we have lost will. . . . I didn't need the next page to finish the sentence: *return.*

I did sleep, eventually—at least, I slid around on the surface of my dreams. The woman with the braid rode out of the vanished day on her blue bike; I called to her, but she melted away into the unreal light, and my own voice woke me. No refuge tonight, certainly. I got up to look at the page again. Even for Kabbalists, these guys seemed incapable of sticking to one topic. I stayed at my desk until I fell half-asleep once more, the dreams intertwining with the Hebrew letters. At dawn I dragged myself into the kitchen to make a thermos of good strong coffee. My pills . . . had I taken them already? Yes. No. Pretty sure not.

At seven a.m. I was back at the bookstore, laptop open and coffee in hand.

Of course I had to do a few fiddly things first—like configure my laptop for the Hebrew alphabet and create an account to search the concordance to the Zohar. But soon I was deep into the database, entering various Aramaic words, roots, and sentences.

I got nothing.

So maybe this text came from one of the lesser-known Kabbalistic works. I tried a general Google search, using "Kabbalah" along with the keywords and phrases I was fairly sure of: "worlds," "the remembered dead," "the sky-blue house of Man." I got lots of hits, but nothing that lead anywhere. The sensible thing at that point would have been to contact my former thesis advisor, old Moishe, but this was my baby now. I searched for anything I could find in other Kabbalistic works—*The Orchard of Pomegranates, The Book of Illumination, The Book of Raziel the Angel*—and scoured the indexes of a dozen scholarly journals. Again, nothing.

It was only when I entered some translated text that I *wasn't* sure of ("Creation is many-gestured") that I found something in an obscure 1965 monograph.

> The idea of Creation as "multi-gestured," consisting of countless worlds (and possibly universes, according to some commentators) was promulgated by the legendary sixteenth-century Kabbalist Rabbi Ezra Ben-Emeth. Known as the Rabbi of the Twelve Winds, Ezra Ben-Emeth lived through the expulsion of the Jews from Spain in 1492. We know of him only through a few allusions in sixteenth-century esoteric texts, including those of the alchemist Paracelsus. Unlike other Kabbalists of the time, he did not travel to

the city of Safed in Israel but went north, pursuing his living as a scribe throughout Europe. He was said to have talked with angels and prophets, including Elijah, Gabriel, and the "wise ones of all the ages."

The Rabbi of the Twelve Winds. What were the chances that Zarandok had found a genuine lost dialogue by this rabbi? About as good as the chances of me getting my face on the next Swiss stamp. Still, I'd go along with it. I liked a crazy literary prank as much as the next guy. But where had he gotten the Aramaic text?

I went back to my rough translation of Zarandok's page. "The remembered dead"—that phrase had been in my head the whole night.

Are remembered dead to be found among these worlds?

As we know from Sefer ha-zohar [the Zohar, the Book of Radiance], though a soul righteous or innocent may depart from this world, she is not lost to Creation, and continues to dwell in other worlds.

She is not lost to creation. Not lost . . . .

Okay, concentrate on the text. Had Zarandok just cut and pasted it from different Kabbalistic sources? The dialogue sure jumped around a lot. I'd only be able to tell when I saw this mysterious manuscript that supposedly smelled of vanilla. Yes, the degraded lignin in old manuscript paper sometimes gave off a whiff of vanilla, but I wanted to smell it for myself.

I looked at my watch: Zarandok was late.

And another thing—why had he come to *me*? Geneva
was home to several real Aramaic scholars. Maybe he just
thought I was an easier target than any of them. Or maybe
he actually didn't want a scholar, didn't want someone who
was part of the academic establishment . . . or part of the
Jewish establishment, apparently. But why not, if he was
Jewish himself? Maybe he wanted someone without *any*
kind of community. Someone less likely to share secrets.

He'd researched me, clearly.

Nine-twenty a.m. I opened in ten minutes. I went to the
door and looked outside: nothing. I took a few quick steps
down the street: the old Calvinist quarter I loved, if somewhat resignedly. Ancient four-sided street lanterns, glo-
ry-crowned horse chestnuts, and the scent of fresh bread
from the bakeries. Tiny, convulsed streets. A sky beyond
the cathedral like a blue ember. Stone fountains. Muted
pastel facades of the buildings: shortbread, cream, oatmeal,
light sorrel, faded ochre, and (especially) the clerical gray
of the molasse stone quarried from the hills nearby. Spring
flowers of white and sweet-pepper yellow in window boxes
of hot scarlet and sea green. Originally I had found Geneva
austere and buttoned-up, a bankers' town. But there was
always the ever-changing light, and the pruned plane trees
that looked like candelabra of coral, and the mountains radiant and dreaming over the lake, and the ghost of Jorge
Luis Borges tapping along the cobblestones with his cane
. . . and the flower boxes. For some reason, my neighborhood always went crazy with the flower boxes.

But where was Zarandok?

Back inside the store, I idly googled his name. All the
results of the first page were in some foreign language: I got

images of people walking with a staff and a cross on their backs, some nuns, a guy on a mountaintop. I kept scrolling until I got some entries in English. Zarandok was a café in London, a Hungarian rock group, and a chess move.

> The Pilgrim's Gambit (Zarándok Gambit in Hungarian), also called Kodaly's Gambit, is an irregular chess opening, classified under the A00 code in the *Encyclopaedia of Chess Openings.*

So "zarandok" meant pilgrim in Hungarian. *That* was the guy's accent—Hungarian.

A ring at the door. Finally. M'sieur Zarandok, I have a lot questions for you.

But it wasn't Zarandok. Before me stood the tiny disheveled form of Madame Lilly, our street book scout. I took a quick look up and down the street.

"How can I help you, Madame Lilly?"

Every big city has a book underclass—itinerants who wander the streets collecting bibliographic detritus. Madame Lilly had been doing it for five decades. She had the face and form of a twelve-year-old boy—wayward hair, caved-in-chest, neck slender as a lute's—except that, being almost seventy, she was mainly silver. Today she wore a frilly white bonnet, a man's gray belted raincoat and rubber boots. An empty beer can protruded from one of the coat pockets.

"I give you this," she said grandly, handing me a plastic shopping bag.

I glanced inside. A few paperbacks in French and German, a fashion magazine, a transit map, and a faded photo in a yellowed cardboard frame. I drew out the picture: a small rodent with a plant in its mouth. "Young water vole," said the caption.

"Thank you, Madame Lilly. I'm not sure I can use these, but thank you."

"Very lovely animal."

"Yes, but not for me."

Every time Madame Lilly approached me with unsellable junk, I vowed to ration myself with the donations. She stood there smiling her tiny folded smile while I glanced over her head, scanning the street.

"Madame, you haven't seen anybody around here this morning, have you? A small man with big ears?"

"No, I'm sorry, m'sieur."

"If you do see anybody like that, please tell me. His name is Zarandok."

"Zarandok. Yes, I will tell you, m'sieur."

I was going to ask her if she knew the woman with the braid who'd ridden by yesterday, but no; that would just get her talking. I gave her a few francs and took the shopping bag.

"Thank you, Madame Lilly," I said stoically.

Back inside again, I refreshed the web page on my laptop. The Zarandok Gambit. . . . What had the guy said? *You move, I counter you, and so we reach the truth.*

That sure sounded like a chess player talking.

*   *   *

Parc des Bastions. Home to Geneva's famous giant chessboards. The pawns came to just below my knee, the queen to just above. In the evenings, old men would gather at one particular board to play slow, convivial games. Among the oldest was Mikaïlou (Mique), eighty-one. From Guadeloupe originally. Now a citizen of the world. He didn't like to stand for too long; sometimes he just played from a bench, strategizing under his breath, directing his buddies to move the pieces.

"Hey, Mique!" I called.

"*Salut,* Tavish!"

The old men's board lay close to one of the park's many horse chestnuts, now flowering in tufts of pale froth. I took a seat beside Mique. The sun had disappeared behind the old city ramparts, with their stolid line of stone Reformation figures, and the park was filled with the clear shamanic light of early evening. *L'heure entre chien et loup*—the hour between dog and wolf. I watched the players at our board: a pair of blue suspenders, a Hawaiian shirt, and a pair of fit-over sunglasses. They were at the start of their game; the Hawaiian shirt had just nudged a plastic pawn into place with his foot.

"And what is happening with you, Tav?" asked Mique. "Are you in love?"

"God, no."

"Why not?"

"Because . . . look." I waved a hand over myself. "Past the best-before date, Mique."

"What?"

"No, I'm not in love. Hey, a guy came into the shop yesterday who looked like Kafka."

He looked impressed. "Things happen to you, Tav. I am

very struck."

"He wanted me to translate a book for him. From Aramaic."

"Recall to me what is Aramaic."

"The language Jesus spoke."

"Another escapade for you, Tav."

Mique always sat with a slight curve to his spine but otherwise remained hale and sharp and unconquered. He liked old fedoras, straw or felt. You might have taken him for a Cuban jazz musician, one of those living-treasure guys, who look fragile and grandfatherly until they suddenly stand up, whip out a horn and blow everybody away with their torrid solos. Sometimes he helped out at the bookstore; the customers loved him.

"This guy was supposed to come back to the store but never did," I continued. "I think he was Hungarian. Called himself Zarandok."

Mique glanced at me sharply.

"You've heard that name?" I said.

"Zarandok," he said, with a faraway look in his eyes. He got to his feet, one hand on my shoulder. "Zarandok!"

He moved over to the chessboard and stood beside a white knight. "Move here," he directed the Hawaiian shirt.

"*Franchement,* Mique!" exclaimed the guy. The suspenders raised one eyebrow—something I had read about in novels but never actually seen. But having just started their game, they were not really put out, and all of them helped Mique move the white knight and then a pawn. After everything was arranged to Mique's satisfaction, he gestured to me.

"Zarandok," he said. "*Le voilà.*"

"Is this the Zarandok Gambit?"

"Very famous."

"That's what the guy called himself—Zarandok. I think he was Hungarian."

"Like many fine chess players."

"Ever play with one named Zarandok?"

"I believe not. But I forget things now." We made our way back to the bench while Mique's buddies rearranged the pieces to restart their game. "Pilgrim," remarked Mique. "Zarandok means 'pilgrim' in Hungarian."

"You clearly don't forget much, Mique. Why is it called the Pilgrim's Gambit?"

"Because the great Kodaly was walking with pilgrims, and playing chess with monks, when he invented it."

"The great Kodaly?"

"János Kodaly. One of the most brilliant Hungarians." Mique placed a hand on my arm to lower himself onto the bench. "But always afraid. Even after he left Hungary, he was hiding himself from the secret police. He never showed at tournaments; he only played by letters."

Mique always insisted on speaking English with me— or rather, a fluid simulacrum of the language, colored by French, Antillean Creole, and dated Hollywood movies.

"Is this Kodaly still alive?" I said.

"No, he died years ago. Maybe poisoned by Russian agents. It is what they do."

The twilight was gently staining my mind, and I was thinking about the woman with the braid. New to the neighborhood. Once I had seen her take off her bike helmet, settle her braid, and then stand tall, chin raised and shoulders back, as if she had been constantly told as a teenager to stand up straight. It was uncanny: that movement sent a jump spark across the years. I almost—

"Nobody plays chess by letters now," remarked Mique sadly. "Only we old men have the time for it. We have such small time left, we have much time."

"Well, I hope you are using some of that time to write your autobiography."

"Mainly I talk about it. Too much papers in my house."

"I told you I can help you organize them."

We listened to the breeze in the park's tall, museful, sane-from-birth trees—the chestnuts and ginkgoes and atlas firs. Zarandok. . . . Was that his real name? Or had he just taken an alias from a famous chess move?

"And you've never seen anybody here who might be this Zarandok," I said. "Looks like Kafka."

Mique gestured to the twilit men who were studying the chessboard. "Tav, they *all* look like Kafka."

*   *   *

For Creation is many-gestured [?], and all worlds are governed by the names of the Blessed Holy One.

All worlds, master?

Know that there are countless worlds beyond the sky-blue house of Man.

At least I was making progress. Root by root, cognate by cognate. And it was pleasant, sitting here in a sunlit corner of my favorite café, beer at hand, reading from right to left (I was getting the habit back), and wrestling with an unruly Kabbalistic passage. My university days all over again.

Going deep into the work, into an imaginative world. Now, twenty-five years after dropping out of grad school, I could truly appreciate the appeal of translation: you couldn't skim. Skimming was how we lived now. Everything was skimmable . . . news, art, emotions, life. We were water striders, barely dimpling the surface of the world and the bubble of other selves. The Kabbalists, though—they may have been wild-brained mystics to a man, but they sure didn't skim life.

Are remembered dead to be found among these worlds, master?

As we know from *Sefer ha-Zohar* [The Zohar, the Book of Radiance], though a soul righteous or innocent may depart from this world, she is not lost to Creation and continues to dwell in other worlds.

In Aramaic, as in Hebrew, the soul was feminine. I took a sip of beer. Keep going. Keep going into their world, and let this one fall away.

I pray you, tell me more of the remembered dead, for I think much of the beauty I have lost.

The remembered dead light candles for us elsewhere in Creation and dream of us in the lost spaces of the night.

Can we ever know all of Creation, Master?

Numbers [stitch, weave] all worlds together; you must know them to know Creation.

Tell me where to begin, Master.

Begin with the foundation, black fire written on

white fire. . . .

Then, after a space—not large, but noticeable—came Schrödinger's equation, just plunked down as if highly relevant. It was definitely Schrödinger's equation; I'd checked it online. Of course, I couldn't tell, from the transcribed page, whether text and equations had been written with the same hand in the original source.

All possibilities and kingdoms are found here, all casts of circumstance, all orderings of nature.

Then came another gap, and the dialogue resumed with a somewhat abrupt plea from the student.

But speak again of the dead, master—will they ever return?

The guy clearly had more interest in the afterlife than in equations.

But what made me curious were these spaces around the equation. I had to assume they were in the original manuscript, since Zarandok had been so careful in transcribing everything else. I remembered reading that traditional Torah scrolls had spaces after certain sections, where the reader was meant to absorb the lesson; could these be the same idea? Or maybe these spaces had once contained lines of text that had been effaced by time . . . in which case, I was missing parts of the dialogue.

And who was this master? Prophet, angel, rabbi? He seemed to be the guy with all the answers.

In the last of the *shemittot* [cosmic cycles], all worlds
will become one, all circumstances and kingdoms will
be woven together, and the garment of the Torah will
be whole. And those we have lost will

It was then that I happened to look down the street;
in front of an old shutterless apartment building, I saw a
familiar bike, a blue one, in a bike rack. The bike I'd seen
outside my window a few days ago.

Maybe that was where she lived. I thought I could see
some books in the oversized handlebar basket. I took another sip of beer. The life of the street flowed around me.
Go now, if you're going to go.

Stuffing my worksheet and dictionaries into my briefcase, I laid down some francs and got up from the café
table.

The books were an intriguing mix. *Cosmos* (the old
hardcover version based on Carl Sagan's television series).
Quantum Information Theory. You're going to Mars! I looked
around—there was nobody in sight—and quickly plucked
out *Quantum Information Theory.*

Quantum theory, as applied in quantum information
theory, really has only a few important concepts. . . .
   1) indeterminism;
   2) interference;
   3) uncertainty;
   4) superposition;
   5) entanglement.

Suddenly she was there, bike helmet in hand. Down her back ran the ever-present braid, as densely plaited as a Shakespearean sonnet.

"Oh, sorry," I said quickly, putting the book back in the basket. "I'm a bookseller, and—"

"I know." Her English was like Himalayan twilight, clear but exotically tinted. I realized that in my confusion I'd been speaking my own language rather than French. I stumbled on: "I can't seem to pass books without . . . anyway, sorry."

Her look wasn't hostile or disquieted; she was studying me as if I were a quaint feature of the street that had just come to her attention. Mid-twenties, I guessed. Dressed in a light-green smock thing that came to her thighs. Eyes dark but sluiced with light. Jeans faded to the milky blue of an August sky. Right pant leg cuffed at mid-calf, to accommodate the bicycle chain. And largish ears . . . one of which had a fine circlet of gold on the upper rim.

"Quantum information theory," I said.

"Yes."

Believe it or not, I couldn't think of a conversation starter on the theme of quantum information theory. I stood looking at the book while she slipped her helmet on.

"Is it good?" I said finally.

She considered, her hands on her chin strap.

"It's not a big-seller book," she said, snapping the buckle.

Getting out a small key, she reached down to unlock the U-shaped lock of her bike, her braid sliding across her back. She straightened, the braid falling back into place; and, placing the lock into the handlebar basket, backed her bike out of the rack. *Tell her.* Before she concludes I'm just a middle-aged dweeb—no, too late—or a creep. Too late, too late.

"Goodbye," she said, from the other side of her bike.

"There's just one thing," I said.

She put a forefinger on the bridge of her glasses and touched them into place. I took out my wallet and, removing an old photo, held it out. She hesitated, her eyes flickering down to my hand and then back to my face.

"It's a picture of my daughter," I said.

She let go of one handlebar grip; the front wheel turned sharply and the whole bike threatened to slide away from her. Now she looked flustered.

"You remind me so much of her," I said. "She was tall too, and . . . anyway, I better let you go."

At her temple I could see a faint mottling of green, as if she had a bit of the sea inside her. She didn't take the photo; she just righted the bike and glanced around with troubled eyes.

I was having a hard time getting the photo back into my wallet. God, I deserved a medal for this. I managed to get the picture back in and then—my face burns to think about it—just walked away. Not one of my better moments. Just walked away because she reminded me so much of Saoirse. It was uncanny. Older than Saoirse had been, but still, that's what Saoirse would have looked like if. . . .

I tried to shut out everything and just walk. I automatically steered myself back to the store, two minutes away. Once inside, I closed the blinds and poured myself a large glass of scotch.

Saoirse, my sweet girl, my sunrise. Was it going to be like this for the rest of my life?

I called my ex-wife Julie, and for once she picked up almost immediately.

"Tav. *Ça va?*"

Julie was married again—another family, another life. She'd had her miracle; why couldn't I have mine?

"I know it's not our usual Sunday," I said, "but I wonder if we can visit Saint-Georges soon. *Very* soon."

A rapping at the door. Had I forgotten to put out the "*Fermé*" sign? No, it was there—somebody was ignoring it. I turned away from the door and lowered my voice.

"I just need a visit," I continued. "Whenever you're free."

"What is the matter, Tav? You don't sound yourself."

"It's just . . . something happened just now, and—"

The knocking continued, more forcefully.

"For *fuck's* sake," I said, getting up. "No, not you, Julie. Hold on."

Setting down my cell phone, I strode across the floor toward the door. Through the drawn blinds I could just make out the silhouette of someone at the doorstep. I unlatched the door and swung it open belligerently.

Madame Lilly stood on the stoop, smiling her infuriating smile. I took a long steadying breath.

"Madame Lilly," I said, "if we are going to do business, you must try to respect my—"

"M'sieur, it is very important."

"What?"

She handed me a large manilla envelope. "From your friend Mique."

"Mique?"

"He wanted you to have it. He is cleaning up his papers."

"All right, but please—"

"Very important. You told me."

"I told you? I'm sorry, I don't . . . okay, okay." I fished in my pocket for some francs. "Thank you, Madame Lilly." *Goddamn it.*

I carried the envelope back to the desk and picked up my phone.

"Sorry, Julie. Back to Saint-Georges . . . can I meet you there on Sunday for ten or so?"

"Fine. But you didn't tell me what happened, Tav."

"What?"

"What happened to you just now? You were about to tell me."

I tore open the envelope and slid out a single well-creased sheet of paper. A list of names and mailing addresses. La Fédération genevoise d'échecs par correspondance.... The Geneva Letter Chess Federation.

"It's nothing," I said.

"It doesn't sound like nothing."

That woman with the braid . . . she had a way of touching her glasses into place with one finger. Saoirse had done that, too.

"Tav?" said Julie.

I smoothed out the paper: it appeared to be a record of competitors for a 2008 letter-chess tournament.

"Don't worry, Julie, it was just me seeing things. Listen, how's Pierre, how's—"

Just then I noticed a name circled in red pen. Mique had highlighted one of the competitors.

M. Zarandok
Poste restante

Post Filiale 1211, Avenue Aurelièn
Genève

*   *   *

The small, worried-looking woman who opened the door
stood peering out cautiously, her chin slightly tilted so she
could see through her clunky bifocals.

"Madame Wasserman?" I said.

"Yes?"

"I am looking for M'sieur Zarandok. I believe he rooms
here."

She reminded me of the man in the moon from that
famous silent movie—was it the first one ever made? Facial
features scrunched into a small area. Large tracts of jowl
and forehead. Gray hair pulled back into a severe bun, ac-
centuating the lunar expanse of her face. She held the door
open no more than six inches.

"Who told you he rooms here?" she said, her eyes narrowing.

"Your local post office. I was just there."

She puckered her mouth at the audacity of the post office but said nothing. Rain fell steadily around us, on the
streets, on the porch roof, on the dripping shrubbery, on
the golden-dead garden. The top part of me, including my
shoulder satchel, was relatively dry thanks to my umbrella;
my lower half was sodden. Behind me I could hear the
damp hiss of car tires on the pavement.

"I am doing some work for him," I continued. "Is he here?"

She looked me up and down and then said hesitantly: "I
have not seen M'sieur Zarandok for some days. He rents a

room here, that's all I can tell you."

"Is there a telephone number where I could reach him?"

"No. I'm sorry I can't help you. Good day."

"I'm afraid something has happened to him," I said quickly. "He gave me something and—"

Her eyes narrowed. "Gave you what?"

Rooting around in my shoulder satchel, I withdrew Zarandok's page with my worksheet stapled to it, encased in a plastic sleeve. "This. The work he requested. He said he would come back for it, but never did."

She opened the door slightly to see the page better. Behind her I could see a bare vestibule and a staircase disappearing into dim light.

"Why do you think something has happened to him?" she demanded.

"He was just so concerned about this work. He said it was his life."

She blinked at me irresolutely. "Give this work to me. I will make sure he gets it."

"I'd rather give it to M'sieur Zarandok himself. I know how important it is to him."

I expected her to close the door then, but she just looked even more uneasy and stole a glance up the staircase behind her.

"His door is locked," she confided, "and he won't answer when I knock."

"You're sure he's there? He hasn't just gone away for a bit?"

"He *never* goes away." She brushed a wisp of gray hair from her eyes, looking even more worried. "I always hear him in the morning. He goes out the front door here to get his coffee and newspaper. But I haven't heard him for days now."

"Does he have any family that you know of? Any friends?"

"Nobody." She hesitated. "He hasn't been well for a little while, and. . . . "

"You have a key, I presume?"

She laid one hand on her chest, fingers spread. "I can't enter his room without permission. He is very particular about that."

"If you're concerned about him, I think he would understand."

She shook her head distractedly. I got out a business card from my wallet.

"Well, when you do find him, could you tell him I called? Tavish McCaskill. Tell him I've finished the work."

Without a word she opened the door wide, gestured me in, closed it after me and slid the deadbolt home. I stood in wet shoes with my folded umbrella, relishing the stale warmth of the vestibule.

"Usually my son helps me with these things," she said agitatedly, "but he is in Zurich."

"I see."

"What should I do?"

"I suggest that you knock on M'sieur Zarandok's door, loudly. Tell him Tavish McCaskill has come with his work. I'll wait here."

"And if he doesn't answer?"

"Open the door and have a quick look. I think you are entitled to that under the circumstances."

"Should we call the police?"

"I think you should have a look first. I will wait."

"No. Leave your umbrella and come with me."

The art-deco stairway, a curving latticework of rusting iron, creaked as we ascended. The light was swamp-light: rheumy, tallowish, faded. The second floor was lit by a single bare bulb in mid-passageway; the wallpaper showed endless rows of flowers, gold and fungus-green.

Madame Wasserman stopped in front of the only door and knocked.

"Please announce yourself," she directed in a whisper.

"M'sieur Zarandok!" I called. "It's Tavish McCaskill. I have that work you requested."

Silence. I put my ear to the door and listened. Madame Wasserman was watching my face.

"M'sieur Zarandok, are you in there?" I called.

Nothing. I took a step back to see if there was any light showing under the door, but the whole place was so dingy it was hard to tell. For a moment we listened to the rain outside, a vast susurration, like locusts settling.

"Do you have the key?" I said to the landlady.

She rapped hard. "M'sieur Zarandok! I am very worried. Please answer the door."

Again there was silence. Biting her lip, she inserted the key in the door and opened it.

The room was tiny—probably one of those little rooms in Geneva's apartment buildings that once housed servants. A narrow linoleum counter slanted along one wall, following the dip of the floor. Beside the sink stood a single plug-in cooking element. On the ceiling and cupboard, I could see the faint sheen of cooking oil residue. In the far corner stood a cot-like bed, and beside that, a small table with a chessboard. I smelled stale tobacco and a damp-washcloth odor.

"He is not here," said Madame Wasserman. "But oh!"

An oriel window looked out over the courtyard; it must have been open for some time, since I saw a moist patch on the rug. Madame Wasserman crossed the floor in a second and closed the window. Immediately the rain lost amplitude, becoming a faint clicking against the windowpane.

"Come, we must leave," she said.

The room was a monk's. No family photos, no artwork, no plants, no cheesy knickknacks, no recycling box, no coin jar. The only domestic item I could see was a fluffy household duster, plastic-handled and very grimy. I sensed in the room a shuttered man living in balked and withered circumstances, but still dusting. I thought uneasily of my own flat.

The fresh air from the open window hadn't completely dissipated the smell of tobacco; clearly Zarandok rolled his own cigarettes. His bookshelf summed up his life—chess, mathematics, cryptography. I saw only one book I recognized: Gaines's *Cryptanalysis*. A first edition. Worth some money. And something called *Steganography: Tools and Techniques*. Steganography. I felt I should really know that word, but—

"We must go," urged Madame Wasserman. "He may come back."

"That window has been open for some time," I said.

Madame Wasserman was making clucking sounds over the state of the rug.

I went over to the chessboard—an old wood-laminate one, wrinkled from water damage. The life of the room seemed to center here. The squares were colored like last year's leaves: tints of weak coffee alternating with gray sand. Some were curled at the edges, and one or two of them had come right off, revealing the fabric background. The pieces were distinctive—tall and roughly carved, with very little ornamentation. Many were as cracked and chipped as the board. They had been set up for a game, and in their ordered stillness they seemed to be waiting, like miniature terra-cotta warriors, elementally alive in their aged and battered casings. Now I noticed an empty square: the white knight was missing. I glanced under the table and saw a scatter of tobacco flakes and more dust, but no chess pieces.

Outside the rain continued to tap softly against the closed window.

The room was so gaunt, so empty of clutter that a small thing like a missing chess knight stood out. I figured it would be around somewhere. I slid over to the wall radiator and ran a finger under it. Nothing but dust.

Madame Wasserman made an exasperated sound. "M'sieur, *please.*"

"Yes, yes."

While she was locking the door, I said, "And he never had any visitors of any kind. Nobody ever comes to play chess with him?"

She shook her head. "He is a hidden man—a man with a hidden life, you know?"

I remembered the cheap household duster. To survive this world, as my wise old thesis advisor Moishe used to say, you must stain yourself with another life; but here was a man living unstained in his own narrow, austere universe. His chessboard made me think of my own, piled under empty picture frames in my crowded closet. I hadn't played since . . . well, since my life had changed.

At the foot of the stairs I retrieved my umbrella and gave Madame Wasserman my business card. "If he should show up, please have him call me. Thank you, Madame."

A hidden man fighting the void.

With the rain falling steadily around me, I walked home through a landscape of echoes.

TWO

Both Julie and I brought flowers—she lilies, I daffodils—
and we put them on the grave together, as we always did,
and then stood listening to the birds. The sunlight came
down in soft obliques through the oak trees. After a day of
rain, the sky had cleared and the lawns gleamed. I smelled
damp mulch and freshly turned earth.

"You look tired, Tav," Julie remarked.

"I'm good. Let's talk about spring or something."

The gravestone was pure white marble; we made sure it
was kept clean of lichen and leaves. The face was smooth
and polished, but the sides were rough, unworked. Saoirse
Lake Gascon-McCaskill, 1992 – 2007. The quote was from
Thomas Wolfe: "O lost, and by the wind grieved, ghost,
come back again."

"So, your spring, it is nice?" she said.

"Well, a lot of things have been happening to me lately."

"What things?"

"Just things. Odd things."

The first time I had stood in Cimetière de Saint-Georges,
I was in far worse shape than any of the underground deni-
zens, my legs cut off at the knees, my heart incinerated into
nothing—ripped out of my body with tongs and torched
before my eyes—and my guts scattered to the winds. Yet
it was such a place of new beginnings. Some of the graves

had little plaster cherubs lying on the bases, chins in their hands, looking up winsomely at the mortal bereaved. Every year we saw a new crop of earnest and believing young trees, supported with stakes and wire, their gamin trunks tenderly wrapped in plastic guards. And now, in spring, the birds decanted their song into the blonded green light, and the earth under the leavening sun smelled damply alive.

"And the day you called?" asked Julie. "You started to tell me something."

Julie looked good, as usual. A natural redhead. Or pretty close to natural. Crow's-feet extended from her eyes in tiny sweepback lines, very fine, and curved as if decorative. A PhD, too—neuropsychology. Everything I knew about memory, stroke rehabilitation, and sexual arousal came from Julie. Today she wore a misty floral-print blouse, a dark skirt and flat-soled sandals. Her hairstyle was pageboy, with ends that curled slightly at her chin. Looking at her, you would never have guessed that her life, like mine, had been blasted apart twelve years before.

"I saw a girl—or young woman—who reminded me so much of Saoirse," I said. "Tall, lanky, glasses. . . ."

"This has happened to me, Tav. More than once."

"Yeah, but I thought I was past that stage."

Julie narrowed one eye at me. She could use just one eye to express an incredible palette of emotions. This time it expressed a carefully guarded pain.

"I showed her Saoirse's photo," I said. "I know, I'm red-faced now when I think about it. The funny thing was—up close she kind of looked like Saoirse, but—"

"But not really."

"Well . . . not as much."

I remembered that Julie had once suggested that Saoirse wear her hair in a braid. Saoirse wasn't keen; she was at that age when wayward hair was useful for hiding behind. But maybe she would have changed her mind . . . eventually.

"As I say," said Julie, "I still see Saoirse in unexpected places."

"But do you see her *grown up*?"

"Sometimes, Tav."

For years after Saoirse's death, I prayed endlessly for the return of my lost heart and limbs, for my body to be stitched up. I wanted my own miracle, as I say. Julie had hers, and that miracle almost destroyed everything between us. Almost.

"Anyway," I continued, "this woman knew me. At least, she seemed to know I sold books."

"You're *un personnage*. How is that in English?"

Geneva-born, Julie spoke a supple Euro-English that was made even more attractive by the occasional eccentricity—she always called a hatchback a "hunchback."

"Character," I said. "Yes, I've become a character. Thanks for reminding me." I stooped to remove a leaf from the gravestone. "This woman had a few books in her handlebar basket—astro-quantum-space stuff. Like all those books that Saoirse got from the Interstellar Academy."

Between the ages of twelve and fifteen, Saoirse had gone to a physics and astronomy camp in Zurich. First she was an Astro-Adventurer, and then Astro-Adventurer Level Two, and finally a Cosmic Teen (two summers). For a costume party one year at the camp, she'd dressed up as the Big Bang—a black jumpsuit with luminescent chemical formulae all over it, to represent the primordial elements.

When I suggested she attach some stars to the jumpsuit, she looked at me aghast. "Dad, stars hadn't formed then!"

Julie gazed down the vast tilted lawn to the mountains, great-maned beings of light beyond Geneva's two rivers, the Arve and the Rhône—the latter a rich clear blue, the former a muddy green. Like a lot of iconic places in Switzerland, Cimetière de Saint-Georges was almost too perfect—too manicured, too orderly, too sculpted. But the view redeemed it.

"I must go, Tav," she said. "The kids have football later and Pierre is working."

"Does that guy ever *not* work?"

This time, her narrowed eye expressed a very different emotion. Only Julie was allowed to criticize her husband.

"Do you take your pills?" she said, in a counterthrust.

"When I remember. Okay, sorry for that remark, Julie."

I felt her cool green gaze wander over me while (I knew) she was replaying our entire conversation in her head, alert for intimations about my inner life—especially whether I was holding things together.

"The last time we talked," she said, "you spoke of a vacation."

"It's all arranged."

"Finally! I never thought you'd do it. Where are you going?"

"Nowhere. I'm going to hang out in cafés and wear my rattiest old clothes and go without shaving and forget about deodorant."

She exhaled, stirring a lock of red hair by her ear. "And how is your vacation different from your normal life?"

"Now, Julie, you know I always wear deodorant when I

have to be around people. Bookstore patrons don't count. Hey, ever heard of Schrödinger's equation?"

*   *   *

The light was strange, a silvery inundation. In the sky, bruise-colored clouds were piled like shoredrift at the far edges of the world. They had the palpability of toadstools, or snowdrifts, or glacial moraine; they drew the eye out across vast wimpling continents of space, as a chain of mountains does. Only Mique and I would have come out for a sky like this. When the rain came, we could always head for the café just across the street.

"He had all these books on cryptography," I said. "Including one about steganography. I didn't even know what that meant—"

"To cache secret messages in ordinary things," said Mique.

"You're a marvel, Mique. Anyway, there was no sign of Zarandok."

"And the room was disturbed?"

"Not really, but something didn't seem quite right. The window was open, and . . . a small thing: the white knight was missing from the chessboard."

Mique glanced at me. "The white knight?"

"Probably nothing."

We sat at our usual bench, our gaze moving between the clouds and their shadows on the grass. The old guys' chessboard had been set up for a game, but with the sky so direful, nobody was here except us.

"János Kodaly was famous for opening games with his knight," remarked Mique.

"János Kodaly. The Hungarian chess master you told me about."

"Yes. His Zarandok Gambit—remember I showed you? A knight moves to the center of the board."

"And you said this Kodaly guy died years ago."

"Yes. Poisoned, I think."

"Here's a thought, Mique. What if he didn't die?"

"You mean . . . ?"

"What if he didn't die but took on a new identity?"

"Zarandok." Mique took off his fedora—straw this time, with a bright blue paisley band—and turned it around reflectively in his hands. "Could it be? But how old was this Zarandok? Kodaly was twelve years younger than me."

"Hard to say how old Zarandok was, he was so . . . washed out." I tilted my head back, to get another view of the sky. "I tried to find a picture of Kodaly, but there doesn't seem to be any out there."

"No, Kodaly was a secret man." He glanced at me. "But he knew cryptography."

I sat up. "Really?"

"This is how he has escaped from Hungary. He put coded messages into his correspondence chess games with a Swiss grandmaster."

"Well, looks like he's on the run again. No doubt with his book."

In the ecliptic light that came and went, I thought of Julie, how she'd fought so hard to keep going after we lost Saoirse, fought hard not to blame me. She just tilted her small body forward, eyes almost closed, like someone fronting a gale. And she started making to-do lists. Before, she had just *done* things, hadn't bothered with any kind of list, but now I would find the lists all over the house. She put Saoirse's things in three big boxes—"Interstellar Academy," "Artwork," and "Misc."—and tucked them far away in the attic, in some place that was impossible to reach.

"This book of Zarandok's," said Mique curiously. "What is it about?"

"Everything, apparently."

"Everything?"

"It's supposedly a sixteenth-century dialogue featuring a legendary Kabbalist, the Rabbi of the Twelve Winds. He seems to be talking with a master—maybe a prophet or angel—about all the big topics. Life after death, other worlds, Schrödinger's equation. . . ."

"Schrödinger's equation. I have heard speak of this."

"Then maybe you know that the equation is not sixteenth century at all. Definitely twentieth century. It apparently describes the behavior of a quantum mechanical system—elementary particles, doing whatever they do."

"A revolutionary equation, I think."

"*Very* revolutionary. So revolutionary that the sixteenth century could never have conceived of it. It would have been like coming up with the specs for the atomic bomb."

"Ah. A blackhead on your Zarandok."

"You said it. Suppose someone came to you saying he'd found a bit of the Bayeux tapestry—and it showed a Norman soldier holding a cell phone. Would you buy it from him?"

"Yes. I collect funny things."

Across the park was an old wall, smothered in greenery, now trembling as if alive. The leaves seemed to be crisscrossed by dozens of breezes, making them seethe and roil like the sea, like the collective unconscious. The absolute worst, after we lost Saoirse, was sleeping together. Julie and I would lie there like two carcasses, mute and inert, and when we finally closed our eyes, our dreams were just riffs of sepulchral cloud, like this sky. But now she slept with someone else, had a family again—Pierre and his kids. I was happy for her. I told her that often. Happy: every time I saw her.

"The Rabbi of the Twelve Winds," said Mique. He got to his feet, hand on my shoulder as always. "I would like to meet this man."

At that moment, a flock of dark birds—starlings, maybe—surged out of the wall greenery in a great cloud, like dust being smacked out of a rug. We both watched them turn and wheel, embayed in the air, then stream off over the city, a single smoky thought. This happened sometimes in Geneva: a movement, a sudden spate of life, and you knew that beyond the endless zithering of our machines was another world—the ocean, the jet stream, the blue-petalled night, the tides moon-tethered and law-abiding, the planet-dandling stars that Saoirse so loved. Yes, rain was coming.

"I'd like to meet this rabbi too," I said. "I'd ask him where he'd been, riding those twelve winds."

As I stood up, my eye fell on the old guys' chessboard, and I remembered the board in Zarandok's room . . . and the missing white knight.

*   *   *

The guy grasped two long narrow poles in his hands—sections of fishing rod, it looked like—which held a long triangular loop of yarn. As I watched, he brought the poles together and dipped them into a blue plastic washtub. From the look on his face, he might have been engaged in surgery or some close, holy ritual. When he withdrew the poles, the yarn loop held an iridescent film of soap. Walking slowly backward, he raised and opened the poles: a huge wobbling bubble drifted out, sea-fluid and glittering with rainbow tints. It elongated languidly, bellied like a sail, contracted like an octopus, entwined itself around invisible obstacles; finally it burst as if it had been erased from right to left, leaving flecks of soap foam on the grass.

"Wonderful," I said.

He ignored me. I was surprised to find him alone in the dusk; a display of giant bubbles should have attracted onlookers. I went closer to him—a big, bristly man with a face like a dead planet, lined and pitted by its long beleaguered orbit through space-time.

"A nice park to make bubbles in," I said.

Evidently he didn't consider this remark worth a reply.

"My name's Tavish," I said. "I'm a friend of Julie Gascon's."

This elicited a quick glance from him. According to Julie, people just called him *le professeur*—a once-brilliant physicist at CERN (Conseil européen pour la recherche nucléaire) who'd had some kind of breakdown. Now he lived on the street and made giant soap bubbles.

"I have something to show you, professor," I said. "Can we sit down?"

I thought for sure he would continue to ignore me, but eventually he rapped his poles on the edge of the washtub and, with a jerk of his head, indicated a nearby bench. He was dressed a bit like a professor—worn corduroy trousers, easy-care dress shirt, a shabby knitted vest—except that he wore old running shoes and no socks. His vest was held together precariously over his expansive belly by a single remaining button. I passed him Zarandok's Aramaic page with my translation stapled to it, and he held them up inches from his face.

"It's Aramaic," I said, moving closer.

He lowered the pages to allow me to point.

"You see Schrödinger's equation there," I said.

"Where did you get this?" he said raspily.

"A guy brought it into my bookstore. He said he'd copied it from an old Kabbalistic manuscript. You know the Kabbalists?"

"I've heard of them."

"Medieval Jewish mystics. This guy wanted me to translate the Kabbalistic text. That second page is what I came up with."

He flipped to the second page and glowered at it. I sensed that I had a limited amount of time to get his attention.

"And here's the *really* wild part," I said. "The guy who brought me this claimed that the equation is in the source manuscript—which is over five hundred years old."

I saw that he wasn't really listening; he wiped his nose and looked out over the park.

"Of course," I continued hastily, "it *couldn't* have been written back then, but I just wanted to check with you about . . . I know modern equations often use mathematical concepts that have been around for a long time, and . . ."

Definitely not listening. I drew back, wondering how to proceed. Julie had met him at the hospital where she worked; he had volunteered for a study on memory. I began to suspect she'd had her own motives in having me talk to him.

"I often think," he remarked slowly, "of the rivers of music, and fireworks, I made in my first life."

I blinked. "Your first life?"

He just continued to gaze sadly out at the empty twilit park, smelling of sweat and dish soap, his bubble wand resting alongside him. The triangle of yarn lay coiled on the grass and I noticed that he had tied a washer to the apex, to weigh it down. Then he sighed and held up the two pages again, as if he knew he wasn't going to get rid of me until he offered up his professional opinion.

"Who did you say brought you this?" he asked.

"He called himself Zarandok. But I'm starting to think his real name is János Kodaly."

He gave me a sharp glance. "János Kodaly the mathematician?"

"The chess player."

"Mathematician," he repeated firmly. "Chess is a game; mathematics is life."

"Yes . . . of course. If we're talking about the same person. Did you know him, professor?"

He shook his head. "I think he was at the University of Zurich for a while. But I'm quite sure he's dead."

"I have this idea that he faked his own death."

He gave me such a look of sour wonder that I continued quickly: "It's just a theory. I can't find any pictures of Kodaly anywhere, so I can't—"

I was cut off by the sudden cry of a North American loon, muted but still haunting.

"Sorry, that's me," I said, putting my hand on my jacket.

He waved a hand. "Don't keep the aliens waiting."

"No, no, I can take it later."

But he had already picked up his bubble wand and gotten to his feet. I took out my cell phone in irritation. Whoever this was, it had better be good.

"Tavish McCaskill, *j'écoute,*" I said.

A gruff voice was speaking French. I caught "Wasserman."

"Sorry, what was that?"

"Henri Wasserman. I am the son of Madame Wasserman. I believe you spoke to my mother about one of her lodgers, M'sieur Zarandok."

"Yes!" I stood up excitedly. "Has M'sieur Zarandok come back?"

"He has not. And I am getting concerned."

"You and me both, M'sieur Wasserman."

"My mother said you are a business associate of his."

"Not exactly. He came to me once for professional advice."

"Professional advice on what, may I ask?"

"Is that important?"

"Maybe. I find it strange that everybody is so close-lipped about our M'sieur Zarandok."

"We just talked about books—I run a bookstore. But why do you say everybody is so close-lipped? Have you spoken to other people?"

In the silence that followed, I watched the professor send out another bubble, a placid ghost shape-shifting its way through a lifetime that lasted four seconds.

"Other people don't seem to *exist*, for M'sieur Zarandok," said the guy on the phone. "But a woman came to our door last week asking about him."

"A woman?"

"She said very little—just that Zarandok was a family friend. She would not give her name."

"Can you describe her?"

"No, I regret that I can't, m'sieur. I was not there." He seemed to be moving his phone around out of impatience. "My mother is personally very concerned about M'sieur Zarandok, and I, frankly, am concerned for slightly less personal reasons. He is not the most conscientious of tenants."

"You mean you're worried about your rent."

"He has been neglectful before."

"Has it occurred to you that he may be injured somewhere, or in a hospital, or . . . ?"

"He is not in any of the Geneva hospitals; my mother has already checked. If you do receive any further information about M'sieur Zarandok, I would greatly appreciate a call, m'sieur. And please contact *me*, not my mother. Thank you."

He rang off. Now there was a warm, caring heart.

I went over to the professor, who was watching a newly formed bubble as it rippled and eddied, a living pellicle both cosmic and protozoan. "What mammal or reptile was that?" he said.

"I'm sorry?"

"Your phone."

"Oh, my ringtone. It's a loon. Takes me home whenever I hear it—Canada. I haven't been back in . . ."

Fourteen years. And then a lost moment resurfaced: we were on the lake near my parents' cottage, Saoirse and I, our paddles stilled. She had been endlessly practicing the rise and fall of the loon's call. *You try it, Dad.* I made a loon call that sounded more like a zombie's lament. *Okay, Dad, that's enough.* Then she did it, and a loon actually answered.

I closed my eyes. Sometimes a memory would flare up like this, a bit of voltage free of its sheath, and people would wonder why I had temporarily dropped out of the conversation.

But the professor didn't seem to notice; his art had captured him again. Rivers of music and fireworks ... the fruits of his first life, he'd said. Now, belatedly, I wondered if he had meant his life as a *physicist.* Maybe that's what physics was to him: music, fireworks.

"You say you can't find a picture of János Kodaly," he remarked.

"That's right."

"I know where you can find one."

I waited. He drew out another slow bubble, turning in my direction as he did so, and it drifted slow as a whale's thought toward me.

"Cross the park to Adhémar-Fabri and go left," he said. "Turn right at Philippe Plantamour and walk two blocks. When you get to the Emmanuel Church, go down the stairs. There is a small lending library there. Walk to the very end of the first row. There is a book on the uppermost shelf. Paperback, blue cover. In the first third of that book you'll find a photo of Kodaly."

"That's great. Um ... you don't happen to know the title of the book?"

"I don't remember. I just know where you'll find it."

"Well, thank you, professor." I thought about giving him money, but something told me that would be the wrong gesture in the circumstances. "Julie wanted to know if you need anything."

He shook his head. I remembered something Julie had told me once: when people are battered and pounded by their own minds, they can only survive through extreme strategies—and those strategies are often taken to be the mental instability itself, rather than just attempts to cope. This guy was coping by creating giant bubbles. Who knew what the shapes, the topology, did for his mind?

"Other worlds," said the professor.

"I'm sorry?"

"Your text speaks of other worlds. They exist." He dipped his poles into the soap solution. "I don't mean other planets; I mean other universes. They may even be inside ours."

"Inside?"

"Like the overtones of a piano note." He stepped backward, opening up his wand. "When you press middle C on the piano, you hear one note. You *think* you hear one note. But inside it are overtones—the third of the scale, the fourth, the C an octave above, and so on. Our universe may be like that: filled with overtone universes, all sounding at different frequencies, so to speak. But I don't know how I could ever test this hypothesis."

"That's a thorny one."

I watched as he released a bubble the size and shape of a beach ball. In the instant before it lost its planetary perfection, I caught a clear glimpse of myself and him standing together. Then it wobbled and wavered, and the two of us blended together, becoming one shimmer on its surface.

*   *   *

There—just where he'd said I'd find it. *Flight of Genius: How Refugee Hungarians Made the Modern World.* That was some memory the professor had.

I plucked the book off the shelf. It seemed to be mainly about the big names in science—Leo Szilard, Edward Teller, Eugene Wigner—but there were passages about the unknown geniuses, the recluses, the shooting stars that burned out early. Kodaly had exactly one page devoted to him. Mathematical physicist, chess master, space enthusiast. An uproar of numbers in his head since childhood, apparently. After escaping from Hungary in the mid-1980s, he drifted around Europe and ended up at the University of Zurich. Hobbies: collecting micrometeorites, devising chess problems, teaching physics to kids. A socially awkward polymath, but by all accounts a gentle, harmless man. He believed children could grasp all the essential concepts of physics; apparently he would teach them general relativity using a trampoline and various kinds of balls—tennis, bowling, basketball. Favorite weekend escape: Baulmes Monastery.

And yes, there was a photo: undated, black-and-white. Two men, one in a monk's robe and cassock. "János Kodaly playing chess with the Abbot of Baulmes Monastery." Their features were hard to make out. The dark-haired man sitting across from the abbot was certainly smaller than the cleric, but as small as Zarandok?

I scanned the text below the photo.

In the last years of his life, János Kodaly spent considerable time at Baulmes Monastery in central Switzerland. It seemed a strange choice of retreat for a secular Jew, but the tranquility and isolation appealed to Kodaly. He felt it was the one place where he didn't have to be watching night and day for the mysterious agents who (he claimed) continued to pursue him.

Baulmes Monastery. . . . I laid my phone on top of the open book and googled the place. About ninety kilometers from Geneva. The monks kept a guesthouse for visitors. A local bus went there several times a week.

I remembered what Mique had said: Kodaly had devised his Zarandok Gambit in a place of pilgrims and monks.

I wanted to have another look at Zarandok's apartment; I couldn't get the missing chess knight out of my mind. And who was this woman that had made inquiries at Madame Wasserman's? I had to talk to the landlady again. But now something else had caught my interest: I'd always wondered what it was like to be a monk.

THREE

A real firecracker, this guy. A bit stooped, a bit of an old-wicker cast to his frame, but his eyes were clear and alert. He wore a denim apron over his monk's cassock and large, authoritative rubber boots. Brother Alphonse, the oldest monk at Baulmes Monastery. I hoped I could wear boots so authoritatively when I was ninety years old.

"János Kodaly." He shook his head. "Of course I remember him. Always at the chessboard. One day he left and we never saw him again."

"Never?"

"Well, not that I know of. Did you ask Brother Didier about him?"

"I've asked everybody."

He seemed to be the general handyman at the monastery. On the walls hung sickles, rakes, drawknives, and pruners. Seed bags were piled on a crib near the bench, and a beekeeper's helmet sat on a post.

"I have reason to think that he might have come back here recently." I said. "He might be using the name Zarandok now."

"Zarandok." He shook his head. "I can't recall the name. But we get a lot of pilgrims passing through."

So much for my hunch.

"Tell me your name again," said Brother Alphonse.

"Tavish McCaskill."

"You are American, Tavish?"

"Canadian."

"Ah, yes. Mounted police." He smiled and waved a hand to take in the work shed. "You like my office, Tavish?"

I couldn't believe the amount of junk on his workbench—wrenches, screw drivers, files, spark plugs, jars of screws and bolts, oil cans of various sizes, rolls of wire, a bench grinder, a small chainsaw with the chain missing, a tool and die set, several dismantled motors. From the middle of the jumble, he plucked out something cylindrical and handed it to me.

"I made that," he said, with satisfaction.

It looked like a very large juice can, topped with a funnel whose narrow end was angled outwards. Attached to the side was something like a bellows, or the squeeze box on a concertina. I didn't have the faintest idea of what the object was.

"There's a local company that makes these now," he said disdainfully. "They're not worth. . . ." I didn't quite catch what they weren't worth; he muttered under his breath.

"I see. But back to—"

"How about in Canada?" he said suddenly, holding the thing up. "Do you still make your own there?"

"I believe . . . they might in a few places, yes."

"Really? Where?"

Well . . ." I was sure that *was* a pair of bellows, to blow air out the funnel, but for what purpose? "In the east."

"The east, eh?"

"I believe so. Also . . . the west. But tell me, Brother Alphonse, are there any hiking cabins or anything around here?"

"No. Do you think this friend of yours is hiding some-where?"

"Well, he's a bit of a hermit."

"It's hard to be a hermit in a monastery, Tavish. This is a community."

Just then the supper bell rang. Brother Alphonse took off his denim apron and sat down creakily to remove his rubber boots. Through the window of the shed, the sunlit mountains were slowly draping themselves in cloud shad-ows.

"It's a bee smoker," he said, smiling.

"Pardon?"

He nodded to the cylindrical object he had shown me. "A bee smoker. You light a fire inside the cylinder and blow smoke at the bees . . . gently. It settles them down."

"Yes. Of course."

He set his rubber boots aside and slipped on a pair of sandals over his socks. "Would you like to try it out tomor-row? I'm going to visit the bees in the morning."

"Oh, thanks for the offer, but I'm catching the bus back to Geneva tonight."

"Things of this world are calling, eh?"

"Well, bills of this world."

He stood up. "*Eh bien*, come along. We must give you a good supper before you go."

*   *   *

What a strange place. I'd never felt so at home. Gray lime-stone buildings, rolling lawns, cinder paths. Six beehives and three goats. Two guesthouses—one for men, another for women. A little chapel where the monks sang plain-chant services seven times a day. Paradise.

Coffee in hand, I took a seat in the monastery's garden café—four rickety tables clustered around a shaggy-barked tree. Leaning against the tree was an old rusted bike, its handlebar basket filled with flowers whose tint fell some-where between tiger-coat orange and warm salmon. Im-patiens, maybe. One of the café tables had a chessboard stenciled on it, with pieces set up for a game. Everyone here, monks and pilgrims, seemed to play chess.

But I'd been wrong about Zarandok—or János Kodaly, or whatever his name was. Not a trace of him. And no photographs. I'd come here for nothing. Or maybe not nothing—the two days here had been a balm. No waking up feeling like dead matter, like the long cold remnants of an exploded star. The plainchant was indescribable: a soft golden skywriting in the mind. And the morning cof-fee . . . walnut-rich, homey, and heady. Like darkness to night-blooming flowers: the needed medium of transfor-mation. Just mixing in the fresh cream, watching the white tourbillions fade, was a pleasure. I could change my life here. The grounds were rivered with smells—lilac, cut grass, rain-dampened topsoil, goat's-milk cheese, fresh bread. In-stead of potato chips, the monks served the edible red and fuchsia petals of the day lily. I wouldn't have minded a few Pringles, but still.

I knew I should start for town very soon, but . . . just a few minutes more. I liked being somewhere I wasn't con-stantly resisting. That was my life now: resisting inertia, distraction, sleeping pills, invasive technology, that fourth drink of scotch. Each day was propped and braced to prevent backsliding. It wasn't enough for me to just live; I had to have a program for living. Maybe I should become a monk, escape everything. The life here would probably kill me, though. That sign over there said it all.

Temps de prière

4H00: Vigiles
7H00: Laudes- Messe
9H00: Tierce
12H00: Sexte
14H00: None
17H00: Vêpres
19H00: Complies

Seven prayer offices a day and plenty of work in between. Maybe the monks played the occasional game of chess, but the life here was basically prayer, work, prayer, work, cocoa, and bed.

I sipped my coffee and read the English pamphlet I had picked up from the men's guesthouse.

One of Europe's most ancient pilgrimage routes, The Via Francigena begins in Canterbury, England, and crosses France, Switzerland, and Italy to conclude in the Holy City of Rome. In central Switzerland, it intercepts the other great European pilgrimage route, the St. James Way. This famous route runs through Switzerland on a north-south diagonal and takes the pilgrim all the way to the shrine of the apostle Saint James in Santiago de Compostela, Spain. Since

Baulmes Monastery is so close to the crossroads of these two pilgrimages, it is a popular meeting place for—

"Hello," said a clear voice beside me.

The woman with the braid stood beside my table, a small daypack over her shoulder and a reusable coffee mug in one hand. I watched her come around to the other chair. My voice felt detached from me, threshed out of my body. All I could do was blink at her.

"May I sit?" she said.

Without waiting for an answer, she set down her cup and, slipping off her knapsack, placed it at the foot of the table.

"I'm sorry, I gave you a jump," she said, taking a seat—or rather, swaying into it and sitting very tall, knees to the side.

"You did."

"Sorry for that."

She unscrewed the lid of her cup, letting off an eddy of steam, and I could smell the spicy apple tea they made at the monastery. She wore a brushed cotton shirt, hiking boots, and a baseball cap whose back gap was large enough to accommodate her braid.

"Are you here because you're interested in the religious life?" I said.

When she smiled, her mouth didn't turn up at the corners; it just crooked fractionally. But very slight dimples appeared in her cheeks, and a faint meander of light went through her black eyes, like a brandy flame in a darkened room.

"No, I am following you." She dabbled the tea bag in her

cup. "You are looking for a man named Zarandok."

"How do you know that?"

"I am looking for him, too. And his book. Which is *not* his book." She screwed the lid back on her mug, opened the little drinking slot, and took a sip. "I am trying to find him since a long time. That book belongs to my father. I want it back."

"But how did Zarandok get it?"

"My father gave it to him—*trusted* him with it."

"Your father?"

"János Kodaly."

I put my fingers to my temples. "Your father is János Kodaly, the mathematician? Then who is Zarandok?"

"Zarandok is . . . Zarandok. I do not know his real name. I do not think he is a bad man, he just has our book."

I remembered my brief conversation with the son of Zarandok's landlady—some unknown woman had enquired about the Hungarian.

"How long have you been following me?" I said.

"A week, perhaps." She took off her glasses—the serious, studious kind, like those of Marcello Mastroianni in the movie *8½*—and, drawing a shirttail out of her jeans, began to clean them. "I thought I lost you, but then the man in your bookstore—"

"Mique."

"Yes. He told me you were here."

I wouldn't have said she was beautiful, but when you added up everything—the height and the glasses and the eyes like the moist plumes of ink made by a calligrapher's brush—she had presence.

"Why did Zarandok want to talk to you?" she said curiously.

"He asked me to translate the book."

"Translate it? You know Aramaic?"

"I told him I wouldn't be much use. Yes, I studied Aramaic for four years, but I've lost a lot of it."

She put her glasses back on and scrutinized me. "Your name is McCaskill and you are Jewish?"

"It's funny how people keep asking me that. No, I'm *not* Jewish, but I'm beginning to think I was in a previous life. So you know my name—can I know yours?"

"Jaëlle."

"Jaëlle what?"

"Kodaly, of course."

When I looked at her directly, I saw features that were not Saoirse; but when I looked at her with the other side of my mind, so to speak, she *was* Saoirse. It was like trying to make out a faint constellation—you saw the pattern better if you didn't look straight at it.

"Did your father ever speak to you about this place?" I said, glancing around.

"Oh, yes. He often came to Baulmes." She was studying me again. "You are here because you think Zarandok is here."

"Yes, but I got it wrong—I thought Zarandok *was* your father."

"He is not, but for some reason he is doing everything my father did. He becomes my father's *shadow*."

"Well, anyway, Zarandok is not here."

"You are certain?"

"Unless he's hiding in the chapel organ—or the women's dorm."

She swept the grounds with her calm, noctilucent gaze, as if she didn't quite trust my judgment.

"So Zarandok left Geneva because you were after him?" I said.

She continued to gaze at the horizon. "I wonder now," she said, "if it was *me* who did that."

The evening sunlight, the clouds, the shadows, the grass, the birds, the earth, the chessboard, the stones, the orange-tawny flowers, the walls, the mountains, the snow on the mountains . . . at that moment, they all seemed oddly lit and ajar. The whole world felt heavy with unraised sparks, to borrow a Kabbalistic notion. I needed another coffee.

"Do you want something?" I said, picking up my coffee mug.

She shook her head. The poise in the midst of gawkiness—that was Saoirse, too.

After getting my coffee, I stood concealed by the shaggy-barked tree, studying her. How was it that this daughter of a Hungarian Jew reminded me so much of *my* daughter? Or my daughter as she might have been. Jaëlle wasn't Saoirse's double; more like her echo. The constellation Saoirse. Her nose didn't turn up at the tip like Saoirse's; her ears were bigger, and no bumps on the lobes that I could see— but looking at her I felt a tremor of déjà vu, a prickling in my head as if lightning hung in the air. I watched her rise and take a seat at the chessboard table. Get a picture of her. Julie would see the resemblance. But what if she didn't? Maybe it was all in my head. Maybe I *really* needed that vacation.

I took a few rapid sips from my coffee, plunked it down unfinished in a dish pan, and strode over to her.

"Listen," I said. "Do you remember when we first met on the street?"

Now she looked up. She was holding one of the chess pieces—the white knight. It was noticeably taller than the other pieces, rough-hewn and chipped. Even before I took it from her, I could tell it was wooden, not plastic like the others.

*   *   *

"Okay, so he *was* at the monastery," I said. "Where is he now?"

"I believe he is on the pilgrimage route." She kept her eyes on the road. "Sorry, we will not go back to Geneva."

Her rental was a red Fiat hatchback, very nimble on the twisty roads. She had her hiking boots and other stuff in the back, and every time she went around a curve, the stuff would slide to the side. She drove fast, shifting fluidly, rarely looking at me.

"Why on earth would he be on the pilgrimage route?" I said.

"There is only one road to the monastery. I think he wished to leave in secret." She shifted down for a curve. "And maybe he has a friend on the pilgrimage route, to help him."

"But what's he running from?"

"I thought you could tell me that."

"Me? How would I know? All I know is that he gave me a page from this book to translate, then disappeared." Out of some indefinable unease, I glanced in the mirror. "You're going to have to tell me more about this book of yours. I'm beginning to think it's more valuable than I thought."

We drove southeast through the rolling canton of Vaud, passing tiny churches, orderly vineyards, and manicured Swiss towns. The evening had been done in quick, soft strokes of mauve and gray—Degas with his pastel crayon.

"I don't know a lot about the book," she said. "I think my father got it in Wiedikon."

"Wiedikon?"

"The Hasidic quarter in Zurich. He was going there sometimes to sell his meteorites."

"He sold *meteorites* to orthodox Jews?"

She smiled her tiny subsurface smile. "Oh, yes. János knew several gem dealers in Wiedikon who dealt in meteorites. And the gem dealers were often inviting him home for Shabbat, and he was helping their children with mathematics, and . . . I think they talked much."

"What did they talk about?"

"God, Torah, the universe. . . . I think they liked him, even though he wasn't Orthodox."

"From what I've read about your father, that's an understatement. You're driving a bit fast."

"I want to get to Lausanne as soon as possible."

"Lausanne?"

"I think Zarandok probably reached Lausanne on the pilgrimage route. We can ask at the hotels and the pilgrim hostels."

"And if there's no sign of him?"

"Then we start to walk."

"What, we're going to walk the whole pilgrimage route?"

"If necessary."

"But that will take weeks . . . longer, if I have to check

every chessboard for a sign from Zarandok."

"We have to think where he might be. And look for other signs."

"You're sure that knight *was* a sign?"

She nodded. "It was the only sign he could leave without revealing himself."

"But who'd he leave it for? Not for *us*."

"He must have friends helping him along the way."

For once in my life, I didn't give voice to my skepticism. I was wondering how many days I could spare for a wild goose chase like this. I'd have to call Mique when I got a chance and ask him if he could look after the bookstore.

"How did you know about the knight, anyway?" I asked.

"I broke into Zarandok's apartment."

"You *what?*"

"I had no choice; the woman there did not let me see it. The knight was gone and also the book."

I remembered the waterlogged rug in Zarandok's apartment. She had climbed the exterior of that house to the second story? After seeing her drive, I thought her quite capable of it.

We drove in silence, with me frequently looking in the mirror.

"What's the matter?" she said.

"I'm wondering if we're going to get picked up for speeding. But back to this book of yours. You think these Hasidic Jews just gave it to your father?"

"I believe so. He knew Aramaic and mathematics and . . . meteorites. To them he was a *hacham*, a wise man."

"But he didn't believe in God."

"Well, not in the Orthodox way. But as I say, I think they

trusted him. I know he spent a lot of time with the *rebbe*, the spiritual leader."

"So maybe the *rebbe* wanted help in understanding the mathematics of the book?"

"Perhaps. I know the *rebbe* gave him other things . . . papers and scrolls and such like."

"And why did your father pass the book on to Zarandok?"

"To keep safe. He knew his life was in danger."

"From the Hungarian secret police."

"Probably the Russian secret police. But I really don't know who they were; I just know they succeeded."

"I understand your father was a mathematician—chess was just his avocation. Did he have access to any scientific secrets in Hungary? Weapons or anything?"

"He wasn't that kind of scientist."

"What kind *was* he?"

An early moon, delicately veined as a butterfly's wing, floated outside the car window. The mountains lay on the horizon like snoozing leopards, snow in the folds of their coats.

"He could see things in his head," she said.

"What kinds of things?"

She waved a hand. "Chess games from many years before. The shapes of animals in the clouds. A crystal structure that existed mathematically but not in nature. Even universes."

"Universes?"

"He said to me once that he will make a universe one day, but first he needed to see it clearly—see all the stages."

"He was talking about modeling a universe mathematically, I presume."

"No, I think he meant making it really. He could be very *farfelu*."

"You must have had a very interesting childhood."

A car passed us, and her face lit up briefly, the lenses of her glasses gleaming. She was unsmiling, her jaw set.

"Well, I didn't see him much," she said. "He was often busy or . . . pensive."

The sky beyond her was the color of a tropical lagoon. A few gregarious stars had drifted in and now nodded to one another across the infinities.

"But you followed in his footsteps," I said, remembering the books in her bicycle basket.

"Well, I was a bit more *pratique*. I did a graduate degree in physics and then went into cybersecurity."

"Very *pratique*. Where do you work?"

"Anywhere that asks. I'm a consultant."

"A consultant! How old are you?"

"Twenty-six."

"You *can't* be a consultant at twenty-six. You have to be old, jaded, and basically unemployable. A lot of people think I'm a consultant."

But I felt a strange relief to hear that she was a year younger than Saoirse. Had she been the same age, it would have been just too weird.

"There's something you're not telling me," she said.

"What?"

"What are you not telling me? You're not easy in your skin."

"There's something you're not telling *me*. Why do you remind me so much of my daughter?"

I could see by her shoulders that she was holding the

steering wheel tighter. "How can I know?" she said. "I would have to meet your daughter to know what is your problem."

"She died twelve years ago."

She bit her lip and took a fresh grip on the steering wheel, as if the road had temporarily gotten away from her. For a minute we both looked down the shadowed expanse of asphalt.

"I'm sorry," she said.

I got the strange feeling that she was indeed sorry, that she felt the loss as keenly as I did.

*   *   *

My sleeplessness came back to me in Lausanne, where I tossed and turned in the stuffy dormitory of a pilgrims' hostel (we'd managed to get the last available bunks). When I finally slept, I fell into my usual debilitating dream.

I was in my car of twelve years before, the last vehicle I ever owned. The smell of the interior came back to me, the mustiness, the unvacuumed floor. My hands were on the steering wheel, and I was turning left when I heard a semi's horn over my shoulder. I knew I had to react, but the steering wheel had frozen, or *I* had frozen, or the whole world had grown calcified and unyielding. Then came a titanic slam like the impact of a locomotive. My blood was slapped hard inside my body; I might have been a tiny bat that had been walloped out of the air with a plank. I was thrown sideways, and I actually thought for a moment that my insides had been flung right out of me. When I raised my head, I saw that the passenger's seat was gone. I had lost the entire side of the car.

And then my dream abruptly changed. I was holding Zarandok's book—somehow I knew it was his book—with the Hebrew letters scrawled in faded brown ink on rough handmade paper. The letters floated off the page and became a great mansion, with pillars and high dormer windows and crow-stepped gables. I found myself wandering inside the mansion, pacing the corridors, trying all the doors; but every door was locked, and outside each door I would stand, calling my daughter's name over and over.

FOUR

"Any luck?" I said to Jaëlle, as she took a seat at my table.

"No. And you?"

"Nothing. As I expected. Hopeless."

Lausanne: the tilted city. Everywhere were road signs featuring a giant open-palmed hand preventing a car from rolling down a hillside, along with four-step instructions for parking on an incline and a bold-font injunction: "*Bouge pas de là!*" (Don't move from there!). We sat in the warm floral light of late afternoon, in a café behind Place St-François. Around us tourists milled, kids scampered, dog walkers meandered, mothers pushed prams, melancholics sieved through the still promising light. I felt a light sprinkle of rain on my face, fine as mist. Rain from a cloudless sky? Then I saw the cause: across the square jetted a good-sized fountain. The wind was carrying invisible drifts of spume everywhere.

"What do we do now?" I said.

We had split up to cover more ground, in vain. Nobody anywhere—not at the pilgrims' hostels, or the men's shelters, or the university dorms—knew anything about Zarandok.

"We still have the Jewish cemetery," she said, glancing at the city map, its edges fluttering in the breeze. She gestured to the ponytailed, soul-patched waiter, who shimmied toward us between the tables, his tray riding the tips of his fingers.

"But first," she added, "I want you to tell me what you weren't telling me."

To the waiter she said, "*Vin rouge, s'il vous plaît,*" and he shimmied away again. I studied the foam on my beer.

"You really think Zarandok is hiding out at the Jewish cemetery?" I said.

"It's something my father might do, visit the graveyard, so it's something that Zarandok might do. Now tell me, Tavish."

I glanced around at the other tables. Nobody was paying attention. I took out the page Zarandok had given me, with my translation worksheet stapled to it.

"I never saw your book," I said. "But Zarandok did show me a page he'd copied out. Here—and my translation."

She ran her eyes over the text in wonder. "This is from the book?"

"*Your* book. Do you know any Aramaic?"

"No. I'm Jewish, but not as Jewish as you, I think." She flipped to my translation, skimmed it, then flipped back to the original. "This is all you have?"

"All I have."

"It's very strange. And this equation . . ."

"Schrödinger's equation."

"Yes, I recognize it, but why is it here?"

"Zarandok claimed it's part of the original text."

She put up one finger to touch the bridge of her glasses. That small gesture said: *Be rational.*

"Crazy, eh?" I took a swallow of beer. "Let's suppose that Zarandok was being truthful—that the equation is actually in the manuscript. As I see it, there are only two possibilities. One, the manuscript can't be that old."

"But it *is* old," she said. "János—my father—"

I held up my hand. "I'm just giving possibilities here. Two: the manuscript *is* old, but it contains modern glosses. It's handwritten, after all. Someone could have scribbled in the equation within the last century."

"But I'm sure no one would write in that book. It's almost a holy text."

"Not your father?"

"*Especially* not him." She went back to studying the page. "Are there more equations in the book?"

"Zarandok said there are a number of them."

"But modern equations?"

"I have no idea."

"Why are these spaces here?" she said, pointing to the line gaps before and after the equation.

"Again, unclear. Torah scrolls do have spaces after certain sections; I seem to remember a famous rabbi saying that the spaces allowed Moses to meditate upon the lesson. Maybe that's what these are—contemplative pauses, kind of."

"So they are in the original manuscript?"

"I assume so. But that's the whole problem: I haven't seen the actual book."

In front of us, a woman did a dog-walker's pirouette to untangle herself from the leash of her eager poodle. The wind fluttered the huge patio umbrella above us. I drained my glass of beer.

"Anyway, what about this cemetery?" I said.

She looked up. "You go. Right now I want to study this page."

"But you're the one who wanted to see the place!"

"Yes, and now I want to look at this page." She handed me the street map with the cemetery marked out. "You can walk—it is for the benefit of your health."

I hesitated. "Actually, I'd rather not let the page out of my sight."

"Why not?"

"I'd just rather hold onto it."

"You do not trust me."

"It's not that. I'm just not quite easy in my skin right now, as you put it, and . . ."

"Very well." She got out her phone. "It is correct to take a picture?"

"I don't think that's a good idea either, because—"

But she'd already snapped a picture and handed me back the two pages. I sighed my wolverine's sigh, which usually had an effect on people, but she didn't look up from her phone.

"Jaëlle, let's go to the cemetery together. You've got the car."

"I have to return my car to Hertz . . . because we start walking tomorrow."

"That's something else I want to talk to you about. Do we even know where we're going?"

She looked up from her phone screen and locked eyes with me. "Goodbye, Tavish."

*   *   *

I took a cab to the cemetery, gritting my teeth when it came time to pay the fare. Something for my diary—underline in red: no more vacations on the Swiss Riviera.

The cemetery was in a suburb of well kept houses with orange-tiled roofs and hedges so carefully trimmed they resembled fine-pile carpets. I thought at first the graveyard was closed, but I just slid open the metal barrier and walked inside. Like so many things in Lausanne, it had been built on a hillside. A number of the gravestones were not marble but something rougher and cheaper—limestone or field-stone. The Hebrew letters were often so weathered or lichen-streaked I couldn't make them out. Write it on the walls: History is just a long discoloring.

As I walked, I thought about my life. I was rapidly becoming nothing more than my own habits. And the residue I had to contend with! Dust, unpaid bills, compost to empty, unmatched socks, food leftovers, unwritten emails, pens to refill, printer cartridges to replace (didn't I just replace that thing?), batteries to recycle, medical appointments to schedule, appliances to repair, furniture to get rid of, people to avoid, people to reach out to . . . and great expanses of the past to shun. I was sure that more humans died of residue than cancer and Alzheimer's. In fact, what were those diseases but residue?

Though a soul righteous or innocent may depart from this world, she is not lost to Creation, and continues to dwell in other worlds. . . . The line from Zarandok's book came back to me and I thought of the professor in the park, the bubble man. *He* believed in other worlds, other universes. And they were inside this one, he had said. Overtone universes. But he was off his rocker, poor guy. And yet. . . . When I saw Jaëlle on the street the first time, I'd felt a barely perceptible dislocation inside me, as if some hidden magnetic field had reversed itself—as if the overtones had subtly shifted. I could imagine what Julie would say to that.

A lot of the graves, I noticed, had piles of stones on them.

I stopped beside one grave. Hannah Jöder, beloved daughter of Hans and Ruth Jöder, sister of Mena, departed this world for a better one in the Hebrew month of *Tishri* (September–October, as I remembered), 1973, aged ten years, may her soul be bound in the bonds of eternal life. The only motif on the gravestone was a carved tree with four branches, one of which was broken off close to the trunk. The gravestone was strewn with leaves and bird droppings. I took a handful of the leaves and wiped off as much of the bird shit as I could.

The decrepit peacefulness got me thinking about death. I liked to imagine (with W. B. Yeats) that when we died, we would find ourselves living our lives backward, shucking off guilt and despair, flaming into innocence as the summer flames into autumn. And at some magic juncture, Saoirse would appear. She'd grow younger with me every day. Time would swell with unlived experiences. That was the only heaven I had ever believed in, and actually, I *didn't* believe in it—it just alleviated and countervailed my life. But this book of Zarandok's . . . it was even crazier than W.B.'s vision, and here I was, chasing it. And now it was mixed up in my mind with Jaëlle. That pulled me along even more, despite my wariness. And I *was* wary, puzzled, and—

Just then I looked up to see a man in an elegant dark suit walking down the twilight path toward me. I could hear his shoes scuffling the gravel. He held a bag or something and seemed to be stopping at different graves. Approaching me diffidently, he said a soft "shalom," and stood looking down at the headstone for a moment. Taking something from his bag—a leather pouch, I saw now—he knelt to place it on the grave; when he rose again, I saw that it was a single white stone.

"*Excusez-moi,*" I said.

He looked up. His squarish face might have been handsome except that one cheek was pocked and scarred, while the other was largely unblemished. The Phantom of the Opera in a bespoke suit. Maybe mid-forties, but it was hard to tell with that face.

"What is the meaning of these stones?" I said in French. "I see them on a lot of the graves."

He squinted down at the stone he had just placed on the grave. "The meaning . . . do you know, I am not exactly sure. We've just always done it. I suppose it's because flowers wither, but stones stay." He smiled and held out his leather bag. "Would you like some? I have plenty."

"Oh, well. . . . I'm just a tourist."

"So am I. Please."

Some of the stones were just ordinary pebbles, some were quartz or colored stones—white, blue, and red. Out of politeness I took a few.

"I bring a few stones with me when I travel," he said.

His suit fit his stocky form very well. His French was excellent but not native: a German speaker, I suspected.

"I save the white ones for the children," he continued, looking down at the gravestone. "They leave us, they are called out of their names, but someday they will return to their names." He gave a shrug, but not a nonchalant shrug—I noticed a tightening of his mouth. "You are American?" he said.

"Canadian. But I live in Geneva now."

"Ah, yes. Beautiful. But you'll forgive me—not the most exciting city."

"It has its moments, as I'm finding. And where do you call home?"

"Israel. But I'm living for the moment in Zurich."

"Now there's a city that ranks high on the excitement scale. If you have money."

He chuckled. "Yes, yes, but perhaps I was unkind to Geneva. Cities are like people—they can be introverted or extroverted, timid or . . . *talk-active*, depending on when you find them. And what do you do in Geneva?"

"I own a bookstore."

He gave me a keen glance. "Really! Old books or new?"

"Old. The older the better."

"I agree. I am in the business of old books myself."

From his wallet he drew out an embossed card—French, German, and Hebrew.

The Tikkun Olam Project
Director and Founder, Jakob Zunz

"Do you know what *tikkun olam* means?" he said.

"Repairing the world."

"Yes! Repairing the world by gathering all the divine sparks that are scattered and hidden."

"So books are your divine sparks."

"As they are for you, I'm sure." Stooping, he took the edge of his coat sleeve to rub at the gravestone, squinting to make out the letters. "I am engaged in the lifelong task of collecting old Jewish manuscripts and fragments across

Europe—the ones that were hidden away during the Nazi era—in order to bring them under one roof." Straightening, he smiled faintly. "My roof."

"You must have a big house."

"I do." He smiled again. "I need a big house, for all those visions. That's what I really like to collect—the visionaries, the seers. Those with the inflaming, as we say."

"Yes, I know a few Jewish writers like that."

"I have visions piled everywhere, visions inside visions . . . in fact, I need a bigger space." He eyed me speculatively. "Perhaps the Clerne Foundation in Geneva."

"They'd love to get a collection like that. Moishe Rivken— you know him?"

"I know the name."

"You'll be dealing with him if you have any medieval stuff. How old are your books?"

"The oldest I have now is fourteenth-century, but I've heard there is an even older one in Bern. I am going there shortly." He hefted his bag of stones. "And you? Are you staying here long?"

"Just passing through. Doing the pilgrimage."

"The pilgrimage?"

"The Via Francigena."

"Where does it go?"

"Across Switzerland as far as Rome. But I'm hoping I don't have to go that far."

I suddenly felt the fatigue of having walked all day— mainly uphill, so it seemed. What a crazy waste of time this was, trying to find Zarandok. The man Zunz sensed my restlessness, or maybe he was just eager to keep distributing his stones.

"Do you have a business card?" he said.

I gave him one and he read it aloud in English. "'McCaskill's Books: Old, Rare and Neglected Literature.'" His English seemed as strong as his French. "Too bad you will not be around longer, M'sieur McCaskill. We would have had much to chat about."

"Well, I *think* I'm leaving, but it's a bit uncertain right now. Where are you staying in Lausanne?"

"Place St-François. The Charlie Chaplin Hotel."

"I am near the cathedral too. If I am here tomorrow I will give you a call."

"Please do. And I wish you the best on your pilgrimage. May you find what you are looking for."

As he turned to go, I called after him: "Herr Zunz."

"Yes?"

"You said something about children, after they die. . . ."

"They will come back to us."

"And take up their names again."

"Their mortal names, yes. They must give up their angelic names and fly back into their old names."

"Is that idea from one of your books?"

"From my library or my soul, I can't remember. But really they're the same." His smile now seemed to be a clenching of his face. "It makes a nice picture, yes? Souls flying back, like Adam's birds, into their names."

He was scrutinizing me as if to determine whether I genuinely considered it a nice picture.

"Definitely," I said. "I'd just like to know where it's from."

He was still half-smiling, but his gaze was somber and somehow bereft. "From some visionary," he said, in a tone that suggested he was looking forward to the day's end.

* * *

Back at the pilgrims' hostel, I concluded I could easily stay another day or two. The calm alacrity of the house plants soothed me. I relished the smell of rosemary and garlic in the kitchen. In the big communal living room hung a sign that said, "I want to fall asleep to the sounds of animals."

Jaëlle was at one of the tables in the living room, completely absorbed in Zarandok's page on her phone. She sat hunched over, one arm across her chest, hand on her shoulder. Just as Saoirse used to sit.

"Solved the mystery?" I said.

She set her phone aside. "Zarandok said there were other equations in the book, yes? What else did he say?"

"He said the equations were beyond him—and beyond Schrödinger."

"Beyond Schrödinger?"

"That's what he said. But look, I'm beginning to think this equation is just a modern bit of literary graffiti. Somebody scribbled it in as a joke."

"That is the most likely possibility."

"It's the *only* possibility. You think some Kabbalist came up with the equation before Schrödinger did?"

"No. It belongs to modern science. Just like Einstein's equations, and lasers, and the expanding universe. . . ."

"At least we agree on one thing. I mean, if a sixteenth-century Kabbalist had come up with the equation, he would have used Hebrew letters as mathematical symbols. Not Latin, not Greek, but *Hebrew*."

She turned and got up very slowly, as if something had levitated her out of this unimportant conversation. At the

window she stood tall but a touch gawky, nerdy-magisteri-
al, like a flamingo. I saw in my mind the souls of children
flying back to this Earth—what had that guy Zunz said?—
flying back and wrapping themselves in their names, as the
wind wraps itself in sheets on a clothesline.

"The page speaks of other worlds," she said.

"Yes."

"How the dead can die in this world, but. . . ." She turned
to me. "Do you believe that, Tavish?"

"Well . . . no. Not when I'm sober."

Still, I liked to imagine Saoirse dreaming of Julie and me
and lighting a candle to us, wherever she was. I looked at
Jaëlle with the other side of my mind and got overtones again.

"Anyway, I'm tired," I said. "I've got blisters. I worry that
Mique is not turning on the alarm every night. Do you
want to hear about the graveyard?"

She returned to her seat at the table. "Yes, but first—may
I see your mobile phone?"

"My phone? Why?"

"I would like to see it, please."

I got it out and handed it over.

"What's your passcode?" she asked.

"No passcode."

She gave me an incredulous look. "You have no passcode
on your mobile phone?"

"No. I just . . . listen, if I had to do all the fiddly things
I'm supposed to, my life would be *all* fiddle."

Turning the phone off, she dug one pointed fingernail
under the edge of the grubby green cover and began to
remove it.

"I think you are lucky," she said gravely, "to meet me."

FIVE

Morning. A sky of fresh-blown cobalt. Breeze in the crowns of the trees and the golden bleed-through of sunlight shifting, winking, transmuting. I had no food except for an apple, given to me by a German pilgrim who looked like John Lennon during his *Imagine* phase. Gala, said the sticker. Jaëlle hadn't come down yet with my phone, but I felt like talking, so I called Mique from the phone at the front desk. He cheerfully enumerated all the books he hadn't sold and told me not to worry.

"Nobody has asked about the Dumas set?" I said. "Or the Hesse?"

"People are waiting for you to come back, Tav. But I hope that won't be too soon."

"Thanks a lot!"

"No, I mean it is a nice divertissement for me. And you need your vacation."

The apple radiated morning in my hand. It had a starburst color pattern flowing up from the stem well and down the sides—a rosy red, dappled with creamy celandine. Morning, yes, but also night: I could see minute dots like stars all over it. The color pattern reminded me of swirling nebulae.

"Are you turning on the alarm every night?" I asked.

"Of course."

"I can't believe nobody has asked about the Dumas."

"Tav, *vacation*, remember?"

I could understand why artists chose fruit for their still-life compositions. An apple wasn't quite as voluptuous as a pear, but—

"By the way," said Mique, "I discovered more about your Rabbi of the Twelve Winds."

"Really?"

"Your friend Moishe came into the store yesterday."

"Moishe! How is the old swashbuckler?"

Moishe Rivken—rabbi, academic, convivial grumpus. Twenty-five years before, I had talked him into being my advisor for a master's thesis on the Kabbalists. He insisted we speak Aramaic as often as we could; Julie started calling me Mr. Ein Sof—the Kabbalistic term for the Infinite—because that term came up so much in our conversation. We were still friends even though I'd dropped out of my program after four months.

"I told him about the book you found," continued Mique. "He was *very* interested."

I was immediately alert. Mique's great virtue as a bookseller—he liked to talk—was now a drawback.

"Listen, Mique, I'd rather you kept quiet about that book."

"Why?"

"Just because. I want to find out more about it on my own. That's actually the reason for my vacation—I'm pursuing some leads here."

"Then you will be interested in what Moishe told me."

"Okay, what?"

Old Moishe. Long ago he asked me why I wanted to study the Kabbalists. Simple, I said: they were wild and

we're tame. They saw thin places everywhere. They embod-
ied the unfeigned self, the raw soul. All in all, I told him,
they reminded me of my much loved and long deceased
Scottish grandmother. And when he still looked skeptical,
I added: Plus, I've fallen in love with Aramaic.

"There's a story about your rabbi," said Mique. "His real
name was Ezra Ben-Emeth of Castile. When he was banished from Spain with the other Jews, he wandered all
around Europe . . . even in Switzerland."

"Switzerland? Where in Switzerland?"

"Moishe couldn't say. But we're doing more research on
it. We're both interested in your rabbi."

"Okay, but listen, please tell Moishe—be discreet." I was
suddenly conscious of other pilgrims milling about, and
especially the rosy-cheeked neo-hippie woman behind the
desk. "I think there might be a bit of history attached to
this . . . thing we're talking about."

"It sounds so."

"I mean a history of contention. It seems to have been
originally owned by Hasidic Jews, who gave it to a guy, who
gave it to *another* guy—look, I'm monopolizing the desk
phone here. Bye for now, old friend. Discretion is the word,
okay?"

Yes, once I had been in love with traditional Aramaic,
even though learning it almost killed me. At some point I
just had to let go of grammar and follow the glittering path
of the words, like moonlight on water. I kept following the
path in my dreams; it sometimes seemed easier in REM
sleep. (My dreaming brain was gathering all my scattered
memory traces of Aramaic, explained Julie—and they were
definitely scattered.) After a while, even Moishe had to ad-

mit I was making progress. But then Saoirse was born, and, in the words of the Hasidic storyteller, the wonder of the near replaced the wonder of the far.

I was about to wash the apple and take a bite when I thought of Jaëlle. Maybe I'd save the Gala for her.

*   *   *

I knew I couldn't continue this wild goose chase much longer. It wasn't fair to Mique. I saw that I'd have to put my foot down with Jaëlle.

"Can I have my phone back?" I asked.

We'd set out to get breakfast. She hadn't bothered with her braid, just drawn her hair up at the back. Her maverick ears, one with its fine circlet of gold, stood out even more. At her nape were impossibly fine hairs, like the lines on old maps that indicated wilderness or the steepness of mountains. With the braid gone, I noticed a tattoo there, half-visible above the neck of her T-shirt. It was so small I couldn't tell what it was—an emblem of some kind, it looked like.

"It wants to be cleaned, I think," she said, and handed me my grubby phone case along with the phone itself.

"Well?" I said. "Is it bugged?"

A pedestrian street dipped away before us: cobblestones, long shallow steps at either side and a water sluice down the middle. The morning was warm and clear, an exhalation of the green earth. Under every city, the living world is trying to breathe through its clogged pores. Gray-faced, petrific, the buildings rose up around us with their bright storefront names: Breitling, Ana Sousa, United Colors of

Benetton.

"That's why you wanted to look at my phone, right?" I pursued.

She was tall enough to be able to take two of the shallow steps at a time. Now, unhurriedly, she began taking three steps.

"Who's Julie?" she said.

I stopped walking. She took one step farther and then turned to gaze up at me. She didn't look defiant, or guilty, or sheepish—just patient.

"You went through my contacts," I said.

She took a stride upwards to bring herself level with me, and at the same time switched into French. "I had to check everything to see if the phone was clean."

"And you had a nice long look while you were at it."

"You keep saying I look like your daughter. I wanted to find out the truth."

"So you *did* have a nice long look."

"Is Julie the mother of your daughter?"

We were each speaking our respective languages, circling each other in our minds like electric eels, creating a charged aura that passersby could sense at once. People slowed as they went around us, averting their eyes but straining to hear; one guy actually took his earbuds out.

"There's something wrong here," I said.

"What do you mean?"

"There's something wrong, and it started that day we met."

"What started?"

"You just *happened* to have the kind of books that Saoirse loved?"

Her eyes flashed. "Yes, Tavish, I just happened to have them. Because I grew up with books like that. János had *shelves* of them."

I started walking again, three steps at a time, and she followed.

"Can you *stop?*" she said at my shoulder.

The street leveled out temporarily, and we came across a cluster of café tables with bright yellow patio umbrellas, green Carlsberg ashtrays, and baby prams. Several Swiss mothers were out with their infants, enjoying the sun.

I stopped and faced Jaëlle. "You know what?"

"What?"

Just then, over her shoulder, I caught sight of a familiar face: Jakob Zunz, the guy I'd met at the graveyard. He looked up from a café table and raised a hand.

Jaëlle followed my gaze. "Who's that?"

I couldn't pretend I hadn't seen Zunz; he had half-risen from his seat, a smile on his heavy, hardscrabble face.

"Tavish?" said Jaëlle.

"None of your business. Listen, I think it's time you and I—"

"He's waving to you."

"I can *see* that." I took a second to compose myself. "You'll understand if I don't introduce you to any of my acquaintances, Jaëlle. You might decide to scroll through their contacts too."

She shifted her weight to one leg and folded her arms combatively. I left her there and walked over to Zunz. He'd gotten out the business card I had given him, maybe to remind himself of my name.

"Please join me," he said, smiling. "Your companion too."

"I'm afraid she has another engagement."

I suppose I intended to say a brief hello to Zunz and then return to the pilgrims' hostel. But now Jaëlle stood beside me, awkward but determined in her waterbird way. Zunz hastily dabbed his mouth with a napkin and got to his feet.

"Hello," she said, trying to soften her features. "I am Jaëlle."

I suspect Zunz guessed he'd interrupted a spat of some kind, but he was evidently well bred enough not to let on.

"Jaëlle," he repeated, offering his hand—palm upwards, so that she self-consciously extended her own into his. He lowered his eyes to it very briefly. "I am Jakob Zunz," he said slowly, as if accustomed to making an impression with his name. "So happy to see you both." Now he let her hand fall as if it had been a floating feather and turned to shake my own; his grip was like iron.

"Please, have a seat," he said. "The babies and I are just watching life walk on."

He was dressed as immaculately as before, in a powder-blue suit and a cream-colored silk shirt; his open collar revealed curling chest hair like steel wool. I saw a copy of *Le Monde* beside his placemat; it seemed to be covering something.

"You are a pilgrim too, Jaëlle?" he inquired as we took our seats.

"In a way."

"Ah."

When he realized it would be up to him to carry the conversation, he held up the card I had given him. "M'sieur McCaskill and I met in a graveyard."

"Oh, yes?" said Jaëlle stonily.

"But we did not talk much about the afterlife, thanks to God. We talked about old books." He gestured a waiter over. "*S'il vous plaît*, coffee for my friends—coffee for you, Jaëlle?—and yes, more croissants."

The waiter left, leaving behind a slightly awkward silence. Since both Jaëlle and Zunz were looking at the babies, I did so as well. Two of the infants were in a double stroller right beside our table. They had the bland, peaceable faces of sunflowers. One wore a frilly bonnet while the other sat inside a shapeless baby suit that made him look like a baggy starfish. Every once in a while, their mother would reach behind and give the stroller a back-and-forth nudge. She was talking to another woman at her table; their sunglasses had reduced them to pure lips and complexion. Zunz toasted the table with his coffee cup, and the women gave him small, contained smiles. The twin babies looked on, serious as jurors.

"Old books," prompted Jaëlle.

"Old *Jewish* books," said Zunz. "I collect them."

"Do people ever come to you with manuscripts?"

"Oh yes. From all over the world."

Jaëlle leaned toward him. "And have you ever been approached by a man named Zarandok?"

I shot her a warning glance, which Zunz could not have missed. Until then he had tried to keep the good side of his face toward Jaëlle, but now he looked away, no longer smiling.

"Zarandok." He put his coffee cup down. "Yes, I've had dealings with Zarandok. Why do you ask, madame?"

I saw I would have to corral the conversation.

"He came into my bookstore not long ago," I said.

"Really?" Zunz turned to me. "Did he try to sell you anything?"

"Not exactly. He said he was looking for a translator."

Zunz nodded, his mouth tight. "Let me guess. He found a manuscript in Aramaic or Assyrian or Hebrew and was desperate to translate it. Because he loved the subject so. Yes?"

Jaëlle gave me a sharp sidelong glance. I kept my eyes on Zunz.

"You have dealt with Zarandok before," I said.

"Zarandok has stolen at least two books from my collection," he said calmly. "He is well-known to the police in Germany and Switzerland. So I am always interested in news about my friend Zarandok. What book did he bring you?"

"He said he had an old Aramaic manuscript, but he didn't actually have it with him."

Zunz grunted. "He was investigating you. Looking for a soft target."

"Well, I must have disappointed him. He left and never came back."

"He may be waiting for the right time."

"I'll be ready for him." I always liked to think I had a good poker face, honed from decades of negotiating first-edition sales, but I was still nervous under Zunz's steady gaze. "What books did he steal from you?"

"A collection of Hasidic tales and a sixteenth-century edition of *Sefer Yetzirah*, the Book of Creation. Zarandok likes the visionaries, as I do." He hunched over the table, and again I was struck by the contrast between his elegant manners and his battered physicality. "This is how he works," he continued. "He says he doesn't want to sell his book, just translate it. But isn't it curious—he never approaches translators or universities, just book collectors . . . . especially small ones without the relevant expertise."

"In this case, I *do* have the expertise," I said.

"You do?"

"I know Aramaic . . . some."

"My apologies, M'sieur McCaskill. I was being superior. My servants have warned me about that." He chuckled. "But you say he didn't have the book with him. Did he show you any proof—photos or photocopies or such?"

"He just described it. He was very nervous."

"Of course. But generally he has some evidence of the book. He gave you nothing at all?"

I remembered reading somewhere how to lie: look steadily but not fixedly at your interlocutor, imagine you're stating your birth date or some other ironclad fact, and (most importantly) plant your lie in a bed of truth.

"No, but our conversation didn't last long," I said. "As I say, I told him to come back with the book. He never did."

Zunz withdrew a Moleskine notebook and silver pen from his shirt pocket, tore out a page, and began writing. "This is the man at the Bern police department who is working on the Zarandok file," he said, handing me the paper. "Dassvanger is his name. You can contact him if Zarandok returns. And I would be glad of a call, too."

"Of course."

This whole subject of Zarandok seemed to have disconcerted Zunz. When the coffee and croissants came, I changed the subject, asking him about literary attractions in Switzerland. Jaëlle sipped her coffee in silence. I think he would've preferred talking to her over me, and observing that she didn't feel chatty, he eventually said he must return to his hotel.

"Please, let me look after this," he said, picking up the bill. "And Jaëlle, if you'll permit, I have something for you."

He lifted the copy of *Le Monde* to reveal the leather pouch he'd been carrying at the graveyard.

"They are for safety in your life journey . . . and beyond." He put two colored pebbles into her hand. "Blue and purple . . . echo and essence."

"Echo and essence?" I repeated.

He smiled. "There is a belief that there is only one soul, the primordial soul, the soul of Adam Kadmon—and we are all part of that soul. We are all each other's essence; we are all each other's echo. Jew, Christian, Hindu, Muslim . . . even Nazi. Have a good pilgrimage."

*   *   *

"I don't understand what you were saying," said Jaëlle. "About the books in my bicycle basket."

Through the kitchen window of the pilgrims' hostel, I could see a table in the corner of the courtyard. Two women in large floppy hats were giving out pilgrims' gifts—water bottles, sunscreen, blister bandages—along with *cartes de bénédiction*, blessing cards. The banner on the front of the table said Les Amis du Chemin de Saint-Jacques, the Friends of the St. James Way. We seemed to have found ourselves in the middle of a pilgrims' convention. The number of guests at the hostel had doubled. I saw people wearing name tags with brotherly affiliations—the confraternity of this or the community of that.

"Tavish?" she said.

"Forget it."

"No, I will *not* forget it. What did you mean about my books?"

I had swallowed my anger at Jaëlle, and I wasn't sure why. Then again, with Saoirse, I never could hang onto my anger.

"Saoirse would have had the same kind of books," I said wearily. "I know I'm sounding like a broken record."

Her look had grown slightly less severe, but now she spoke as if explaining matters to a child. "You know, Tavish, it can sometimes happen by hazard that two people from different places in the world will resemble each to each. It is a mathematical likelihood. In fact, there is a website—"

"Yes, yes, all right. You're definitely your father's daughter."

We sat at a wobbly, toffee-colored wooden table that seemed to have been put together from scrap—the legs looked as though they came from an old piano. From close by came the scent of roasted sunflower seeds and coffee. I picked up a blessing card that had been left on the kitchen table. *Pilgrim, know that your path takes you upward into the angelic houses.* From a group called the Malta Brethren of the Holy Way.

"Anyway," she added, "I'm quite sure your phone isn't bugged."

"Thank goodness for cybersecurity consultants. Listen, you told me that maybe Zarandok had a friend on the pilgrimage route."

"Yes, because he left the sign, the chess knight."

"So we have to find this friend of his."

She was gazing out the window. "I'm thinking now that maybe the friend was *you*."

"Me? How did he know I'd be there at the monastery?"

"He guessed you would follow him." She fingered the circlet of gold on her ear and—once again, I couldn't help it—I thought of Saoirse, fingering her own earring. "I think he trusts you," she continued. "I don't know why. Maybe because you are like him."

"I'm *like* him?"

"Yes . . . in the eyes."

"Here's another possibility: he left that chess knight for *you*."

She gave a bitter smile. "He is running from me for years. I think now he *stole* the book of my father. You heard what your friend Zunz said."

The book of my father. Earlier, she had called him "János." I wanted to delve more into their relationship, but I suspected that now was not the time.

"Actually," I said, "I just met Zunz yesterday, so I would take what he says with a grain of salt." I unfolded our map and laid it out on the table, and her gaze moved from my face to my hands, as if alert for some legerdemain.

"There's a more pressing issue right now," I said. "You know why there's a pilgrims' convention here? Lausanne is a crossroad for *two* pilgrimage routes."

"Yes, somebody told me that."

"The question is, which route did Zarandok take?"

She peered at the map. "Where do the routes go again?"

"The Via Francigena goes east to the Great St. Bernard Pass and into Italy. The other one is the famous Camino, the Way of St. James—the Jakobsweg, in German. It goes south from here into France and eventually into Spain."

"The *Jakobsweg*. It goes where if you follow it north?"

"Right through Switzerland . . . Fribourg, Bern, Lucerne, Interlaken, Lake Constance." I picked up another blessing card. "So which route?"

She shrugged listlessly; maybe she was finally starting to see the hopelessness of our enterprise. *The world is scripture, voyager,* said my blessing card. We were knee-deep in blessings, it seemed. Except the blessing of a clear destination.

"You never told me how Saoirse died," she said.

She said the name with assurance, as if already familiar with it. I sat with elbows on the table, fingers gently massaging the back of my neck. The world is scripture, voyager. The world is scripture.

"Car accident," I said.

"Were you in the car too?"

"I was driving."

My dream flickered through my mind: the world-severing slam, the squall of glass, the shattering inside me. I had flashbacks continually in the hospital afterward, where I nursed a skull fracture and broken ribs. The accident had happened on the way to Saoirse's summer camp, the Interstellar Academy. And I lay in the hospital bed trying to die, trying to follow her among the stars.

"May I see that picture of her?" said Jaëlle.

She took it from me, and I saw her draw a tiny breath, as if readying herself for the sight.

"I don't really think I look like her," she said shortly, handing it back.

Earlier she had re-braided her hair, and now, tilting her

head slightly and reaching behind, she drew the plait in front of her and began fingering the end. She had asked to see the picture and yet handed it back almost immediately.

"Your tattoo," I said.

"Yes?"

"What is it?"

She put a hand to her nape. "The Hebrew word *chai*. It means—"

"I know. 'Living' or 'alive.'"

Chai: Two letters, one word. I could understand why she chose it. With its horizontal stroke and two graceful arms, *chai* closely resembled the mathematical symbol pi.

"When did you get it?" I said.

"A long time ago. It's just *chai*. Nothing special. " She sat up, brushing her braid over her shoulder. "Listen, I think we must get another rental car and return to the monastery."

"To Baulmes? Why?"

"Those monks know something. That old brother, the beekeeper . . ."

"Alphonse."

"Alphonse, yes. He was not at ease with me."

"*I'm* not at ease with you, Jaëlle. Look, I talked to Alphonse myself, and I'm pretty sure he knew nothing about Zarandok."

"All right, Tavish," she said with asperity, "what is *your* proposition?"

"Let's go back to Geneva."

"But we can't give up now!"

"We're not giving up; we're going back to get more information about Zarandok."

And about you.

"We can't just drive aimlessly all over Switzerland," I added. "Or *walk.*"

She raised her chin and became still, looking across the room; when she was irritated or disaffected, she always looked as though she were sitting for a portrait painter she didn't particularly like.

"Anyway," I said, "I have a bookstore to run."

"This is more important than your bookstore, Tavish."

"For you, maybe. But the store is all I have."

She gave me a long appraising look and got to her feet. "Well, I do not want to take away your *life.*"

"Good. I've only got one, despite what the Kabbalists say."

"We meet in the lobby in half an hour," she said, and strode off. I tried to catch another look at her tattoo, but it was covered by the black familiar that followed her everywhere, her braid.

With almost nothing to pack, I was ready in fifteen minutes. There was no sign of Jaëlle in the lobby. For once I felt like walking; the day had remained blue and buoyant. I shouldered my knapsack and stepped outside. The Way of St. James route, the Jakobsweg, led across a bridge and up the hill behind the hostel; I could see the green Via Jacobi sign, with the miniature Swiss flag in its corner. Beyond the sign was a wooden awning like a well roof, which sheltered a bulletin board. An information station for pilgrims, I guessed. I made my way across the bridge and up the cobblestone path. Under the awning, I stood before a wall map of central Switzerland, with the pilgrimage route marked out in red. Beside the map, a bulletin board held a scatter of blessing cards, business cards, and handwritten notes. On a shelf beneath the map was a battered ledger-type notebook, along with a pen on a string.

That tattoo of hers . . . *chai*. Which looked a lot like pi. Saoirse had wanted to get a tattoo. When you're sixteen, we told her. What would she have chosen? I could have guessed. . . .

The pages of the ledger book were lined in the faded aquamarine of an unused swimming pool. A pilgrims' registry. Names, dates, nationalities. Scrawled comments about the journey along with the occasional doodle—crosses, hearts, suns. I began flipping back through the pages. Swiss, French, Brits, Italians. *It helped my PTSD,* wrote one pilgrim. *J'ai vu un ange,* said another—I saw an angel—

Just then my eye was drawn to a small drawing at the bottom of the page. A horse's head. No, it had a base.

A chess knight.

April 27th, three days ago. No name, just the knight. I let the register book fall. Zarandok had gone north on the Jakobsweg. Not east to Rome, not south to Geneva, but *north*. Whoever the clue was for, there it was.

I ran back to the hostel, my hiking boots scrabbling on the cobblestones; two people stepped hastily off the sidewalk to allow me passage. In half a minute, wheezing, I had bounded up the stairs to Jaëlle's dormitory room.

"Jaëlle!" I called. I knocked loudly and opened the door; two middle-aged women, one of them half-dressed, glared at me.

"*Excusez-moi.*" I raced back downstairs to the front desk.

"I'm looking for the young woman who was with me," I said to the guy. "Dark hair, braid . . ."

"I am sorry, m'sieur, I did not see her. This is yours."

He handed me my cell phone.

"It fell from your pocket just now," he added.

"What? Okay, thanks. . . . Are you sure you haven't seen her?"

"I am sure, m'sieur."

Okay, easy. Breathe. I could feel my heart beating in my ears as I went out the backdoor into the courtyard. The sun-hatted ladies were still giving out pilgrim's gifts. They looked up benignantly as I approached. *Excusez-moi, mesdames . . . avez-vous vu une jeune femme aux cheveux noirs?* No, they hadn't seen a young woman with black hair. Inside again, I stood bewildered before the front desk. Goddamn it, did she just . . . ? Maybe she just decided, *enough*.

I went outside once more and skirted the hostel, passing under arcades, over the bridge, and around rows of parked scooters. Nothing. I was breathing noticeably now. Back to the hostel.

"Are you all right, sir?" said the guy at the desk.

"Yes, yes. She didn't appear while I was out, the woman with—"

"No, sir."

"And you have no note from her? She didn't leave a note?"

"No note, sir. Sorry."

SIX

Think. Think. She wouldn't just leave. Or would she? Maybe I had finally weirded her out, with all my talk of . . . Saoirse, my sweet girl, O lost and by the wind grieved, how could I *not* be drawn to Jaëlle if—it wasn't a fixation, it was just—not a sexual fixation, anyway—was it?—okay, stop with these thoughts! She looked like my *daughter*, for God's sake. Young enough to be my daughter. She must have decided to go back to the monastery—on her own. Stop thinking about it.

I went over everything that had happened today: we'd shared that apple, exchanged a few words with the guy at the hostel desk, walked out into the street, seen the man Zunz, had that conversation—

Zunz.

I took out his business card from my wallet. Had she gone to find him, for some reason? To learn more about Zarandok? I called the number and waited impatiently for the end of the voice-mail greeting—in German, French, and Yiddish.

"Herr Zunz, this is Tavish McCaskill. My friend Jaëlle— you met her today—seems to have gone off somewhere, and I'm trying to. . . . I'm just wondering if you've seen her today. Thanks so much. Or talked to her. Thanks. You have my number."

Four-thirty p.m. She'd been gone for almost two hours. I had to decide if I wanted to stay at the pilgrims' hostel another night. I put my hand in my pocket, looking for the hostel receipt, and felt something small and round: the white stone that Zunz had given me. For the children, he'd said. I studied it in my hand, feeling Jaëlle's absence fluttering inside me like a netted bird. A perfectly smooth white stone. Maybe a beach stone, polished by the ocean for millions of years. I remembered that he'd given stones to Jaëlle, too. Purple and blue: echo and essence.

My loon vibrated inside my pocket; I jumped and scrabbled for it. "Herr Zunz?"

"No, sorry, Tav! Just me."

"Mique," I said dully.

"You were expecting somebody else?"

"Well . . . yes, but it's okay."

"Maybe I shall call you later?"

"No, no." I needed something to distract me from the tremor of Jaëlle's disappearance. "Listen, did you find out anything more about the Rabbi of the Twelve Winds?"

"Yes. But everything is fine, Tav? You sound very—"

"I'm okay, it's just . . . never take a vacation on the Swiss Riviera, Mique. What did you find out?"

"Your rabbi *was* in Switzerland. Do you know the name Paracelsus?"

"Yes, yes. Alchemist and doctor."

"Paracelsus wrote about your Rabbi of the Twelve Winds. He said the rabbi stayed at the house of his father, in a place called Einsiedeln."

"Einsiedeln. That's on this pilgrimage route."

"The pilgrimage route?"

"I'm walking the St. James Way."

"You, Tav! Things are always happening to you."

"I'm starting to wish they wouldn't. Listen, what does Paracelsus say about our rabbi?"

"Not much; he was a youth at the time. Just that the rabbi was. . . . Let me get my paper." Pause. "Yes, here is the citation—'A bent reedlet of a man, who had lost everything in his exile and whose only solace was his visions; he would see Creation as Adam saw it, with all the ages of the world laid out like islands in an archipelago; he would speak to sages from the past and future, to generations unborn and the children of his house. . . .'"

"The children of his house?"

"His descendants, according to your friend Moishe. 'And he would cry out and pray in anguishing wonder.' End of citation."

"But this is the sixteenth century, right? Paracelsus's father must have been very broad-minded, to shelter a rabbi."

"Yes, especially since—again, says Moishe—Jews had been officially banished from Switzerland."

"Listen, Mique, could you and Moishe find out all you can about our rabbi's travels in Switzerland?"

"Unfortunately I think I've found out all I can. He's very elusive."

"See if you can dig around a bit more, okay? But don't call me—I'll call you."

"Why, Tav?"

"I'll explain later. Got to go, Mique. And listen—can you handle the store for a little while longer?"

"Of course. Julie helps me when she can. I'll tell her about your adventures."

"Actually, please don't, Mique. As I say, I'll explain later. And remember, I'll call you. I owe you, bud."

I checked my phone for the twentieth time. Okay, gear down. Breathe. What was I going to do before Mique called? Yes, register for another night. There were three people in line at the front desk, and the pilgrims kept coming in. I'd be lucky if I got a place.

Then a thought struck me: Suppose Jaëlle had somehow seen the chess knight in the pilgrims' register. Could she have decided to go north on her own?

Once again I went out the front door and across the bridge. She wouldn't have gone ahead without me, would she? Restless, I kept going, past the pilgrims' register and through the manicured Parc de l'Hermitage, into the Bois de Sauvabelin, where I climbed the circular wooden tower and spent ten minutes scanning the countryside. The mountains were bathed in the soft mango light of late afternoon. I had the absurd thought that I'd be able to see her on the path somewhere, see the tiny line of her braid swaying to and fro. If she'd gone ahead without me, I'd have to return to the hostel, get my pack, and—

I descended the tower and began retracing my route. I went slowly, barely noticing my surroundings, feeling more drained than I'd felt for weeks. FaceTime Julie. Get her opinion on it all. I could just see her, narrowing one eye at me, as she used to do when I committed some domestic misdemeanor—like returning a box of rice to the cupboard with exactly eleven grains in it (she had shaken them out into her palm to count).

Once inside the pilgrims' hostel, I marched up to the ponytailed guy at the desk.

"No, sorry, m'sieur, I haven't seen your friend. But a package came for you."

He handed me one of those manilla shipping envelopes, about the size of a small pillow and almost weightless in my hands. It bore my name, written in felt marker, and a single phrase at the top left corner: "From the Friends of the Shared Path."

"What's this?" I said.

They man leaned over the desk to see. "I think it's a pilgrim's gift."

"Who are the Friends of the Shared Path?"

"A pilgrims' association, I guess. I don't know them, but—"

"Did you see who left it?"

"I'm sorry, m'sieur; it was here at the desk when I came back."

At that moment, my loon called, startling us both. I drew out my phone: private number. I brushed it open with nervous fingers.

"M'sieur McCaskill," said a deep, accented voice.

"Yes?"

There was something *off* about the voice, as if it had been electronically distorted.

"Walk outside to the back courtyard," said the voice.

"What?"

"Take the package and walk outside to the back."

"Who is this?"

"The back courtyard. Do not talk to anyone."

The ponytailed guy at the desk was looking at me expectantly. Package in hand, I turned away and walked through the hostel to the back door. In my head was a kind of aura, very close (I suppose) to what epileptics feel before a seizure. People were talking and laughing around me, but I barely saw them; I had retreated into a pool of my own breathing.

"Into the corner," said the voice.

Could he see me? *How* could he see me? In the corner of the yard I stood near a bench, under a tree, scanning the yard and the buildings beyond. Easy, easy. The tree was a laurel, something like laurel. The package rested feather-light against my arm. I leaned against the laurel, trying to put a bit of space between each breath.

"You haven't opened your pilgrim's gift," said the voice.

Whatever was in the package, it occupied only about half the space, so that the lower part of the envelope was contoured out. The bulge was soft to the touch, like. . . . I put the thing hastily on the bench.

"I'm not going to open it," I said harshly, "until I know what's going on."

Was it something toxic, some kind of—? I looked at my fingers. No, it seemed irregular in form, something *lumped* but compressible. . . .

The telephone line breathed a faint static, a measureless emptiness, like the background radiation from the Big Bang.

"You know where Zarandok is," said the voice.

"How do you know about Zarandok?"

"We propose an exchange. You give us Zarandok. We give you the girl."

Blood or darkness swam before my eyes. I leaned against the tree, trying to get my breath. Focus. *Focus.*

"I *don't* know where Zarandok is," I managed. "Yes, he's gone north—I think he's gone north. But I don't know where."

Long pause.

"Open the package, M'sieur McCaskill."

I closed my eyes. Dread had completely invaded my body, a slow-working poison.

"The package," repeated the voice.

I picked it up gingerly: the flap was sealed with two diagonal pieces of transparent tape. In fumbling with them I must have touched the keypad of my phone, since I heard an electronic chirp.

"I'm *opening* it," I said desperately.

I tore open the flap. Something dark. . . . My fingers touched a silkiness and I drew out a mass of black hair. Jesus. The length of hair was tied at the tip with a green elastic band—the same one I'd seen on Jaëlle's braid.

Then everything grew distorted around me: my breathing, the laurel, the world. The voice on the phone seemed to be speaking white noise, smeared and distant, as if coming from beyond Pluto. Vaguely I became aware of his words.

". . . the Friends of the Shared Path. We will be watching over you on your pilgrimage."

No blood. . . . . Thank God. I could see that the braid had been cut close the roots, but no blood, no—

"Listen to me," I said hoarsely. "Zarandok doesn't trust me, but he trusts Jaëlle. Let her go. She'll lead you to him."

"We will contact you again. Say nothing to the police, or you will receive more gifts. And may the angels with their radiant strides keep pace with you."

"What?"

"A pilgrim's prayer, m'sieur."

The line went dead. I leaned against the tree, half-con-

cussed, my phone in one hand and Jaëlle's unraveling braid
in the other. A breeze detached a small tuft of hair from
the braid, and I dazedly watched it drift to my feet.

*   *   *

The hour between dog and wolf. I was walking through
shadows. Jesus, what a thing. Call the police. No, too risky.
I was sure that prick had been watching me while . . . the
forest. Call the police from the forest. But what if my phone
was bugged? Jaëlle had said it wasn't bugged. No, she'd said
she was *pretty sure* it wasn't bugged. That voice seemed to
be everywhere. Talking to me from beyond Pluto. A *scaly*
voice. Fuck you, Mr. Friend of the Shared Path.

Headlights swam by me; the cars were strange evanesc-
ing shapes in the dusk. I was following the same route I
had already walked—Parc de l'Hermitage, Bois de Sauvabelin—but everything had changed. I didn't like the cars,
didn't like the headlights, but I was also leery of the shadowed woods. Steady. Ride it out. That voice . . . it had almost
sounded computer-generated. Not human. A voice made
of atmospherics, charged particles, solar wind. The Friends
of the Shared Path. . . . Who were they? Find Zarandok.
Find Zarandok. Find Zarandok. He'd gone north. Fribourg
or Bern. Or farther?

Into the monsoon of my mind blew a small seed from
the day—my conversation with Mique. I slowed my pace.
What was the story? The Rabbi of the Twelve Winds in
Switzerland. All of Creation laid out before him. He took
shelter somewhere . . . yes, at the house of Paracelsus *père*,
in . . . Einsiedeln. That was it. I'd seen the place on the map,

maybe a week's walk away. A famous stop on the pilgrim-age.

And I was a pilgrim now.

SEVEN

Like the pilgrims of old, I went warily, my senses stretched tight across the shapes of things—through parkland, and around a small beehive-fringed garden, and across a road, and through a long stretch of heavily ivied trees, and down wooden steps that were wrapped in chicken wire to prevent slipping, and under a motorway, and into a woodland again. Slowly the world drained itself of light and a few faint planets came close and my phone battery died. Eventually I found myself in a shallow, treed ravine with a creek on my left and a bluff on my right. How long had I been walking? Two hours, more? The bluff on my right turned out to be sand, not rock—the surface crumbled in my fingers. Because of the urban glow, only a few stars showed. The darkness resonated with crickets. I kept going cautiously until the path rose and turned to the east, and I emerged from the ravine into the pallid glow of street lamps. Chemin des Croisettes, said the street sign. From my knapsack I got out my map of the pilgrimage route: Les Croisettes, in Épalinges—a northern suburb of Lausanne.

By some miracle I had managed to keep to the pilgrimage route.

I walked aimlessly through the streets, past a school and a bakery and a Let's Go Fitness, and soon came to a main intersection. No hotels, no B and Bs. I continued down the main road and then went west again, back into the residential area, and eventually I saw a small sign—the Wimli Café.

"A place to meet yourself," said the sign. Just what I needed.

The place was spotlessly clean but radiated a hard hospital light. I took a seat at a table close to a wall socket and plugged in my phone. The tables and chairs were institutional style, plastic veneered, no frills; but my own table had a mason jar stuffed full of flowers that set the place alight. Purple hyacinths and yellow daffodils and tulips of a hot living pink. Even their stems in the clear water were a cluster of fresh greens—citrine and celery green and the rich tint of an unripe banana. I could smell the flowers as I sat down, especially the brassy, perfumey hyacinths. After everything that's happened, I still remember those flowers, their aplomb, their hospitality. They were flowers for a pilgrim.

A leached-out spirit had emerged from the back and now stood at the small counter. He seemed to be all fadeaway points and vignetting, like a hasty pencil sketch. We were the only two people in the place.

"I don't have any food," he said blankly.

"But you have croissants." I nodded to a plastic-wrapped dish on the counter.

"I mean I don't have any dinners or anything. Our cook has gone home."

A young man, so it seemed, but with a face of old porcelain and a wispy, sand-colored beard. His eyes were like rainwater, with no discernible tint. I noticed he kept glancing at points near me, but not directly at me, as if gauging the amount of space I occupied.

"A croissant and a coffee would be great," I said. "Actually, how about two croissants?"

He moved over to the coffee machine, and at that moment my loon called. I crossed the room and scooped my phone off the table. It took me a second to recognize the number: Jakob Zunz. I hesitated as the loon kept calling. When my phone went to voice mail, I turned it off and stuffed it deep into my knapsack, under my clothes and under Jaëlle's braid. I really had no idea how telephone bugs worked, but I seemed to remember reading that some could eavesdrop even if you weren't using the phone.

When I had paid for my coffee and croissants, I said to the guy, "Could I possibly use your phone?" I had noticed a landline tucked away at the far end of the counter.

He nodded and watched as I got out Zunz's card and picked up the receiver. I thought I'd have to make the call with him standing there, but at the last moment he wandered into the back room.

"Herr Zunz?" I said. "Tavish McCaskill."

"M'sieur McCaskill! I just tried to reach you."

"Yes, sorry about that. I'm having problems with my phone. Are you alone?"

"Quite alone, but—"

"I really need to talk to you. Where are you now?"

"Bern. Where are *you?*"

"Just outside Lausanne. Listen, I wonder if we could meet somewhere on the pilgrimage route tomorrow."

"Well, that's possible. But tell me, did you find your friend Jaëlle?"

"She . . . went on ahead. Listen, it's very important that I find out more about Zarandok."

"Zarandok?"

"I'll explain when we meet." I got out my map. "Tomorrow I'm going to be walking to . . . Moudon, I think it is, and then Romont."

"I know them both. M'sieur McCaskill, you sound very upset."

"I'm fine, just. . . . Let's say Moudon for tomorrow. I don't know if I can make it to Romont."

"But why don't I pick you up in my car?"

"I prefer to stay on the pilgrimage route. Is there a place in Moudon where we can meet?"

"There is a café right beside the main church, the Church of St-Étienne."

"I'll find you. Let's say five p.m." The dissimulated spirit came out of the kitchen, and I said into the phone, "I appreciate your kindness very much, m'sieur. Until tomorrow."

After I'd hung up, the counter guy turned his gaze to me.

"We close in a few minutes," he said apologetically.

I suddenly felt exhausted. "I don't suppose you'd know of a hotel around here?"

He shook his head and fingered his wispy beard, looking obliquely at me with those colorless eyes.

"Or a B and B?" I added.

"Not around here. You must go into Lausanne."

"I'm actually going the other way. On foot."

He came a step closer, and for the first time he was looking directly into my eyes.

"You are a pilgrim," he said.

"Yes, but . . . I'm going in the wrong direction."

He smiled. "Ah. *That* kind of pilgrim."

He disappeared into the back room. While I was waiting, I noticed a few pamphlets beside the tip jar. I plucked one out; the text was in French and German.

Welcome to Wimli Café!
   A place to meet yourself.... Come and enjoy our delicious baked goods and home-cooked meals. Wimli Café is a venture of Les Croisettes Residential Housing and is run by, and for, people with mental health challenges. Amuse yourself on our trampoline out back!

The guy emerged with two thick folded blankets.
   "There is no hotel," he said, handing the blankets to me, "but there is a bench."
   "A bench?"
   "I show you."
   On the back of a napkin he drew a detailed map, labelling several streets, a medical center, and a park. "It is under two big trees, away from the street," he said. "You won't get wet if it rains—at least, only a little bit. Nobody will bother you. You can leave the blankets there; I will pick them up."
   "Well . . . thank you. Thank you very much."
   Knowing Switzerland, I was sure I would invite disapproval, or maybe even a fine, if I were found sleeping on a park bench. Seeing my hesitation, the guy drew out something from under the counter.
   "Here, " he said. "In case anybody asks you what you're doing."
   He handed me a well-worn scallop shell—not plastic

but a real shell, with a small hole drilled in the edge.

"The symbol of St. James," he said. "It says you are a pilgrim. Hang it on your pack."

"But I don't want to take your . . . personal shell."

"I give it to you." He smiled. "I was a pilgrim myself, once."

"Oh, yes?"

"Going the wrong way, like you. But I survived. As you will."

*   *   *

The first thing Zunz said to me was, "You've gotten a lot of sun, M'sieur McCaskill."

My day had been spent amid the green of early hay and the yellow of canola and the burnt umber of freshly tilled earth. Swallows had dipped and risen over the crop fields; the buzzards (I think that's what they were) had floated like cinders in the fresh blue air; wildflowers had flowed hot and sociable around the stone walls of the villages. I'd gotten lost briefly in a forest but then backtracked and rediscovered the walking route that eventually took me to Moudon. The wind had kept me company most of the way, along with the wind-chime melody of Swiss cowbells. And yes, the sun.

"I need a decent hat," I said.

Zunz himself wore a peach-colored polo shirt, white slacks, and jet-black sunglasses, now propped up on his forehead. I was sure his gold-rimmed Rolex was beautifully luminescent at night. He didn't look like any antiquarian bookman I had ever known, and I wondered how he had made his money.

"The way of the pilgrim is not easy," he said, swirling the coffee in his cup.

"You're telling me. I slept on a park bench last night. But to continue our conversation . . ."

He took off his sunglasses and tucked them into his shirt pocket. He'd gotten a haircut since I last saw him, and I could see his scalp through the short bristles of black hair.

"What I have to tell you is between you and me," I added.

"You can be assured of my discretion."

"I need more than discretion; I need absolute secrecy."

"You have it."

Moudon: a perennial contender for Switzerland's prettiest village. A valley, a river, a Reformed church. Standard issue for Swiss villages. I was sure there was a gnome garden around here somewhere. The afternoon light in the square was a warm clear element, like chardonnay held up to the sun. I glanced around at the patrons: a few students, a few families and kids, a middle-aged couple who I suspected were other pilgrims. Near me sat a woman with a Renaissance face—a hint of the cherubim in her features, and the most sensual mouth possible, full but decorous. Nobody looked suspicious, but after all that had happened, *everybody* looked suspicious. I wasn't even sure I could trust Zunz, but I badly needed help from somebody—and Zunz seemed to be the only person who knew any more about Zarandok than I did.

"I told you that Zarandok came into my store with a book," I said, lowering my voice. "But I didn't tell you the whole story. That book belonged to Jaëlle's father. I am trying to find it for her."

Zunz raised his eyebrows. "And you think Zarandok has

it?"

"I *know* he has it. We tracked him to Baulmes Monastery, and then he disappeared. We think he took to the pilgrimage route."

"When you say 'we,' you mean . . ."

"Jaëlle and I."

He studied me while I furtively watched the woman with the Renaissance face. She drew on her cigarette, inhaling deeply. Her eyelids fell and her lips parted; a curling wafer of smoke appeared between her tongue and her upper palate. She straightened to exhale—eyes full-lashed, chin tilted, mouth in a languorous "o"—as if she had just felt the touch of a lover's tongue between her shoulder blades.

"You seem to know Zarandok better than me," I continued. "Can you think of where he might be on the route? Maybe he's hiding out somewhere, or . . ."

He shrugged. "Your guess is as good as mine. I doubt if he is doing the pilgrimage for the good of his soul."

"You mentioned a police detective in Bern who was investigating Zarandok. Maybe he would know something."

"Dassvanger. Yes, I can ask him. But I'm puzzled. . . . You think Zarandok is on the pilgrimage route to escape the police?"

"Maybe."

He raised his eyebrows again. "On foot?"

Not for the first time, I had doubts. And that chess knight drawn in the pilgrims' registry . . . If Zarandok had indeed left it for me, as Jaëlle had suggested, had he left it to guide or mislead me?

"I don't really know what he is doing," I said. "Originally I thought he might be hiding out somewhere along the route. I've seen places today—little huts in the forest and so on. . . . But now I'm not even sure he *is* hiding out. I'm beginning to think there is some other reason why he is on the pilgrimage route."

Zunz shook his head. "I think it is a very low chance you will ever find him."

"That's why I need all the help I can get."

He spread his hands wide on the table. "I will see what I can find out. What will you do now?"

"First I have to find something for my sunburn. Then I will get a B and B for the night."

"And start walking in the morning."

"I hope to make it to Fribourg if the weather is good."

He raised his eyes to the green foothills surrounding Moudon. "That's a good long walk. And after that?"

"A place called Einsiedeln. It's on the pilgrimage route."

"Why Einsiedeln?"

"Because the man who wrote Zarandok's book, the Rabbi of the Twelve Winds, visited there. It's not much to go on, but it's all I have. Listen, Herr Zunz, could I use your cell phone?"

"Please," he said, touching open his iPhone.

Getting up, I scanned other patrons to see if anybody followed my movements; nobody did. In the far corner of the square, facing the tables, I called Julie. I wasn't sure how much I wanted to tell her but I badly needed to hear her voice, just to get myself on even keel again. When I got the voice-mail greeting on her cell, I tried her home number and, as luck would have it, got her husband, Pierre.

Docteur Pierre LeSwain. Brusque and unfinished as a new mountain, craggy and sharp-jawed, fault lines everywhere. One of Geneva's top neurologists. We had a delicate relationship.

"Sorry, she's in Bern for work," he said, in answer to my question. "Won't be back until late tonight."

"Okay. Well . . . how are you doing, Pierre?"

"Very well, thank you, Tavish."

For almost two years after Saoirse's death, Julie and I never talked. It got so bad that she left, married again, and acquired another family. But then something strange happened . . . we drifted back into each other's orbit. Started talking again. And I don't think Pierre ever got used to that.

"Listen, Pierre," I said, "I'm in a little place called Moudon. I'm doing a pilgrimage, the Jakobsweg."

"Wonderful."

"I'm aiming for Fribourg tomorrow if I can walk that far. Please tell Julie I called. But tell her *not* to call me on my cell."

"Why not?"

"Because my cell is . . . doing funny things. It's better if I call her. I hate to bother you with all this, Pierre, but it's kind of important."

"Which is important, Tavish? That you will call her, or that you're going to Fribourg tomorrow, or that your cell is doing funny things?"

"All of them. Sorry, I am a bit dazed from the sun today."

"I'll tell her. Fribourg and *not* your cell and you'll call her later." Pause. "Is everything all right, Tavish? You sound funny."

"I just . . . need a hat. I'll let you go. Thanks, man. Don't worry, I won't become all religious on you. Ha!"

When I rejoined Zunz, his coffee cup was empty. He

glanced at his Rolex and got out his wallet. "I will talk to my friend Dassvanger," he said.

"Herr Zunz," I said.

He looked up.

"Can I ask—why were you putting white stones on the graves of children?"

He paused with a twenty-franc bill in his hand, his eyes on the bill.

"It is a tradition," he said.

A tradition. Fair enough. I drained my coffee cup while he watched me, the bill still in his hand.

"I have no children myself, you see," he said at last, "and . . . well, it's just my personal *tikkun olam.* A few stones to repair the world." He placed the bill on the table and slipped his wallet into his back pocket. "Do you have children yourself, M'sieur McCaskill?"

My dream of two nights ago came back to me—the car accident, the book, the mansion that *was* the book—and I was walking through the corridors, trying all the doors, calling Saoirse's name. What had the Kabbalists said? Holy scripture is a great house of numberless rooms, all of them locked. Outside each door is a key . . . but it is *not* the key to that particular door. I wanted to explain to Zunz why this crazy book drew me so strongly, and why I was *really* on this pilgrimage, but I just said, "My daughter, Saoirse. . . ."

"Yes?"

I had to step back and take another run at it.

"My daughter, Saoirse, died twelve years ago. She was my only child."

"Oh, I'm so sorry. What a terrible thing."

I watched the woman with the Renaissance face stub

out her cigarette. The waiter came to retrieve Zunz's twenty-franc bill and he waved away the change. I had effectively stopped the conversation with my reply, but he was still looking at me curiously.

"Is there anything else you want to tell me, M'sieur Mc-Caskill?" he said.

"No. Is there anything else you want to tell *me*?"

"Yes." He put on his sunglasses and stood up. "Don't forget the hat."

*   *   *

Evening. Walking aimlessly through Moudon, aimlessly speculating. Maybe I should have told Zunz everything. He could have helped me; he knew a police officer. But I was wary of everybody now—my fellow pilgrims, the monks, Zarandok, the woman with the Renaissance face, the leached-out guy in the Wimli Café, the families with their kids, everybody. Those Friends of the Shared Path. . . . Who were they? Swiss gangsters? I had always thought Switzerland had no gangsters any more than it had hill-billies. And I couldn't figure out why they had decided to kidnap Jaëlle now. If they had just waited a bit longer, we could have led them to Zarandok . . . maybe. With a bit of luck. Were they getting impatient? At least they'd left me alone for twenty-four hours. But I knew that once again I wouldn't get much sleep that night.

Where are you, Jaëlle? Why is this happening?

I found myself back at the central square, in the shadow of the Church of St-Étienne. I had thought that nothing was open in the vicinity, but then I noticed a tiny bookstore,

Le coin du livre suisse, The Swiss Book Nook. Rents here were probably nothing like Geneva's Old Town. When I'd opened my own bookstore all those years ago, I'd had to borrow money from various friends and relatives, including my thesis advisor, old Moishe. I'm no scholar, Moishe, I told him (he nodded at that), and anyway, I have a kid to support now. He was sad I had to drop out—I was surprised at how sad he was—but he told me I could still be an *amateur* Kabbalist. I suspect I disappointed him there, too.

The picture window of the bookstore was not much bigger than the desktop at my own shop. I stepped into a space of two aisles and books stacked unevenly in every corner, the piles precarious, half-twisted like sections of spiral staircase. Nothing really to interest me. *Shapers of Religious Traditions in Switzerland. A Concise History of the Reformation. The Birth of Calvinism.* Translations of works by Zwingli and Martin Luther.

Then one title caught my eye ... *Jews in Christian Switzerland: History, Conflict, Reconciliation.* I plucked it off the shelf. By one Alexandre Alphonse Valentin. The University of Basel Press. I opened it at random.

> Jews were officially exiled from most cities and cantons in the fifteenth and sixteenth centuries—from Bern in 1427, Fribourg in 1428, Zurich in 1436 and Basel in 1543. Nevertheless, a number of Jews returned to Switzerland during the sixteenth century to work for Christian printers, who had begun producing Hebrew texts and needed proofreaders.

Jewish proofreaders ... I remembered that the Rabbi of

the Twelve Winds had pursued his living as a scribe across
Europe. Visionary mystics were not always your best men
for catching typos, but maybe he had managed to find work
as a proofreader in Switzerland.

Idly I skimmed the dust jacket blurb. "Alexandre Alphonse Valentin is a historian and member of the Cister-
cian Brotherhood. A former Vice President of the Swiss
Friends of the Hebrew University, he makes his home at
Baulmes Monastery, in the canton of. . . . "

Baulmes Monastery.

The author's photo had been taken years before, but I
recognized the face immediately: Brother Alphonse, the
ninety-year-old handyman monk. So he had avocations
beyond beekeeping and metalwork. I wondered if his
scholarly interests included old Aramaic manuscripts.

I paid for the book and walked quickly back to my B and
B, only three streets away. A typically immaculate Swiss
B and B: there was a sign in the bathroom asking men to
kindly pee sitting down. The owner of the place was a small
dark bunting of a woman, long widowed, lightly mousta-
chioed, who would apparently do anything for her guests.

"Madame, could I use your telephone?"

"Of course, m'sieur. And would you like some tea? I'm
just making some."

Rooting around in my knapsack, I found the pamphlet I
had picked up at Baulmes. I was sure I would get their voice
mail—didn't those monks go to bed at seven o'clock?—but
to my surprise I got somebody named Frère Matthieu.

"I am afraid Frère Alphonse has retired for the night," he
said.

"I need to talk to him about his historical research. It's

very important."

"If you give me your name and telephone number, he can call you. But I must tell you, he uses the telephone rarely. The best thing is to write him a letter."

The charm of the monastery's backwardness was rapidly wearing off.

"My name is Tavish McCaskill," I said. "Here is my message: the Rabbi of the Twelve Winds."

There was a silence.

"Could you repeat that?"

"The Rabbi of the Twelve Winds. Please make absolutely sure Frère Alphonse gets that message."

Another silence.

"And your name again?" asked the monk.

I told him, keeping calm.

"Please wait, m'sieur," he said.

I picked up a table knife and sat turning it over in my hand while the B and B proprietress busied herself with the tea. Something told me that Jaëlle had been right: the monks did know something. . . . *Though a soul righteous or innocent may depart from this world, she is not lost to Creation, and continues to dwell in other worlds.* I had almost memorized that entire page from Zarandok's book. Black fire written on white fire . . . and that equation: Schrödinger's equation. With those curious spaces around it. *Was* there text missing? Or were the spaces just meant to symbolize the white fire of Creation, to set off the flaming black letters of God's word?

I was beginning to think the monks had forgotten me when finally somebody picked up the phone. A paper-thin voice said, "Brother Alphonse here."

"This is Tavish McCaskill."

"Could you speak up, please?"

"*Tavish McCaskill.* The Canadian guy. Do you remember me?"

"I believe I do. The Mounted Police."

I lowered my voice because my proprietress was still hovering. "You weren't quite straightforward with me, Brother Alphonse."

"I am always careful what I say around the police."

"I am *not* the police. Tell me about the Rabbi of the Twelve Winds."

"What do you want to know?"

"Everything you told Zarandok."

The monk's breathing was a faint pebbly wheeze, like the backwash on a remote beach.

"I am afraid I don't know that name," he said.

"Stop playing games, goddamn it. Zarandok came to the monastery to find out about the rabbi. So now you can tell me what you told him."

"You are mistaken in all this, m'sieur. *And* you are using rather impious language. I feel the need to return to bed."

"Then you will be condemning someone to death. János Kodaly's daughter is involved in this now."

"His daughter?"

"Have you got your hearing aid turned on? Yes, Kodaly's daughter. We're in it up to our necks."

Again I heard the scratchy breathing.

"I don't believe János Kodaly had a daughter, M'sieur McCaskill."

I stopped toying with the knife. "What?"

"At least, he never mentioned a daughter. But please go

on—you say this woman is in danger?"

"*Yes.* Jaëlle is her name. Does that ring a bell?"

"I'm afraid not. What has happened to her?"

I sat staring at the knife, which rested between my thumb and forefinger. He claims he knew Kodaly, but maybe Kodaly hadn't confided in him about *anything*, least of all about his daughter. . . .

"M'sieur McCaskill?" said Brother Alphonse.

"Listen to me," I said. "I need to find Zarandok fast and I don't know who I can trust. Why didn't you help me when I asked you? I asked for your *help*. Why didn't you help me?"

The proprietress turned; I must have raised my voice. So much for keeping things secret. I resisted the urge to throw the knife across the room.

"I couldn't be sure of your intentions, m'sieur," said Brother Alphonse quietly. "I am still not sure."

"What would convince you?"

"You don't have to convince me. You have to convince Lavichet."

"Who?"

"Go to Fribourg, to the Convict Salesianum."

"What's that?"

"A place for pilgrims. Lavichet will find you there."

"Who is Lavichet, dammit?"

"I prefer not to talk much on the telephone, m'sieur, partly because I'm deaf, and partly because . . . well, I just prefer not to. Good night now. God bless."

EIGHT

The tiny woman opened the window, letting in a breath of lilac. A medieval city, dotted with the terra-cotta of tile roofs, sloped down before me to a river valley. The early evening light was arctic-clear, as far from ordinary light as Venetian glass is from mica. The atmosphere seemed to have been distilled and purified a dozen times over. A single bird idled far above the idling river. The mountains ranged themselves on the horizon like battle-worn kings, blue as smoke. Even I, who, after thirty years had grown blasé about the Swiss scenery, stood still at the window.

"Are you in Fribourg long, m'sieur?" said the tiny woman.

"With this view, I'd like to be."

"We have plenty of space until next week."

I turned from the window to face her. "What happens next week?"

"Theology conference."

The room was Shaker-simple: hardwood parquet floor, low futon bed, a single table and chair, superangelically white walls. The only bit of color was a cornflower blue duvet, spotlessly clean like everything else. I was suddenly conscious of how grubby I was.

"I'm curious about the name of this place," I said. "In English—"

"I know," she said, smiling. "A convict is a felon."

She was barely five feet tall—a lay sister of some kind. Small wattle under her chin, heavy glasses, eyes the color of chert. A face lined through long abrasion by the world, by work and duty and devotion, not by neuroses and introspection. She wore a pager—a black rectangular device with a greenish display window. I hadn't seen one of those in years.

"'Convict' comes from *convivere*, to live together," she continued, clearly happy to explain. "And 'Salesianum' means 'House of Sales,' after St. Francis de Sales, Bishop of Geneva in the early seventeenth century. So Convict Salesianum is a place where people live together in the spirit of St. Francis."

"Can anybody stay here?"

"Yes, but we especially like students and pilgrims." She had obviously caught sight of the scallop shell on my knapsack. "Are you going all the way to Spain?"

"I'm actually going in the other direction. Toward Einsiedeln."

"Oh, yes. A very spiritual place. Well, whichever way you go, you're on the route of our beloved St. James."

She held up her hand, as if to quiet a crowd, and for a moment I thought she was going to bless me.

"O help for all ages," she intoned, "O honor of the apostles, O bright light of the Galicians, O advocate of the pilgrims—James, lead us to the port of safety." She smiled again. "A prayer to St. James."

"Thanks. I think I need all the prayers I can get."

From outside, we heard the sound of children's voices raised in song; they must have been standing on the front steps.

"They are still singing, *les petits*," said the woman fondly, going to the window.

"Yes, I've heard them all day. Why are they singing?"

The whole time I'd been on the pilgrimage route, kids had come up to me to sing songs and then wait expectantly—for monetary recompense, as I'd figured out pretty quickly.

"A tradition of the Fribourg canton," she explained. "On the first of May, children go out singing to collect coins or treats. Did their songs inspire you, m'sieur?"

"Yes. One kid even sang 'My Heart Will Go On.'"

"I don't know that one."

"From the movie *Titanic*."

"Oh. I haven't been to a movie since . . . *The Love Bug*." She put two fingers up to her mouth in an understated laugh. "What are you going to see in Fribourg, m'sieur?"

"I guess the cathedral. Anything else you can recommend?"

"Well, we have some interesting museums. Do you like puppets?"

"Not really."

"How about sewing machines?"

"Maybe I'll just walk around the old town."

"Of course. Oh . . . what about bees? We keep our hives at the university's botanical gardens. I could take you there."

"Thanks . . . if I have time." I turned back to the window. "Is there a synagogue in Fribourg?"

"Oh, yes—you can walk to it from here. Rabbi Franks is a member of our philosophical book club." Again she held up her hand. "'A stranger is a friend to another stranger, on account of their strangeness on earth.' That's from the Baal

Shem Tov, who—"

"Yes. The founder of Hasidism."

She looked at me with a new interest. "You know the Baal Shem Tov! Perhaps you'd like to come to our book club, m'sieur. It's very ecumenical."

"I'm not really a book club person."

I thought of asking her if she knew somebody named Lavichet, the name Brother Alphonse had given me, but first I wanted to find out a bit more about this place . . . and about her.

"If you have your pilgrim's passport," she said, "I can stamp it for you."

"I don't have a pilgrim's passport."

"Oh, you must! I'm sure we have a few in the office."

"Can't I do the route without it?"

"But the idea is to get it stamped at the places along the route. Then you're part of the pilgrims' community."

I wanted to tell her that I wasn't a real pilgrim and had never been part of *any* community, and that I badly wanted to sleep, to escape my fears, but I just said: "Okay, yes, but—I'm sorry, I've forgotten your name, madame."

"I am . . . *Cléance LaBonté!*"

She held the name up like a flag, as if her soul were there—a soul frayed by time, but still vigorous in the wind.

"A woman of the mountains," she added, nodding out the window. "That's the Moléson there."

"Cléance," I repeated. "Well, let's get that passport, Cléance, and then I think I might have a rest. I must have walked thirty-five kilometers today."

We went down the wide staircase of marble and wrought iron, past the stained-glass windows on the landings, and into the spacious lobby. The place was like a castle in its sprawling stateliness. In the lobby we saw more kids—or maybe they were the same ones we'd heard through the window—two girls, perhaps seven or eight. They were dabs of color in that solemn, echoing space. Both wore bulky, multi-zippered school knapsacks. One girl had differently colored shoelaces for each shoe, sky-blue and green. The other wore glasses, red-framed. She was taller and more freckled than her companion, but still, they were as alike as two spring ephemerals. Sisters, probably. Or perhaps just good friends who had come to resemble one another from a close sharing of their lives. They stood shyly in front of the Convict Salesianum office, rolling their song sheets in their hands. Cléance beamed at them.

"Children, do you know . . ." She turned to me. "What was the song you mentioned, m'sieur?"

"'My Heart Will Go On.'"

She turned back to them. "'My Heart Will Go On.' Do you know it?"

The girls shook their heads as one, like two leaves in a breeze.

"Well, perhaps he'll sing it for you," said Cléance, turning back to me.

"No, Cléance—unless you want to send them screaming into the street." To the girls I said: "Sing whatever you want, ladies. Sing your best song." I felt in my pocket for some francs.

The girls sang hesitantly, eyes rarely leaving their song sheets, singing to the space in front of them rather than to us. I moved a bit closer to hear.

Enfant au visage de printemps
Joue dans un hiver qui semble éternel....

And the song, like the mountains outside the window, made me stand still—an awkward, halting, half-tuneful air that filled the vast cloistral space. *Child with a face of spring . . . plays in a winter that seems eternal.* Listening to the two girls, I couldn't always distinguish one voice from another. They were two notes, one chord. Like Hebrew and Aramaic. I thought of Jaëlle's tattoo: the Hebrew letters *cheit* and *yod,* joined to spell out "living." Two letters, one word. Or, if you looked at it with the other side of your mind, one mathematical symbol, pi. The elements of Creation mirror one another because they all share divine sparks.... Which Kabbalist said that? Or maybe it was just me, speaking like a Kabbalist.

The girls sang on.

Où est l'enfant ? Où est le printemps ?

I had to close my eyes against the lacerating edge of the song. When I opened them, I saw that somebody had come in the front doors and now stood listening to the girls—a woman wearing a sun hat, sunglasses, and white capri pants with notches at the side of the knee that showed narrow triangles of skin.

When the kids' song ended, she said, "Bravo!" and clapped enthusiastically.

The girls turned together, startled and pleased. With a shock I recognized the woman's voice and smile: my ex-wife, Julie.

* * *

"Pierre gave me your message," she said. "Your very *disordered* message."

She sat on the bed, legs crossed, sun hat beside her. Her sunglasses, now fitted on the open neck of her pineapple-yellow blouse, were the sixties movie-star kind—classic white rims, midnight-dark lenses—designed to slay the paparazzi.

"But how did you find me?" I said, from the window seat.

"I called the pilgrimage office. They said there were two principal places in Fribourg for pilgrims: a nunnery and this Convict place. I didn't think you would be sleeping with the nuns."

We had grabbed two beers from the dining room and, on my insistence, carried them straight back to my room.

"Here, pilgrim," she said, standing up to hand me a package: Dr. Scholl's blister bandages.

I wanted badly then to take her in my arms, but I let memory fill the need—I saw her as I had seen her for the first time, in the cafeteria line at the University of Geneva, standing with her weight on one leg, tapping a forefinger against her lips as she pondered the menu. Strange powers were at work around Julie. She was small and slender, but when she moved—or stood still after moving—she seemed voluptuous.

"You came from Bern just to see me?" I said gratefully.

"It was on my way home." She was sitting on the bed again, narrowing one eye at me. "Is everything all right, Tavish?"

"Sure."

"Pierre said you sounded a bit strange."

"I just had too much sun."

She took a sip from her beer bottle, turning her head away slightly but keeping a skeptical eye on me. I wondered if she saw before her the person she had once saved me from becoming.

"So this is your vacation," she said.

"This is it."

"You're doing it alone?"

"Well, I'm meeting other pilgrims. Look, here's the hat I got. Not quite the brim that yours has, but pretty effective."

Her glance flickered to the cloth hiking hat in my hands and back to me.

"What's this about a book?" she said.

"A book?"

"Mique told me you were looking for a book."

I turned to glance out the window. If they were watching me, they might have seen her arriving earlier. But how would they know she had any connection to me? I thought of Jaëlle's braid, still tucked away inside my knapsack in the cupboard, and my phone, buried at the bottom. Sufficiently buried, I hoped.

"Listen, Julie," I said in a low voice, "forget about the book, and please tell Mique, *again*, to forget about it."

"Why, Tav?"

"Because . . . it's just another old book I'm chasing. I'm trying to keep it quiet because other parties are interested in it. Look, you should probably go."

She blinked. "I just got here."

"Pierre and the kids are waiting for you, and I want you safe. I want you *safe*."

She didn't move from the bed. "Now you've got me worried, Tav."

I put my hat on the window seat and went to sit beside her, keeping her own sun hat between us. At that moment she was the woman I had married, all fire and pith, and I didn't trust myself to get too close.

"Don't be worried, Julie, just be . . . you. Your old self. Tough and reliable and . . . not that interested in my vacations."

Her eyes searched my face. "Are you in some kind of trouble? If you are—"

"I'm *not*."

"—I want to help."

I sidled a few inches closer. "Okay, here's how you can help," I said in the smallest voice I could manage. "Find out everything you can about a guy named János Kodaly."

"Who?"

"*Shh*. János Kodaly. A Hungarian mathematician and chess master. He was at the University of Zurich for a while."

"Why do you want to know about him?"

Someone knocked on the door. I froze, putting my finger to my lips. The sound of traffic came to us from the open window. I got up quietly and crossed the room.

"M'sieur McCaskill?" said a familiar voice. "I just wanted to tell you I'm going to see the bees now."

"Another time, Cléance," I said through the door.

"Certainly. Oh, and we have our book club tomorrow evening. It will be fun—we're discussing Spinoza."

"Cléance, please, I'm exhausted. Could we talk about this tomorrow?"

"Of course. Very sorry. Good night, m'sieur."

Julie watched me return to bed. "You're right about meeting other people, Tavish."

"That's just Cléance of the mountains. They must lead jam-packed social lives on the slopes, if they're all like her. But back to János Kodaly. Can you find out about him? Especially about . . . his personal life."

"What about his personal life?"

"Anything at all, like . . . whether he had a daughter."

"A daughter." She turned her face away slightly, as if to study me from a new angle. "All right. And then you're going to tell me what's going on?"

"Okay, yes, yes."

She put her sunglasses on and studied me darkly. "So you're back on the pilgrimage route tomorrow?"

"No. I'm supposed to meet someone here named Lavichet. Don't ask me about him because I don't know anything." I was whispering again. "Listen, I'm going to call you in two days . . . but not on your cell and not at home."

"So where?"

I thought for a moment. "Where Saoirse is."

"What?"

"You know where I'm talking about. Go to the caretaker's office—what's his name, the old Italian guy who looks after the grounds. He's got a landline. Can you be there at . . . let's say, around seven on Wednesday evening?"

"Yes, yes, all right. You are a very annoying pilgrim, Tavish."

I picked up her sun hat and placed it gently on her head. "And Julie, please, *please* don't tell anybody about any of this."

*   *   *

"'If the bee disappeared off the face of the earth,'" said Cléance, "'man would only have four years left to live.'" She handed me a bee helmet, similar to a Victorian explorer's pith helmet, except with a broader rim and a heavy dark veil attached. "Maurice Maeterlinck."

"I didn't know anybody still read him," I said, putting on the helmet. I was already wearing the beekeeper's jacket, with its elasticized sleeves and waist.

"I certainly do. I hope you slept well."

Around us, trees were treading the soft air—all native European species; the exotics were at the other end of the garden—and I stood half-awake in a wash of light that was like chlorophyll extract. Sleep? I wondered if I'd ever get a decent night's sleep again. And no sign of this Lavichet. I really didn't want to see this woman's bees, but she seemed to know everybody at the Convict Salesianum, and I needed an ally.

"You can attach your veil to your jacket," she said, showing me the velcro straps. "And you better take the gloves, too."

"These aren't African killer bees, are they?"

"Don't be silly, Tavish." She had taken to using my first name, which made me a bit uneasy. "Do you have a cell phone? You can leave it here." She indicated the gym bag she'd brought.

"I need to keep it with me."

"If it rings, the bees will be bothered."

"I'll put it on vibrate."

She eyed me sternly through her beekeeper's veil. "Tav-

ish, are you one of those people who can't be parted from
their cell phones? Leave it here. I will need your full attention."

Since that first call from the Friends, my phone had indeed begun to feel like a parasite—I never knew when it
might twitch under my skin.

"We're only going to be out there a few minutes, right?"
I said.

"Just a few minutes."

I put my cell inside the gym bag, glancing around warily.
We were inside a fence that separated the beehives from
the rest of the botanical garden. The hives were fifty meters
away, encircled by tall hedges—a "bee break," said Cléance,
to keep the flight path of the insects well above the heads
of people.

"Your job is to carry the smoker," she said.

She held up a metal canister like a long narrow coffee pot, with a small bellows attached. I remembered that
Brother Alphonse had shown me a similar object.

"What have you got in there, cannabis?" I said.

"You like to joke, Tavish."

"It keeps my mind off my worries."

"What are your worries?"

"Well, right now I'm wondering if I'm going to get stung
till I swell up like a pumpkin."

"These are Convict Salesianum bees, Tavish. They want
only world peace."

For a moment she basked in her own joke, eyes closed,
and then bent to remove the lid from the smoker. Once
lit, the contents sent up tendrils of rich balsamic smoke,
much more aromatic than that of cigarettes. "We want *cool*

smoke," she said, feeding the smoker with handfuls of grass. "You have to mix in lots of green." After a minute, she put the top back on and handed it to me. "Ready?"

The smoke followed us in piquant drifts as we made our way through the trees. In the clear spearmint light, even the age-bitten conifers took on blood and glow; the trickles of sap down their trunks stood out like arteries. Flowers went speckling beside us, white as cream in the green air. My hiking boots were already wet with dew. Stepping through a gap in the bee hedges, we reached the hives, which were basically just stacked wooden boxes. Like so many things in Switzerland, they were painted pastel colors. The lid of the uppermost box was held down by two bricks; Cléance plucked them off, swept the weather-stained top with a gloved hand and held up a finger to show me golden grains of pollen.

"I love this place," she said. "It's so alive. Now, a bit of smoke."

She directed me to wave the smoker around. "You quiet down, bees," she said and, getting out a tool like a narrow metal spatula, pried open the lid to reveal a series of wooden slats. No, not slats, but frames hanging downwards (she'd withdrawn one and was now holding it up). The bees were thickly carpeted across the honeycombed surface. I involuntarily took a step back.

"Closer, please," she instructed me. She hung the frame on a hook and, with the smoke all around, pretended to draw on a cigarette through two fingers of her beekeeper's glove, raising her chin to exhale theatrically. The bees did seem rather somnolent, fortunately; they just crawled lazily over the hanging frame. Cléance turned to look all around her.

"Something wrong?" I asked.

"No. Beekeepers just like to know what's happening in their vicinity. Closer, please."

Now I was standing right beside her. She unhooked the frame and replaced it, but instead of drawing out the next one, she began reciting something in a language that was neither French nor German. I caught a few gutturals, along with the familiar "ch" sound, and recognized it.

"Aramaic," I said in wonder.

"Yes. Keep smoking."

"Is that another of your quotes? Say it again."

"I will, but first . . ."

I waited impatiently while she withdrew the next frame; without looking at me, she recited the sentence again. My spoken Aramaic was not strong, but now I caught the words "exile" and "righteous."

"Something about exile," I said. "Is it from Daniel?"

I couldn't see her eyes through the veil, but she seemed to be calmly studying the bees.

"No," she said, "it is from the book you seek."

I stared at her, the smoke eddying around us. A dove or something wistful cooed from beyond the hedge. She swept a bit of dried honeycomb from the edge of the frame.

"At this time of year," she said, "I'm always watching for mites. They can destroy a hive."

"How do you know about that book?" I demanded.

"All in good time, Tavish. First, the sentence—you might want to memorize it."

She put the frame back in and said the sentence again, clause by clause. I repeated the words after her and she corrected me. There was one word that didn't sound Aramaic—she gave it a clear French intonation—and with a shock I recognized it.

"Lavichet." The name Brother Alphonse had mentioned. "Lavichet is in the *book?*"

She gave a quick glance around her. "Not so loud. And please . . . a bit more smoke."

In my distraction I squeezed smoke directly into her face.

"At the bees, *s'il vous plaît,*" she said mildly.

"Please stop what you're doing and talk to me. Lavichet is in the book?"

"I'd rather not stop what I'm doing, Tavish," she said imperturbably, "because I came here to see the bees and that's what I intend to do. Just say the passage—and keep looking at the bees. Aren't they wonderful?"

I said the passage again and got most of it. I had been translating it in my mind, and now I murmured it through the smoke: *My exile took me into the land of Schwytzerland, and there I met another sojourner named Lavichet, a righteous gentile, who helped me.*

"Tell me how you know about the book," I said.

"As I say, Tavish, all in good time. We still have a few frames to look at. Can you say the sentence again?"

*   *   *

The book club was small: just Cléance along with her friend Rabbi Franks and a tall guy in sunglasses named Benesh. The rabbi was in a wheelchair, the non-motorized kind. We sat in a flood of pale-sherry light admitted by the big bay window. The dining room at the Convict Salesianum had thinned out; we were the only ones in this part of the room.

"Do you belong to a book club in Geneva, Tavish?" asked the rabbi, in excellent English.

"No, rabbi, I'm not really a book club person."

"Please call me Aaron. And don't worry—we're not typical book club people either."

With his wayward red hair, ear stud, and massive chest, he seemed about as book-clubbish as one of Van Gogh's stars. Leather vest, blue-jean shirt, bolo tie. And a pager, oddly. It looked like one of the old Motorola models, same as Cléance's. The other guy, Benesh, was a long daguerreotype of a man with close-cropped silver hair and skin the color of light equatorial wood. I couldn't guess his age; he had an old-young smile. I had the sense that I had strayed into some recondite, insular gathering—amateur archaeologists, stamp collectors, cameo-glass aficionados—who preferred to meet away from prying eyes.

"Usually we start with biographical information about the author," said Cléance. She took a sip of mineral water. "Baruch Spinoza! His brain was surely gigantic."

My exile took me into the land of Schwytzerland. . . . We hadn't left the beehives until I had memorized the Aramaic sentence; then Cléance had suggested firmly that I have a nap. "And don't forget the book club this evening," she'd added.

And now here we were at the far end of the Salesianum dining room, with the end-of-the-day silence pooling around us, and the evening beyond the window volumed out with stillness. I could hear kitchen clatter from the other end of the room, but in this spot, we could have been in a comfortable old house: an aged piano sat just behind us, and the walls were hung with large abstract paintings, all thick dabs and swirls, pleasantly amateurish; they could have been done by somebody's aunt. Cléance and Benesh drank mineral water while Aaron and I had bottles of the Swiss beer Cardinal.

"Do you know much about Spinoza, Tavish?" said Benesh.

His English dipped and rose as if riding a tropical breeze. Sri Lankan or Indian, I guessed.

"Not much."

"Maybe you need a bit more of an introduction than Cléance gave us," he said, with a smile. "Spinoza was born in 1632 in Amsterdam of Portuguese Jews. Bertrand Russell called him 'the noblest and most lovable of the great philosophers.' He knew Latin, French, German, Hebrew, some Arabic, and some Paleo-Hebrew. Interesting biographical tidbit: he owned a signet ring engraved with the Latin word *caute*, which means . . ." Slowly he put his hand out for his glass of mineral water. "Cautiously," he finished, taking a sip.

I saw Cléance's gaze move beyond me to take in the entire dining room. Aaron had turned slightly so he could see out the window. Benesh smiled at me again, but I had the sense that his entire being was alert, alive to his surroundings. The rush of the present slowed, and I too became attentive to the waning light, the enfolded shadows in the window drapes, the distant clatter of pots, the murmur of the last few diners.

"Aaron," said Cléance, "perhaps you might read some words from the book, to begin."

"Of course," said Aaron, opening his book. I noticed

that Cléance and Aaron had different paperback editions of Spinoza's writings—*The Essential Spinoza* and *The Ethics and Other Works* respectively. Benesh had no book at all. I wondered when he was going to take off his sunglasses.

"I'd like to begin with something from one of Spinoza's little-known works, *The Celestial Gate*," said Aaron. "I'll read it in the original language—I apologize in advance for my accent."

As he spoke he lowered his voice, and I had to lean forward to catch the words. His eyes were on the open book, but he clearly wasn't reading from it. And the language . . . Aramaic. His accent was as good as I'd heard from anybody. Straining to hear, I caught the words "exile" and "righteous."

He read the sentence twice and then put the book on the table. A quiet fuse had been lit in the back of my mind.

My exile took me into the land of Schwytzerland, and there I met another sojourner named Lavichet, a righteous gentile, who helped me.

"This is the book we are here to discuss," said Cléance, looking straight into my eyes.

I nodded. Benesh ran a hand through his silver hair, and Aaron took a careful sip of beer.

"*Allez-y*, Aaron," said Cléance easily.

Aaron moved himself closer to the table using the turning rims (or whatever you called them) on the back wheels.

"There's an old Jewish legend," he said quietly, "that God created the universe using the Torah to guide him. I think He could have just as well used this book, *The Celestial Gate*. The book describes comprehensively, in both words and numbers, the structure of our universe . . . and other universes."

"Other universes?" I said.

"The author was much ahead of his time," Benesh put in.

The last few diners rose and deposited their trays on the racks near the kitchen. Aaron waited until they had gone.

"*The Celestial Gate* has a curious history," he continued. "The author didn't wish to publish it—he was already in trouble with the authorities—so he circulated the manuscript to his friends. They were fearful that the manuscript, or maybe even the author himself, would be seized at any time. So they decided to memorize passages of it."

"It's not a long book, I believe," put in Cléance.

"About as long as *A Brief History of Time*. No pictures, though. Anyway, the friends met for years to discuss and memorize the book, and eventually their beloved friend, the author of the book, died, and the manuscript disappeared. The circle of friends—they called themselves the Talmeeds—were determined to keep the text safe for future generations. But given the political and religious climate, that meant *not* writing it out."

"So the book was passed down orally?" I said.

Aaron nodded. "It became a memory book—recited collectively and handed down through the centuries."

"Were these only Jews, Aaron?" said Benesh.

"Initially. But eventually a few Christians joined, and even a few freethinkers. And the group continues today."

"Today?" I said in surprise.

"Well, a remnant still exists," said Aaron, holding my gaze.

In fact, they were all looking at me.

I sat back, studying them in turn. A recondite circle, for sure. But I wasn't sure I believed anything yet; I was burning to ask them some direct questions, to be rid of this charade.

Just then Benesh said, "You haven't told us the end of the story, Aaron."

Once again he reached for his glass of mineral water, and the way he did it—with studied deliberation, as if the glass might have moved from its previous location—told me what I had already sensed: he was blind. At that moment, he turned slightly in my direction as if aware of my discovery.

"I hope it's *not* the end." Aaron was looking directly at me. "Yes, the impossible happened not long ago, Tavish: the original manuscript of *The Celestial Gate* was found."

"I can imagine the excitement," I said.

"Excitement, yes . . . but also turmoil. The history of the Talmeeds has not been continuous; in some eras, war and exile scattered the members. For the modern-day members, the discovery of the manuscript was the greatest test of their existence. Would it prove the *faith* of their memories?"

They were all silent for so long I said: "Well? Don't keep me in suspense."

"*Everybody* is still in suspense," said Aaron. "The individual with the book is being very . . . cautious. But we are confident he will meet with the Talmeeds soon. You see, it appears that the manuscript of *The Celestial Gate* has degraded in a number of places. Sections of the text, and at least one equation, have been lost. The Talmeeds' memories have therefore become very valuable. That's why—"

At that moment, Cléance sat up, alert. Aaron turned in his wheelchair to scan the room. The silence grew taut around us.

"But let us return to the *Essential Writings*," said Cléance briskly, holding up her book. "Spinoza knew Leibniz, I think, Aaron?"

"He did. Leibniz even sought him out to discuss God and the universe. That reminds me of another passage—you'll like this." He picked up his book again and removed a marker. "'I do not know how to teach philosophy without becoming a disturber of established religion. . . .'"

Okay, so they were back to talking about the *real* Spinoza. Something had spooked them, or maybe they just made a rule of discussing the rabbi's book in snippets.

"Another beer, Tavish?" said Cléance pleasantly.

For the rest of the evening, I listened impatiently to a rather dry discussion of Spinoza and his era. Eventually, somebody from the kitchen came out to flick the dining room lights, and Cléance said, "Well, *mes amis*, I think Tavish must go to bed for an early start tomorrow morning."

"An early start?" I said.

"On the pilgrimage."

"No, I'm staying here for a while. I want to learn more about . . . Spinoza."

"You need to keep going, Tavish," said Benesh. "Hold on to the good weather."

"We think it is best," said Cléance.

I leaned across the table. "Listen, I've sat here this whole evening and haven't said a word about my own situation. But I'm caught in some pretty *bad* weather, believe me, and I need your help." I lowered my voice to a bare whisper. "Zarandok has the book, right? And you say you *haven't* met with him yet?"

Backing his wheelchair away from the table, Aaron

rolled toward me and placed a large veined hand on my forearm.

"Let us continue our conversation on the pilgrimage, Tavish," he said. "I'm coming with you."

*   *   *

I lay on my bed, the window open, the night breathing around me. It was a good thing I'd napped this afternoon; I wouldn't get much sleep now. These three people—Cléance, Benesh, and Aaron—*they* made up this five hundred-year-old book club that had memorized this book of Rabbi Emeth's, *The Celestial Gate?* Unbelievable. But I had to admit, they looked the part. And it finally might explain why Zarandok was on this pilgrimage route: his pursuit of Rabbi Emeth had led him to the Talmeeds. He needed them, according to Aaron—needed their knowledge to fill in the gaps of his degraded manuscript. But it seemed that he was being his usual skittish self and hadn't contacted the Talmeeds yet . . . because of the Friends, presumably. But what was his end game for the book? And where was he now? Turmoil—that was Aaron's word. Somehow I got the feeling that Zarandok was stirring up more worry than goodwill.

And this Lavichet . . . he seemed to have been a contemporary of Rabbi Emeth's. A righteous gentile, according to the passage I had memorized. Had he been one of the first Talmeeds? *Talmeed*—Hebrew for "student" or "disciple." And these Talmeeds seemed ready to trust me, though I didn't know why. Maybe Brother Alphonse had told them about me. And speaking of Alphonse, how did he fit in?

Was he a Talmeed, or—

From somewhere in the darkness, my loon called. I sat bolt upright. The phone display glowed on my bedside table: private number. Dread had once more invaded my body, diffusing outward from my racing heart. I tried to still my breathing.

"Yes?"

Again I heard the staticky silence I remembered, and then came the scaly voice, the voice from beyond Pluto.

"M'sieur McCaskill. We told you not to talk to anybody about our business."

NINE

I stood up and went to the window, smelling the lilac once again. Nobody in the yard and no vehicle on the street. Only a brilliant moon over the cathedral, and the city lights flowing away from me like a phosphorescent wake on a midnight sea.

"I *didn't* tell anybody," I said.

"Your ex-wife," said the voice.

I closed my eyes. These pricks were blindsiding me at every turn.

"I swear I never said a word to her," I said. "She has nothing to do with this."

"She does now."

There was another long silence; the night and its moon remained calm, respiring gently, but I felt as if I were trying to breathe underwater.

"Are you sufficiently devoted to your task, m'sieur?" said the voice. "I ask myself this."

"What are you talking about?"

"I'm talking about devotion. Perhaps you need a deadline. You have four days to find Zarandok."

"Four days! For God's sake—"

"Never be without your phone. Sleep and eat with it. Do not turn it off."

Easy. Root yourself like a tree. If they get the book,

they'll leave me alone, they'll leave Julie alone . . . and Jaëlle.

"Listen to me," I said. "I can get you the book. I met these people today, the Talmeeds—they've *memorized it.*"

"We don't want memories, M'sieur McCaskill. We want Zarandok."

My anger and fear finally got the better of me. "How the fuck am I supposed to find him when *you* can't?"

In the silence that followed, I could hear the crickets out the window. Shit, that's done it.

"Because he trusts you, m'sieur," said the voice. "Two residual men, walking the great pilgrimage. You'll find each other."

I was so dizzy I had to sit down once more. "I don't understand any of this."

"Good. Just keep your phone with you always. If you tamper with it, we will know."

Breathe, breathe. But I couldn't breathe, there was too much happening, too much he knew. He kept on saying "we"—how many people did he have with him? If they knew about Julie and the Talmeeds, then they probably knew about Jakob Zunz.

"Let me speak to Jaëlle," I said.

"She is unable to come to the phone right now." There was a ripple of static, as if to underline the words. "I repeat, you have four days. And pray that your ex-wife does not contact you again."

Anger called me out of my fear for a second. Go fuck yourself, you—I almost said it, but then put one hand on the chairback to steady myself. My head cleared temporarily.

"Tell me what to do," I said. "I don't know what to do."

The voice made a clicking sound, as if in impatience. "You must win the trust of the Talmeeds."

"How do I do that?"

"Your daughter."

I held the phone away from me, staring at it. "My daughter?"

"Talk to them of your daughter. They will understand. This is your path."

"How do you know about my daughter?"

"I repeat: this is your path. When the Talmeeds say that the soul lives forever, nod your head. When they tell you that one day you will see your daughter again, cry. Soon they will lead you to Zarandok."

*   *   *

Dark bouffant clouds lolled on the horizon, manatees in shallow water. Far off, lightning skimmed the mountain-tops. Ten o'clock in the morning and already the day was a guttering candle.

"Well, this is not fun," said Rabbi Aaron Franks, looking out the café window from his wheelchair, a mug of coffee in front of him.

"What do we do now?" I said.

"Enjoy our coffee."

Fribourg loomed below us in gray air. At least we'd managed to get to the other side of the river. We'd just gotten up a steep flight of stairs—me carrying the folded wheelchair (largely titanium and aluminum, I found out) and the rabbi, unbelievably, hoisting himself up each step using the handrail. I was in awe of this guy. We'd taken a break in this café, watchful of the lightning. Aaron sat with his long hair hanging damply over his forehead, his padded wheelchair gloves on the table. The steam from his coffee made an eddying shadow on the wall.

"You said last night that you'd got caught in some bad weather," he remarked.

I was conscious of my phone in my pocket, resting under my windbreaker like a tick, invisibly feeding. I took it out and, holding it under his eyes, gave him what I hoped was a semaphoric look. He nodded slightly.

"Had a ton of rain coming out of Lausanne," I said, replacing the phone.

"We can get big weather coming off the big lake."

"I got cold and wet right through, caught a fever. It seems like I've been carrying it with me since then."

Again he nodded. "The thing for me," he said, looking out at the sky, "is that I can't travel in mud."

"Maybe we should go back to Fribourg and get the train."

"Let's wait a bit longer." He took a sip of coffee. "So is this your first pilgrimage, Tavish?"

First and fucking last, I wanted to say, but I just nodded.

"And are you a *believing* pilgrim?"

"At this stage in my life, I'm beyond believing or disbelieving. I just grind away at the days while they grind away at me." I glanced out the window, thinking of what the Friend had told me: to talk about Saoirse. "Are we just going to sit here?"

He smiled. "No, we can talk. Share some life hacks."

"Life hacks?"

"That's correct English, yes? Things to make better your life."

Reaching into his shirt pocket, he withdrew a notebook, fluttering it briefly to separate the pages, which had stuck together with the humidity.

"We discuss life hacks in the book club sometimes," he said.

"I believe you."

"My kids give some of the best ones."

There was nobody in the café except two female cyclists in lycra and sports tops, their curves as streamlined as dolphins'.

"What's your birth date?" asked Aaron, getting out a pen.

"Why?" I hadn't slept since that call in the middle of the night, and I really wasn't in the mood for life hacks.

"It's just my *pastime*, Tavish," he said patiently. "What year were you born?"

I told him, and added, "Listen, maybe I can keep walking on this route and *you* can catch the train."

"And the month and day of your birth?"

I ended up not only giving him my birth date information, but my street number, at work and at home, my Swiss heath card number *and* my library card number. All of them he wrote down in his notebook.

"Would my credit card number be useful for your hacks?" I said.

"No, this should be fine. Twenty-nine digits, yes?"

He took no more than half a minute to glance at them, then closed the notebook. "Another coffee?" he said.

"I'll get it."

"No, no, my treat. You carried my wheelchair."

The café was a self-serve coffee place, like a lot of Swiss cafés. He paid for two coffees and then rolled himself back to our table, the cashier following with the steaming mugs. Once the cashier had gone, he wrote out the numbers on a napkin and then opened his notebook. He'd gotten every one.

"Impressive," I said.

"Here is my first life hack for you, Tavish: how to remember numbers."

"*That's* your life hack? I was expecting some rabbinical wisdom."

"This *is* wisdom, Tavish. Memory is the architecture of the soul. Think of the visionaries from very old times: their culture was mainly oral, and books were rare. Memory let their visionary fire leap from generation to generation . . . and century to century." He turned his notebook around in front of me. "Look, this is how it works. You make each digit into an image—an animal or person or such. We remember images better than letters, yes? So, number one is a pencil, two is a swan, three is a butterfly . . . "

"I get it."

"And then you make a story out of the images. So, one-nine-six-four. A pencil draws an elephant, and the elephant walks along to pick up a pregnant lady, and then they both get into a sailboat—it's a bit tipsy, but—"

Four days. How the hell was I going to find Zarandok in four days?

"And you can even use this method to memorize equations." He had written the symbol Ψ in his notebook. "The Greek letter psi. Very common in mathematical formulas. To me, it looks like a phoenix . . . you know, the mythical bird that is born from ashes. We have many storytelling possibilities there."

I watched as he wrote out an equation that included a "d" over a "dt"; an H with a kind of a hat, like the *accent circonflexe* in French; and this psi symbol. I would never have recognized it except that I had seen it a lot recently. Schrödinger's equation.

He looked up, his pen poised, smiling faintly. Yes, rabbinical wisdom—the wisdom of the Talmeeds.

"You know," he said, looking out the window, "I think the rain might delay itself for a while." At the same time, he was writing—not numbers but letters, large and cursive. Hebrew letters. I recognized an Aramaic phrase when he turned the notebook around for me.

Who is after you?

I was so caught off guard that I said, "I don't know."

"Oh, yes, it's definitely clearing," he said briskly. He laid his pen on the table and gave me a brief, charged look.

I took up the pen. Would it even make sense to him? I wrote it down anyway: the Friends of . . . What was "shared" in Aramaic? In the end I just wrote סיטרא אחרא, *Sitra Achra*—the Other Side, the Kabbalistic term for the realm of evil.

Aaron studied the notebook gravely and drained his mug. "Are you ready?"

"Now?" I said.

He swept his wheelchair gloves from the table. "We're over the steep part."

I definitely wasn't keen on walking right then—the lightning was still there—but I figured he had a good reason to keep going.

*   *   *

The Kabbalists held that whenever God wanted to communicate something important to humans, He used Aramaic, since that language could not be understood by angels—neither the good ones nor the fallen kind. The Talmeeds clearly had some experience of the latter.

These Friends . . . they want the book?

They want Z. I must help them or they kill a woman.

We carried on this dialogue in tiny snippets throughout the day, writing Aramaic on my map, his notebook, the page inside my pilgrim's passport, anything available. He knew the language better than I did and was also more adept at slipping it unobtrusively into the spaces of the day. But I persisted; all I could think of was *four days.*

Where is Z? I wrote.

He wrote a question mark, and then *B is looking*, using the letter *bēth*, the Hebrew form of "B."

B? Who was B? Then I remembered: Benesh, the other Talmeed. The tall blind man.

About two kilometers from the café we came across a sign intended for walkers coming from the other direction: *Bienvenue en Suisse romande*, "Welcome to French Switzerland." Rolling past it, Aaron turned his wheelchair to face south.

"Au revoir, Suisse romande," he said, and then turned his wheelchair around to face northward again. *"Hallo, deutsche Schweiz!"*

I stood looking out across the bucolic Swiss landscape, scanning both earth and sky, wondering if the Friends were anywhere around.

"It's interesting, Tavish," said Aaron. "There is a strong divide between French- and German-speaking Switzerland. It's like a border."

"My German is very basic," I said.

"Don't worry, I can do the talking."

"I just saw lightning there."

He followed my gaze to the horizon. "The old pilgrims walked in any kind of weather."

"They weren't traveling in a metal wheelchair."

Using a Biblical language to talk about digital technology can be a challenge. A few minutes later, when we got out my map and were calculating distances, I scribbled down on the map: *My machine follows me.*

He nodded, tracing out a route with his finger.

"We're making pretty good progress," he said.

"No, we're not. We'll never make it to Schwarzenburg at this rate."

"Do we need to hurry?"

I wrote *four days* and underlined it twice. He glanced at me uncertainly.

"But Schwarzenburg is certainly doable," he added.

Just then, as if to undermine his words, a rustling filled the air and the rain swept across the field in a rippling curtain. We flipped up the hoods of our rain jackets.

"You said yourself you can't travel in the mud," I said. "Pretty soon the path will be impassable."

"Don't worry. There's a medieval road coming up."

"A medieval road?"

The hem of the rain had become a furious stippling where it met the earth—an artist's scruff lines, frenetically alive. Water was already flowing in the ditch beside us, carrying bubbles, leaves, and bracken.

"The Torenöli," said Aaron, above the sound of the rain.

"A welcome sight to pilgrims for seven hundred years."

*   *   *

The Torenöli turned out to be a sunken lane in a forested hillside, flanked by sandstone walls that were streaked with lichen and climbing vines. The wall on the left rose at least two meters and was topped by a fledge of forest; the wall on the right was half that height, and crumbled and patinaed with the centuries.

"We're going up *that*?" I said.

"This is the path," said Aaron.

Under a tree, I flipped off the hood of my jacket so I could hear better. I thought at first the lane was paved with cobblestones, but up close they looked more like large beach stones, smooth and dark with rain. On a beautiful day, it might have been a pleasant hike. But on a day like this . . .

"You can't get up that on a wheelchair, Aaron. Be serious."

"You might have to give me a push now and then."

"But we won't be able to get any purchase."

"This is the path, Tavish. We must stay on the path."

I stared at the road, despair soaking into me with the rain. How would we ever find Zarandok if we were mucking around on a medieval road?

Aaron had already nosed his wheelchair ahead. He had gotten out an umbrella and fixed it to the back of his chair, but it didn't want to stay upright, and several times he had to adjust it. The rain continued to fall, a steady demoralizing drizzle, and the sky above us was all ashlight and seethe. I could still see weak flashes of lightning on the horizon.

I took a hold of the grips on the back of the wheelchair, planting my feet sideways, so I could fit a boot tread into the spaces between the stones.

"It's easier if we keep as close as possible to the wall," he said.

We grunted and strained up that medieval road while the surrounding foliage quivered and fluttered in countless small places from the rain. We had given up writing in Aramaic, and Aaron had given up on his umbrella and stowed it in his bag. At one point, when the walls on either side were high and we were surrounded by forest, he paused and motioned me close.

"Let's stop here," he said.

"Why?"

He reached out to touch the sandstone wall. "Stone and forest around us, lightning and rain above, and no telecommunication towers. We're back in the medieval world now." He held out his hand. "Can I see your phone?"

I shook my head urgently, but he continued to hold out his hand. Finally I retrieved the phone and opened it; he pointed to the reception fan. No bars were lit.

"We're in a natural dead zone," he said and, taking the phone from me, pressed the button on the side to power it off.

I lunged for his hand. "Are you crazy?"

"The phone has to be off or it can still record." He watched the powering-off animation fade. "We've got a few minutes now. So talk to me, Tavish. What did you mean by four days?"

"Are you sure about this?" I whispered hoarsely.

"I'm sure. You said four days."

"Yes, or they kill this woman, Jaëlle." I was scanning the tree line above the path. "They might have a drone or something—"

"Only an idiot would fly a drone in a lightning storm. Who is Jaëlle?"

"She's after the book, too. She said it belonged to her father, but . . . I don't know what's true any more. Listen, where the hell is Zarandok?"

Aaron shook his head glumly. "No idea. Alphonse set up a meeting, but then Zarandok just disappeared. As I said, Benesh is working on it."

"We have to find Zarandok *fast*."

"We won't find him fast."

"We *have* to. They cut off Jaëlle's braid and sent it to me."

"What?"

"Yes. And I don't want to get any more packages with . . ."

I leaned against the wall, feeling broken, unselved, an empty sack. A memory had leapt out of the grayness: fragments of windshield glass in my hair and down my shirt. Lying in the hospital bed after the accident, I seemed to feel broken glass everywhere—against my skin, behind my eyelids, inside my lungs. No—no more packages, no more broken glass. . . .

Removing the shoulder straps of my daypack, I slipped it off and began sliding down the wall into a sitting position. "I need my pills," I said.

My knapsack rested upright at Aaron's feet, against his knees. "Where?" he said, unlatching the flap.

"I'll be so glad when I'm out of this. Right at the top there."

Aaron was rummaging in my knapsack when his hand

became still; evidently he had found Jaëlle's braid. He gave me a somber glance from under his rain hood and then, feeling around to the sides, withdrew three bottles of pills. Meanwhile I had taken off my raincoat and stuck it under me, and now sat surrounded by damp fungal smells and the soft tattoo of the rain. I shook out three pills in my hand—a capsule, a smaller one like a kid's aspirin, and a larger one like a vitamin C tablet—and got out my water bottle.

"Suppose I do find Zarandok," I said. "What am I going to do then? Just stand back and let the Friends take him?"

"That is the problem. They've arranged it so that you have no choice but to betray *somebody*."

"Who are these Friends, Aaron?"

"No idea. As you say, *Sitra Achra*. Enemies of God."

"They seemed to know everything about me. They even know about . . ."

"Yes?"

"Just everything. My entire life."

I took the capsule first, feeling it melt on my tongue, becoming pliant and slippery before I washed it down. The small one, meant to boost the capsule, had a powdery bitterness to it. Heart taken care of.

"Why did you decide to help me, Aaron?" I said.

"Alphonse told us about you."

"Is he a Talmeed as well?"

"No, just an ally. Sometimes a skeptic of our work, but an ally."

"Alphonse couldn't have told you much about me. He doesn't know much. So again, why did you decide to trust me?"

Aaron was about to take a swig from his water bottle and then paused, studying the contents as if uncertain about them. "Maybe you have noticed that the Talmeeds are a bit . . . different."

"Yes, I've noticed that."

"Me, I was paralyzed from the waist down after a motorcycle accident. Cléance and Benesh—well, they have their own stories to tell . . . or keep silent about." He took a swig of water and eyed me over the rim of the bottle. "We saw that in you also, Tavish. A story you tell through silence."

I swallowed the last pill. Cholesterol taken care of. I only half-believed that these things did me any good, but they were all I had.

"The Friend, the *Sitra Achra* guy, said you believe in an afterlife," I said.

He put his hands on the back of his neck and tilted his head back. "I believe that, yes."

"Because it's in *The Celestial Gate*?"

"Because of my experience. The book doesn't give new arguments . . . although it does give new mathematics."

"You're saying it contains *equations* about the afterlife?"

He took off one of his wheelchair gloves and massaged the back of his neck, moving his head all around.

"It contains one," he said.

He brought out my phone from under his rain jacket.

"But thanks to God, I don't have to worry about the equations," he said. "That's Aveu's department."

He said the name distinctly, as if he wanted me to remember it.

"Aveu?" I repeated.

"Our other Talmeed. Though he's not really a Talmeed."

Wiping off the face of my phone with his sleeve, he handed it to me. "We saw very early that we would need somebody to help us with the mathematics in the book. After years of searching, we found Aveu."

"I gather he's not a regular part of your book club."

Aaron shook his head. "He's a kind of wandering math elder. He's in Zurich for the next month, giving seminars." He tilted his water bottle and took a gulp. "He may be one of the few people in the world who can make sense of those equations."

"Does Zarandok know about him?"

"No. He's . . . how do you say it, a shadow partner." He looked at his watch. "We should go, Tavish."

"You're *sure* Zarandok doesn't know about him?"

He gave me a long look. "What are you thinking?"

"I don't know what I'm thinking, exactly, I'm just trying to—"

"You're thinking that if Zarandok found out about Aveu, then this can explain why he just disappeared. He's gone to find the one who *knows*. Yes?"

"Well . . . is it possible?"

"But how could Zarandok have found out about Aveu? Even Brother Alphonse doesn't know about him."

"You're sure about that as well?"

Aaron was looking at the phone in my hand. I stuck my head over the wall to have a glance around but, seeing only a gray pointillist landscape, I turned back to him.

"You say Aveu is in Zurich now?" I said.

"For a while."

"Maybe we need to go to Zurich."

"It's two hours away by train. We'll have to abandon the

pilgrimage."

"Fine. We can dry out."

"But the pilgrimage is safer, Tavish. That's why Zarandok used it."

"I've only got four days, Aaron. Three days, now. I'd rather act on a hunch than just . . . wander."

He considered for a moment while the rain continued to fall around us.

"Very well, we'll take the train from Schwarzenburg," he said. "You should turn your phone back on. But from now on, we just talk about *innocent* subjects, yes? I will practice a few sermons on you."

*   *   *

T-shirt sermons, he called them—homilies short enough to write on a T-shirt. "All men are the abode of wandering souls," a quote from Martin Buber. "Fill your hours with days." (He was very proud of that one, since he'd made it up himself.) And the one I'd already heard from Cléance: "A stranger is a friend to another stranger, on account of their strangeness on earth." Apparently his synagogue had printed up these mini-sermons on T-shirts—in German, French, and English—and sold them as a fundraiser.

"I brought a few with me," he said. "I'll give you one, Tavish."

The rain had ceased, unexpectedly. The new sunlight, shining through the cloud gaps, seemed to have a substance, like spun glass. We passed fields of asparagus, their leaves still beaded with rain droplets; and sunflowers in their tattered bonnets; and a line of slender beeches, several of them tilted slightly, like a row of women inclining their heads as their necks are being kissed. The changeling earth in its mud and limpidity seemed potent and alive. I felt that the old alchemical recipes might have held true here: Had you placed a bit of crushed basil into a rock hollow, the nubile sunlight would have made a butterfly out of it.

But all the while, my gut told me that we shouldn't have talked so freely on the medieval road.

"How long have you been a rabbi, Aaron?"

I figured this belonged in his category of innocent subjects, and I needed to distract myself.

He steered his wheelchair around a patch of mud. "Eleven years. Since my accident." He smiled faintly. "I couldn't be a cowboy, so I became a rabbi."

"I see that as a natural transition for you."

"This is what my wife says." He stopped to remove a twig that had caught in his wheel mechanism and then continued along. "In my young years, you see, I was sometimes going to a dude ranch in Wyoming. You know what this is?"

"Of course."

"It was wonderful. Riding and catching small cows and every kind of cowboy thing. Then I had my accident, and I had to find . . . another way."

Head lowered, he began rolling ahead of me, but then slowed to let me catch up. *From maladies he hath devised escapes* . . . How did that go? From *baffling* maladies. Sophocles, yes: Man the skilled, the brilliant.

"And you, Tavish?" he said. "How long have you been"—he smiled again—"whatever you are?"

"Whatever I am?"

"Theologically."

"Theologically, I guess I'm . . . non-participating."

"*Everybody* participates, Tavish."

"You sound a lot like my old thesis advisor."

"Who?"

"My master's thesis advisor, Moishe Rivken. He used to say that there were two crazy, unbelievable propositions about the world. One, a loving God made it. Who could believe such a crazy thing? Two, there is no God, and this incredible world just *happened*. Who could believe such a crazy thing? But we all have to believe one of them, he said. The question is, which is the *least* crazy?"

Aaron kept his eyes on the path ahead. "I can answer that for you, Tavish. God is much more crazy than any of your propositions—and much more real. But look, I think we are at Schwarzenburg."

We had actually made decent time despite the mud.

At the *reisezentrum*, the little travel center in the heart of the town, we discovered that we had just missed the train to Bern. But there was a bus leaving in less than ten minutes. We could see it through the window, waiting at the curbside, the door to its storage compartment open.

"It's the local PostBus," I said to Aaron. "It'll take forever. We'd be better off waiting for the next train."

"I don't want to wait," he said, getting out some Swiss francs. To the attendant he said in German, "Two tickets, please."

"But it will stop at every little place," I protested.

He took the two tickets from the attendant and handed me one. "We can catch up on our sleep."

Outside, the early evening light lay in feathery riffs on the horizon. I remembered that I was supposed to call Julie at Cimetière de Saint-Georges. Too late now. But what if she got worried and tried to contact me? What a mess.

"This says Köniz, not Bern," I said, looking at my ticket.

"That's a suburb. Downtown Bern is just a few minutes from Köniz by train. Could you get my bag for me?"

I unhooked his wheelchair bag and placed it on his lap, and after rooting around he drew out a bright blue T-shirt, neatly folded. "Yes!" he said. "An English one."

He unfolded the garment and held it up.

To change one's life:
Start immediately.
Do it flamboyantly.
No exceptions.
    – William James

"I'm sure I'll treasure it," I said.

"Try it on. There's a washroom inside." He handed me the shirt and began rooting around in his bag again. "And while you're there, could you get a bus brochure?"

"A bus brochure?"

"I saw them at the counter." From his bag he had withdrawn a pair of lightweight khaki pants, also neatly folded. Now he had gotten out the pen and the map, the latter damp from the rain, and was writing on the edge—in English this time.

And put on the pants with the shirt.

I stared at him; he nodded distinctly.

"Why?" I blurted.

"Because I want to see where the bus stops." He was writing again: *And bring out your clothes—belt, too.*

Had he lost his mind? I scooped up the T-shirt and trousers and went inside the *reisezentrum*, making my way to the washroom. Empty, fortunately. Stripping off my shirt and pants, I donned the William James T-shirt (too small) and Aaron's trousers (too big). With my rain jacket over my shoulder and my clothes under my arm, I stopped on my way out of the building to get a brochure—I figured that was just a pretext, but I took it anyway.

"Here," I said, handing him the brochure and clothes.

He stuffed the clothes into my knapsack and held out his hand for my rain jacket. When I reached into the pocket for my phone, he shook his head vigorously, his hand still extended. I gave him a good hard eye-bite (as my Scottish grandmother called it), but he just looked stern. Then, without warning, he reached out, grabbed the jacket from me and began stuffing it into my knapsack. I leaned close to mouth at him, *What the fuck?* He ignored me. Rolling his wheelchair to the storage door, he tossed the knapsack into the back of the undercarriage compartment.

"Okay, we're ready to go," he said cheerfully.

I gave him a furious glare and bent down under the open door, trying to discern a crawling route over the baggage. He put a hand on my shoulder; when I stood up, he turned in his wheelchair and began rolling away at a rapid clip. After a moment's hesitation, I sprinted after him.

"What are you doing?" I whispered savagely.

"Keep walking, Tavish," he said, his hands churning.

I turned to see the bus driver come out of the *reisezentrum* and close the door to the undercarriage storage compartment. Aaron was already thirty meters away.

"But my phone!" I said.

"It will be fine there," he called over his shoulder.

Catching up to him, I grabbed the handle grips of his wheelchair and applied decelerating force, with no effect. Then I heard an engine start and, turning once again, watched in dismay as the bus pulled out of the parking lot.

TEN

Schwarzenburg is a friendly, handsome, old-world village with a mystical, whimsical, amusing sculpture park and a quaint, charming, picturesque church for fairy-tale weddings. So the guidebooks say. I wasn't paying any attention to my surroundings.

"If they call my phone," I said heatedly, "I will blame *you* for whatever happens."

"Hopefully they think we're on the slow bus to Köniz," said Aaron. "They'll pick up the trail there."

"*Hopefully.*"

"Whatever we do now is a risk, Tavish. At least we're free of them for a while."

"One thing I've learned about these guys, Aaron—you don't get free of them. You think you're free of them, and then *bang.*"

"So we must bang them back." He came to a stop, rotating his wheelchair to face me. "I'm afraid that medieval road we were on wasn't so safe after all."

I closed my eyes, fighting an upheave of vertigo.

"I'm pretty sure your phone was on the whole time," he continued, "even though I turned it off."

"My phone was *on?*"

"The screen was dark, but I think it was still in surveillance mode."

"How is that possible?"

"Malware—the latest kind."

"But there were no cell phone towers around!"

"I'm sure they don't depend on cell towers. They probably have their own portable one."

What infuriated me was his complete lack of contrition. He put his hands on the turning rims, but I grabbed the back of his wheelchair.

"So now they know *everything,*" I said.

"No, they know what we want them to know."

"But they heard all about this Aveu guy, this math whiz—"

"There is no Aveu, Tavish."

"What?"

"There is no shadow Talmeed who knows all the equations. As I say, we have to bang them when we can."

He was rolling away at a good pace now, and I had to stride to keep up with him.

"For God's sake," I said, "they told me not to say *anything.*"

"They wanted you to find out about Zarandok. You did what they wanted."

He had apparently forgotten what was at stake for me—namely, Julie and Jaëlle. I wanted to point this out very forcibly, but it's hard to heap fire and brimstone on a guy when you're trotting to keep up with him.

"Tell me again why I'm wearing your stupid pants," I said, when we got to a crosswalk.

He threw a glance to either side of him and, despite the red light, began rolling ahead. "Possibly they placed a mini-GPS tracker on you, as a backup to your phone. I wasn't going to waste time looking for it."

"You think they put a GPS tracker in my *pants*?"

"Maybe in your pants, maybe in your knapsack, maybe in that braid of hair they sent you. I got rid of everything, just in case."

I stumbled along after him, thinking about Julie; if she didn't hear from me, she might be tempted to call my cell. God, I'd never survive this.

"We absolutely have to get to Köniz before that bus does," I said.

"We will. But now we have a bit of breathing space. So breathe."

*   *   *

I was able to breathe for about twenty minutes. Then I found myself in the back of a sedan doing 130 kilometers an hour, weaving in and out of other vehicles on a darkened highway, a wan moon keeping pace with me outside the window. Benesh the blind Talmeed was at the wheel.

"A lot of traffic tonight," he remarked.

My gaze was fixed on a computer screen in the center of the dashboard. It showed a bird's-eye view of our car moving through the twilight. Everything around it—other vehicles, road signs, lampposts, roadside fences, the median, the highway guardrail—was outlined in colored rectangles. Shadowy vehicles, encased in pink, flowed past our car like diatoms in their silica houses. Stationary objects stood eerily inside yellow oblongs. At first I was puzzled by the green lines that formed and reformed, amoeba-like, in front of our moving car; then I realized they charted the safe trajectories on the road ahead.

"Do you drive a lot, Benesh?" I said, trying to sound casual.

"Not usually by myself," he said, and nodded to Aaron in the passenger's seat. "I like to have a co-driver."

"Always wise."

But he must have driven to Schwarzenburg by himself, because he was waiting for us in the car—Aaron had apparently gotten a message to him—and soon we were out on the highway, streaming through the dusk, me still wearing the William James T-shirt and Aaron's pants. Tycho: that was the name of the car's operating system. Every few minutes, it would issue spoken bulletins in calming British English: "Exit twenty-five will be coming up in two kilometers. A vehicle has pulled out and is preparing to pass on your left." I had settled into a state of uneasy vigilance.

"How long will it take to get to Köniz?" I said.

"We don't go to Köniz yet," said Aaron. "First, we go to downtown Bern."

"Aaron, for God's sake—"

"For once we have a chance to get to Zarandok without these Friends on our backs."

I leaned forward. "Zarandok is in Bern?"

"Benesh found him," said Aaron.

"Well . . . I actually just found someone he's been in contact with," corrected Benesh.

"God, *finally.*"

It was unsettling to see the leather-wrapped steering wheel turning by itself. "An autonomous vehicle-human interface" was how Benesh had described the car. I was in the future. I didn't want to be.

"What's Zarandok doing in Bern?" I said.

"He seems to be spending a lot of time at a neo-Nazi bar," said Benesh.

"Did I hear you right? A *neo-Nazi* bar?"

"We must find Zarandok before he disappears again," interjected Aaron. "And to do that, we must find this friend of his. What's his name again, Benesh?"

"Kovag. He's a *straßenfeger*."

"A what?" I said.

"A traditional street sweeper. He and Zarandok seem to have struck up a friendship."

I went back to keeping an eye on things. Generally Benesh sat with his hands in his lap, but every now and then, he would touch the wheel in an exploratory way. Was the wheel somehow communicating to him through vibrations? I was badly outside my area of expertise here. Apparently the car had both radar and "lidar," whatever that was. The sensors were on the roof, hidden in the components of a ski rack.

"Okay," I said, "but goddamn it, Aaron."

"What?"

"No more made-up mathematicians. I don't know what you were thinking with that Aveu dodge."

"You must remember, Tavish," he said evenly, "what these Friends are really interested in."

"What?"

"The equations in the book. If they think there is a secret Talmeed in Zurich who knows all the numbers, they might leave you alone to find him."

"They'll figure out pretty quick that Aveu doesn't exist."

"He *does* exist," put in Benesh. "Virtually, anyway. I gave him just enough of a presence online to make him a plausible recluse."

Slumping back into the seat, I felt my pulse. I decided I would just concentrate on surviving. *You have a minor electrical problem with your heart,* my doctor had told me years before. I was sure this pilgrimage had turned a minor problem into a major one. And my pills were somewhere on the way to Köniz. . . . Breathe. Again.

Benesh must have sensed my distress. "You all right, Tavish?"

"Yes, yes. Keep your eyes on the road, Benesh. I mean . . . you know what I mean."

We were passing a truck, and I watched the digital speedometer click progressively higher—126 kilometers, 132, 144—and then fall again as we regained our lane.

"Listen," I said, "is there really an equation in this book about the resurrection of the dead?"

In the silence that followed, Tycho announced that we were thirteen minutes from our destination.

"We *think* that's what it is," said Benesh.

"'Cosmic dust comes together and starts remembering,'" put in Aaron.

"What?"

"That's how the chapter starts," said Benesh. "And yes, it contains an equation. The numbers of reawakening, the book calls them. I'm very far from figuring them out, but sometimes I think they could be translated into computer science terms: they relate to the retrieval of information in the universe. *All* information that ever existed, in all universes."

"So it's about the resurrection of everything."

"Seems to be."

"That's a looney idea even for a Kabbalist. You can't have an equation about everything."

"Why not?"

"Because you *can't*. How far are we from Bern?"

"Tycho just told us," said Benesh patiently. "Around thirteen minutes. And since you've given your opinion on the numbers of reawakening, Tavish, I'll give you mine. I think it *is* possible to have an equation about everything. Alexander Friedmann came close to that back in 1922, with his equations about the expansion of the universe. But as I say, we're still trying to figure out these numbers of reawakening. That's why we have to keep them safe."

"You can't keep them safe if they're in the rabbi's book. They're already out there."

Aaron turned in his seat, speaking over his shoulder. "They're not in the book."

"What?"

"They *were* in the book, but it seems this section is water-damaged. According to Alphonse, Zarandok always asked about that chapter; he suspects something big was lost. Those numbers exist only in the Talmeeds' memory."

The night outside had become unreal; the moon had grown more insubstantial in the urban glow.

"Anyway," continued Benesh, "it's the one part of the book I've written down. I had to risk it—I had to explore the numbers. I've got pages and pages of notes on them."

"In Braille," added Aaron. "Almost as safe as Aramaic."

Sitting there in the semi-darkness, watching the steering wheel turn itself and the neon-vivid shapes float across the computer screen, I thought: I am *not* in the future. I'm in the past—the far-off past. The world is scripture, voyager.

That's the kind of past I was in.

"Listen, what's this about Zarandok hanging around a neo-Nazi bar?" I said.

"We are also confused by this," said Aaron. "It's this man Kovag he seems interested in. "

"What do you know about this guy?"

"Very little. By day he is a street sweeper; by night he visits this neo-Nazi bar. The city has a thousand stories, eh, Tavish?"

*   *   *

Bern came into view in all its glitter, the reflections of the streetlights serpentining in the River Aare, the Gurten (the city's mountain) lolling salmon-pink on the horizon, the traffic stuttering over the bridges, the trees of the Botanical Garden speaking to each other under the earth, the fountains embroidering the air, the city's iconic bears dreaming untamed dreams, the famous tower clock (the Zytglogge) keeping human and astronomical time. Like all great cities, Bern was part history, part tale.

But we weren't going into the famous old town. We skirted the city center, the diaphanous moon still keeping us company, and after a few minutes on the autoroute we exited onto a boulevard. Soon we found ourselves moving under a stringy network of unused streetcar wires. The car would drift almost imperceptibly, right then left; at first I thought something was wrong, but then Benesh said it was avoiding potholes. We passed *stripteaseklubs* and boarded-up buildings and piles of rubble. And I had always thought that Bern had no sketchy neighborhoods.

"Are you sure about this, Benesh?" said Aaron.

"No," said Benesh. "Let's see if this Kovag is there. If not, we leave." He leaned forward. "Tycho, speed up five kilometers."

Aaron and I both sat hunched and intent, our eyes darting from the computer screen to the streetscape. Waves of yellowish dead-leaf light—from the sodium street lamps— slid and rippled across the car interior. The buildings grew smaller, the darkness scruffier. Graffiti appeared: fat, pale letters like uncooked dumplings, squeezed together so that the interior spaces were just slits. Often they had layers of secondary graffiti written over them, anarchist daubs seeping into lewd snarls. We drove deeper into the shifting harlequinade of grimy light.

Then the car turned down a small street and slowed.

"Park, Tycho," commanded Benesh.

As the car inched into the space, Aaron and I alternated between craning to see behind and peering at the dashboard screen. The angles and distances were all there, flickering like changing stock prices. Benesh told Tycho to unlock the doors and trunk, and I retrieved Aaron's wheelchair.

"You really think we're going to find Zarandok at a neo-Nazi bar?" I said.

Benesh unfolded his cane imperturbably. "First we need to find this man Kovag. With luck he can point us to Zarandok."

We moved together through this neighborhood of ruck and tumbledown, past lattice-covered windows and old padlocked warehouses and vandalized fire hydrants. Two kids on bikes, incognito in their hoodies, darted by, tossing out epithets in German. Aaron and Benesh, moving beside each other, were fluid and sure. Benesh was clearly leading. I saw him hesitate several times, taking in the space around him; I learned later that he used echoes from his cane as well as smells, sounds, and air currents as navigational aids. In a few minutes he had guided us to a dingy street corner.

"There," he said.

Ahead of us, a staircase led down to a basement entrance that was lit by a single bare bulb. Even at this distance, we could hear the thumping bass from inside.

"Hold on, for Christ's sake," I said.

They both stopped, Aaron's hands on his turning rims.

"We're just going to walk into a neo-Nazi bar?" I said. "A blind guy, a rabbi in a wheelchair, and a guy in a William James T-shirt?"

The two of them considered me for a long moment.

"You're right, Tavish," said Aaron. "You should turn your shirt inside out."

I was starting to wonder if Aaron had some strange personality disorder where he thought he was in a movie.

"You don't have any kind of a plan, do you?" I said.

"The last time I was here," said Benesh, "this guy Kovag was outside. He seemed to know the doorman."

"Well, there's nobody there now, so—"

Just then, somebody appeared at the foot of the stairwell—shaved head, Odin beard, beef-carcass torso. One combat boot followed another up the stairs. The man drew himself up and barked something in German.

"That's not Kovag," whispered Benesh.

The guy seemed half man, half landform: a face of solidified lava above an elephantine gut and baggy camouflage pants. His visage was the only hard thing about him; otherwise he might have been filled with sand to the top storey. I'm sure it was just the turning of the earth that maintained his circulation. He held his slab-like arms out in a stock gesture of strength, but what really caught my eye was the machete at his belt.

Benesh, speaking calmly in German, asked about Kovag. The doorman just moved closer to us, arms still curved outwards.

"I think we should go," I said to Benesh.

The doorman caught my voice. *"Engländer,"* he said, turning.

Aaron said something placating in German, but the guy ignored him and took a step toward me.

"You come for fun, *Engländer?*" he said, his English so heavily Teutonic he could have been parodying Arnold Schwarzenegger. "You like Nazi men?"

Aaron moved his wheelchair forward so that he was in front of Benesh, who placed a hand on one of the back grips.

"You come inside, *Engländer,*" said the doorman.

"Thanks," I said, "but we really have to get going. Another time. But I love this city."

The guy reached across his body and, holding the machete scabbard with one hand, drew out the blade.

"Engländer inside," he said, gesturing with the blade. "You two go."

When none of us moved, he barked, "Now!"

I heard my own voice say, "All right. Yes."

"No, Tavish," said Benesh. "Let's go."

The doorman turned to him. You idiot, Benesh, I thought.

Maybe he shared that personality disorder with Aaron.

"*Yes,*" I said. "I'll go inside. I need a beer."

The doorman gave a rictus of a grin. "*Bier,* yes." He pointed to Benesh and Aaron with his machete. "Fast!"

Go, I mouthed desperately at Aaron. They didn't move fast, but they went, both looking fighting-grim. The doorman came close to me, machete in hand; I smelled sweat and beer.

"Now we have fun, *Engländer,*" he said.

*   *   *

The music inside was chain-saw rock, cranked high. It came from a DJ dressed in the stock neo-Nazi getup—combat boots, thick braces, a T-shirt that read "White Rex." But I was disoriented to see how much of the crowd looked normal. As normal as me, anyway. I saw standard barbershop haircuts, rugby shirts, Van Dyke beards, loafers. I saw an eager-faced guy in a short-sleeved shirt and loosened tie who could have been a Mormon missionary. The women, in contrast, were mainly Goth, heavily tattooed and pierced. Their Ziggy Stardust makeup gave them the dead fluorescence of an airport interior at midnight. I walked through drifting cannabis smoke as I might have walked through the Valley of the Shadow of Death, trying not to look like a tourist. Passing the Mormon missionary, I glimpsed a Viking tattoo on his bicep. Two of the normal-looking patrons, greeting each other, took hold of each other's forearms rather than shaking hands. Was that how neo-Nazis said hello?

At the bar, the enormous doorman held up two fingers,

and the barman, a sweating wifebeater (judging by his shirt), began filling our steins from a keg. It wasn't really a bar, just a makeshift plywood counter. We had squeezed in among patrons who exhibited a broad evolutionary range. I stood next to a flabby tuberous type wearing large headphones that pulsated neon blue and green. The neo-Nazi next to him was all shaved head and kestrel gaze. He held a cardboard box that contained . . . what? Cans of something. I didn't want to lean over to see; I just took out my wallet, since the doorman clearly expected me to pay.

"Speak Hanglish, yah?" bellowed the doorman.

"Yes, okay."

"For my girl!" He'd gotten out his phone to show me a picture of a bovine woman with a nose ring and purple hair.

"Very nice," I yelled. I didn't understand why I was supposed to speak English for his girl, but I wasn't going to argue.

"She's good vibrations!"

Our beer arrived. He began quaffing it down but paused in mid-chug, wiping his mouth and staring at my torso.

"Was ist das?" he said. He leaned close, peering, and sounded out the first line like a preschooler. "To change your life . . . "

Suddenly he grabbed my beer from me, plunked it on the counter and, gripping the shoulders of my T-shirt, yanked upwards with both hands. Struggling with the shirt half over my head, I felt again that I was in the Valley of the Shadow and decided to cooperate. The doorman finally got the shirt off and, holding it at arm's length over the tumult of his belly, read out the words with difficulty. Bare-chested, I took a sip of beer, trying to look as if I didn't mind a bit of brainless horseplay now and then. The guy with the cardboard box was smiling his raptor's smile. His shaved head was as pitted and scored as pumice. Those cans in his box . . . I had the wild thought that they were containers of *air freshener.* The flabby man in the headphones looked away, as if he wanted nothing to do with this scene. The earpieces of his headphones still pulsed neon blue and green, like bioluminescent sea creatures.

"Vilhelm Jems!" said the doorman, reading the attribution on my shirt, and added something I didn't catch.

"What? . . . Sure. You can have the shirt if you really—"

"Yes! For my girl."

Did this guy do *everything* for his girl? He drained his glass of beer in about ten seconds, banged it down on the bar and gestured for a refill. Benesh, Aaron . . . please be waiting for me. If I can get away from this guy I might be able to lose myself in the crowd . . . Okay, for his *girl.* I understood now . . . maybe. His girl was English-speaking, and he wanted to practice English. A William James T-shirt would be the perfect gift. So talk to him in English. Ask him about his girl.

"Now we dance, Vilhelm Jems," said the doorman, plunking down his beer.

"Actually, why don't we talk some more and—"

"Dance!" he bellowed. "It's good vibrations!"

Sweeping up my beer, he chugged it down and wiped his mouth with the T-shirt. Then, grabbing my arm, he dragged me onto the dance floor—not forgetting his own beer, however.

We were swallowed up by the sweating, thrashing throng. It seemed only a shade away from a war rally. There seemed to be more women here than in the crowd: black bustiers, fishnet stockings, bear-claw tattoos. The doorman was at my shoulder, watching my feet like a dance instructor and stomping in rhythm with me. His belly-filled shirt billowed like a spinnaker in the wind.

The only thing I could do was stomp along with everybody else. Mimesis, the biologists call it. Imitating vile, poison-fired things. I knew enough not to get too far from the doorman. He seemed completely intent on his slampunk moves, but I knew he was keeping an eye on me. Köniz ... the bus must have long since arrived. I just hoped that Benesh and Aaron had retrieved my stuff and come back to wait for me. God, what a mess.

The doorman had drunk or spilled most of his beer. Catching his eye, I raised one hand in a chugging gesture and pointed to the bar. He gave me a wild-eyed look and kept dancing, which I decided to take as a yes. I dipped out of the throng and made my way to the bar. I hoped he could clearly see me, ordering another round. When I turned, he'd disappeared among the dancing hordes.

I saw at once that I wouldn't be able to make it out the front door with all the bodies. Besides, Pumice Head was still at the bar with his cardboard box. He wasn't looking at me, but if I tried to squeeze by him, he'd notice. A back door? I slipped away, skirting the wall, keeping as far as I could from the dancers. All the windows I could see had bars on them. But at the back ... yes, a worn exit sign.

And then I saw the flabby guy I'd seen at the bar, the one with the headphones.

He was standing by himself just under the exit sign; his headphones, now unlit, rested around his neck. At first I thought he had just retreated into his own space, but as the seconds went by, I felt that something was wrong. His eyelids fluttered and his lips moved tentatively, experimentally, as if he was exploring a subtle flavor. Drugs? He gestured spasmodically with one hand and then went back to staring fixedly at nothing. I moved a step closer. He had a child's head atop an obese man's body; he might have been a small boy who had stuck his face into one of those life-size cardboard cutouts in a museum—of Orson Welles or Jackie Gleason or somebody of that girth. Low forehead, sunken jaw, a fringe of hair around his pate like a resurrection plant. For some reason, I thought of Mique's description of the Rabbi of the Twelve Winds, from Paracelsus: *He had lost everything in his exile, and*—how did it go?—*his visions were his only solace. . . .*

I hesitated, wondering if he was having some kind of attack; and just then, from out of the throbbing music, came a yell: "Vilhelm Jems!"

Four of them streamed around me, all beer-breath and combat boots. One was the doorman and one was Pumice Head with his cardboard box. I had no idea where the other two had come from. They ignored the man with the earphones and hustled me out the back door. The cold spring air kissed my bare torso. The doorman had one hand on the back of my neck and was forcing me along. Pumice Head withdrew something from the cardboard box and handed it to the doorman.

"Time for fun, Vilhelm Jems," said the latter.

Not air freshener. Definitely not.

They spun me around, and two of them locked my arms from behind. The doorman rattled the aerosol can of spray paint and raised the nozzle. Eyes shut, face averted, I felt the cool needling spray across my chest. The doorman did a few quick passes—*fhhht, fhhht*—angling and curving the line; then I heard the can being dropped into the box.

"You Nazi now!" he exclaimed.

He'd drawn a thick dark swastika on my chest, its cross just below my sternum. One of the guys was breathing loudly and hoarsely. What was up with *him*? Then I realized he was only mimicking me. They hurried me roughly toward the street, laughing and belching.

Pallid darkness, grit under my stumbling feet, the sour metallic smell of acetone from the spray paint . . . then I saw an old Vauxhall sedan with a well-dented exterior. The doors were wrenched open and I was pushed inside. The doorman took the wheel, and I was squeezed into the back seat between the two unfamiliar neo-Nazis. Pumice Head sat in the passenger's seat, the box of paint cans on his lap. He half turned with a grin to show me something in his hand—my wallet. I hadn't even felt it leave my pocket.

The tires squealed as the Vauxhall pulled out.

Everybody in the car was drunk, although thankfully the driver seemed less drunk than the others. As we approached the old town, he slowed down—I suppose he didn't want to jeopardize his mission. For I knew they had a mission and that I was part of it. From the outside, his car attracted no attention; from the inside, it was even more of a pagan zoo than the dance floor. Chanting and belching and *Sieg Heil*-ing. The raptor in the front seat was now handing around the bills from my wallet; then he tossed it out the window. Braying all around. The guy sitting next to me raised one buttock to fart and miraculously found a lull in the cacophony. More braying.

We crossed the river on one of the modern bridges and then made our way down a broad avenue, maybe Bollwerk. Passing the railway station and a Burger King, we ended up on a street I didn't know, quiet and unlit. The paint had almost dried in my chest hair, though the odor lingered. I realized only then how cold I was.

The doorman pulled into a darkened spot, the front fender touching a construction barrier, and suddenly everybody was freakishly quiet. They all got out—the doorman left the engine running—and Pumice Head silently distributed the cans of spray paint. The doorman thrust one into my hands. I wondered what we were going to decorate.

We moved to a building with stained glass windows, and I saw a Star of David over the door. Of course.

One guy took the position of lookout, facing the street, while the others spread themselves out against the wall, rattling their paint bombs. The doorman was right beside me.

"Vilhelm Jems first!" he said.

The two guys on either side were watching me, cans of spray paint poised. I put a touch of spray paint on the wall—just a touch.

"Swastika!" snarled the doorman.

Then, from close by, came the sing-song, two-note tone of a European siren.

They all turned their faces toward it, and I ducked away from the wall as fast as my faulty heart would let me. The doorman lunged; I blasted him full in the face with my spray paint. Then the moment smeared around me. I swerved to avoid one of the louts and clipped a construction barrier as

I pounded across the street. A can of spray paint whizzed by my head. Normally I would never have outrun guys like that, but I had the advantage of being both sober and terrified. I sprinted on a diagonal across the street and around a corner, heading toward what looked like a lighted security guard's hut. I thought I heard the Vauxhall rev up behind me.

I wasn't really taking in details apart from the whoosh of light and shadow. I was running faster than I had in thirty years. A car braked violently to avoid me; I flagged it desperately but it just disappeared down the road. The lighted hut turned out to be empty, so I just hitched up Aaron's oversized pants and kept going. My surroundings became even more blurred. I remember coming to a stop beside a Porta Potty, slowed by the throbbing in my chest. This is it, I thought. The big one. You can't sprint like that and avoid a heart attack.

I was astonished when the neo-Nazi doorman appeared out of nowhere, machete in hand. Just materialized. Another of his cronies joined him, and then the Vauxhall pulled up behind; they must have done a loop. I remember holding a garbage can defensively in front of me as they closed in.

But the siren we'd heard before was growing louder. A police car swung around the corner and bumpily climbed the sidewalk. In retrospect, I think somebody in one of the adjacent buildings had seen us when we first arrived at the synagogue. The Nazi brotherhood was either very dumb or very brazen, since the main police headquarters of Bern was only a few minutes away from the synagogue.

"Halt!" said a female police officer, getting out of the car.

Another police car now pulled up behind her.

"You're dead, *Engländer*," yelled the doorman, before scattering with the others. He moved pretty fast for a mountain.

Two police officers from the second car went after them while the first pair approached me cautiously. Now reality slid back into place and I came to, wheezing hard. I was weakly holding one hand at shoulder level while the other clutched the waistband of Aaron's pants. The officers were both wearing fluorescent orange vests with shoulder microphones. The woman held something in her hand—a taser, I presumed. She said something in German.

"*Français?*" I said.

It couldn't be a real gun, could it? I was relieved when I saw a bit of green at the end of the barrel—no real gun was *colored*.

"I'm not with those guys," I said.

"Identification," she demanded, keeping the taser up.

"I don't have it. They took my wallet . . . and my shirt."

I could imagine the figure I presented—no shirt, pants barely on and my chest swastika smudged but still clearly identifiable.

"I'm not a neo-Nazi, I'm a *pilgrim*," I said.

"Keep up *two* hands."

I did, even though Aaron's pants were drooping precariously. "Don't taser me or my heart will explode. I've got a major electrical problem there."

"We must search you," said the male officer, taking out a pair of latex gloves.

He patted me down while the female officer watched warily, occasionally speaking into her shoulder mike.

Standing with my hands up, feeling finally safe from the neo-Nazis, a wisp of memory floated into my mind: my conversation with Jakob Zunz. He had spoken of a detective in Bern. A guy working on Zarandok's case. What was the name? Started with a D. Dass somebody . . .

"We take you to the station," said the woman.

"You're arresting me? But I'm an innocent bystander."

"Please come with us."

"But I have to get to Köniz right away, I have to—"

At least they didn't handcuff me; maybe I looked too beaten and battered. The male officer took me firmly by the elbow, as if I were his infirm but still crazy grandpa, and led me down the incline to the police car. The woman, her taser holstered, opened the back door and stood beside it impassively. As I was getting in, I remembered the name that Zunz had mentioned.

"Dassvanger," I said, half-straightening. "You have a detective named Dassvanger, right?"

The woman raised a hand but then I guess remembered that she wasn't wearing gloves; it was the male officer, his hand on the top of my head, who steered me into the car.

"I *know* Dassvanger," I said urgently from the back seat.

The male officer didn't look at me. "You know him?"

"Yes! At least . . . I know a friend of his, Jakob Zunz."

The woman spoke impatiently to the male officer, who closed the door.

"Can you call Dassvanger?" I said, when they were inside buckling up. "I'm sure we can straighten this out."

The woman just started the car while the man began snapping off his gloves. I slumped against the back seat. Could this possibly get any worse?

ELEVEN

At the police station, they gave me a shirt—pinstripe gray flannel, neatly pressed, with a scarlet bear (the city's emblem) on the breast pocket. Say what you will about the Swiss, they believe in maintaining sartorial standards, even in jail. The flannel still gave off the lemony scent of laundry detergent. I was tempted to ask for a pair of jailhouse pants—I was sure I could have worn them to the opera—but the desk officer didn't look accommodating.

He was a man of stormfall and gleanings: bits of dark, bits of light, surfaces rough and smooth, deteriorating essences, discolorings, wood and leaf, shake and shingle—all the things that end up against a fence after a gale. He took me to a cubicle that had a wall map of Bern, a phone, a wide-screen computer, and a pinned-up pamphlet called "Freewheeling along with the Bern Bike Police."

"Name and birth date."

He keyed in the information without looking at me. In contrast to his face, his uniform was impeccable—the deep gentian blue of the Bern Cantonal Police, with gold-trimmed epaulets and the Bernese coat of arms above the breast pocket.

"You say you are a clergyman or some such thing," he said.

"No, I'm a *pilgrim*. I'm walking the Jakobsweg. The path

for pilgrims?"

I thought of him as the Reconstituted Man, shattered by something in his past and then reassembled slapdash. Hobo kings had faces like that, and veteran oil-rig rough-necks, and old ranchers living out their days at rehabilitation centers for alcoholic cowboys.

"You say the neo-Nazis kidnapped you," he said.

"Yes. I was at a bar and they dragged me away."

"A neo-Nazi bar."

He sat staring at the computer screen, fingers on the keyboard, waiting for an explanation. The digital clock on the desk said 00:17.

"I didn't *want* to be there," I said. "I thought a friend of mine would be there, another pilgrim. But I got mixed up with those cretins. Look, I told the other officers that I know Dassvanger, one of your detectives. Have you—"

"What happened to your shirt?"

"The neo-Nazis took it. It had life advice written on it."

His severe eyes flickered to my face and then back to the computer screen. I noticed that his epaulets had two gold stars. A sergeant?

"Look, my things are at the Köniz bus station," I said. "I have to get there immediately. Could we wrap up here?"

"Where are you staying in Bern?"

"I . . . don't have a place yet. I'm a pilgrim; I just find a place when I need to."

This was probably the wrong thing to say. He got up and crossed the room to the reception area. We had been sitting behind a door that had to be buzzed open; the public part of the reception desk was outside the door. Even if I managed to get out into the public area, I'd have to sprint by the reception window, down the marble stairs and . . . not worth thinking about.

I was discreetly scratching my chest (itchy from the dried spray paint) when the man returned.

"You will stay here tonight," he said.

"*What?*" I stood up. "What are you arresting me for? I didn't do anything."

"We are not arresting you. You said you have no money and no place to stay. And you do not want to meet those neo-Nazis again."

"But I have to get to the Köniz bus station."

"The Köniz bus station is closed. I just checked."

I sat down again, eyes closed. This was like being broken on the wheel.

"In the morning, Detective Dassvanger will be in," he continued. "You said you want to talk to him, correct?"

I contemplated then telling the guy everything—about the book, about Jaëlle, about the Talmeeds, about the Friends. Would he believe me? Unlikely. I didn't think he even believed the little I had already told him. I figured I'd be better off unburdening myself to this Dassvanger, who at least knew Zunz.

"Can I make a telephone call?" I said.

He nodded to the desk phone and went back over to reception.

I picked up the receiver. Benesh and Aaron . . . Had they managed to make it to the Köniz bus station? Barely possible. So where were they now? I put the receiver down. Maybe they were still waiting for me outside the neo-Nazi bar. I could only hope they hadn't gone in after me. How could I reach them? I stared at the logo of the Bern police on the computer, which the Reconstituted Man had locked. Pagers . . . Both Aaron and Cléance had worn pagers. Old technology was more secure. So maybe Cléance's main communication line was the Convict Salesianum office. . . .

I picked up the receiver again and dialed the only personal number I knew by heart. After four rings, a sleepy voice answered.

"Tav?"

"Hi, Julie. I'm so sorry to—"

"Are you all right?" I could imagine her sitting up in bed.

"Yes, yes. I'm in Bern . . . at the police station."

"The police station! What happened?"

"It's a long story. Listen, I really need you to do something for me."

I heard the sound of the phone being moved around; she was saying something to her husband Pierre, evidently awake now as well. Just what I needed.

"Are you there, Julie?"

"Tav, why didn't you call me? You said you would call me at Saint-Georges!"

"Sorry, sorry—things got crazy. Look, Julie, remember the place in Fribourg, the Convict Salesianum?"

In a tumble of words I explained what I wanted, while police officers passed and phones buzzed and somebody plunked down a coffee beside me. Coffee, thank God.

"You'll get the voice mail of the Salesianum," I said, "but I'm hoping the message will reach Cléance."

"Yes, all right, but Tav—why are you at the police station?"

"The police thought I was a neo-Nazi."

"Tavish, I thought you were on a *pilgrimage*."

"Yes, yes, I just . . . I got mixed up with some bad company. Fortunately I was able to talk my way out of being tasered. But listen, can you call the Salesianum as soon as possible? And remember—tell Cléance to contact Aaron *now*."

"All right, yes. Listen, I found out about this man János Kodaly."

"Great. And?"

"I don't think he had a daughter."

"You're sure?"

"Well, I can't find much biographical information about him, but there's no mention of a family. So are you going to tell me what's going on?"

"Very soon, I promise. But don't call me on my phone because—"Just then I noticed the Reconstituted Man hovering. "—because I don't have it any more."

"What happened to it?"

"Stolen, along with everything else. Don't worry, it can all be replaced—except my photo of Saoirse." The Reconstituted Man made an impatient movement, and I said, "Got to go, Julie. Tell Mique to hang in a bit longer."

"*No*, Tav."

"What?"

"You're going to tell me right now what's going on."

Another officer had buttonholed the Reconstituted Man, and the two were consulting over a clipboard. I huddled close to the phone, lowering my voice.

"Okay, okay. The short version. There *is* a book—a very valuable book. So valuable that people are willing to kill for it."

"Tav, come *home*."

"I can't, Julie, because . . . listen, remember I told you I met this young woman who reminded me of Saoirse? Well, she's involved in all this."

I could imagine Julie's look at that moment: lips parted, green eyes kindled, the whole room seemingly staring with her.

"She's *involved?*" Julie repeated.

"Yes, yes. I can't figure it out, but . . . she reminds me so much of Saoirse, Julie. I wish you could see her. It's like a stab in the heart to see her."

"And how is she involved, exactly?"

"Sorry, Julie, I have to go." The Reconstituted Man had finished his conversation and now strode purposefully toward me. "I'll contact you soon. *Je t'aime.*"

I hung up over her protestations and realized I had just said that I loved her. God, what a mess.

The Reconstituted Man gave me a long contemptuous look. "You were *not* almost tasered," he said.

"What?"

"We don't use tasers. That was a pepper-spray pistol."

"Really. Maybe I should have made a run for it."

He gave a grim smile, as if he'd heard this before. "Those guns shoot a liquid cayenne extract at two hundred and ninety kilometers an hour. The spray opens up into a fan at face level. It feels like a bath of acid."

"Somehow I get the feeling that you don't do outreach work with school kids. Okay, where's my bed?"

*   *   *

My holding cell could have been a room in a college dorm. No bars, no iron cot, no concrete floor that sloped to a drain. The linen was spotless. The only cell-like features were an intercom and a thick wire lattice over the window. I was too tired even to try and wash off the swastika; I just lay down and gave in to my monologuing mind.

Vintage pagers. *That* was how the Talmeeds communicated. Kodaly: he *didn't* have a daughter, according to Julie and Alphonse. *Cosmic dust comes together and starts remembering.* The numbers of reawakening. They weren't in the book, Aaron had said. Only in the Talmeeds' memory . . . and in Benesh's papers, I guess. Memory: the architecture of the soul, in Aaron's words. It carried the visionary fire across time. . . . Time: the element we all swim in, whales and galaxies and people; and in the end (according to this crazy book) it will slow, and eddy, and finally reverse itself. Everything will be born anew. Absolutely crazy. I had always loved the Kabbalists because they saw the numinousness in the ordinary: a bird was a magic letter, ice a God-feathered thing, a mountain a continent, surfeited and dark with astonishments. But never for a moment did I take their metaphysics seriously. They weren't even *wrong*, to borrow a line from a famous physicist, I forget who. And yet, Benesh and Aaron clearly took it seriously. The Friends took it *murderously* seriously. . . . Two days. Two days to find Zarandok. God, would I ever survive this?

The questions blurred, hope and fret softened; the equation of reawakening slid away from me like a retreating wave.

In the morning I was woken by an intercom buzz. A voice (presumably the Reconstituted Man) said: "Ten minutes. Please be dressed. What do you take in your coffee?"

Some minutes later, a styrofoam cup of coffee in hand,

I followed the Reconstituted Man out of the holding cell area, through another door that had to be buzzed open, and into an interview room.

"What now?" I said.

"Somebody will be with you soon," he said, looking even more worn—I presumed he was at the end of his shift.

Plastic-veneered table, chairs, wastepaper basket, fire evacuation poster—the room was as sterile as a dentist's waiting room. I finished my coffee in a series of rapid sips. I had scrubbed at the swastika but only managed to blur it; now it was itching again. When nobody came, I began picking at the rim of the styrofoam cup, crumbling bits onto the table.

Finally the door opened, and a plainclothesman came in—a big, slope-shouldered guy with chin stubble like iron filings standing up under a magnet. He took something out of his pocket and tossed it on the table. A small booklet in a plastic sleeve.

"This is yours?" he said, in gravelly English.

The booklet featured a photo of a carved wooden statue—a saintly-looking bearded man with a staff and book. Behind him were two backpackers on a country road. *Pilgerpass... Carte de pèlerin... Credencial del peregrino.* My pilgrim's passport. Last I knew, it had been in my knapsack, which Aaron had rashly put on the bus to Köniz.

"Yes!" I said. "How did you get it?"

He took off his suit coat and draped it on the chairback. His features were coarse and graphite-dark, as if roughed out by a carpenter's pencil; he looked as if he had only just gotten out of bed.

"I am Dassvanger," he said curtly.

"Detective Dassvanger! Finally. I think we have a mutual friend—Jakob Zunz."

He didn't say, "*Small world, mon ami!*" He just studied me with his hooded eyes, and I sensed depths—maybe good depths, maybe not so good, but I knew he wasn't your average plod.

"How do you know Zunz?" he said.

I caught the imprimatura of German in his English, like an underwash in a painting, but he spoke the language well in his heavy, brooding way.

"We both collect old books," I said. "He told me that he'd had a problem with book thefts and mentioned a man named Zarandok."

"Go on," he said impassively.

"I don't have to tell you that this Zarandok specializes in stealing old books. The kind I deal in." After a week on this pilgrimage from hell, I was chary about revealing too much. I wanted him to talk. I wanted to hear about Zunz, especially how long they'd known each other. Most of all, I wanted to hear about Zarandok. But he wasn't talking, and he still hadn't said how he had gotten my pilgrim's passport.

"How does a bookseller become involved with neo-Nazis?" he said.

"Unintentionally. I ended up at that bar by accident, and then they stole my wallet and my shirt, and—"

"Your cell phone, too?"

"They took everything."

"What is your number?"

"What?"

"Your cell phone number."

I briefly contemplated lying, saying it was a new phone

and that I didn't actually know the number, but I wasn't
sure I could pull it off. I gave him the number and, while he
was dialing, slipped my pilgrim's passbook into my pocket. I
didn't want him to see the Aramaic jottings that Aaron and
I had exchanged. Or had he already seen them? He studied
the table, phone to his ear, and I started picking at the rim
of the cup again. He listened for a moment, his eyes on the
fragments of styrofoam, and then ended the call.

"Anything?" I said.

"No. But we'll track the phone."

With the side of his hand, he carefully swept the styrofoam bits into his palm and let them fall into the wastepaper basket.

"Let me give you some advice, Herr McCaskill," he said.
"First, do not go to neo-Nazi bars. Second, do *not* say you
know a ranking police detective when you don't."

He stood up abruptly and plucked his suit coat off the
chairback.

"Fair enough," I said. "But you haven't told me how you
got my pilgrim's passbook."

"Your friend brought it in."

"My friend?"

He opened the door, scowling. "Your blind friend."

*   *   *

A morning sudden with light and rush: flurrying pigeons
and whirring motor scooters and tourists taking selfies and
an old woman buying cheese and a strange spiral fountain with moss growing all over it. Waisenhausplatz, the
orphanage square. Benesh and I stood outside the police

station, heads raised toward the unblemished spring sky. He wore a light blue windbreaker, crisp white shirt, and the ever-present sunglasses. A few minutes before, he had produced my knapsack without a word, and from it I had retrieved some clothes (I'd had to give up the police-issue shirt).

"Where have *you* been?" I said to him.

He raised a finger to his lips. So we still had to worry about being surveilled. Jesus, would this ever end?

"You're probably hungry," he said. "I know a good rösti place."

My phone was in the jacket of my raincoat, buried in the knapsack that was now slung over my shoulder. I wanted to get away from the police station before checking it.

"I'll take your elbow, if you permit me," he said. He carried his foldable cane but hadn't opened it up.

Two minutes away from the police station, I unshouldered my knapsack and fished inside, slowing my stride. Benesh took his hand away from my elbow but continued to walk along easily beside me. The phone log said one missed call, one voice mail. The missed call was from ten minutes before—Dassvanger, I presumed. The voice mail . . . I took a long breath.

"M'sieur McCaskill. This is Jakob Zunz. I know you told me not to call you on your cell, but I didn't hear from you. Please give me a call. I am staying at the Bellevue Palace Hotel in Bern. I am worried. *Shalom.*"

Relief flooded my being: the Friends hadn't called. But was that good or bad? I glanced at Benesh, who stood calmly in the center of the morning; once again I had the feeling that he was taking in far more of his surroundings than me. When I went to stuff my phone back into the knapsack, he shook his head and indicated one of the outer pockets. Okay, so he *wanted* them to eavesdrop.

"Got the tickets to Zurich," he said. "Aaron's going to meet us there. We have time for breakfast."

We moved through the Old Town—arcaded streets, Swiss flags, and baroque facades. Two bicycle police officers in short pants rode by; each had a miniature Bernese flag sticking out from his back panniers.

"You know the police here use pepper-spray pistols?" I said.

"Yes. They're safer than tasers." He took his hand away from my elbow for just a second. "You've been to Bern before, have you, Tavish?"

"A few times. I've always liked the city."

Benesh seemed to have an internal map of the place; at one point, he came to a stop and nodded to our left. I saw a little hole-in-the-wall café. Its outdoor patio was bigger than the interior, but Benesh preferred to sit inside. He steered me toward the very back and had me sit against the wall, presumably so I could be the lookout man. We gave our orders and sat drinking excellent coffee while Benesh told me about his memorable dining experiences at the café. He was clearly a devotee of rösti, the traditional Swiss potato pancake, and knew the menu by heart.

"Rösti *aux légumes*, rösti with garlic butter, rösti with spinach and cheese, mushroom rösti . . . "

Without pausing in his litany, he took out a cell phone from his jacket pocket, along with a folded sheet of paper, and laid them on the table in front of him. Since his body was blocking the sight lines, nobody could have seen what now lay on his placemat.

"Macaroni and cheese rösti, rösti with oregano and onion, rösti with blue cheese and caramelized pear . . ."

Aaron had suggested sermons as a safe conversational subject; for Benesh it was rösti.

"Where's the washroom?" I said.

"Right behind you."

I swept the interior with my eyes; nobody was looking. Scooping up the phone and paper, I slipped them into my pants pocket and got to my feet, leaving my knapsack at the table. Once inside the washroom, I locked the door and took out the phone that Benesh had given me—an old flip model from the nineties. The paper had a seven-digit number written on it. I dialed the number and stood watching the light pattern under the door.

"Tavish," said Aaron. "So glad you're safe. What happened to you?"

"The neo-Nazis took me on a graffiti outing." I stood in the far corner of the washroom, speaking low to the wall. "What happened to *you?*"

"*Eine scheußliche Nacht,* this is what happened. How do you say that? A *villainous* night. We waited outside the neo-Nazi bar but we didn't see you. So we decided we must go to the Köniz bus station—"

"I just hope you weren't followed."

"As I said, we have to take small risks to go around the big ones. Anyway, we got your knapsack and came back to the bar . . . and waited. For two hours."

"I was worried sick that you'd go inside looking for me."

"That wouldn't have been wise. Eventually we got a call from Cléance, who explained what had happened. Who's

Julie?"

"My ex-wife. Thank God. I don't mean Thank God she's my ex, I mean—"

"Yes, yes. Listen, you and Benesh must find this street sweeper we talked about."

"Street sweeper?"

"Kovag, remember? We weren't able to get inside the bar, so we'll have to find him on the street."

"How on earth do we do that?"

"Just start walking. He'll be in the old town somewhere."

"We just walk around till we find him? I don't even know what he looks like."

"You'll have to talk to each one you meet; there won't be many. Benesh will know his voice." He continued on above my objections: "Approach him *very* carefully. I think he likes to proselytize—carries pamphlets in his cart. If he trusts you, he might speak about Zarandok."

"We still haven't solved the really big problem, Aaron. Even if we find Zarandok and the book, what do we do then? We can't just hand him over to the Friends."

"Yes, we're . . . thinking hard on that. Listen, we believe your cell phone is still bugged. Only call me on this phone."

"If my cell phone is still bugged, I'm screwed. They haven't heard my voice for . . . what, ten hours?"

"You went to Bern, you got a place to stay, you slept. They don't expect you to talk in your sleep."

"I wish I could be as optimistic as you, Aaron. How do I talk to Kovag if they're listening in?"

"You'll be asking him about Zarandok—that is what you're supposed to do. Just remember what we communicated to them before."

"About Aveu, you mean."

"Yes, and Zurich. Benesh probably told you he got train tickets. He didn't. That was for the Friends."

"Jesus Christ, I have to keep all this in my head?"

"Just follow the lead of Benesh. He has more experience than you. I must go, Tavish."

"Where are you now, anyway?"

"At the Bern Technical School for the Blind. Benesh teaches here. Memorize the number you called, Tavish; use that life hack I taught you. Then discard the paper."

I was almost out the door of the washroom when I remembered Zunz's message. I got out the flip phone again and his card, which, luckily, I had put in my pants pocket instead of my wallet.

"Herr Zunz. It's Tavish McCaskill. I am in Bern and yes, I would like to get together with you. The Bellevue Palace Hotel, right?"

*   *   *

Leaving the café, I felt calmer, faintly salved in the spring light that was like mixed humors of lemongrass and honey. I had ordered the blue cheese and pear rösti—crisp, lightly browned, creamy-sweet at the center. As we walked, Benesh called my attention to prominent landmarks.

"You know Bern well, Benesh," I said.

"Well, I spent four years here working on my PhD."

It occurred to me that if the police had succeeded in tracking my phone, they'd see now that it was in the Old Town and would come after us. I had to have a story ready. But I was tired of working up stories. Born to trouble as the sparks fly upward. Now I knew how Job felt.

"Albert Einstein lived and worked in this neighborhood," remarked Benesh.

"I remember reading that. When was he here again?"

"Early twentieth century. His miracle year was 1905, when he published his four great papers—on the photo-electric effect, Brownian motion, mass-energy equivalence, and special relativity."

"Is that what your PhD is in—physics?"

"Astronomy. We should be at the Zytglogge by now."

"Right here. Astronomy . . . interesting."

The Zytglogge—Bern's famous medieval clock tower. We joined the small crowd waiting for the mechanized display that happened every hour. I cast my eyes around the square. What were the chances we'd ever find this guy Kovag?

"What time is it?" said Benesh.

"Exactly seven minutes to nine."

"Just another few minutes and we can see the mechanism in action."

Astronomy. I had the inclination to ask him to take off his glasses, so I could see his eyes. He was so poised, so attuned to his surroundings, that I wondered if he was *totally* blind.

"Tell me if I'm being too nosy," I said, "but . . ."

"You're wondering how somebody can be an astronomer if he can't see the stars." He smiled. "That was actually the subject of my PhD. I looked at ways of translating astronomical data, including visual and radio signals, into sound."

"Very cool. Listening to the stars."

"Something like that."

"I once knew a guy who did that."

"Really?"

I was reliving vanished summer nights with Julie and Saoirse at our little alpine cabin, Maiensäss Ana: a luxuriance of darkness, the stars in their eternal tremolo, and our eccentric old neighbor, Herman, wearing a pair of oversized headphones. . .

"Well, he *said* he could do that," I continued. "He had this crazy set-up in his front yard—a telescope, and solar cells, and amplifiers, and—"

"What was his name?"

"Herman . . . something. Near a village called Renz, in the north. I'll think of his last name in a minute."

"Vonn," said Benesh with a smile. "Herman Vonn."

"Don't tell me you know him."

"We're a small community, we star-listeners."

"I remember the first time we took our daughter Saoirse to Herman's place. She would have been about nine or so. She said that Alpha Centauri sounded like a crowd of people humming—people just standing around humming. . . ."

And then everything seemed to close down for a second. All this strife, this pursuit I was caught in . . . what did it matter? Saoirse was gone and everything about her was gone. My dream from Lausanne came back to me: the rabbi's book changing into a house, the Hebrew letters growing into walls and beams, and me wandering through endless corridors of words, calling her name. . . .

"How old is your daughter, Tavish?" asked Benesh conversationally.

Calling her name forever.

"Tavish?" said Benesh.

"She seemed to be able to hear the stars better than any of us," I continued as if he hadn't spoken. "One summer she was planning to give a presentation about it at her summer camp. We were on our way there, just leaving Geneva, and there was a lot of traffic. . . ."

We had stopped, but he still kept his hand on my elbow.

" . . . And this semi came out of nowhere—it was terrible, like being hit by a bullet train, and I thought I'd never get free of the broken glass. I thought I'd have to die to get free of it, and I've always asked myself: Was I paying attention when it happened? I mean *really* paying attention, as much as you should when—"

Just then, on the facade of the clock tower, a wooden jester began striking a bell. Below this figure, a carousel with miniature bears and mounted knights began turning. The tourists raised their phones to take pictures.

"She was fifteen," I said. "Sometimes now I imagine her as grown up, a young woman. . . ."

On the clock tower, the king moved his scepter, the hour struck, and another bell sounded. Benesh kept his hand on my elbow for a few more seconds while we watched the display. I was searching desperately for something to cut me loose from the memories that thronged like a boil of hawks in my head, and maybe he sensed this, for he said, "I used to pass this clock every day on my way to the lab."

I let a long breath float me out of the past.

"I couldn't resist stopping to watch it," he continued, "although eventually I could only listen to it."

I turned to him. "You went blind *while* you were doing your PhD?"

"I began losing my sight the year I started. But the university helped me out—gave me a sighted assistant and so on."

"And now you teach at the Technical School for the Blind."

Benesh's face changed then. He was still tree-like in his poise, but now he could have been a tree that had been dealt a glancing blow by lightning—no visible scar, but some charring deep inside.

"It wasn't originally part of my career plan," he said.

"What *was* your original career plan?"

"To work for NASA. To work with people who see the world as I do."

I badly wanted to ask him what Aaron had asked me— where he stood, theologically—but I wasn't sure if this question would fit his definition of a safe subject.

"Aaron told me that he wanted to be a cowboy but became a rabbi instead," I ventured.

Benesh smiled. "A different kind of home on the range."

"You said it. And I guess Cléance . . . well, I suspect her home is not exactly Aaron's, but I'm sure she's just as devoted to it, and . . ."

We stood there in silence before the clock. *And you, Benesh? What's your home?* I didn't say it out loud but maybe he picked up on it. He gazed up at the astronomical clock as if he could see it, with its ornate gold leaf and zodiac dial and projecting circles of blue (to represent shades of the sky). The sidereal system that turns our wheel of time. Einstein himself, so the story went, often stopped to ponder this apparatus; it supposedly inspired some of his theories. I had only the vaguest idea of what everything meant on the clock face, but I'm sure Benesh knew exactly.

"I would love to be the person in charge of the Zytglog-ge," he remarked. "He's got a great job title: Governor of Time." He took my elbow again. "Shall we keep going?"

We hadn't gone a few paces when I came to a sudden stop.

"I am so sick and tired of this," I said.

Benesh's long stride had taken him slightly ahead of me, and when I stopped he took a small, unhurried step back, like a man keeping pace with an awkward dance partner.

"Sick of what?" he said.

"Of being followed and watched and *listened to.*"

I swung my knapsack from my shoulder, turned it around so the outer pocket was facing me, and held it up, the pilgrim's shell jumping on its string.

"Whoever is listening," I said, "fuck you."

Benesh didn't try to shush me or hurry me along; he just applied slight pressure to my elbow.

"I'm talking to *you*, motherfucker," I said to the scallop shell. "You want to call me? Then *call.*"

After that, my memory is a bit hazy. I must have plunked the knapsack on the ground and scrabbled at the pocket to get at my phone. I remember my Guild of European Booksellers reusable coffee tumbler clattering along the cobblestones; I presume I flung it away in my frenzy. By now I was the center of attention on the street. I have a vague image of an enormous woman in pigtails grabbing the hands of her two tiny, bespectacled children—although that could have come from a dream, or a Fellini movie.

"Let's get a coffee, Tavish," said Benesh.

I came to then, slid back into myself, and saw passersby staring at me. One guy actually had his cell phone raised—I guess I was just another kind of street entertainment. I'm sure I would have gone after him, but at that moment I noticed a stocky man in an orange workman's jumpsuit moving among the passersby.

He picked up something from the pavement—the bottom casing of my coffee tumbler. Then he shuffled along a few steps to retrieve the lid. Completely oblivious to everything else, turned in on himself. Like the guy who sweeps up all the glass at the scene of a car accident. Multiple fatalities, but he just sweeps.

When he straightened, I saw that he was wearing a large set of headphones that pulsated in waves of neon green and blue.

*　　*　　*

"Wir sind Pilger," said Benesh.

The street sweeper Kovag eyed us warily, headphones around his neck. In the sunlight he looked even paler than he had in the neo-Nazi bar. A flabby, shapeless man with bad teeth and a ruined gaze, he seemed strangely fragile, like one of those transparent jungle frogs whose hearts can be seen beating in their squat bodies. In contrast to him, his witch's-style broom was tall and svelte, with a long untidy brush like a comet's tail. It leaned against his pushcart, an old fashioned two-wheeler with tin sides and the ever-present Swiss and Bernese flags sprouting from the corners. Faint music sounded from his headphones. I couldn't identify it, but I caught no pounding blitzkrieg bass such as I'd heard in the bar.

"Pilger," Kovag repeated. Pilgrim. We are pilgrims, Be-

nesh had told him, which seemed as good an opening as any.

"Yes, Jakobsweg," I said.

The guy glanced at my knapsack, with the pilgrim's shell attached. I remembered the strange, suspended state I'd seen him in—not exactly a trance, but a tidewater place of mind. He slipped his headphones back on, as if he felt safer surrounded by the music.

Benesh asked him in German about Zarandok, and I caught the word *Pilger* again. Kovag was studying me curiously. Afraid he would recognize me from the neo-Nazi bar, I said preemptively, "Do you speak English?"

He gave us both a suspicious look. "I think you are *Polizei*." His English was slow but surprisingly good.

"No, no. I am a pilgrim. My name is Tavish." Now I was speaking as slowly as he had been. "I am walking the Jakobsweg with a man named Zarandok, but we've lost him." Conscious of the phone bug, I added, "I think he's in Zurich somewhere, but—"

Kovag shook his head. "They learn he is a Jew. So he left."

"Where did he go?" I asked.

Kovag just shrugged.

"*Who* learned about him?" asked Benesh.

"Ludi and the others."

"Ludi?"

"My half-brother. He is neo-Nazi."

Ludi and the others . . . maybe the creeps who took me on that graffiti outing? Again I caught the sound of music from Kovag's headphones; there didn't seem to be any beat to it, just voices.

"But you're a neo-Nazi too, aren't you, Herr Kovag?" said

Benesh.

He looked uncomfortable. "I'm drinking with them. Just drinking and clean up sometimes."

I presumed the guy still suspected us of being police officers.

"I see," I said. "But how do you know Zarandok?"

"We met here," he said, glancing around uneasily.

"Here? On the street?"

He nodded. "We talk."

"What did you talk about?"

He turned away, banged open a little door in his cart, and drew out a pamphlet. "Eine Vision vom Operationstisch," read the title. It showed a very childlike drawing of a man lying on an operating table, with shadowy figures all around. I read the title out loud.

"'Eine Vision vom Operationstisch'," repeated Benesh. "'A vision from the operating table.'"

"Yes, vision," said Kovag.

"So you and Zarandok talked about your vision?" I said.

He nodded. "I show him this." He pointed to a scar running the length of his nearly bald crown. For Benesh's benefit I said, "He's got a scar on the top of his head, but I'm not sure—"

"Here," said Kovag, and taking Benesh's hand, he leaned over slightly, holding his headphones in place, to guide the other's fingers to the top of his head. Benesh touched the scar gingerly; even with his sunglasses, he looked as bewildered as me.

"I had a surgery," Kovag continued. To stop the . . . *Anfälle.* The storms."

"Seizures," said Benesh to me.

"You know this surgery?" said Kovag. "The surgeon must take out some of your brain."

"That sounds . . . " I began, but Kovag plunged ahead: "And you are *awake.*"

"Awake?"

"Not sleeping from anesthetic. You must talk to the surgeon."

"You're kidding," I said.

"*No* kidding," said Kovag earnestly. "Your skull is gone and the membranes are gone. You are awake. The surgeon touches your brain with the *Sonde*—"

"Probe," whispered Benesh.

"—and you tell him what is happening."

"What is happening?" I said.

"In your head."

Something chimed far back in my mind: Julie had once told me that patients can indeed be conscious during certain neurological operations, since the brain has no sense of touch or pain. And the surgeon's probe can sometimes elicit mental phenomena, like—

"Memory flashbacks," I said. "That's what's you experienced?"

"Not memories," said Kovag. "*Visions.*"

"Visions," repeated Benesh. "And what exactly did you see, Herr Kovag?"

It was then that I glanced across the square and saw, about fifty meters away, a great juggernaut of a man shambling in our direction. Beard, shaved head, suspenders . . . Now I recognized him: the doorman from the neo-Nazi bar. The guy who'd spray-painted a swastika on me.

"Let's go, Benesh," I said, seizing his arm.

He stumbled. "Easy," he said.

"Sorry, but we really need to get going."

"Let me take your elbow."

We walked away hurriedly without looking back. As we turned a corner, I cast a quick look over my shoulder; the crowd obscured the street sweeper and the other neo-Nazi. The doorman—Ludi, I presumed—was probably on his way to talk to Kovag. What were the chances that Kovag would tell him all about us? Pretty good, it seemed to me.

"Do you still have that pamphlet of Kovag's?" asked Benesh.

I put it in his hand.

"You'll have to read it to me, Tavish," he said dryly.

"Of course, sorry. But let's find a place to sit down. Well away from here."

After fifteen minutes of walking, we came to a tiny park and spied a bench half-obscured by shrubbery. I figured by then we were far enough away from the doorman to be safe. Anyway, from the bench we would see him coming before he saw us.

"I'm at a loss to figure out that Kovag guy," I said as we sat down.

"You and me both," said Benesh. "Can you read the pamphlet to me?"

"I'm going to mangle the German, but okay."

As I ran my eye down the pamphlet, a word jumped out at me: *epileptisch*. I remembered Kovag's strange absent state in the neo-Nazi bar.

"Kovag has epilepsy," I said.

"Do you know what was playing in those headphones of his?" said Benesh. "Choral music. Go ahead, Tavish."

I read: "*Mein Name ist Hans Kovag. Ich bin Straßenfeger. Vor einigen Jahren hatte ich eine Operation, bei der ich seltsame Visionen hatte. . . .*"

"'My name is Hans Kovag,'" translated Benesh. "'I am a street sweeper. Some years ago I had an operation that brought me a strange vision. . . .'"

Aaron had apparently been right: Kovag *did* like to proselytize—but not for the neo-Nazi cause. The pamphlet described a religious vision that Kovag had experienced while undergoing a seizure operation. I read on, trying to get the accent as best I could while keeping an eye on the street.

"Wait a minute," said Benesh. "Read that again."

"Did I really butcher it? '*Eine gute und unschuldige Seele mag diese Welt verlassen . . .*'"

"'A good and innocent soul may leave this world,'" he translated.

"'*Ist jedoch nicht für Gott verloren . . .*' Is that right? '. . . *sondern lebt in anderen Welten weiter.*'"

"' . . . But it is not lost to God, and continues to live in other worlds.'" Benesh turned to me. "Does that remind you of anything?"

Eventually I forgot about the threat of the neo-Nazi doorman. I had the odd feeling that Benesh had *become* the author of the pamphlet: he would sit silent after I read a passage, his head slightly raised, and translate in a faraway voice. Black fire inscribed on white fire, the dead lighting candles for us, Creation as an ocean of worlds. . . . Slowly the city retreated, and Kovag's vision—a bewilderingly familiar vision—filled the space between us.

TWELVE

The latte before me was a work of art—the cinnamon color of buttered toast, with the traditional leaf design in steamed milk, served in a porcelain bowl of unearthly white. I took a sip: just the right balance of espresso and dairy. The steamed milk was not too foamy, not too thin. Cost: seven Swiss francs, about nine American dollars. Zunz had paid.

"You are walking fast on your pilgrimage, Tavish," he said.

We sat in a café just across the street from the Bellevue Palace, the grande dame of Bern hotels—four hundred bucks a night, spectacular view of the Bernese Alps, ninety-nine kinds of gin in the lobby bar. This neighboring café was only slightly less pricey. Everything here was quaint and high gloss and very Swiss, with roses on every table and a tiered fountain in front of us. Zunz had ordered a "luxury oolong tea," and along with the pot and cup, the server had brought him a small wooden rack containing three tiny hourglasses—to keep track of various steeping times.

"Well, I cheated," I said. "I took a bus from Schwarzenburg."

"Ah. Where are you staying?"

"At the Bern Technical School for the Blind."

He looked impressed. "You move in many worlds."

The colored sand of all the hourglasses—pure white, apple green and yolk yellow—had run out. Zunz poured himself the tea while I watched the lamé of waterlight from the fountain, wondering if Benesh and Aaron had located Kovag again. A vision from the operating table. . . . We had to find Zarandok, yes, but we *absolutely* had to find out more about Kovag and his vision. It was *very* familiar.

"I met your friend Dassvanger," I said.

"Excellent!"

"I asked him about Zarandok, but I couldn't get anything out of him. He seemed suspicious of me."

Zunz chuckled. "I think he has been a policeman too long."

"He didn't seem to believe I was a pilgrim."

"But are you, Tavish?"

"Well . . . kind of."

I couldn't make up my mind about Zunz. He seemed very interested in me and my life, and I wasn't sure why.

"And what about the book you came here to see?" I said.

"Pardon?"

"You told me that you were going to see an old book in Bern."

"Oh yes. I did see it. A legal treatise—not very interesting. I am more interested in the visionaries."

"So am I. Especially lately."

"Then you understand their appeal. Perhaps you are a bit of a visionary yourself, Tavish?"

"You've got to be kidding."

"But you can see pictures in your mind, yes?"

He was studying me intently, and I remembered our encounter in the cemetery several days ago, and the spirits of dead children flying back into their mortal names—as he'd described.

"If, for example," he continued, "I asked you to close your eyes and imagine this scene around us"—his gesture took in the glittering fountain, the flow of passersby, the hour-glasses with their falling colors—"you could see it in your head?"

"Well, basically. But can't everybody do that?"

He took a sip of tea. "Not me."

"Really?"

"I have no ability to see images in my mind. When I remember, I do not see pictures of places or people. I never dream at night. My imagination is blind."

"I've never heard of that."

"It is called aphantasia. It doesn't seem like such a big thing, no? But I assure you, it is." He reached out to the rack of hourglasses, turned it over, and watched the colored sand flow in delicate grained columns. "Only once did I ever see pictures in my mind. I was trying to decipher an old book, written in a language I barely knew, and that night, I dreamed of things from the book. It only happened once. I couldn't explain it."

"That sometimes happened to me when I was studying Aramaic. What was the book?"

Smiling his effortful smile, he slipped his sunglasses down over his eyes. "An old, forgotten book of *science* . . . or at least, of what they once called natural philosophy. Now long gone, sadly. Such books have a curious power, Tavish. Look at Galileo's *Dialogue Concerning the Two Chief World Systems.* You move through it as through an old museum: here is an astrolabe, there is a suit of armor or a parchment map of the night sky." His gaze was on the flowing sand in the hourglasses. "But my visit to the museum only lasted a night."

"Well, if it happened once, it can happen again."

Again he smiled his labored smile. "Sometimes I wonder if I can *train* myself to see mental images. Is there a way to do that, do you think?"

"No idea, but I know a neuropsychologist I can ask."

"You do?"

"My ex-wife Julie. She knows about that kind of stuff."

He suddenly looked a bit embarrassed, maybe regretting he had disclosed so much. "Well, thank you. But I neglected to ask about your friend Jaëlle."

"It seems she has . . . gone her own way."

I had to believe she was still alive; she was more important than Kovag, or Zarandok, or the book. . . .

"I'm sorry to hear that," said Zunz, seemingly unperturbed by my vague answer.

"But that reminds me. You gave two stones to Jaëlle, one blue and the other purple. You used an interesting phrase—echo and essence."

"I remember."

"Where does that phrase come from?"

"Oh, I don't know. It's just an idea. We get echoes of people everywhere."

"I guess we do. But I think it's time I told you about one of *my* echoes."

I was about to reach into my pocket for my wallet, to show him the photo of Saoirse, but then I remembered I no longer had my wallet.

"In Kabbalistic thought," I said, "there's this idea of the *ibbur*. Do you know it?"

"Yes. A spirit that possesses a living person—often with good intentions."

"Right. Because the spirit has something it desperately needs to do in life, some unfinished task. To me, it's just a picturesque conceit, but . . . "

"Yes?"

"I'm surrounded now by people who actually believe these Kabbalistic conceits. Anyway, when I look at Jaëlle, I see—"

Just then I felt my phone vibrate inside my jacket—my old phone, not the one Benesh had given me. I fished it out: private number. My pulse beat ramped up a notch. Zunz was looking closely at me.

"I'm sorry . . . I have to take this," I said.

"Of course."

I got up and walked away to a corner, brushing open my phone as I walked.

"M'sieur McCaskill," said an electronically distorted voice. "You are still in Bern?"

It was him, the Friend. I stopped walking. But *was* it him? There was something different about the voice.

"I'm here because we are trying to find Zarandok," I said.

"But you were planning to go to Zurich, yes? Why are you still in Bern?"

"Listen," I said, "you have to give me more time. We're getting close to Zarandok, but—"

"You do *not* seem to be getting close. You do some crazy zigzag. First you take a bus, and then it's a neo-Nazi bar, and then you sleep at the police station. . . . "

I closed my eyes. How, *how* did they know all that? Okay, no more subterfuge.

"We went to the bar to talk to a guy named Kovag," I said. "He apparently knows Zarandok."

"How does he know Zarandok?"

There—I caught it again. A different coloring to the name "Zarandok." Definitely not the same Friend. So what happened to the first guy?

"They met on the street," I said. "We didn't learn much from this Kovag, but we think Zarandok left Bern in a hurry. For Zurich, we think."

"So I ask again: why are you still in Bern?"

"For God's sake, we have to be sure we're on the right track. But yes, we are going to Zurich. *Yes.*"

I was looking at the fountain, tall and layered like a wedding cake. Everything swam in my mind, and I remembered my conversation with Benesh and Aaron about the book, about the numbers of reawakening. . . .

"Listen to me," I said. "Even if you get the book from Zarandok, you'll be missing a big equation. Maybe the biggest."

I said this in a kind of spasm, desperately, as you might yank the steering wheel hard when an air horn sounds and something huge is bearing down on you—

"The biggest equation?" said the voice.

Shit, that's done it. I closed my eyes.

"Listen," I said. "Please let me speak to Jaëlle. I just need to know she's still alive."

"What equation do you speak of, m'sieur?"

No, I can't, I can't betray Aaron and the others. . . . But could we give them *something?* Just to win us some time?

"M'sieur?" said the voice sharply.

"The numbers of reawakening,' I said. "That's what they

call them."

The voice made a short contemptuous hiss, or maybe that was a flicker of static in the background.

"You think that's bullshit," I said. "Well, Aveu doesn't think so."

"Aveu," repeated the voice.

"Yes, Aveu. You don't know about him, but—"

"We know about him, m'sieur."

Okay, so Aaron had been right: they *had* been listening on the medieval road. Though I still didn't know exactly what he had in mind with—

"But we are not sure if he exists," continued the voice.

"What?"

"We suspect the blind man is Aveu."

"What are you talking about?"

"Aveu. Short for *aveugle*—'blind' in French. A little joke of the Talmeeds, perhaps? But you were speaking of an equation."

I had the sudden urge to throw the phone away and just get the hell out of there.

"M'sieur?" said the voice.

"I can't keep on doing this, I can't. Let me speak to Jaëlle."

Long pause.

"What about this equation, m'sieur?"

Easy. Root yourself. Like hemlock on rock, immoveable.

"So this is something you *don't* know, is it?" I said. "Okay, listen—and this is the truth. This equation apparently describes the reconstitution of all information in the universe. And it's gone from the book, thanks to worms or water or something. But I can get it for you."

"How can you possibly do that, m'sieur?"

"Because Benesh has written it down—he's studied it and made notes. And I can get you all of it. Just let me speak to Jaëlle."

"I don't think you would betray your friends."

"I'll manage it somehow. Anyway, I'm giving you just one equation, not the entire—"

"The answer is no," said the voice. "We will see you in Zurich, m'sieur."

"What about the other guy, who called me before?" I said quickly. "Will he say no, too?"

In the silence I heard the static on the line waver and ripple. Why would they distort their voices like this?

"Do not think you are in control here, m'sieur," said the voice.

"I *don't* think I'm in control. I'm making you a reasonable offer. I want you to pass it on to the other guy."

"We will see you in Zurich, m'sieur. We hope you are going there."

He hung up. I knew it was hopeless to try and trick these guys. But what had I been thinking, to offer the equation to that guy?

I glanced over to our table: Zunz was tranquilly reading the paper. Thirty meters away, the fountain overflowed glitteringly in the sun. I walked over to it, took out my cell phone, and put it on the stone ledge. Zunz looked up at me curiously as I approached the table.

"Herr Zunz," I said, taking a seat, "you have to help me."

"What is it?"

I looked back at my cell phone. Was the flowing water enough to drown out our voices?

"I want to tell you what is really happening," I said. "Jaëlle has been kidnapped."

His face twitched. "Kidnapped?"

"By these guys who call themselves the Friends of the Shared Path. The ransom is Zarandok's book."

"His book? I'm sorry, I don't—"

"An Aramaic manuscript. It's worth your entire collection put together." I looked back at my phone. "I have to deliver Zarandok and his book to them or they'll kill Jaëlle."

"But you must tell Dassvanger about this." He half rose from his seat. "We will go now."

"No, I can't take the risk. I don't know who to trust. These guys are everywhere."

Zunz lowered himself into his seat again, his eyes on my phone. If there were any of the Friends watching us, they'd see the phone there. But I was past the point of caring.

"I just have to get my breath," I said. "I have to think."

He made no attempt to conceal his bewilderment; I'm sure he thought I had a screw loose.

"We can't talk for long," I said. "I just . . . anything you can do for me, I . . . I know I sound crazy, but—"

He glanced at the fountain. "*That's* why you didn't want me to call you." He cast his eyes around our vicinity. "Who are these kidnappers?"

"No idea. Murderous pricks to a man."

His ugly-handsome face was somber, his jaw set. "I will find out who they are."

"Listen to me, Jakob. Don't mess with these guys. They are *not* amature."

He gave a grim smile. "You may not believe this, but I have experience with such people."

"Experience?"

"My life task is to find books that were stolen from my people. Along the way I have met cheats, criminals . . . and demons." He stood up. "The Bern Technical School for the Blind, you said?"

"That's right, but—"

"I will contact you there. It's best not to call me."

*   *   *

Close your eyes. Let your neglected senses take over. Sun on your face and the warlocking wind in the trees and the moist, grained wood under your hand and water flowing and a flower faint in your head, a smudge of pastel scent. The Garden of the Senses. I was doing what the lawn sign had told me, leaving sight behind and following other avenues into the world. It was supposed to relax me, but that state seemed pretty unattainable right now.

"What about Kovag?" I said, opening my eyes.

Benesh shook his head. "He didn't show up for work today, and his supervisor had no idea where he was."

"Great. One step forward, three steps back."

"But we did learn that Kovag has a half-brother," said Aaron. "Name of Ludi."

"Yes, I'm pretty sure that's the doorman at the bar. The guy who took me on that graffiti outing."

"So you probably don't want to come with us when we ask him about Kovag."

"You're actually going to talk to Mr. Machete? I give up on you two."

We were in the backyard of the Bern Technical School for the Blind, clustered around a picnic table in the Garden of the Senses. A single note of birdsong moved the trees, but I couldn't see the bird. Beyond us, on the first floor of the building, I could see my bedroom, where the shower was running. My phone sat right beside it, on the bathroom sink. A reprieve, just for a few minutes.

"What's going on with those visions of Kovag's?" I said. "Black fire on white fire, the dead lighting candles, worlds like waves on the ocean...."

Benesh nodded. "Rabbi Emeth's visions ... or at least, elements of them."

"I would not go that far," said Aaron, frowning.

"There are *strong* similarities," I said.

"Kovag is a *neo-Nazi*," said Aaron shortly. "Do you think there is a connection between a neo-Nazi and a sixteenth-century rabbi?"

"Well, anyway," I said, thinking it best to change the subject, "now we know why Zarandok was so interested in Kovag. Speaking of Zarandok, where's he got to now?"

"I have a feeling Kovag can tell us, if we win his trust," said Benesh. "We just need to find him."

"Is it just me," I said, "or are we going in circles here?"

We listened to the sound of the miniature waterfall. I hadn't told them about the call from the second Friend, and how I'd completely lost my head and offered up the numbers of reawakening. Best if they remained ignorant about that.

"Please get your phone, Tavish," said Aaron.

"Why?"

"Because it's time we shared some information with the Friends."

"So what's our plan?" I said.

Aaron ran his hands through his hair. "We don't have a lot of choices now. We're going to tell them exactly what's going on and ask for more time."

I got up without a word and walked past the bamboo grove and the miniature windmill to the dormitory building. Zunz . . . was he another mistake of mine? He had said he wanted to help, but if he started to meddle. . . . Visionaries. He was obsessed with them. Because of . . . what was the word he used? Aphantasia. He couldn't see mental images. Only once in his life had he seen them, he'd said— when he was reading some old book of natural philosophy. In a language he barely knew. It had pulled dreams out of his mind. . . .

Inside my room, I turned the shower off, retrieved my phone and made my way back down to the garden. Pulled dreams out of his mind. . . . Yes, an old museum of a text could do that. I remembered years ago breaking my brain on the Aramaic of the Zohar, the Book of Radiance, and then going to bed in frustration—only to dream vividly of the passage that had defeated me. I saw the rabbis on the road and heard their famous riddle-filled conversation with the old donkey driver. The next morning, the Aramaic had come a bit easier, as if . . . Had I told Julie about it? I must have . . . as if the words somehow carried a bit of illuminant from my dream. I'm sure I told Julie. I need you now, Julie.

I stood before Benesh and Aaron, feeling raw and light-headed from lack of sleep. Should I tell them about the call from the other Friend? Yes. No. Not now.

"I need to know that Jaëlle is still alive," I said.

Aaron glanced at Benesh, who stretched out long-limbed, sequoiac, on the picnic table.

"Why won't they let me talk to her?" I said.

"We just have to keep going, Tavish," said Benesh. "We're close. Kovag is the key."

My loon called at that moment, making us all start. Benesh stood up from the picnic table, knocking over his water bottle. My hand moved spasmodically to my phone: private number. I brushed it open.

"M'sieur McCaskill?" said a crackly voice. "We hope we are not disturbing your bathing time."

It was the first Friend, the voice from Pluto. I scrabbled around to switch the cell to speakerphone. I was tired of being the only one dealing with these pricks.

"I understand you made an offer to us," said the voice. "A certain equation."

Aaron raised his eyes to me. Benesh sat very still, his body turned toward the phone on the picnic table.

"An equation about the end of the universe," continued the voice.

Now Aaron's face was flushed. Benesh removed his sunglasses to rub his brow, but his eyes were concealed behind his hand; the next moment, the sunglasses were back on again.

"We accept your offer," said the voice.

In the silence, all the sounds of the sensory garden flocked around me. Water, birdsong, wind chimes, the breeze in the trees, the rush and troubledness of the world.

"Did you hear me, m'sieur?" said the voice. "We want the equation. Then you can speak to the young woman."

Benesh's mouth was tight; he sat hunched toward the phone, bent to some inner chaos.

"Do you accept this arrangement, m'sieur?" said the voice

impatiently.

Aaron hadn't taken his hands from his turning rims; from his look, he might have been at the start of a wheelchair race.

"Yes," said Benesh. "We accept."

The tension went out of Aaron; he exhaled and leaned back in his wheelchair.

"Is this the blind man?" asked the voice. "Do you make the decisions now . . . M'sieur Aveu?"

"I'm speaking for all of us. We accept."

"Make sure you understand what you accept. We want more than the equation. We want to know what it means."

"Nobody knows what it means. You already know that."

"But you have your ideas. Give us everything—notes, calculations, theories. On paper, not in electronic form."

"It will take some time to get it all together."

"You have until four p.m. today."

"And then what?"

"When we are satisfied that we have everything, you will be able to speak to the girl. We will contact you later with instructions."

The line went dead. Benesh and Aaron sat unmoving in a cache of waving tree shows. Aaron sat rigid in his wheelchair, his body like a bent sapling, ready to whip upright.

"We don't give them the real equation," I said, completely forgetting that the Friends might still be listening.

Aaron turned his wheelchair around to face one direction, then immediately pivoted to glare into the other corner of the garden.

"No, Tavish," said Benesh tiredly. "We will give them the real equation." He took off his sunglasses, hand over his eyes. "I thought we were a team here," he said, replacing the sunglasses. "Nobody strikes off on his own."

"Yes, yes, it's just . . . I didn't want to lose her, I couldn't— I'd be *responsible* then, and you don't know what that's like, you have no—"

Some of the tension seemed to leave Aaron; his body was no longer a knuckled fist in his wheelchair. Benesh had stretched out his legs and seemed to be contemplating them as if he'd never realized how long they were. I got the odd sense that both Talmeeds were listening to each other's thoughts.

"Is an equation more valuable than a life?" I said. "Really?"

After a moment, Benesh picked up my cell phone and held it out to me. As I took it, my fingers touched his, and I remembered our conversation at the Zytglogge.

"Okay," he said. "But Tavish—we work together from now on, right?"

"Yes, but . . . okay. Together."

"*Together,*" repeated Aaron, looking frazzled.

*   *   *

I made my way to the bottom of the stairs below Lorraine-brücke Bridge, alert for syringes (there was a needle exchange close by), and then continued along the bank of the Aare to a secluded patch off the pedestrian path. With the binoculars that Aaron had lent me, I scanned the Botanical Gardens, a hundred and fifty meters away across the river. I couldn't see into the witch hazel grove, which wasn't surprising: that was probably why the Friends had chosen it as the drop-off place.

We'd seen Benesh off less than half an hour ago, watching him tap his way resolutely along Lorrainebrücke Bridge. Our plan was for Aaron to be in Benesh's car on the bluff, overlooking the river, and I was to be at water level. The Friends had been very particular in their instructions. Benesh was to come alone. He was to carry the papers in a satchel and not have anything electronic or mechanical on him, not even a wristwatch. At exactly four p.m., someone would sit beside him and relieve him of the satchel. Aaron and I were not to be anywhere in the vicinity.

"Sorry I got us into this, Aaron," I had said, once Benesh had left us.

He kept his gaze averted. "Let us not worry about it now, Tavish."

"I know *The Celestial Gate* means everything to you."

"It's not that, Tavish. You can't just—" He sighed and, turning to unhook his wheelchair bag, fished inside it for the pair of binoculars. "At any rate, we're doing what the Rabbi of the Twelve Winds would have wanted . . . in a way."

"We are?"

He handed the binoculars to me. "The rabbi would have wanted his teachings to be shared with the world—even with his enemies."

"But with *Sitra Achra*? The antagonists of God?"

"Even with them—if there was a possibility of converting them."

They must have had a talk about me, Aaron and Benesh . . . maybe Cléance, too. And I had the strongest feeling that Benesh had told them all that I had lost a daughter.

Now I sat on the ground, hidden behind a thick cluster of sumac shrubs, scanning the opposite shore. Clouds had begun to convene and the world was less blue than in the morning. Throughout the afternoon, Aaron had helped Benesh transcribe the content they had on the equation (a lot of it was in Braille). Speculations, glosses, derivations: Benesh kept it all in a safe at the Technical School for the Blind. And now here I was, binoculars in hand, a dark fume of anxiety in my head.

A cyclist passed on the pedestrian path and then two rollerbladers, an expert and a novice. The expert glided along in a rhythmic sway, her movements as regular as windshield wipers; the beginner struggled by with wading, stiff-legged steps as if she had cats clinging to her ankles. Benesh should be at the hazel grove by now. I let my breath out and drew it in again slowly, trying to loosen the knot in my stomach.

Just then I felt my cell phone vibrate. Is it *them?* But instead of the "private number" I had come to dread, it was a Bern exchange. I brushed open my phone.

"Tavish speaking."

"M'sieur McCaskill. Detective Dassvanger here."

Dassvanger. Zunz's friend, the police detective. I tilted my head back in relief, but the next moment I was wondering how I could end the call quickly.

"I see you found your phone," he said.

"Yes . . . yes, I did. You're not going to believe this, but I went back to the neo-Nazi bar and it was lying in the gutter."

If the Friends are listening, I thought, they'll think I've been in contact with the police. Get rid of the guy, fast.

"Please come out of the bushes," he said.

"What?"

I looked up. He was standing thirty meters away, just off the pedestrian path, phone in hand. He must have just walked down from the police station, only five minutes away on the bluff. What now?

"You should have told us you had found your phone," he said, when I got up to him.

"Yes, sorry about that. Listen, I'm wondering if we can put off this conversation; I have an appointment shortly."

"In the bushes?" Unsmiling, he looked me over with his dark-lantern gaze and added: "I need to show you something. It relates to the man you told me about, Zarandok."

I gave him a sharp glance. It was the spin he gave the name: *Zahr-ahn-dahk*.

"Tell me," I said.

"No, I need to show you. It's rather urgent."

I wanted to turn to see if I could spot Aaron in the car, but I didn't want to do it with Dassvanger's eyes on me. He nodded down the path toward a squat tower almost under the bridge. I fell into step with him.

"The Blood Tower," he said, nodding to a large turret-like structure farther down the path. "Anatomy students used to keep corpses here. Now it is a . . . how do you say, an urban space. For the leisure of citizens."

We were at the staircase now, where he stopped and looked down, frowning. I followed his gaze: a syringe lay on the bottom step.

"We need to get somebody new to keep these stairs clean," he said disapprovingly.

Taking out a handkerchief, he gingerly picked up the needle by the capsule end and indicated the path again.

We kept going under the bridge, into shadows. Now I noticed a small wooden shed set back from the river and surrounded by a few ancient oaks. The single window was covered with iron lattice; the door was padlocked. Dassvanger bent to place the needle on the grass and then selected a key from his very cluttered ring of keys. A musty, oily smell hit me as he opened the door. A small table of cracked linoleum stood in the center, and on the walls hung pruners, rakes, a Weedwacker, a crowbar, and a coil of hose. Apparently the place served as more than a tool shed; the fissured wall held a calendar, and I spied a cot and sleeping bag in the corner.

Just inside the door was a street sweeper's metal cart, decorated with Swiss and Bernese flags.

Having retrieved the handkerchief-wrapped needle, Dassvanger closed the door behind us and placed the needle on top of the cart. "Please," he said, nodding to the chair at the far end of the table.

He sat down in the chair near the door, pulled out a pack of cigarettes and offered me one. I shook my head warily.

"The stairs haven't been cleaned," he remarked, "because Herr Kovag hasn't been around to do them."

I stared at him. "You know Kovag?"

"We know most of the neo-Nazis in Bern."

"He seems an odd kind of neo-Nazi."

"I agree." He fished in his coat pocket for a lighter. "You only have to look at all the books he kept in his cart to see that."

"I *thought* I recognized his cart," I said, with a glance in the corner.

"That's his cart, and this is his home."

He clicked open the lighter, lit the cigarette, and drew on it lazily. I was trying to think where I had heard his accent, but I had experienced such a menagerie of accents in the last few weeks that I couldn't place it.

"The city allowed him to live here," continued Dassvanger, looking around. "They didn't know he sometimes shared the place with addicts and vagrants. Like Zarandok."

"Zarandok hid out here?"

"Kovag was of great interest to him."

He glanced out the window, smoke drifting out his nostrils. If there was something urgent he wanted to show me, he sure was taking his time. My unease deepened. What was happening with Benesh?

"It's bizarre, eh?" he continued. "A neo-Nazi and a Jew meet and talk and share lodgings. I believe they came to trust one another."

Rising, he took a few steps to the cart, unlocked the lower compartment, and took out something wrapped in cloth. I half thought about ducking out the door, but he was right in my line of escape.

"The other neo-Nazis were not quite as tolerant as Kovag," he continued, returning to the table. "And when they found out Zarandok was a Jew, he had to flee for his life. But he left something behind."

We sat looking at the object wrapped in dark cloth. The sound of the traffic came to me from the bridge beyond. Now, belatedly, I remembered where I'd heard that accent: in the voice of the second Friend. The guy who'd called me that morning.

Dassvanger unwrapped the cloth to reveal a small leather-covered book. I could see in a glance that it was old, maybe centuries old. Calfskin binding, a frayed spine . . .

"It's over, M'sieur McCaskill," he said.

He put his cigarette in his mouth and, very easily, took out a pistol from his inner coat pocket and laid it on the table. I sat very still, smelling the cigarette smoke and eyeing the pistol. It was relatively small and stubby, with a very large trigger guard. I seemed to be caught in a held moment, like the instant before a tsunami, when the breakers on the shore go silent and everything is still.

"All we need is the equation," he said. "And we probably have that by now."

I gripped the sides of the narrow table, feeling something sharp against my palm. Dassvanger watched me through slitted eyes, his hand six inches from the gun.

"Jaëlle," I managed.

He turned to glance out the wire-covered window. "Your pilgrimage together is over, m'sieur."

I stood up quickly, knocking over the chair. His hand moved to the gun.

"Sit down," he said.

"Where is she?"

"*Sit down.*"

I sat down, my pulse loud in my ears. I figured if I kept him talking, I might stay alive for just a bit longer. Maybe Aaron would find me, or Benesh, or Zunz . . . somebody.

"Give me your phone," said Dassvanger.

When I took it out, he said sharply: "Not that one. The flip phone."

I passed him the phone that Benesh had given me. He considered it with a faint smile. "They made them to last, yes?"

I was staring at the book. No, it couldn't be. It couldn't be that *easy*. After all this fraught chase, the flesh-eating anxiety, the book had just dropped into this guy's lap?

"Let me see it," I said.

He narrowed his eyes at me, drawing on the cigarette.

"If I'm going to die," I said, "I want to see it."

He spread his hands on the table. "You are after revelations, perhaps?"

"You must be after revelations, too, if you're willing to kill for it."

"Yes, we're after revelations. The kind that can be used."

"Like the numbers of reawakening? Good luck with that."

"Thank you."

"Where's Jaëlle?"

A shadow moved outside the window. He saw it, too, and taking a last drag on his cigarette, dropped it on the cement floor and ground it out with his foot. The door opened.

She was standing in the doorway wearing a baseball cap, sunglasses, and a scarf bunched up around her neck. The braid was gone, along with the gawkiness; only the poise remained. She stepped into the room, and I saw that she was wearing the shoulder satchel that Benesh had taken to his rendezvous.

"Well?" said Dassvanger, keeping his eyes on me.

Opening the satchel flap, Jaëlle withdrew a sheaf of papers and laid them on the table.

"They look genuine," she said.

"And the blind man?"

"He's not going anywhere."

Her face was hard, the face of a woman bent on survival. I sat back against the chair, trying to blink away the whole hallucinatory scene.

"And there's this," she said, reaching into the satchel again.

In a second she had drawn out an odd, elongate pistol— black with a green barrel tip.

Everything turned fast-frame then, but afterward, when I replayed the scene in my mind, each frame presented itself to me in lucid detail. As Dassvanger looked up, Jaëlle fired directly into his face. I heard a soft plosive sound, like the *phhtt* from a pellet gun. Something split the air, a red spark. Jaëlle's gun hand jumped and Dassvanger's head jerked sideways. The calendar behind him ruffled in the rush of air, and a large red stain appeared on the wall. Surprisingly, Dassvanger made no sound. Even more surprisingly, he managed to lunge for his pistol on the table.

But Jaëlle beat him to it and, tossing away her weapon, levelled his own gun at him.

"Don't move," she said, "or you'll get a real one in the head."

It was like an LSD dream: I'd just seen a man get shot, and yet there he was, upright and wheezing in his chair, eyes tightly shut. His face was coated in red, but it wasn't blood. Even in my dislocated state I could see that.

"Cunt," he gasped, "I will tear you apart."

I became aware that I was on my feet. I smelled a sharp smell—not gunpowder but something piquant and oddly clean. Jaëlle backed up a step and swung the pistol around to me.

"Sit down, Tavish," she said.

"Jaëlle, for God's sake—"

"Don't make me shoot you. Sit down."

Dassvanger looked like a man riding one of those human centrifuge machines used in astronaut training—face scrunched up, eyes closed, mouth in a grimace. He gave a hacking cough and lurched forward. Still holding the pistol, Jaëlle laid the satchel on the table and swept the papers back inside. My fogged brain finally recognized the sharp smell in the room: cayenne.

By now Jaëlle had stuffed the cloth-wrapped book into the satchel as well. Pistol raised, she backed up to the door, one hand on the body of the satchel to keep it from swinging.

"If you come after me," she said, "you're both dead."

Thankfully, Dassvanger had put the padlock on a side table out of sight, so that she wasn't able to lock the door behind her. If I'd been shut in with him, he would have had a broad choice of implements with which to murder me. He waited maybe ten seconds and then exploded from his chair. I dove away, thinking he was coming after me, but he made toward the door, coughing and spitting, one hand to his eyes. He was only a few steps outside when he went sprawling.

I dodged around him and sped under the bridge. No sign of her anywhere along the pedestrian path. The stairs . . . I took them three at a time. At the top, panting, I scanned the bridge. Passersby gave me a wide berth. Where *was* she? Dassvanger would be after me in a second.

I sprinted away from the staircase and into the heart of the old town.

THIRTEEN

Rain moved across the city, blurring and effacing the world. The cars made a tidal sound as they plowed through the streets. Rufflets of water flowed down inclines, cresting as they slid into one another, sweeping along leaves, bracken, old tree seeds, coffee cup lids, stir sticks, cigarette butts, all the detritus of a metropolis. I crouched under a storefront awning, drenched to the skin but grateful for the deluge to hide behind. A few feet from me, a woman, sodden and sighing, had taken off her tiny leather knapsack and was shaking it out. When she raised a hand to smooth her damp hair, I saw water droplets flowing down her bare forearm and off her elbow. We stood in silence, looking out at the pixelating gray air. Free, finally. Free of those murderous pricks. I'd gotten rid of my phone, dropped it into a garbage can. But Dassvanger was out here somewhere; he probably had his officers scouring the streets.

I tried to settle my head. No use going back to the Technical School for the Blind; the Friends would surely know I was staying there. The Bellevue Palace Hotel? No, I couldn't risk it: Zunz and Dassvanger were friends. But did Zunz know what Dassvanger was up to? Regardless, I couldn't risk it. The police would seek him out anyway. First I had to find out if Aaron and Benesh were safe. Would Jaëlle have really shot me? No, she wasn't a killer. She could have killed Dassvanger and didn't . . . though I was sure this was calculated. If you want to disappear in Switzerland, you don't leave behind a dead police officer. You just shoot him with a pepper-spray pistol.

You were *in* on it, Jaëlle?

I flipped up the hood of my windbreaker and moved into the street. I had indeed memorized the telephone number Aaron had given me; I just had to find a phone. But public telephones are about as common as butter churns in contemporary Switzerland, and I had no choice but to keep going. I drifted southeast, away from the old town center. The clouds hung low, massed and swirling like choral voices. The sidewalk was alive with countless watery eruptions like tiny sparklers; they seemed to be coming from below rather than above. Faint yellow headlights showed behind the wash of rain. Gray gouache figures passed me, umbrellas angled against the wind.

The bedraggled river was grainy with rain. Currents meandered in splotches. As I crossed the bridge, I saw a small Gothic church the color of fossilized bone, rising out of the mist. It sported a drenched spring bazaar banner—with letters smeared by the rain. At the front doors, a hand-drawn arrow directed me around the side. Rain poured out the eavestroughs into a rain barrel; I passed a long patch of rich black earth containing tiny flecks of grass seed. I would have to go back into the heart of the old town and find Aaron and Benesh.

Inside, the hall was crammed haphazardly with tables; clearly they had started their bazaar outside and had been forced inside by rain. The bounty was piled high: jellies, pickles, seedlings, seeds, homemade garden ornaments—

gnomes, flamingoes, swans. Books of all kinds. Bee products: honey, candles, lip balm, deodorant. Even a set of carpentry tools.

"Can I help you?" said a short churchy-looking woman.

I explained that I was doing the Jakobsweg and asked if I could use her phone.

"Yes, of course, pilgrim!" She looked me over. "But you're traveling very light."

"A friend of mine has my stuff."

"Would you like some honey for the pilgrimage? Pickles, maybe? And we must get you some tea."

"Thank you. But about that phone?"

She ushered me into a small office at the back of the hall and left me. I picked up the phone. Aaron's number . . . I knew it. Or at least, I *had* known it. I put the phone down and picked it up again. Think. I closed my eyes. No use: I needed the actual flip phone in my hand to remember. The events of the last few hours had completely expunged the number. Once again I marveled at the Talmeeds' ability to memorize the whole of *The Celestial Gate*.

The short woman entered with a cup of tea. "Is everything all right?"

"Actually, no. I need to get in touch with the Convict Salesianum in Fribourg. Do you know them?"

"Oh, yes. We run our summer day camp there."

"You wouldn't happen to have their number?"

She searched the bulletin board on the wall and plucked a pamphlet off the board. I punched in the number. A man answered and explained that Cléance had been called away on family business.

"Do you know where I can reach her? It's very important."

"May I ask who's calling?"

"Just a pilgrim."

"And can I ask your name, pilgrim?" said the voice briskly.

For two weeks I'd been surveilled and menaced and followed; I could no longer afford the pilgrim's traditional openness.

"Lavichet," I said shortly. "She'll know me."

Lavichet, the righteous gentile who had helped the Rabbi of the Twelve Winds. I spelled the name for the guy at his request, and then he said: "And your number, M'sieur Lavichet?"

"I don't have one. I'm calling from a borrowed phone."

"Can you borrow it for a while longer, m'sieur?"

"Pardon?"

"Please borrow it for a while longer. I will contact you soon."

He rang off. I went to the doorway: the gardening table was within a few easy steps. I really should buy something but I had only eleven francs to my name. Before me were flowers, and packets of seeds, and young tomato plants. I should buy something small and cheap—seeds? I turned from the gardening section to the bee products table. Honey, candles, lip balm. Lip balm . . . I picked up a tube. It was by far the cheapest thing there. Organic, and the container degradable.

The phone rang inside the office. I let the churchy woman get up to answer it while I hovered.

"Lavichet?" she said. "I'm sorry, I don't know if there's anybody—"

"Thank you," I said, taking the phone from her.

She noticed the lip balm in my hand and smiled uncertainly at me, maybe wondering now if I was a pilgrim or just a tramp.

"Tavish," said Cléance.

"Cléance, thank God. Where are you?"

"Bern. Arrived here yesterday." Her breathing seemed wheezy. "Can you talk now?"

"For a few minutes. Listen, are Aaron and Benesh okay?"

"Yes, more or less. As for me, I nearly died from an asthmatic attack."

"What ?"

"I was in the botanical gardens, too, keeping an eye on Benesh, when I saw this woman take his satchel." She gave a muffled cough. "I followed her at a distance, but she waited for me behind a tree and shot me with pepper spray."

"That seems to be her weapon of choice."

"Who is this woman, Tavish?"

"It's Jaëlle, the woman we've been looking for."

"The one who was kidnapped?"

"Yes. It's all very . . . confused."

I recounted the events of that afternoon, and when I'd finished, I thought Cléance had hung up, the pause was so prolonged. She must have already known that I'd bartered away the numbers of reawakening, and now *this*.

"So this Jaëlle has the book now as well as the equation," she said finally.

"Yes, but . . . at least she's safe."

From the ensuing silence, I guessed that Cléance didn't share my relief.

"She was clearly working for the Friends from the beginning," she said.

"No. She wouldn't do that."

"She faked her own kidnapping, Tavish."

"She wouldn't do that. She *wouldn't*." Would she? I couldn't bring myself to think too deeply about it. "I'll get them both back for you, Cléance. The book *and* the equation."

"Don't be foolish. They'll be looking for her now. You want to stay out of it."

"All this happened because of me. I'll get them back."

"And what are you going to do, exactly? No, don't tell me."

Where would Jaëlle go? She was probably on a flight by now. Hopeless.

"The Talmeeds need to disappear for a while, Tavish," said Cléance. "They know all about us now."

"That's my doing, again."

"You're being foolish, again. I'm sure they knew about us long ago; now they're just taking us seriously. We won't be able to communicate with you for a while."

"I understand. Listen, did you find out what happened to Kovag?"

"I heard that this man Dassvanger took him away two days ago—and not gently. According to one of the addicts at the Blood Tower, Kovag had a seizure in the middle of it."

"God. Is he all right?"

"We're trying to find out. As for Zarandok, he did what he always does—vanished. You might want to do the same, Tavish."

"Where should I vanish to?"

"Anywhere—but don't tell me." There was a pause. "I must say goodbye now. May St. James watch over you wherever you go. Do you still have your pilgrim's shell?"

"No! But listen—"

"You must get another one. To keep you safe until the end of the world."

"God, I have to go all the way there?"

"It's just an expression. Pilgrims who complete the Compostela to Santiago sometimes do an extra leg out to the coastal town of Fisterra. In medieval times it was considered to be land's end—as far as you could go on this Earth. So I'll say it again, Tavish: stay safe until the end of the world."

She rang off abruptly. What was that all about? *Stay safe until the end of the world.* I had the strong feeling she was advising me to keep going on the pilgrimage route. Why? It held nothing for me now. I had to get back to Geneva. But that's exactly what Dassvanger expected me to do. He might come after me, thinking I might know Jaëlle's whereabouts; he might even go after Julie. . . .

Jaëlle, how could you do this to me? In it from the beginning. From the *beginning*.

When I went to pay for the lip balm, the churchy woman said vivaciously, "For the pilgrimage?"

I looked out the window; the rain was starting to let up. Yes, I had to get out of Bern. Dassvanger and his men would be scouring the streets and probably watching the airport and train station. I had no credit card, no ID, no phone, no change of clothes, and only eleven francs to my name . . . no, nine now. There was only one place I *could* go.

"For the pilgrimage," I said.

*   *   *

Two hours out of Bern, I sat against a tree in a small wood-ed park, thinking about Julie.

What's the word for the small groove between the upper lip and the nose? I've forgotten it now, but I once put it into a poem to Julie. Also the waved green of her eyes. Also the ripple of vertebrae down her back, like the pattern of water flowing over stones. I put all these things into a poem and said that her beauty and intelligence were enough to light up the whole of Egypt, as the rabbis said of Sarah. I wanted to write the poem in Aramaic but my vocabulary was too limited. Take her breasts. They weren't biblical or classical or heroic quest-style breasts; they weren't like two young does that were twins, as the *Song of Solomon* puts it; they were just the ordinary breasts of a small woman, each a pearled overfullness, like a water droplet on the underside of a leaf, with a slightly upturned nipple. Breasts that were calmly, self-reliantly going about their business. When she bent over, naked, they took on form, filling a more slender space—as a soap bubble does, trembling on a wand, when a child breathes it into fullness. (The miracle of skin: it's actually two miracles, flow and containment.) Could even the author of the Zohar have done justice to all this?

Mr. Ein Sof, she called me. Mr. God-in-His-Primal State. Moishe and I used that Kabbalistic term so much she decided it should be my nickname. What a long time ago that was.

I liked to think she still had that poem I wrote for her, but it had probably been lost in the shipwreck of our mar-riage. To the best of my knowledge, the only things she kept of our shared life were the boxes of Saoirse's belong-ings—"School," "Interstellar Academy," and "Misc."—that she'd put in some unreachable place in her new house. She couldn't bear to have them really close to her; she just wanted them nearby. And then, when we began talking, circling cautiously closer, she asked me if I wanted to have them for a while. No, I said, it was enough that she kept them safe. I had just a single picture of Saoirse; that was sufficient. Now, with my wallet gone, I didn't even have that.

It occurred to me that tomorrow would be the third Sunday in the month—the day Julie and I usually visited Saoirse's grave together.

Adrift in these thoughts, I watched an old Volkswagen van drive into the parking lot and discharge four people who seemed appropriate to the vehicle: a small fortyish man in a ponytail, a rotund woman with hennaed hair, a teenage girl, and a spiky-haired guy in his early twenties. The rotund woman wore a T-shirt that said, "Muggles for Harry Potter."

The ponytailed man carried a cooler, and the others held jugs of juice and bags that I presumed contained foodstuffs. Hoisting myself to my feet, I went over and gave my usual preliminary—did they speak English or French?

"All of them," said the ponytailed guy expansively. The teenage girl smiled, showing braces.

"This is a bit embarrassing, but I'm wondering if I could buy some food from you. I'm doing a long hike and I stupidly didn't bring enough."

They gave me long, appraising looks, curious but not suspicious.

"Of course," said the ponytailed man. "But please, eat with us. No money is needed."

"Oh, I can't impose."

"We have too much!" He hefted his cooler and then turned to look across the grass. "But first we must do an offer."

"An offer?"

I followed them across the park to a good-sized oak tree, cleft and scabrous but still robustly leafed. Setting down their picnic stuff, they removed various items—a paper bag of something, a plastic jar of nuts, a bouquet of flowers. The ponytailed man unfolded a paper towel to reveal slices of apple.

"He is on the list of sacred trees," explained the Harry Potter woman, nodding to the oak.

We stood in a semicircle before the tree, each of them holding their chosen item. The teenage girl started to speak in German, but the woman coughed lightly.

"Oh, yes, English," she said. She closed her eyes and raised her hands. "Old One, we say thank you for yourself, to shelter the birds, to let the ants and rodents walk on you, to hold up the ... *Himmel*, what is that? ... hold up the sky, yes, and give people breath."

Opening their eyes, they went individually to the tree and laid down their offerings. The teenage girl seemed keen to educate me about the ritual, for as she emptied her paper bag (it turned out to contain soil) she said, "Earth for strength. It is like chocolate for trees."

The spiky-haired guy placed the flowers at the base of the trunk, the woman shook out some mixed nuts near the bouquet, and the older man laid his apple slices between the roots. I began to feel like a visitor in a church who stays seated while everybody else receives the Eucharist. I wished now I had bought a packet of flower seeds or something vegetative at the church bazaar. Feeling in my pocket, I discovered the lip balm. Better than nothing. I self-consciously stepped forward and placed it among the other items.

Back in the semicircle, we spaced ourselves out and then took each other's hands. We stood like that until the ponytailed guy said, "That's nice!" Which seemed to end the ritual.

On a blanket spread not far from the tree, we sat or sprawled to eat the food that hadn't been offered to the Old One. I was wondering if I could ask to borrow a cell phone, but none of them had even glanced at a phone since they arrived.

The ponytailed guy explained that they all belonged to a "grove" near Lucerne.

"A grove?" I said.

"Yes. We're druids."

The subsequent exchange revealed that they were driving south across the country and visiting the sacred trees of Switzerland.

"By dinnertime we shall be in Fribourg," said the ponytailed guy, "and then Geneva."

"Geneva?" I said. "When will you get there?"

"Oh, early evening. The Spring Pagan Festival starts tonight."

I was still wary of anybody I met, even druids, but I was getting desperate. "I wonder if you could deliver a message from me," I said.

"A message?"

"I know I'm imposing again—"

"Yes, we can give your message," put in the teenage girl.

"I'm the senior druid and I say yes."

"You're the *senior* druid?"

"We take turns," explained the spiky-haired guy.

As they packed up their food, I sat at a nearby picnic table and wrote on a piece of notebook paper torn from the girl's "book of consciousness."

> Mique: so sorry for leaving you in a lurch. I have to ask for one more favor . . . no, two. Please take this note immediately to Julie; make absolutely sure she gets it in person. I will call her tomorrow (Sunday) morning at around ten at our special place—she'll know where. Secondly, lock the store tomorrow and put up a sign saying that we're closed indefinitely. Please PLEASE do not tell anybody about any of this. Your grateful friend, Tav.

I folded up the paper, wrote Mique's address on it, and gave it to the ponytailed guy.

"You don't know how much I appreciate this," I said.

The ponytailed guy waved a hand. "Nothing. Keep the pen. It's our Grove pen."

I held it up: on it was written *Ár nDraíocht Féin.*

"It's Gaelic," he explained. "It means 'Our own Druidry.'"

"Nice. Maybe I'll start keeping a book of consciousness."

"It's a beautiful practice. Are you walking far?"

I had only the vaguest idea myself where I was going. *Not* back to Geneva. But if I went in the other direction, where would the pilgrimage take me? Vanish for a while, Cléance had said. I didn't want to, but maybe people's lives depended on it.

"I'll just follow this route a bit," I said. "I better let you go; I don't want you to miss the Pagan Festival. Stay safe until the end of the world."

"Pardon?"

"That's just what pilgrims say."

He smiled. "Well, stay safe until the next sheltering tree. That's what druids say."

After they had gone, I went over to the oak tree and retrieved my lip balm. I figured I needed it more than the Old One.

FOURTEEN

Eternity tented above me, a deep violet falling away. The stars in their ancient need-fire had come close and now occupied the bit of sky directly above. Some of them were just faint dots, but others were vivid nicks and gouges of light, and Jupiter (*was* it Jupiter? Saoirse would know) lay like a tiny bright apparition in a dark pool. Even the darkness among the stars was suggestive, filled with *possible* stars. The peripheral mind was at work here. Maybe this was what darkness was like for the ancients: when the night is enormous, all kinds of presences reveal themselves. That's how constellations get made.

Stay safe until the end of the world. How far was I from there?

I had found what the druids called a sheltering tree: an immense European maple whose vast steps of foliage had kept off most of the earlier rain. I lay down on a fluffy bed of moss, a bit damp at the edges but reasonably dry in the center. My sleep was an odd semiconscious kind of sleep, with the huge trunk sharing my breathing and the occasional small animal skittering by and the branches questing above, veining the night. The tree was more than an ecosystem; it was a firmament. Now and then I would feel a winged seed land softly on me. I couldn't be sure if I was awake or dreaming; the leaves and the stars rustled together and the endless blue carol of the night filled my head.

Maiensäss Ana.

That's what we had called our little alpine hut in the northeast of Switzerland. The place where Saoirse had listened to the stars, as I'd recounted to Benesh. When she was almost three, I hung a swing from a tree branch behind the hut, and Julie would swing her very gently, one hand on her back and the other on the plastic swing seat. With each upswing, her eyes would widen slightly, and then she would fall back into Julie's hands and wait, eyes closed, for another push. She did all this with the grave insouciance of a flower. Julie would catch her on the backswing, holding her just long enough to kiss the top of her head, and then let the swing go once again.

Another summer: she was six, and we were all out in the garden at Maiensäss Ana when she ran up to Julie in her yellow flip-flops, saying she had a secret to tell her. Julie, on her knees, said *Oui, chérie?* and kept gardening. Maybe Saoirse had expected more attention, a suspension of our activities so that we could hear her secret. *I have to think what it is*, she said, and flip-flopped away.

And then a winter in the hut—she was thirteen, and a blizzard was raging outside. She came to me with a large book under her arm and asked me to touch my toes.

Now? Why?

I just want to see if you can do it.

Yes, I can do it, but I don't like to do it when people are looking.

Come on, Dad. It's an experiment.

It's unethical to conduct experiments on non-consenting dads.

But in the end, of course, she got me to touch my toes,

and after I had righted myself, face flushed, she held up the book, her finger on the page.

In the time it took you to do that, the universe expanded by one hundred trillion cubic light-years.

My thoughts, spinning and turning in the slipstream of time, left Maiensäss Ana and traveled south. The Interstellar Academy. Robotics classes and Big Bang Cookies and micrometeorite hunts on the rooftops of Zurich . . . Zurich. János Kodaly had taught at the University of Zurich. I guessed there was some connection between Kodaly and Jaëlle, even if they weren't daughter-father, since she'd known all about him. Conceiving universes in his head. I saw her tattoo again: the Hebrew word *chai*. And drifting off in the camaraderie of shadows, I suddenly had a wild thought: Maybe Jaëlle and Saoirse had somehow *known* each other. I had an image of two transparent worlds, like the giant bubbles of the professor in the park, touching and becoming one.

*   *   *

Ten o'clock in the morning and the mountains young with the sun. Another quaint Swiss town where, amazingly, the tourist information place was open on Sunday. Even better, they offered free coffee. I had woken up to the pale aquarelle light of early morning, with the moon a soft creaturely thing in the pellucid sky. All around me lay the blue dolphinade of the mountains—bone-wreathed, varicosed, but auroral and sharp in the dawn. I hiked three kilometers to this tourist office and found nobody there but an elderly woman behind the desk. I asked her if she could find the number for Saint-Georges Cemetery in Geneva and then put down five of my remaining nine francs on the desk, to cover the cost of the call. She told me to keep the francs.

I needed to hear Julie's voice, tap into her memories. I wished I had a photo of Jaëlle to send to her. Again I wonder if Julie would actually see the resemblance to Saoirse. What if it was just me?

The office of Saint-Georges Cemetery would not be open, but I hoped the caretaker would hear the phone and pick up. What was his name? Italian. Not Giovanni, but . . .

"Hello, my friend! Long time no speak. It's Tavish Mc-Caskill."

"Tav, hello! I was waiting for your call." Not Giovanni, not Giacomo . . . After a few pleasantries he said, "I give you your friend, Tavish."

"Thanks, Gi . . . Thanks, buddy."

A voice I knew well came on the phone. "Hello, Tav."

"Mique! What are you doing there?"

"I had to come instead of Julie—I know this is your special place. Julie has gone away."

"Gone away? Where?"

"On a weekend escape, it seems."

"God, what a time for that!"

"Well . . . she needs to get away, too, Tav."

"Of course, of course." I gazed out the window in the still deserted streets of the town. "So the druids came through."

"Oh, yes. Where did you meet these children of nature, Tav?"

"In a parking lot. Listen, you don't know where Julie went?"

"I don't know. It was meant to be a *discreet* escape. That's what the neighbor said. And Tav, *en passant*—a man called the bookstore yesterday asking for you. A Herr Zunz."

"Jakob Zunz?"

"That's him. He wanted badly to speak to you. I have his number."

I wrote down Zunz's number on the receipt for the lip balm I had bought, using my druid's pen. Could I risk getting in touch with Zunz? Dassvanger had probably sought him out by now and told him God knows what. That I was a criminal, that I had helped another criminal escape, that he was looking for me. . . .

"What's happening with you, Tav?" said Mique.

"Everything. I'm still chasing after this book, but everything is happening at once. Look, Mique, Julie wouldn't just go off without telling me."

"But she doesn't know where to contact you. Tav. Nobody does. Where *can* we contact you?"

I sighed. "You can't. I have no phone and no money to buy one."

"Please stop this, Tav. I can send you money."

"Don't worry about me, Mique. I'm traveling light now."

"But you need to *eat*. Where are you?"

"I don't know, actually. Somewhere on the path to Lucerne."

"Isn't your customer Duvalsin near Lucerne?"

"Duvalsin the taxidermist?"

"Yes. Go and see him. He owes you money."

"He has no money to spare, Mique."

"How many books on wildlife have you given him? And the bills never get paid."

"I can't remember where he is exactly."

"The town with the glassworks. I'll think of it in a second."

At that moment, I was looking out the window of the tourist place, into the heart of the town. A sign was visible just across the street: Café Ende der Welt. Under the name was a bright picture of a pilgrim's shell. The phrase sent ripples through my mind: I *almost* seemed to remember it.

"Are you there, Tav?" said Mique.

"Mique, what does *welt* mean in German? As in *ende der welt.*"

"I don't know. Do you want me to call Duvalsin?"

The tourist woman seemed to have been discreetly following the conversation.

"Café Ende der Welt, yes," she said, following my gaze. "Very nice. So friendly."

I cupped the receiver. "What's the name in English?"

"Hmm. It's . . . how do you say, the end of the world. The Café at the End of the World."

I uncovered the phone. "Got to go, Mique. I'll call you soon at home."

I cut him off in mid-expostulation.

Stay safe until the end of the world. So Cléance had indeed given me a message in her last call.

*   *   *

Chunky wooden furniture, chalkboard menu, a rich jumble of sunlight and shadow. An espresso machine at the end of the counter. A battered table with pots of cream, milk, sugar, and cinnamon. And framed collages of people—pilgrims, I assumed—that filled the entire back wall. Some of the portraits were black and white; some were paintings that had an air of antiquity. I wondered how long this café had been around.

There was only one other person in the place—a tall angular woman with a wind-scathed, outdoorsy air, wearing tiny granny glasses that didn't suit her face of clear horizons. She wiped her hands on her blue-jean apron and unhurriedly came out from behind the counter, smiling an asymmetric smile.

"Welcome to the end of the world," she said, in German-accented English.

"It's very cheerful, for the end of the world."

Her eyes were like the glass of old bottles that have been in the sea for a hundred years and grown transparent as amber.

"You are a pilgrim," she said.

"Yes. Coffee, please. A small one."

She nodded. "Anything else?"

"Just coffee."

She went behind the counter but didn't get me the coffee immediately: soon I heard the sizzling of eggs on a grill. The menu was in German and French: I saw an inset paragraph giving the story Cléance had previously told me. Fisterra, from the Latin, *finis terrae*—land's end. Where the world stopped. Pilgrims on the St. James Way in Spain often did the extra leg from Santiago to Fisterra, to see the end of the world. Wonderful sunsets there, apparently.

It *must* have been a message from Cléance. She knew the pilgrimage well; she knew the route passed right through this town—and by this café.

The woman brought me the coffee. "Your omelet will be

ready soon."

"I'm afraid I don't have money to pay for an omelet."

She smiled her lopsided smile. "Well, it will be ready anyway."

She served it to me, and I ate with a combination of wariness and gratitude. When I was almost finished, she brought out a coffee pot to refill my cup.

"I have news about the man Kovag," she said, in a low voice.

"Yes?"

"He has disappeared. Cléance fears the worst."

"But the police should know where he is. They arrested him."

"The police say he was never in custody."

Goddamn that Dassvanger. I sat silent. I had the odd thought that Kovag's picture should go on the wall here, among all the pilgrims.

"He had visions, I understand," said the woman.

"Yes, and not the kind of visions you'd expect from . . . somebody like him."

Who *was* Kovag? Not a neo-Nazi at all, I suspected. Maybe he had formerly been one, along with his half-brother, and maybe he still hung around that bar because . . . why? He had no other community, or he feared reprisals if he made a complete break . . . or he had some hopeless need to find someone who might actually listen to the story of his visions. I was wondering now if he had surreptitiously helped Zarandok escape the others. And what about those visions of his, anyway? Judging from his pamphlet, he himself didn't know exactly what to make of them. They certainly seemed to draw on those of the Rabbi of the Twelve Winds, but in imagery, not doctrinal content. His pamphlet didn't even mention the Bible. It was as if his mind, his memories, held the glowing coals of the rabbi's fire . . . though I probably wouldn't have put it that way to Aaron.

"I presume these photos are of pilgrims," I said, nodding to the wall.

She nodded. "The history of the pilgrimage resides here, in the Café at the End of the World."

"I see. And how do you know Cléance?"

"Oh, we've walked the pilgrimage together several times. And that reminds me—do you have your pilgrim's pass-port?"

"Why?"

"I'll stamp it for you. We're an official way station."

She took my pilgrim's passport behind the counter, stamped it, and brought it back to me. Café Ende der Welt. Mique would be very impressed to hear that I'd reached the end of the world. I noticed there was something tucked inside the plastic sleeve of the passport, about the size of a business card. A bus ticket to Lucerne.

"I can't accept this," I said.

"A stranger is the friend of another stranger . . ."

. . . *On account of their strangeness on earth.* Yes, okay. We were all strangers on this pilgrimage route, apparently.

"The Post-Bus will stop right there very soon," she con-tinued, nodding out the window. "Once you get to Lu-cerne, go to the conference center."

"And why exactly am I going there?"

"I can't say. I was just told to get you there."

"Well, thank you." I put down my fork. "So if you know

Cléance, you must know about her . . . book club."

I could see two silk-fine, straggly lines encircling her neck and tiny stria on the side of her nose; I began to think she was older than I had first thought. But the way she moved, I guessed she was quite capable of walking forty kilometers a day on the pilgrimage route. The wrinkles around her eyes were like the craquelure in old paintings. She was as tall as Benesh, maybe taller; and in fact, she reminded me of Benesh in some ways. I had a feeling she had traveled the pilgrimage route as far as it could be traveled.

"Oh yes," she said. "I was a member of the club, for a while."

"Really."

"For a while."

"I always thought that if you were a member of that club, you *stayed* a member."

She shrugged. "In a way you do. I don't go to the meetings, but I still help them when they need it."

"On account of their strangeness on earth."

She smiled and turned away, busying herself behind the counter. I finished the last of my coffee, and when she came to refill it, I said, "Is it true that the club has been going for many generations?"

Stepping back, she surveyed me with her eyes of starburst brown. "Cléance should be the one to tell you the history of the club."

"Well, for reasons I won't go into, I've had a problem having anything like a real conversation with her. With any of them."

"You don't have to tell me your reasons. I know all about them." She went back behind the counter to set down the coffeepot, and then turned to me, casting a quick glance out the street.

"Each of us has done research on the club," she said, "and when we put it all together, it's not much. There are no club annals, as you know. Nobody takes minutes."

"But you must have found out *something*."

Again she looked out into the street. "In all my searching, I found exactly two references to the club. Paracelsus in the sixteenth century refers to the rabbi and some of his friends, the Talmeeds, who met secretly to discuss"—she held up her hands to make air quotes—"the miracle work. And then there is a gap of more than four hundred years."

"So the Talmeeds were very successful at keeping it secret."

"Maybe. All I can say is that, in 1929, the *Zurich Jewish News* carried an article about a small circle of Orthodox Jews who also called themselves the Talmeeds. They met weekly to memorize and discuss a book that apparently contained"—again came the air quotes—"angelic visions and holy numbers."

"So the memory of the book was passed down by Orthodox Jews all that time."

"That's what Cléance and Aaron believe. But Benesh . . ."

"Yes?"

"He wasn't so sure. That gap of four hundred years bothered him. He began to wonder if their little book club owed its origins not to a secret fraternity from the sixteenth century, but to the meetings of orthodox Jews in the 1920s."

"Okay, so the pedigree of the Talmeeds is shorter than we think. Is that important?"

"It seemed to be, for Benesh. But I never did understand

why." She was silent for a moment. "I worry about them sometimes. All of them."

"They seem very capable, very strong."

"Yes, but I think their strength comes from each other. From the club itself." She shook her head. "I wonder what would happen if one of them left the club."

"Why would one of them leave?"

She shrugged. "It happens. A change, a retreat, a going forward, a new wilderness, a lost wilderness. . . ." She began running water into the sink, keeping her back to me. I figured I would not get another chance to enquire further about the Talmeeds.

"If you left the club," I said, getting to my feet, "then I'm guessing you don't think there is any miracle associated with . . . well, the miracle work. The thing that holds them together."

She turned off the tap, withdrew her hands from the sink and faced me.

"Sometimes I've felt that there is a miracle there somewhere," she said. "But it might not be the one *they* see." She glanced out the window and gave her lopsided smile. "Your bus is here."

FIFTEEN

Lucerne: an airbrushed dream of a city, flower-suffused, swan-embellished, hemmed by a teal lake and sun-smitten mountains, scrubbed clean of mold and gimcrack and bumptiousness. I'd had enough of it after fifteen minutes. I was wary of cities now, wary of crowds; I couldn't tell if I was being followed. From Bahnhof Luzern, the main station, I walked down Zentralstrasse to the KKL Luzern, the Culture and Congress Center. Now and then I felt twinges in my lower back, probably from sleeping on a tree root. I badly needed a shower. Soon I stood before the postmodern conference center, all glass and austere angles. The banner above the front doors said, "Thirty-ninth European Congress on Cognitive Neuroscience, Lucerne, Switzerland."

What the hell was this, now?

Once through the revolving doors, I found myself in a poster hall with rows and rows of dense scientific displays. This was surely the last place that Cléance would be. I moved from one polysyllabic realm to another—neuroinformatics, electro-analgesia, biomolecules structure, neuralgia, nano-toxicology, brain pathways and barriers, neural networks, simulations and stimulations. After a while I grabbed a free coffee and donut from a side table and stood apart from the crowds, baffled. Had the woman at the End of the World Café sent me to the wrong place? At least I might be able to score enough free food to keep going. But where *was* I going?

Maybe I would have to follow Mique's advice and find Duvalsin, the taxidermist. Though the guy was a bit off-center, to put it kindly. A complete Luddite—even more so than me. Lived in his Wunderkammer, an old-fashioned cabinet of zoological curiosities. I doubted whether I'd get any money out of him, but maybe I could wrangle a shower and a meal. Where had Mique said he was? The town of the glassworks. No idea where that was.

Not far away stood a poster presenter—a short, homely man with ears that seemed to have been put on backward. We exchanged *guten tags*, and clearly he caught my accent, for he said: "English, yes? Welcome to my display! It is the only poster here on this topic."

The poster title was in both German and English: *Die Neurobiologie spiritueller Zustände*, the Neurobiology of Spiritual States. The board had half a dozen bright images of brain scans, taken from both the side and from above. The skulls of subjects were haloed in deep luminous blues, and the brains themselves were variously aglow, their topography traced out in flaring reds, yellows, and oranges.

"Very colorful," I said.

He smiled. "To allure the eyes. It is a kind of speed dating here for eggheads. You are a presenter too?"

"Just a visitor."

I was willing to bet he hadn't abided by the poster presentation rules, because the print was too small to read unless you went very close. Or maybe he just wanted people to approach. It worked on me.

"I didn't think that brain scientists bothered with spirituality," I said.

"Oh, our lab does. Once, a person in my lab was a theology student. He left years ago to become a brain scientist." He smiled. "I avow, that is me."

"What kind of spiritual states are you interested in?"

"All kinds. Prayer, meditation, awe . . ."

"Visions?"

"We would like to capture visions, but they are so rare."

Not so rare, I was about to say. Even in modern Switzerland. Even in this secular world of digital systems that surrounded us like the infinite jeweled net of the god Indra. But just then I noticed, among the colorized images on the board, a black-and-white brain scan that seemed delicate, wraith-like, a fragile map of some lost geography. It got me thinking not of Hans Kovag and his bright visions, but of Jakob Zunz, a man who couldn't see mental images. What was the word for it?

"Aphantasia," I said.

"I'm sorry?"

I turned to him. "Do you know anything about aphantasia? It's when—"

"Aphantasia, yes. I've never studied it myself, but I have colleagues who have. Why do you ask?"

"I just know someone who has it. The severe form, I suspect."

He nodded. "Some people see it as a real disability, and others . . ."

"He seems to be in the first category." I moved closer to the black and white image. "I think he hopes he can somehow . . . *develop* the capacity to visualize."

"I have never heard of such a thing, but then, I never underestimate the brain's capabilities."

"He told me that the only time he ever visualized anything was in a dream." With all the other uncertainties surrounding me, this topic somehow felt tangible—and I had a willing listener. "He had been reading a book in a language he barely knew, and . . . I don't know, maybe he was working so hard, trying to get *behind* the words, that it unlocked something in his mind."

Given my own experiences of dreaming in Aramaic, I found this explanation highly plausible. The poster guy looked as if he needed more convincing.

"Possibly," he said. "There *is* some evidence that the visual faculty employed in dreams may be different from the one we use in waking life."

"I'll tell him that. But is there anything he could do to *train* his mind to—"

At that moment, I felt a touch on my forearm. I turned to see Julie eyeing me through slim elegant glasses with lozenge-shaped lenses.

"Julie! What are you doing here?"

She withdrew her hand from my arm and glanced around quickly, as if she didn't want to be seen with me.

"You look as though you slept outside," she remarked. She replaced her hand and I felt the press of her fingers on my forearm. "Excuse us," she said to the poster guy. "He still has a long way to walk."

The poster guy was proffering a pamphlet to me, but Julie had already hustled me away.

"I'm so glad to see you," I began. "Mique told me—"

"I don't have a lot of time, Tavish. Pierre is giving the

keynote address."

"Pierre's here?"

"Of course. It's his thing."

Her outfit was classic Julie—pencil skirt of a soft cloud-like blue, crisp white blouse open at the neck, silver stud earrings, a small wallet-purse on a shoulder strap. I suspected she had left a blazer somewhere.

"So this is your escape—a conference on neuroscience," I said.

"It's Pierre's escape." She avoided my gaze. "I came along for the fun."

"And where are we going now, to the fun section?"

"We're going somewhere quiet. I went to the trouble of getting you here, so now you're going to tell me everything."

"You got me here?"

"Well, it was mainly your friend Cléance. I don't know this woman but thank God for her."

She plunged ahead of me to catch the revolving door; I wasn't quick enough to get inside the same space with her, and she turned to make sure I followed. Once outside, she steered me down the steps toward the lakefront, past the immense fountain and the sapling trees in their elegant wooden boxes. We didn't quite make the green light at the crosswalk, and as she came to a stop, she rose up on her toes slightly in impatience.

"You *did* sleep outside, didn't you?" she said, giving me a once-over.

"Yes. I'm a pilgrim now."

"You mean you don't have any money."

"Not for frivolities."

She put her hand on me again, as if afraid I would try to

make a getaway. When the light changed, we crossed the street and made for a park bench. The lakefront was alive with people under a gush of blue sky. At the bench, she took a seat and brought her wallet-purse around so that it sat in her lap.

"Start talking," she said.

"There's a lot to tell."

"Give me the short version."

"Aren't we going to say hello first?"

"Tavish."

I was about thirty seconds into the short version when she said: "Wait. This woman Jaëlle . . . She's the one you told me about, who reminds you of Saoirse?"

"Yes, yes. Not so much in her face, but in her . . . aura."

"Her aura," repeated Julie, in a tone that counseled a trip to a specialist.

"It's hard to explain. Anyway, she escaped with the book, and . . . I think I've seen the last of her."

I hadn't gone into any of the important details, and I was pretty sure she divined that.

"But there are still a few loose ends," I continued. "Like this guy János Kodaly, the genius recluse. Did you find out anything more about him?"

"No, because I don't have time to be your research assistant, Tavish. Keep going."

As I continued, her look changed from impatience to pained incredulity. Her conference pass, dangling on a string around her neck, was getting in her way, so she briskly tucked it inside her blouse.

"Why didn't you go to the police?" she said, when I had finished.

"Julie, Dassvanger *is* the police." I put my head back and stretched out my legs; my lower back still ached. "But the Talmeeds are in charge now, and they're very capable of handling things."

"So what are they going to do?"

"Probably go to Interpol or somebody—anybody but the Bern police."

I had no idea if the Talmeeds planned this course of action, but I knew this is what she wanted to hear.

"I'll help the Talmeeds if they need it," I said. "I'll even testify if it comes to that. But that's the extent of my involvement now."

She gave me another once-over, clearly skeptical.

"And it's nice to see you, Julie," I added.

She turned away, her green eyes clouded like the meltwater of glaciers. We watched in silence as two ducks flicked, chinked and whirring, across the sky; their shapes reminding me of the star twists in barbed wire.

"I guess I better let you get back to the conference," I said.

But she just kept staring out at the lakefront with her clouded green eyes.

"Pierre is wondering . . . why you call me so much," she said finally.

"What?"

"Yes. And why I'm often distracted. He doesn't say it, but I'm sure he thinks you're the cause." She gave me a sharp glance. "We have to go back to being as we were, you and I."

"As we were?"

"Before all this *merde* happened. You have to stay out of *merde*, Tavish."

I turned to face the lake. For years, Julie and I had made

up a single, albeit untidy, self—two tones, one chord, if not always in tune. Often, when couples split, they become strangers to one another. Not us. So I liked to think.

"Listen, Julie," I said, "the last thing I want to do is cause problems for you and Pierre. Absolutely the last."

No, we were never strangers. Even during the years I hadn't seen her, I could imagine the inscape of her life, to use Hopkins' wonderful term. I could see her doing all the small things I knew so well. Reading research papers in bed. Saying goodbye at house parties—unlike most people, she never prolonged her farewells with chat but just breezed out with a wave. Breathing on me to see if she smelled of garlic (she loved the seasoning but always wondered if she was eating too much). Now, I guess, she breathed on Pierre.

"Would it help if I talked to Pierre?" I said.

She stood up. "No, *I'll* talk to him." She hesitated and, dipping into her wallet-purse, withdrew a photo and handed it to me.

"What's this?" I said.

"You said you lost your photo of Saoirse."

It was the last photo we had of Saoirse: a group photo from her fourth summer at the Interstellar Academy, showing a dozen kids holding hands while jumping as high as they could. Saoirse was second from the end on the right; her baseball cap had come off in the air. For the first time in days, I smiled.

"I only need one photo to keep me going," I said.

She took a step toward the lake and was gazing out at it, so I couldn't see her face, just wisps of her hair being stirred by the wind.

"Tavish," she said.

"Yes?"

"Maybe you think that now that I'm with Pierre . . ." She hesitated. "Maybe you think that things are easier for me. That I don't miss Saoirse."

"Julie, I never said—"

"I still miss her. Sometimes terribly. But the thing is . . . a big part of me has stopped crying for her. Because I've cried enough. You have, too."

When I made no answer, she turned to face me.

"We've cried for years, Tavish. We've cried enough for all those other people in the world who lost their own children. But you know what? Twelve years of crying is enough."

I was looking out at the lake and the people, but I wasn't really seeing them. I was wondering where the pilgrimage would take me now.

"I should get back to the conference," she said. "Do you need any money to get home?"

"Absolutely not . . . but thanks, anyway."

"Goodbye, then," she said. "And Tavish . . ."

"Yes?"

"Please stay out of *merde*."

"I will. A new leaf. Bye, Julie."

I sat on the bench, photo in hand, watching her go. Before I'd met Julie, I was on the fast track to a life of emotional penury. I probably would have ended up a hermit. But she had saved me—or *they* had, Julie and Saoirse together.

Fatigue in my head, in my entire body. . . . A big part of me wanted to leave the Talmeeds to their book. As for Jaëlle . . . Julie had communicated her feelings without actually articulating them: *Forget about Jaëlle*. Maybe she was right; she usually was. I glanced at the photo in my hand. What a group of nerds. Saoirse was fifteen then. How the years run together, blur like the type in wet newsprint.

And then my eye fell on the kid on the far right, a pudgy dark-haired girl who was holding onto Saoirse's hand. Even taller than Saoirse. And glasses, too—she had one of those sports straps holding them in place. She was grimacing at the camera, but it wasn't a happy grimace: she was straining to appear joyful and carefree. I held the photo closer and the shadowed glade around me seemed to dilate inside my head.

Jaëlle.

*   *   *

I pounded up the steps of the conference center. The Interstellar Academy—of course. They'd met *there*. Saoirse had never told us anything about it, but then, she'd entered an uncommunicative phase. And Jaëlle's tattoo, the one that resembled the pi symbol—two Hebrew letters making up the word *chai*. Alive . . .

The poster hall seemed even more crowded than before; people must have been waiting for the plenary to start. I was engulfed in waves of neurologists, neuropsychologists, nano-toxicologists, neural networkers, simulators, stimulators. I dodged up and down the display aisles, trying not to look panicked. Could I find her without—

And suddenly she was there, standing in a corner with her phone. I made a beeline for her.

"Julie! I have to show you something."

Beside her, Pierre turned around and scrutinized me.

Shit—I hadn't even noticed him. Tall and authoritative, Pierre was a lodestar to his students and research assistants. He looked like an idol in the original sense of the word: flakes seemed to have been chipped off his face, as with those Stone Age flint tools, so that it was all planes and shadows.

"Hello, Tavish," he said pleasantly. "Enjoying the conference?"

"Ah . . . Hi, Pierre. Yes, quite good."

"I thought you were doing a pilgrimage."

"I am. Lucerne is on my route. I just . . . stopped in to say hello."

Pierre ran his hand through his close-cropped sandy hair, which always struck me as part of his weathered skin, a roughening and splintering of the grain; his head actually looked like the top of a much hammered stake. Julie's silence was that of a root fire, invisibly seething and sparking.

Well," said Pierre, "I'd like to stay and chat, but I have a talk to give. I'll leave you two together."

"I'll just be a minute, *chéri*," said Julie to Pierre. Once he was out of earshot, she turned to me with eyes like lance-heads.

"Sorry, Julie," I said agitatedly, "it's just—look at this photograph. *That's* Jaëlle."

She didn't look at the photo. "I thought you said you were finished with all this."

"Please look. They were at the camp together."

She took the photo and gazed at it sullenly. "That's Jaëlle?"

"That's her. Can you see the resemblance?"

"No."

"Look at how they're jumping."

"What?"

"You can tell they're both physically awkward." I moved closer to her. "Jaëlle reminded me so much of Saoirse, but I see now that it wasn't really her appearance but her way of walking and moving and . . . everything. Touching her glasses, fingering her earring, straightening her shoulders. You should see how she sits. Pure Saoirse."

"You're saying she *imitated* Saoirse?"

"I think it went deeper than that. Jaëlle unconsciously adopted Saoirse's mannerisms and gestures because . . ."

"Because . . . ?"

"Because I don't *know,* exactly, and I don't know why she would use me the way she did, I can't figure out any of it, but I'm starting to think that Jaëlle and Saoirse were *very* close."

Julie heaved a full-body sigh. "You *haven't* finished with all this, Tavish."

"What?"

"You told me you have finished with all this *merde,* but you haven't."

"I have, Julie, I have. Except for this one loose end, and it's very important—to *us.*"

She drew back, her eyes all clamor. "What on earth do you mean?"

"I don't know exactly, it's just . . . I'm starting to think that more things happened at that camp than Saoirse told us about." I hesitated. "Did she ever say anything to you about a friend at the Interstellar Academy?"

She gave me a mute, ulcerated look. I felt as though I were looking at her from a distant island in the past, separated by an entire ocean, beckoning frantically.

"Don't you see what's happened?" she said.

"What?"

"We were doing fine before all this. We were friends, we got through it all, and we were friends, but now—"

The tears were clearly there.

"Okay," I said. "I better go."

"Where are you going, exactly?"

"I'm going to keep walking."

"No! Go home, Tavish."

"I'm going to keep walking because that's the only thing that helps. Don't worry about me."

"Stop telling me not to worry."

"You better go; the plenary is starting."

The room was emptying around me. Nice one, Tavish. Pierre would see that she was badly upset, and would ask her about it, and . . . I winced inwardly. No, just get out. Repair the damage later, if it's repairable. I walked quickly through the crowds toward the entrance, taking in nothing. Nowhere to go except the pilgrimage route. I'd have to try my luck with Duvalsin the taxidermist. Now I just had to find him.

I was almost out the front door when I ran into the poster guy I'd talked to earlier. I hoped to pass by with just a nod, but he held up a hand.

"You're not going to the plenary?" he said.

"Not for me. Listen, is there a place around here that's known for its glassworks?"

"That would be Hergiswil. South along the lake, maybe ten minutes."

"On foot?"

"No, no. By car."

My heart sank. Another two hours of walking. But I had to go south anyway, to get back on the pilgrimage route.

"I guess I better get going," I said.

He was studying me intently. "You asked me about your friend with aphantasia—how you might help him."

"That's right."

"You said he saw dream images in his head, after . . . what was it? He was studying something—"

Julie. I wanted badly to go back and find her. Our life together, everything I'd lost, poured down on me like a biblical rain. She had once suggested that we have another child—years ago, when Saoirse was a toddler. I had temporized. How could I have messed everything up so completely?

" . . . And re-create the exact conditions of that experience," the poster guy was saying. "To see if the dream imagery reoccurs. He should retrieve the text he was studying, and—"

"Yes, yes, good idea. Thank you. Goodbye."

He hesitated, smiling faintly. "I'd be curious to know what text caused his dreams."

"Natural philosophy or something, like Galileo or . . . But he says it's long gone. I really must go."

SIXTEEN

A magnificent ibex with its head raised, horns curving over its back. A gray seal with pelage mottled like a moth's wing. A flying fox with the face of a terrier. Rows of sea urchins gray with age. A jar of porcupine quills. A meter-high skeleton (real or plastic, I couldn't tell) of a great auk. A giant wolf eel with the face of a ghoul, mounted on a wooden plaque. This was Duvalsin's Wunderkammer, the cabinet of zoological curiosities, and the chief zoological curiosity was Duvalsin himself.

He sat surrounded by smells of sawdust and resin—a short, lumpish man in an old Adidas sweatshirt, sporting a sleeve tattoo of Cat Woman. When I stepped into his store, he was repairing an item from his stock, a two-foot-high model crocodile that stood upright and wore a miniature captain's hat.

"Tavish!" He set down the crocodile, which immediately fell over. The hat must have been glued on, since it didn't budge.

"What are you doing here?" he said.

"I'm here to take money off you, Duvalsin."

"Oh, help. Have a seat." He tried to make the crocodile stand up, but its base was clearly faulty and he ended up just laying it on its side. He hadn't changed much since I had last seen him—same scuff in his voice, same blear in his eye, same hair like a furious chalk scribble on a black-board.

"Yes. Old debts have come due."

On his desk were spark plugs, a fishing knife, a file with a string-bound handle, two pipes (one with a broken stem), an old teal-colored desk phone, a few taxidermy tools, a scatter of pipe tobacco, and an apple core in a tin ashtray. There was also something that might have been a curved bone, maybe six inches long, sprouting long feathery hair the color and texture of old oakum. Some dried animal part. I had fully expected his store to look like this.

"You look tired," he observed.

"I just walked all the way from Lucerne."

"You joke!"

"I'm doing the pilgrimage route, the Jakobsweg. And I'm traveling very light—which is why I am depending on the kindness of strangers."

"I'm not a stranger, Tavish," he said, sounding slightly hurt. "I'm your friend."

"So you'll give me the money?"

"Well . . . no. But I can give you pizza and schnapps and . . . this." He held up the crocodile in the captain's hat.

"You disappoint me, Duvalsin."

"I disappoint most people, Tavish."

I nodded to his shelf of books on everything from taxidermy to sea voyages to wildlife of the Swiss Alps. "Half of those books I just *gave* you."

"I know, I know," he said earnestly. "I will pay you, Tavish. But it's been very hard for me lately, financially and morally." He reached into his desk and got out a bottle of schnapps and two glasses. "But listen! You can stay here in the store, if you want."

"With all these stuffed animals?"

"It will be like camping."

"I can't wait. What is that thing on your desk, by the way?"

He picked up the feathery artifact I had noticed earlier. "Dried whale baleen," he said. "Did you know, Tavish, that there are two kinds of whales, baleen and—"

"Yes, Duvalsin, you've told me before. Well, maybe I'll have to take you up on your offer to stay here. Nature's balm and all that."

"Excellent!" He poured a glass of schnapps for both of us. "And then in the morning, we will go to Entlebuch, yes? Hike and enjoy."

His English had only the faintest coloring of Swiss German; he'd spent a number of years in the U.S., practicing taxidermy and camping in the great lonely places.

"I don't have time, Duvalsin. I'm heading to Zurich."

"Is that on the pilgrimage?"

"It's on *my* pilgrimage."

Yes, a detour. If the Interstellar Academy was still around, I figured there might be someone there who would remember Jaëlle. And I recalled what I had learned at the End of the World Café: the Talmeeds may have begun in Zurich, among Orthodox Jews. I was curious about that.

Our schnapps consumed, I followed Duvalsin into his tiny living space at the back of the store, where he rooted around in a cupboard and found a sleeping bag and a foam mattress for me. In contrast to the rest of the store, they looked almost new; I suspected he spent the little money he had on camping gear. I took a much needed shower in his less-than-spotless bathroom, and then he served me cold pizza and more schnapps. All the time we ate, he spoke of Entlebuch, Switzerland's first UNESCO Biosphere Reserve, forty minutes' drive away. His living space held corners into which he apparently hadn't ventured in a while. At the end of the room I saw old paint flecks seemingly frozen in mid air; I stared in astonishment, until I realized they were caught in a spider web.

"Why are you doing this pilgrimage, Tavish?" he said, a slice of pizza balanced on his stubby fingers.

"To see the country. To meet people. To look for books."

"Any interesting ones so far?"

"People or books?"

"Both. Big souls, small souls. Books are like people."

I figured if I stayed here and drank his schnapps and listened to his talk about wildlife, then I might be able to wrangle something out of him. Maybe not money, but a lift to Zurich. I was being reprehensibly mercenary, but then, being mercenary was not a personal failing in Duvalsin's eyes.

"I got interested in a rabbi who might have done some of the pilgrimage long ago," I said.

"How long ago?"

"Five hundred years ago. But sometimes I think he's still among us, walking the pilgrimage."

"Religion!" said Duvalsin, with robust contempt.

"Your religion is nature, I guess."

"It's part of the family tradition, Tavish. My father was a mountain guide, and his father also."

"It's good to have a tradition. That's the big soul you spoke of."

I briefly saw old Moishe before me, his beard a thicket

and his hands talking—fluttering and pointing and even climbing the rungs of an imaginary ladder—as he held forth on his own family tradition. Coming from a long line of scholarly rabbis, he often felt that he wasn't learning new things but *remembering*—reliving the discoveries and epiphanies of his ancestors. In this (he said) he agreed with Carl Jung: that sleeping and waking, we were constantly tapping into ancestral memories. And that's one guy I almost *never* agree with, he'd added.

"Exactly!" said Duvalsin. "Listen, Tavish, you rest here for tonight. In the morning we go to Entlebuch, just for the day. Then I'll drive you to Zurich."

"I really need to keep going, Duvalsin. Sorry."

"But it's the mountains. We need mountains for the adrenalin."

"My adrenalin levels have been doing fine lately."

We drank more schnapps while Duvalsin talked about all the wilderness places of the world he had visited. I nodded in agreement now and then, but I was thinking of Julie, her tears and anger. I drank more schnapps that evening than I should have.

Eventually I took my sleeping bag, the mattress, and (at Duvalsin's insistence) the bottle of schnapps, and made my way back to my sleeping space. I decided I would camp out between the great auk and Duvalsin's desk. The sleeping bag, fortunately, was a light summer one. I spread it out on the foam mattress and lay down beside the great auk, which stood with its head raised, its vertebrae curving in a snake-like S. The wings were tiny, no bigger than a jay's, and held away from its body. Its breastbone, keeled like a racing sailboat, was detached from the rest of it and floated at the base of the neck, suspended by three delicate jewelry chains. With all the spaces between the bones, it looked almost ethereal. The only thing heavy about it was the beak, which had the solid, clunky look of an antique nutcracker.

That must be worth a bit, I thought. Unless . . . I reached over and touched the beak: yes, plastic.

Gradually the street outside quietened. The animals around me resolved into contoured shadows, though the heavy ridged horns of the ibex still glinted in the residual light from the street. Duvalsin's door was closed, but I could hear the sound of his refrigerator, going off and on. After a while, faintly from the distance, I heard his snoring.

I couldn't have been asleep for more than a few minutes when the desk telephone rang, jerking me awake. No light showed from under the door into Duvalsin's living space. I lay unmoving as the phone rang six times; a thirty-second silence followed, and then it began ringing again. I struggled to my feet and groped among the desk detritus for the phone.

"Duvalsin's Wunderkammer," I said.

There was a long pause. "M'sieur McCaskill," said a voice. "It is you?"

I immediately had a flashback to the demonic Friend, but no, the accent wasn't right. Yet I'd heard the voice not long ago—or *was* it long ago? A voice both near and far in my mind.

"I am lucky," continued the voice. "To find you."

Yes, near and far. Zarandok had stepped back out of the shadows.

Duvalsin's door opened, and the light came on, illuminating all the animals in their petrified aliveness. I had the odd sense they'd been caught listening. Duvalsin himself appeared, shirtless, his belly sagging over a pair of capacious shorts.

"Zarandok," I said in wonder. "We thought you were dead."

"I escape. That is my life."

In response to Duvalsin's enquiring gaze, I cupped the mouthpiece and said, "It's for me."

He looked puzzled, but then shrugged and, taking the schnapps from the desk, shuffled back into the kitchen. I heard the clink of glasses again.

"How on earth did you find me?" I said to Zarandok.

"I call your bookstore. The man say, try this number. The Wunderkammer."

Why, oh why, was secrecy so difficult for Mique? But then I remembered—he knew that I'd been looking desperately for Zarandok. That Zarandok was the very reason for my pilgrimage.

"We do not have much time to talk," said Zarandok. "What happened to the book, m'sieur?"

When he'd stepped back out of the shadows, Zarandok must have found Kovag gone, along with the book, and the Talmeeds incommunicado. No wonder he'd gone to the effort of tracking me down.

"Jaëlle took it," I said.

He said something sharp in Hungarian, and I could hear his raspy breathing.

"Who is she, Zarandok?" I said.

"I ask this many times. A strange woman." Before I could press him on this, he continued: "We must work together now, Tavish. The story is repeating."

"What story?"

"Lavichet and the rabbi. Jew and gentile. They help each other—like you and me."

"If I'm going to help you, you have to be completely honest with me. Do you know a man named Jakob Zunz?"

"Zunz? Zunz? No."

"He knows *you*. He says you stole books from him."

"A lie. Who is this Zunz?"

"He runs the Tikkun Olam Project. A library of Jewish manuscripts."

"I never hear of this Tikkun Olam."

"Well, anyway, you haven't told me the full story of the book, and you're going to do it now."

I could hear his breathing again. The door to Duvalsin's kitchen was ajar, and from inside came a listening silence.

"János gave me the book," said Zarandok. "To keep safe."

"Safe from whom?"

"Russians. Murdering men."

"The same men that are after it now?"

"Maybe. They wanted János. His knowledge."

"Knowledge of what?"

"To make a universe." Zarandok's wheezy breathing was audible now. "He had an experiment. It was ready."

"An experiment to make a universe? Sorry, I just can't believe that."

"Fine. No more talk. We must meet."

"I mean, an entire *universe?*"

"Do we meet?"

"Yes, yes. And listen, what's going on with this guy Kovag?"

"We meet where Lavichet and the rabbi met. You know

it."

"I do?"

"Tomorrow morning. At the *flohmarkt*."

"The flea market? *Which* flea market?"

A click answered me. I replaced the receiver. Kodaly knew how to make a *universe*? Jaëlle had said the same thing. Looking up, I saw Duvalsin in his doorway, blue Crocs on his large feet and the schnapps in his hand. He had put on a T-shirt, but it didn't quite cover his ungovernable belly, with its patterns of hair swirling around his navel as if tracing out the shape of a magnetic field.

"Sorry to wake you," I said.

He nodded blearily. "Who was that?"

"Just another pilgrim. A very annoying one."

I took a seat at his kitchen table, and he passed over my glass of schnapps. The town where Lavichet and the rabbi had met . . . Einsiedeln. I remembered. The home of the alchemist Paracelsus. I was about to explain to Duvalsin that there'd been a change of plans, that Zurich would have to wait; but his appearance silenced me.

Unshaven, bilious, hair in his eyes, he sat as if he could barely maintain the weight of his head. His gaze was ghosted over, like that of a particularly dusty specimen from his dead menagerie. I thought of an ice-girt Arctic explorer, looking out from his trapped ship at a white forever. He breathed as if he were lightly snoring, with a tiny high-pitched wheeze.

"Tavish," he said.

"Yes?"

He drained his glass of schnapps and sat with eyes closed, as if willing the revivifying alcohol through his veins. "I will take you to Zurich," he said, opening his eyes. "I will take you anywhere you want. But please . . . come with me to the mountains."

*   *   *

In the morning we set out in his old hatchback, me with tourist brochures and a stuffed alpine marmot on my lap. Einsiedeln, followed by the mountains—that had been our deal. At first Duvalsin had been tepid about it; he'd had his heart set on Entlebuch.

"A lot of tourists in Einsiedeln," he had said.

"We'll go for a hike after the flea market."

He waved a hand listlessly. "The place isn't wild, Tavish. Not like Entlebuch."

"Well, what about their flea market?"

"What about it?"

"It's pretty wild, I hear."

He sighed. "I thought you wanted to go to Zurich."

"Something came up. Look, it says here there's a walk around Lake Sihl we can do."

A day in Entlebuch was impossible now, with Zarandok waiting for me in Einsiedeln; still, I felt very shabby. Fortunately Duvalsin cheered up when it came to choosing items for the flea market. Into the hatchback went a stuffed adult lynx, various fake-pelt rugs, a plastic scale model of the HMS Beagle, catalogs of dried plants, several fiberglass dinosaurs of various sizes, a stuffed cobra in the act of striking, lizards and bats in wooden frames, cheap prints of Rousseau (the jungle paintings), dozens of books on everything from navigation to fungi identification—and two small, folded card tables.

With the marmot on my lap (it would fit nowhere else) we drove to Einsiedeln in an hour.

It somehow seemed fitting that this ancient cloistral town, home of a famous monastery with its stately library, should have a lively, very human market of chintz and knickknackery. The *flohmarkt* took place at Paracelsuspark, the park of Paracelsus, and we arrived just in time to set up for the nine-thirty start. I observed that all the vendors had stalls or large tables except us. Duvalsin just backed his car into an unoccupied space and opened the hatchback.

"Are you allowed to do that?" I said.

He glowered at me while unfolding one of his skeletal card tables. "Don't be so Swiss."

While he laid out his wares, I took a quick tour of Paracelsuspark, stopping at every stall and table; after that, I skirted the perimeter. No sign of Zarandok. I wondered what on earth he was doing here in this pilgrimage town. The story is repeating itself, he'd said.

Back at Duvalsin's car, I asked to borrow his cell phone.

"I don't have one," he said.

"Let me guess. You don't believe in them."

"Neither should you, Tavish."

"You don't need to convince me. But I need a phone."

He jerked a finger behind him. "There's one in there."

It was a small official building of some kind, gray stone and mullioned windows and well-kept flower beds. Sure enough, I spied a wall phone just inside the entrance—and not a pay phone, just a phone for anybody to use. The Swiss are like that. They assume nobody would monopolize such an amenity or use it to order pizza. I started to dial Julie's number but then put the receiver down quickly. I stood there at a loss, and then, feeling in my shirt pocket, I got out Zunz's number that Mique had dictated to me the day before. Again I wondered if I should risk contacting him. Had he known what Dassvanger was up to? I'd just had to feel out the situation, trust my ganglia.

Miraculously, I got the man rather than the voice-mail message.

"I am so glad to hear from you, Tavish. Where are you?"

"At . . . a flea market. I can't talk long, Jakob. Listen, it's your friend Dassvanger who's behind everything."

There was a long pause. "He is not my friend."

"I understood he was."

"I did, too. But he came to my Bern hotel two days ago, very savage. He wanted to know where you were—you and the young woman, Jaëlle."

"What did you tell him?"

"Nothing. Because I knew nothing. You say he is the leader of these criminals?"

"*One* of the leaders. Look, I'm sorry for getting you involved in all this."

"No, no, I said I wanted to help. But Dassvanger . . . he's an *articulate* anti-Semite. I thought I could tell Jew-haters immediately, but . . ."

Zunz seemed to have lost some of the bravado he'd displayed at the Bern café, when he seemed quite ready to take on all my enemies for me.

"Was Dassvanger physically aggressive with you?" I said.

"No, but he said he could easily find my family in Israel, and . . ." He paused. "Tell me, what *did* happen to Jaëlle? Is she safe?"

"I don't know what happened to her. She's disappeared with the book."

"So what are you going to do now?"

I had learned my lesson about revealing my plans. "I'm going to find out all I can about a sixteenth-century rabbi." *And Jaëlle.*

"What rabbi?"

"Rabbi Ezra Ben Emeth, the Rabbi of the Twelve Winds. Author of this crazy book we're chasing. And that reminds me: Do you know anybody in Zurich's orthodox community?"

Just then, I caught a whiff of tobacco and turned. Zarandok was standing a meter from me. With a spasmodic movement, he reached out to hang up the receiver.

"Follow me," he whispered.

"Nice to see you, too, Zarandok."

"Do not speak. Follow. Not close."

I followed as soon as the big oak door closed on him, keeping twenty meters behind. He wore an old flap cap (much too large) and cheap aviator sunglasses—presumably his idea of a disguise—along with what looked like the same shabby suit jacket he had worn at our first encounter. Eventually he veered off to a small park set back from the road and took a seat at one of the benches, facing the street. In his oversized peaked hat, he looked like a bent roofing nail. He retrieved a crumpled cigarette from his breast pocket and watched me approach with a defiant gaze.

"I am not a thief," he said as I sat down.

"Okay, okay. That's not important now."

"It *is* important. I have many enemies. I don't need more." He jabbed the unlit cigarette at me. "Who is this Zunz?"

"A book collector. Listen, where have you been for the last week?"

"And his library, this Tikkun Olam . . . I am *sceptique*." He put the cigarette in his mouth, his jaw set, and ripped a match from a matchbook. "Where have I been? Making researches. Also, running from death."

"From Dassvanger, you mean."

He struck the match and hunched into the cigarette. "From Dassvanger, from Nazis, from everybody."

He waved out the match and exhaled moodily in my direction. From his world-weary tone of voice, fleeing was his life.

"What about Kodaly and this universe of his?" I said.

He took off his sunglasses, stuffing them in his sports jacket pocket. He looked even gaunter than before, wizened almost to translucency. Touch this man, I thought, and he will bruise.

"János designed an experiment," he said.

"To make a universe."

"Yes."

"And the Russians were after him for the design of this experiment?"

"After him, and the book. It was part of the design."

"This is just too crazy to believe."

"Then do not believe it."

I slid away from him on the bench; the smoke was getting to me. "I thought we were going to be open with each other."

"I *am* open. You are not." He drew on his cigarette and moved closer, till we were squeezed together at the end of the bench. "Tell me about your friend Jaëlle," he said.

"I know nothing about her."

"But she has a power. Some catch on you." He studied me quizzically through the cigarette smoke. "We must find her. Before Dassvanger."

"So you can get the book from her, is that it?"

"I do not want the book."

"Try another one. You've been obsessed with it since I met you."

"This is changed."

"What's changed, exactly?"

He drew on his cigarette, eyes closed, as if the smoke nourished his soul, looking as frail as one of the Desert Fathers. For some reason I thought of Duvalsin in his T-shirt and boxer shorts, trying to hold up his head.

"Do you know this town, Tavish?" he said, looking around. "Where Paracelsus is born. Paracelsus the alchemist."

I noticed he rarely looked at me; his eyes were on the road and the passersby.

"Lavichet and the rabbi met at the house of Paracelsus's father," he continued. "They talked about the book. And many years later, Paracelsus remembered."

"What did he remember?"

"Paracelsus said the book is not of this world. So the world cannot understand it. Even wise men, scientists—no. But Paracelsus said there is somebody. Who *can* understand it."

"Who?"

"The children of the rabbi. And *their* children. And such."

"The rabbi's descendants, you mean."

"Descendants, yes. Of the rabbi's house. His house holds the knowledge, the visions."

It made me think of what old Moishe had said—that in his rabbinical work, he always felt that he was remembering the discoveries of his ancestors. Coming from Zarandok, however, it didn't quite carry the same weight.

"Okay," I said impatiently, "but how does that help us?"

He took a long drag of his cigarette and exhaled through his teeth. "Because maybe a descendant of the rabbi lives today."

"Where? Who is he?"

"She."

He flicked the ash off his cigarette and studied it in his hand. I stared at him.

"You're talking about *Jaëlle?*" I said. "How do you know this?"

"I don't know, for sure." He drew on his cigarette reflectively and tilted his chin to exhale. "The monk Alphonse . . . he knew of records. So I make researches." He stared at the street through the smoke of his cigarette. "Strange, eh? The Swiss exiled us Jews. Run away or we kill you. For centuries. But still, we were here. In archives. In guild records. In graveyards. I found us."

"But . . . this is crazy. If Jaëlle is a descendant of the rabbi, surely the Talmeeds would know."

Running his tongue around the inside of his teeth, he picked out a fleck of tobacco. "The Talmeeds think they know all things," he said sourly. "But . . . " He flicked the tobacco shred off his fingers.

It almost made sense, in a rococo way. But why couldn't Jaëlle have just *told* me? Why did she have to dupe me?

"Where is she, m'sieur?" he said.

I was suddenly wary. Was this something he just made

up, to find out where Jaëlle was?

"I have no idea," I said.

"You speak of Zurich. On the telephone now. She is there?"

"As I said, I don't know."

He flung away his cigarette and got to his feet, his gaze fierce. "You do not trust me, Tavish. But I always trust you. Always."

"Come on, sit down. There is still a lot we need to talk about."

"You are part of her story, somehow. You are not telling me."

"Sit down so we can find out how much we're not telling each other. I want to know about Kovag."

But he just ground his cigarette into the lawn with his tiny shoe and glared at me. "Perhaps I will see you in Zurich." He had walked no more than five paces when he turned. "I am *not* a thief," he spat, and quickly lost himself among the tourists.

*   *   *

Duvalsin had been right: the hiking country around Einsiedeln was not exactly wild Switzerland. But he had a remedy at hand. His stuffed lynx had not been sold—I suspect he changed his mind about getting rid of it—and before setting out on the hiking path from the monastery, he tucked the animal under his arm. We climbed past the stables into the countryside, and beside the statue of St. Benedict, he set the lynx down and got out his camera. The lynx became, in fact, the focus of our hike. At certain points he would place it beside a tree and then photograph it from all angles. We took turns carrying the thing. Once, despite my lack of enthusiasm, he planted it in the middle of a forested footpath and insisted we hide behind a tree. He was gleefully ready with his camera, but no hikers showed up to be startled by this manifestation of wild Switzerland. Eventually, disappointed, he tucked the lynx under his arm and again we proceeded, with Duvalsin constantly alert for good staging areas.

At the bluff overlooking Lake Sihl, we stood in silence, taking in the view.

"Tavish, have you ever loved anybody?" he said.

I kept my eyes on the scene in front of me. "Yes. My wife and daughter."

"Do you still love them?"

"More than ever, but . . . Yes, I still love them."

Duvalsin didn't inquire further; he just kept looking out over the panorama, one hand on the stuffed animal beside him. The mountains stood ambered in the waning light, their cold faces softened by the alpenglow. The unfinished parts of the world—so Henry David Thoreau called mountains. Maybe that's why we're drawn to them: we are unfinished ourselves. We go upward into the luminous air to remake or extend our lives. Again I felt a pang of guilt for not having gone to Entlebuch with Duvalsin.

"You know," he remarked, lightly stroking the tufted ears of the stuffed cat, "lynx are coming back in Switzerland."

"Is that right?"

"There's maybe a hundred and fifty of them now. But it's hard to get numbers. They stay away from people."

During the walk back down to the monastery, he was

silent, carrying the lynx with both arms. By the time we got back to his car, it was close to sunset. He put the stuffed animal in the back and turned to me.

"Are you sure you want to start walking now?" he said.

"Yes. I'll be fine." I had a knapsack he'd given me—actually just a small Coors Lite cooler bag with shoulder straps—containing cold pizza in a Tupperware container. "Thanks for your help, Duvalsin. Next time I see you, we'll go to Entlebuch. I promise."

"And I'll cover expenses. Lots of schnapps."

"Great."

"And we'll camp, right? At least one night?"

"At least one night."

"And if I'm paying for the trip . . ."

"You can forget about your debts."

"If you insist."

I began walking away, but he called out after me. "Tavish, why are you *really* doing this pilgrimage?"

I looked beyond him: clouds blanketed the sky except at the western horizon, where the sun was setting, and through this opening washed a tender rose light. The trees around us seemed illuminated from within. The red brick of nearby buildings glowed like cherry blossoms, like skin, like the sun shining through the closed fingers of your hand.

"I told you about my wife and daughter," I said.

"Yes?"

"Well, my wife is now my ex-wife, and my daughter. . . ." I hefted my knapsack and turned to look at the horizon. "Anyway, on this pilgrimage, my ex-wife is my wife again, and my daughter is my daughter. We're on this pilgrimage together. That's all."

"I see."

"I know it sounds crazy but there it is."

Duvalsin hitched up his trousers. "Good luck, Tavish."

"Thanks. Send me a postcard from the mountains some-
time. Let me know how the lynx are doing."

SEVENTEEN

Big and boutiquey, metropolis of swans and stained glass, home to the world's largest this and most silvery that— Zurich could get on my nerves. But it gave onto infinities, according to the Interstellar Academy.

We'd chosen the camp for Saoirse because it offered sessions in English and because it was so wackily creative. It had to be; it was competing with kids' summer programs at CERN and at Niederlenz's Space Museum. During her four years there, Saoirse had made lego robots, camped out under the stars, and hunted for micrometeorites on the city rooftops. On parents' day, Julie and I had helped her bake cosmic cookies (the dough mimicked the expanding universe, with raisins standing in for galaxies). Later we'd gotten a tour of Urania Observatory and seen the craters of the moon and the clouds of Jupiter. Yes, Zurich had a view, I'll give it that.

I was sure I could find the Interstellar Academy from memory.

I had slept in a house under construction not far from Lake Zurich and set out before dawn. The lake was unearthly, a membrane of twilight in the lap of the hills. I got a coffee at a gas station and continued through the cookie-cutter suburban towns—Thalwil, Horgen, Kilchberg. The mist blew off the hilltops, and the lake turned a deep blue.

Soon I was swept up in the urban wave of Zurich. I kept to the boardwalk along the lake until I started to recognize landmarks: Museum Rietberg, the FIFA World Cup Museum, the Arboretum. The Interstellar Academy had used facilities all over the city, but the main office had been near the Wiedikon transit station, just a few kilometers away. My feet remembered: northwest on Alfred Escher-Strasse, over the River Sihl, left on Birmensdorferstrasse. . . . Then where? The jangled carousel of the city carried me around several times. Eventually I saw the familiar Pile of Books Bookstore, which led me to the Amazing Toys Comic Shop, which in turn led to the three small storefronts that ran under a row of apartment balconies, the middle one being the Interstellar Academy.

Except that it wasn't.

I was looking at a bagel shop with a blue and white striped awning and a sandwich board saying *Koscher.* I gazed up and down the block—I was sure this was the right street—and then approached the storefront window. A mom and pop place. A Coca-Cola vending machine, a few wooden tables, collapsible chairs. I went inside. Pop was a baggy man—baggy trousers, baggy chef's hat, bags under his eyes—and Mom was stout and florid, with a toothy smile. They were serving a Hasidic Jew in a frock coat and wide-brimmed hat. I said *shalom* to them all. Pop nodded and Mom showed me her teeth. I figured now might be a good time to part with some of my money.

I ordered a toasted sesame seed bagel with cream cheese and asked Pop if he spoke English. He grunted as he popped the bagel halves into the toaster.

"Have you been here long?" I said.

"Maybe five year," he said.

I noticed a desk phone at the other end of the counter and a tip box beside the cash register. No, not a tip box: it bore Hebrew lettering. A *tzedakah* box. I'd seen one at the home of my thesis advisor, old Moishe—the traditional Jewish charity box.

"There used to be a science summer camp right here," I continued. "The Interstellar Academy."

"*Interstellar Akademie?*" He kept his eyes on the toaster. "Oh yes. Bankrupt."

"Bankrupt! That can't be."

"They go and we come."

I couldn't believe it. The camp had drifted off my radar after Saoirse's death; at some point I must have stopped getting their newsletter, but I had no idea when.

"My daughter went to their summer camp and I'm trying to find out what happened to them," I said. "You wouldn't know how I might contact the owner?"

"No, sorry."

"Or anybody else who might . . . I'd really like to find out."

"Sorry." The bagel halves popped up, and he plucked them out with plastic-gloved fingers and began slathering on cream cheese. "You wish something more?"

"No, just the bagel."

I really didn't have money to spare for the *tzedakah* box. Would they let me use the phone anyway? Zunz must have been wondering what happened to me, since (thanks to Zarandok) we'd been so abruptly cut off in Einsiedeln. As Pop handed me my bagel in a paper bag, another customer came in—a tattooed party in skinny jeans, a U2 T-shirt and mirror sunglasses. This was the Wiedikon neighborhood: hipsters and orthodox Jews got their bagels at the same place.

"Excuse me—could I use your phone for just a minute?" I said to Pop.

He didn't look up. "Sorry, it's not for customers."

I knew I should have put something in the *tzedakah*. I glanced at Mom, who seemed the more sympathetic of the two, but she was busy squirting whipped cream onto cupcakes. The paper bag was warm in my hand, and I was ravenous. Let it go. As I turned away, I caught sight of the hipster's bicep tattoo—a hand with thumb and pinky outspread. The Hamsa hand, a traditional Jewish symbol. Even hipsters remembered their roots here.

"That's a great tattoo," I said. "Could I ask where you got it?"

*   *   *

"Hello, boss," said Mr. Death.

The tattoo parlor turned out to be a mom and pop place as well, though much more pagan. The man had a shaved head and a wavy black-and-mauve tattoo on his bare pate; the woman had a silver brush cut and a stud through her lower lip. Otherwise they were identical—sallow, sinuous, black-clad. Mr. and Mrs. Death, I thought of them. But the decor was warm-dark, all chocolates and mochas, with lots of colorful framed photos of body art. A foot-long model of an orange Camaro, hood open, sat beside the cash register.

"Good morning, *guten morgen*," I said. "I want to ask you about this." Getting out my druid's pen and my much crumpled piece of paper, I quickly sketched Jaëlle's tattoo, the *chai* symbol. "Do you recognize it?"

"Oh, yes," the guy said. "*Chai*. We've done some."

"You have?"

The guy shrugged. "This is a Jewish neighborhood."

Now I saw that the tattoo on his pate was the Swiss flag. They weren't kids—both in their mid-thirties, I guessed. Mrs. Death was good-looking in a Vampirella kind of way, though her eyes were a sad, alkaline blue.

I got out the picture of Saoirse and Jaëlle at the Interstellar Academy. "I know this is a long shot—*crazy* long—but I don't suppose you remember doing a *chai* tattoo for this girl here?"

Instead of coming close to the man, the woman strained to peer at the photo in his hands.

"Sorry, boss," said the guy. "I make many tattoos. I don't remember the people."

"She would be taller now," I continued. "With a braid and glasses."

The guy shrugged again. Mrs. Death briefly raised her weary eyes to me and went back to craning her neck to see the photo.

"She went to summer camp with my daughter," I said hopelessly. "The Interstellar Academy. It used to be just a few blocks away."

"Oh, yes?" said the guy, clearly losing interest.

Mrs. Death took the edge of the photo in her fingers, but the guy didn't relinquish it. Her pointed fingernails—the only bit of color on her—were pure shrieks of pigment, a scarlet so hot and staring that you could find it nowhere in nature. Just then, the bell on the door rang and another customer stepped into the store. With a frown, the guy let go of the photo and turned to the customer.

"Well, I won't take up more of your time," I said.

Mrs. Death's attention was on the photo in her hands. Her black T-shirt had a generously open neck; I saw a dolphin tattoo, tiny and blue as a compass needle, riding the upper wave of her breast.

"Micrometeorites," she said, looking up.

"Sorry?"

"They looked for micrometeorites on our roof."

Mr. Death said something curt to the woman, who retorted: "They *did*. They said flat was good. A flat roof collected them."

She handed the photo back to me and tossed her head. "Come. I show you."

Ignoring Mr. Death's disapproving look, she led me past several tattooing beds and walls of designs—skulls, superheroes, cuckoo clocks, aliens, angels, peace signs, Escher motifs. At the back, we went up a short flight of stairs and through a low door. Wind and space met us, and Mrs. Death closed her eyes briefly.

"Here," she said, turning to me.

We stood in the center of a featureless industrial roof—black tar, grit, pigeon droppings. A brick parapet, maybe three feet tall, ran around the edge.

"The kids came *here?*" I said.

"Only four at a time. They weren't allowed to go near the edge; they had to stay in the center."

In the open air, she seemed even paler, more death-like, and the emptiness in her gaze became more acute. Kneeling down, she wiped a finger in the grit and held it up.

"There's stardust here," she said.

"Yes, amazing. How big are these micrometeorites?"

"Very small. You need a magnet to find them."

"You don't remember any of the kids' names?"

She shook her head and, getting to her feet, brushed off her fingers.

"How about the staff?"

"I remember the man with the magnet. He made sure the kids didn't go near the edge."

"Was he one of the camp counselors?"

"I don't know what he was. He had the magnet and he kept the kids from the edge." She gazed out over the rooftops, adding, "He was the one who died."

"Died?"

"It was in the newspapers. What was his name?" She took her phone out of her back hip pocket. "He was famous, a little. A Russian chess player. No, not Russian . . ."

Something touched the inside of my head, light as a spider web.

"Not János Kodaly?" I said.

She looked up from her phone. "That's it. Kodaly."

I stared at her. "János Kodaly was an *instructor* at the camp?"

"I don't know if he was an instructor. He was the meteorite man. He had the magnet."

Kodaly, the reclusive genius, helping out at a kids' summer camp? But maybe that's what recluses needed—and he *did* enjoy teaching physics to kids, I remembered. The meteorite man. . . . Had Saoirse ever spoken about a meteorite man at her camp? I'd have to ask Julie, but I had a vague sense I'd heard the phrase before.

"I wish I might go to a camp like that," she said, looking out over the rooftops of Zurich. "When I was young. Maybe I wouldn't be working here now."

For a moment we both stood silent, sharing the view. I could faintly see the clock tower of St. Peter's Church near the river, and to the south, the green copper spire of the Fraumünster. Rain was in the air again. I wondered if I'd actually have a roof over my head tonight—a real roof, not one under construction.

"You don't know where else I could go for information about the camp?" I said.

She thought for a moment. "Maybe the gemstone dealer."

"The gemstone dealer?"

"Kodaly took the rooftop dust to a man who sold gems, minerals, and meteorites. And the man would put their dust under a microscope. If he found meteorites, he gave them back to the camp."

"And you don't remember the name of this gemstone dealer?"

"I shall find him."

While she checked her phone, I went to the roof parapet again. I had been looking at the horizon rather than our immediate neighborhood, but now I glanced down at the street. Parked across from the tattoo parlor was a Vauxhall sedan. An *old* Vauxhall sedan.

"Benjamin," said the woman, looking up from her phone.

"Benjamin?"

"I'm sure that was the gemstone dealer. It says here, '*Edelsteine, Mineralien, Meteoriten.*'" She looked up. "Gems, minerals, meteorites."

"Where is he?"

"No far. In Löwenstrasse."

"Sorry, where?"

The neo-Nazis in Bern had driven a Vauxhall sedan. I immediately stepped away from the parapet. My paranoia was kicking in again. How many old Vauxhall sedans could be found in Switzerland? I hazarded a step back to the parapet. I thought it was the same color, a weak blue, but I hadn't really noticed details on that night of the graffiti outing. I watched it intently for half a minute and then retreated again.

"What is the matter?" she said.

"It's just . . . I think it's going to rain. I should get going."

"But do you want a tattoo? I can give you a small one for free. As a memory."

"Thanks, maybe another time. Listen, is there a back door out of your place?"

*   *   *

My shirt and pants clung to me, and I could feel the rain soaking through my boots. I stood under a storefront awning, scrunched against the wall, but still the wind brought in the rain. For God's sake, the neo-Nazis again? *Was* it the neo-Nazis? My ganglia were hypersensitive now; I was constantly feeling a cold wind from nowhere, a snake's tongue against my skin, vines constricting my heart . . . but *was* it them? Why would they have driven all the way to Zurich after me?

The intercom clicked on and a staticky voice said, "*Bitte.*"

I leaned close. "*Guten tag.* Do you speak English?"

"*Nein.*"

"French?"

"*Non.*"

I could see nothing through the dark curtains that covered the iron-latticed storefront window. The sign was austere as everything else: "Calev Benjamin's Gems and Minerals: cutting, polishing, sales." In German, English, and Yiddish. No pictures of engagement rings or beautiful women in diamond earrings.

"János . . . Kodaly," I said, enunciating each word above the rain. "I am interested in . . . János Kodaly."

In the silence I could hear the rain flowing in the gutters. When the door buzzed open, I stepped inside a warm, well-lit space. Behind the counter sat a bespectacled man with a thin pewtered face and chevron wrinkles above his eyes. The frost of time lay on him; he was all crystallized surfaces. He wore an old-fashioned black frock coat, and his broad-brimmed fedora sat beside him on the table. I hoped my surprise didn't show: the gemstone dealer was a Hasidic Jew.

"*Shalom,*" I said.

He nodded warily. A jeweler's eyeglass lay on the countertop; I suspected he had been in the middle of studying gems. I could see no gem cutter's equipment, though there was a small door ajar at the back; I guessed the store had a workshop room.

"So," he said. "János Kodaly."

For a gem shop, the display was subdued: a few torso mannequins wearing necklaces; rings and earrings on black velvet; some jade carvings—I think it was jade—in heavy glass cabinets. On the wall hung a woven tapestry that said in Hebrew, "Make of your heart harbor and refuge." The rain drummed on the roof above us. I was painfully conscious of how wet I was.

I hazarded a halting sentence about myself in German, but clearly he didn't have a lot of time to spare, for he stood up impatiently and called through the open door at the back: "Tova!"

A woman appeared—maybe late twenties, dressed in a knee-length dark skirt and a white blouse with a high neck and long sleeves. I was pretty sure her hair was a wig, and not very flattering. The man said something in Yiddish—I caught Kodaly's name—and she cast a nervous glance my way. She disappeared again and returned a moment later with a towel.

"I am his daughter," she said, in thickly accented English, handing me the towel.

"Thank you. My name is Tavish. Sorry for dripping on your floor."

"You ask about János Kodaly."

I looked out at her from above the towel. "I believe he used to come here to talk to your father about meteorites— very small ones."

She translated this for her father, who returned a short reply.

"János Kodaly is dead," she said.

"I know, but I want to find out all I can about him . . . and about this summer camp of his."

"Summer camp?"

"A science camp for children. The Interstellar Academy."

At the name, the woman glanced again at her father, who kept his eyes on me. Handing the towel back to Tova, I withdrew the photo that Julie had given me, slightly damp, from the pocket of my Coors Lite daypack.

"I am trying to find people from the camp who knew Kodaly," I continued, and placed the photo on the desk in front of the man. "Do you recognize anybody here?"

The woman came around beside her father to look, but the man barely gave it a glance and said something terse to his daughter. When she continued to study the photo, he spoke even more tersely. She straightened.

"My father says he didn't know anybody from the camp." Her eyes slid back to the photo. "I'm sorry we can't help you."

I was looking at the Hebrew scroll on the wall. *Make of your heart harbor and refuge. . . .* I was in the world of the Hasid, the spiritual descendants of the Kabbalists . . . and the spiritual ancestors of the Talmeeds, if I were to believe the woman at the End of the World Café. I looked right into the eyes of the gem dealer and said in Aramaic, "I need help, friend."

The man blinked. The woman, also startled, said something in Yiddish to her father, but the man just regarded me steadily.

"You know Aramaic," he said in that language.

"A bit."

"Where did you learn it?"

"The University of Geneva."

Again the woman spoke to her father but he remained silent, gazing at me. The dynamic had changed now.

"You know the old language," said Tova.

"I learned it many years ago because I got interested in the Kabbalists. Like Rabbi Ezra Ben Emeth, the Rabbi of the Twelve Winds. Do you know him?"

The man picked up the photo, turned it over, and spoke several phrases in Yiddish.

"My father never met any person from this camp," Tova translated. "But yes, he knew János Kodaly."

"They were friends?"

"They . . . liked to discuss things," she said, touching her hair awkwardly. I wondered if she disapproved of her father talking about meteorites with an outsider.

"You have not told me everything," said the man in Aramaic. I suspected he was speaking more slowly than was customary for him, so I could catch everything.

I smiled at him. "What do you wish to know, sir?"

He took off his spectacles and sat back in his chair. "You have read Rabbi Ezra Ben Emeth, of blessed memory? His writings are rare."

"Well, I found one of them, and . . ." I hesitated. He must have understood that I didn't have the Aramaic vocabulary to express my ideas, because he nodded curtly at his daughter. "*Englisch.*"

I turned to the woman Tova. "I want to explain why I am interested in Rabbi Emeth. The rabbi's writings include numbers—equations. They are not the usual Kabbalistic numerology; they are equations from modern physics."

She held up her hand and translated for her father, who gave a slight smile.

"Some of these equations even seem to describe *undiscovered* physics," I continued slowly. "It is as if the rabbi saw many hundreds of years into the future. I was very curious about that." As she turned toward her father, I added, "And I bet János Kodaly was curious, too."

After she'd conveyed this to her father, they exchanged Yiddish phrases; clearly the woman was remonstrating with him.

"He wants you to have dinner with us," she said, evidently unhappy with the turn of events.

I was completely caught off guard. Orthodox families rarely invited an outsider into their houses.

"Thank you, but . . . I'm afraid I have no dry clothes."

"We can get you something." She looked me up and down. "You are about the same size as my husband."

I was hungry, cold, and wet, and the Vauxhall sedan kept resurfacing in my mind. Was I becoming like Kodaly himself, seeing threats everywhere?

"My father insists," said Tova.

I hadn't seen the sedan on my way here, though I had kept a careful eye out for it. Maybe it *was* all in my mind.

"We have children," said Tova, and I didn't know whether this was meant to persuade or dissuade me.

"Even better. Thank you, I'd be honored to have dinner with you."

She forced a smile, and once again I saw her eyes dart to the photo on her father's desk.

*   *   *

There were two girls and two boys, all very polite. The boys wore the traditional side curls, the payess, and the girls wore white button-up sweaters over fifties-style dresses. We sat at a large oak table and ate latkes, kosher beef, and steamed vegetables. I would have killed for a large scotch, but I had to make do with mineral water. Benjamin's wife Esther, a tiny hummingbird of a woman, presided in her darting, hovering way. I wore a clean white shirt and black trousers courtesy of Tova's husband, who was away on business.

"You look like a fine Hasidic man!" said Esther, beaming.

She added she could get more clothes if necessary; apparently one of her many volunteer pursuits was running a charity clothing store.

Gefilte herring, spiced pickles, horseradish . . . I was back in the house of my thesis advisor, old Moishe. The decor complemented the cuisine: on the doorway to the kitchen I saw the oblong case of the *mezuzah*, the parchment that bore a Hebrew blessing for the home, and on a side table sat the ram's horn that is blown like a bugle on Rosh Hashanah. And there was at least one household item that Moishe hadn't had: in passing the kitchen, I glimpsed twin kitchen faucets. Two sinks, I guessed—one for meat and one for dairy products. This wasn't just a Jewish home; it was a Hasidic home. On the wall of the dining room hung a framed photo of a distinguished-looking man whose beard made two long swaths, as if it had been snipped up the middle. Tova explained that this man was a former *rebbe*, the spiritual leader of the Hasidic community, who had only recently passed away.

When dinner had finished and the children gone with Esther, Benjamin said something to his daughter. Again I heard the name Kodaly.

"Meteorites," translated Tova.

"Yes?"

"They are the hobby of my father."

"And one of János Kodaly's hobbies, too, I believe."

She nodded. "Sometimes they talked about meteorites,

and sometimes . . . bigger things."

"What bigger things?"

Calev Benjamin began speaking Yiddish directly to me, calmly explaining as if I could understand every word.

"My father says that Kodaly left God out of the explanation," Tova translated. "That was his problem. Without God there is no explanation." She glanced over at the framed photo of the man with the beard. "Our *rebbe* of blessed memory tried to tell Kodaly this often."

"Your *rebbe*? He knew János Kodaly?"

"Knew him and liked him. They came from different worlds, but they had much to talk about."

I remembered that Jaëlle had said that the *rebbe* had given Kodaly papers and scrolls . . . and maybe *The Celestial Gate* as well. Perhaps the *rebbe* had known the whole history of the book and the Talmeeds—I mean the *true* history. I was beginning to think that Cléance and Aaron were missing an important part of the story.

"I'm wondering," I said, "if the *rebbe* or your father ever met anybody else from Kodaly's world—friends or fellow émigrés."

Benjamin apparently didn't need a translation for that; "friends" was basically the same in English as in Yiddish (*fraynds*).

"My father remembers a few foreigners," said Tova. "He didn't have much to do with them."

"What about a man named Zarandok?"

"Zarandok?" repeated Benjamin, and added something in Yiddish.

"He wants to know if Zarandok was the false Jew," said Tova.

"The false Jew?"

"A Jew who was no Jew. A *shvindler*."

I didn't know that Yiddish word . . . a *swindler*, maybe? A Jew who didn't follow the Torah? Zarandok seemed indeed to be a secular Jew, but somehow I didn't think of him as a *false* Jew, a swindler. I was wondering how I could discreetly enquire further when Esther returned, bearing tea things along with a plate of those triangular cookies I had tasted at Moishe's house. What were they called?

While Esther busied herself with the tea, Benjamin turned toward me and said in Aramaic: "You spoke of numbers in the rabbi's writings. The numbers of Creation."

I nodded.

"You ask how he could know them."

"English or Yiddish, please!" said Esther briskly, offering me a cookie.

Calev Benjamin sighed, and I turned to Esther. "Your husband wants to know about my interest in Rabbi Ezra Ben Emeth," I said.

"Rabbi Ben Emeth!" exclaimed Esther. "How do you know our blessed rabbi, Tavish?"

"I've read some of his writings. They are very . . . modern, in many ways."

In deference to his wife, Benjamin said several phrases in Yiddish. Tova made a few inquiries to clarify before she turned to me.

"He wants to tell you about the numbers," she said.

Her father inclined his head and spoke several phrases, using his hands to explain.

"He says . . ." Tova posed a quick question and, receiving elaboration, continued: "Numbers are like souls: they live outside time. God charged our rabbi to keep the numbers safe. Because he also lives outside time."

In the silence that followed, Esther said, "Another *purim*, Tavish?"

"Thank you, they're delicious."

Purim. That was the name of those triangular cookies.

"Do you know, Tavish," said Esther, who clearly never liked to be out of the conversation for long, "that Rabbi Emeth of blessed memory was seen in Zurich less than a century ago?"

"Seen?" I said.

"People *think* it is the rabbi," added Tova cautiously.

"Where was he seen?"

"Our oldest cemetery, the Unterer Friesenberg. In 1927 there was a funeral there for Hans Bulcher. Have you ever heard of him?"

"I'm afraid not."

"A great man, a scientist, and pious Jew. Many people came to his funeral—both Jews and gentiles. And in a photograph of the event, there was a man standing at the back, dressed strangely. We believe it was Rabbi Emeth."

When I said nothing, Tova added, "You are a skeptic."

"I would like to see this photograph."

"You can," said Esther. "It's still there at the cemetery."

"And where is the cemetery?"

"On Friesenbergstrasse, not far from my clothing store. I can show you."

"Thank you, Esther. Um . . . have you been running your store for long?"

I listened while Esther talked about her own work as part of Israelitische Cultusgemeinde Zürich, the Jewish

Cultural Center of Zurich, where apparently she was a one-woman volunteer army—visiting hospitals and nursing homes, arranging weddings for people who couldn't afford them, and running a charity clothes shop.

"I can find you a wife, Tavish," she said. "Unless of course you're already married."

"I'm divorced."

"Oh, too bad. Maybe it's time to try again. In nice clothes, of course."

Outside the dusk deepened. I felt comfortably protected, shut off from the modern world and its more malign influences. Esther got out a map to show me where I might find the cemetery she had spoken of, writing down the address for me. When she and her husband went off to hear the grandchildren practice violin, Tova began clearing the dishes.

"My father says you can stay the night, if you wish," she said.

"That's very kind, but I should go. You've done enough for me and I thank you from the bottom of my heart." I leaned closer to her. "Listen, Tova, when your father was speaking about the people who knew Kodaly, what did he mean by the false Jew? He said—"

"I don't really know what he meant. A Jew who was no Jew."

"Who didn't observe Torah?"

"Maybe. I don't think my father really trusted Kodaly's friends." She paused with dishes in her hands; from upstairs came the weak strains of a violin. "Quickly," she whispered, setting down the dishes. "Let me see your photograph."

I got up and quickly retrieved it from my Coors Lite daypack in the entranceway. When I put it into her hands, she held it close, and then nodded.

"Yes, that's Avi." She was pointing to Jaëlle.

"Avi?"

"Avriella. My best friend."

I stared. "You knew her?"

"Once." She sighed. "She grew up very close to here."

"She was Hasidic?"

"Yes, but then everything changed." She handed the photo back to me. "I'm sorry, I shouldn't be talking about this."

"Please, Tova, it's very important. What do you mean, everything changed?"

She stacked two plates in her hands, arranging the cutlery on top of them, and then paused, not looking at me. "Everything changed when . . . Avi looked through a telescope."

The violin stopped, and Tova looked up, alert. Only when it resumed did she continue speaking.

"It happened when Avi and I were perhaps nine or ten," she said. "One evening we were coming back from Shabbat, and we saw people from the science camp—children and a few teachers. They had set up a telescope in the park and were taking turns looking through it. Avi was very curious. She went near and asked one of the girls what they were doing, and the girl said they were looking at other worlds. Avi was amazed—*other worlds*. All the way home, she couldn't stop talking about it. Other worlds in the sky. She wanted badly to join the camp."

"But her parents wouldn't let her?"

"I think her mother was willing, but not her father. This was usual in that family. Always arguments."

I tapped the picture. "But she *did* attend the camp, eventually."

"Only after her mother left."

"Left her husband?"

Tova nodded. "And our community. Taking Avi with her."

"Where did they go?"

She shrugged. "We don't know. Her husband tried to find her, but she stayed hidden, and eventually he gave up. And then he became sick and died—everybody said it was because he missed his wife so *much*." She held her body stiffly, as if carrying around a breakage inside her, something shattered but kept together by force of will. "I know that Avi did go to the camp, because I saw her there several years later. But we didn't talk because . . . we just didn't."

"And you don't know what happened to them?"

"Somebody told me not long ago that Avi's mother Ruth was not well. That's all I know." She was looking at the photo again. "Please, say nothing about this. It's still painful for us."

"Yes, of course . . . but Tova, what was Avi's family name?"

"Baruch, but it may be different now."

I was on the point of asking about Jaëlle's family history—specifically, if she was in fact the descendant of the Rabbi of the Twelve Winds—but just then we heard Esther's voice on the stairs. Tova turned to me and said in a clear voice, "We will give you some food, yes?"

*   *   *

An American expat gave me shelter that night—one *Sequoia sempervirens,* a California redwood. Having slipped into the Arboretum, I lay down in the bracken around its trunk, hidden from the path and greenhouses nearby. I slept poorly: my head was filled with everything I'd heard from Tova. Jaëlle had grown up Hasidic? And then—an encounter with a telescope, of all things. I wondered if Saoirse had been among the group of kids in the park who had introduced Jaëlle to other worlds. I racked my brain for the names of Saoirse's camp friends, but I couldn't recall her ever mentioning an "Avi" or "Avriella." But I knew the pair of them had connected, somehow. Two souls from completely different worlds. The work of the stars.

The wind moved in the trees, bats jagged through the darkness, and several times I awoke, thinking about the Vauxhall sedan. For the second time in forty-eight hours, I got up before dawn. Sipping coffee at a nearby McDonalds, I felt more optimistic than I'd felt in a long time. Finally I had a name—Avriella or Avi Baruch. Daughter of Ruth Baruch. Zunz could help me find them, I was sure. My head was bursting with all the questions I wanted to ask Jaëlle, or Avi, or whatever her real name was—about the book, her ancestry, and her various lies and deceptions. But most of all, I wanted to know more about her relationship with Saoirse. I wanted Saoirse's past back—or at least, that part of it.

Getting out my crumpled piece of paper with Zunz's number, I noticed the address that Esther had written—the cemetery where the Rabbi of the Twelve Winds had been photographed.

That might be worth seeing.

I stepped out of the McDonalds and into the street. The city flowed by me in waves: Latin faces, Scandinavian faces,

African faces, faces medieval and punk, faces coffee-dark and pear-white, confections of dusk and honey, *beurre frais* and *crème caramel*. The start of the day in Zurich's Bahnhof Enge quarter. Swiss cities are not known for their heterogeneity, but this train-station neighborhood seemed to embrace the whole world. Including the police, I noticed. A gray and red Kantonspolizei Zürich car was parked in front of the station. I glanced at the address Esther had written. Friesenbergstrasse. Not far away, I knew, but I wasn't sure how to get there. Maybe down Agnes Robmann-Weg?

And then, looking up from the paper as I walked, I came to an abrupt stop. The Vauxhall sedan was parked directly in front of me, and two men were getting out. I recognized them at once: the neo-Nazi doorman, Ludi, and Pumice Head. My fellow graffiti artists.

Strangely, I never thought of making a dash for it. I was tired of running, and anyway, I figured they wouldn't try anything on a busy street, in full view of the Kantonspolizei.

"*Engländer!*" said Ludi. He wasn't wearing his machete this time; just the camouflage pants and suspenders. Instead of coming toward me, he leaned against the front of the sedan. Pumice Head, in the lead, stopped and looked back at him uncertainly.

"I just want to talk, *Engländer*," said Ludi.

"Really. Last time you wanted to kill me."

"Just talk now."

He had inexplicably lost some of his menace. The face above the wild beard was mottled, the eyes sunk in puffiness. He seemed all contusion beyond his bulk.

"Where is the Jew?" he said.

"The Jew?"

"The little Jew who murdered my half-brother."

"You mean Zarandok? He didn't murder your half-brother. You want the police detective Dassvanger."

So they'd found Kovag's body? I was curious to get the details, but I didn't really want to engage with the guy.

"Somebody help him," said Ludi.

"What?"

"Somebody help Zarandok. They kill my half-brother."

"It wasn't me, if that's what you're thinking. Look, I'm very sorry about your half-brother, that's a terrible thing, but I had nothing to do with it and neither did Zarandok."

He just folded his arms. Pumice Head, clearly nervous about the police car, joined his companion at the sedan.

"You help me," said Ludi, "I help you."

"I *am* helping you. Go back to Bern and find Dassvanger. He's the one you want."

When they didn't move, I stepped into the street. Horns blared and a scooter slowed, the driver yelling. I held up my hand and negotiated my way through the traffic; on the other side, I glanced back to see both neo-Nazis inside the sedan, the doors closing. I kept an eye on it as I edged around the front of the police car and tapped on the driver's side window. It hummed down.

"Ja?" said a young, clean-cut officer.

The sedan was already pulling out of the parking space. The police officer followed my glance and turned back to me.

"Sorry to disturb you, officer," I said. "I'm a tourist and I'm wondering how to get to Friesenbergstrasse."

*   *   *

The main building of Unterer Friesenberg cemetery turned out to be a striking polygonal structure, faintly Middle Eastern, with an exterior of red and cream tile and circular windows. I didn't think it would be open at that hour, but I saw a man in overalls pruning shrubs. We made rough conversation for a few minutes (his English was much better than my German). He managed to convey that he wasn't the main caretaker, just the early morning man. But he did have the keys to the office, and when he'd understood the nature of my errand, he opened the front door and ushered me in. Just before we entered, I scoured the surroundings for the Vauxhall sedan. I hoped I'd lost the neo-Nazis— or they'd given up on me. Very bizarre. Ludi was after his brother's killer? So Kovag *was* dead. Somehow they'd managed to find me in the middle of Zurich. And if they could do it, then Dassvanger could.

Inside the cemetery building, the morning man and I stood before a framed black and white photo, very grainy, of a gathering at the cemetery.

"The rabbi," he said, pointing to a young bearded man in vest and skullcap, who stood apart from the others.

"Why do people think it's the rabbi?" I said.

"The *tallit katan*. You see?"

He pointed to the poncho-like garment the man wore under his vest. The *tallit katan*: the lightweight version of the Jewish prayer shawl. Orthodox Jews wore it daily.

"We know the rabbi wears it so," continued the morning man. "And he is different from the others, yes? A holy face."

That was one way to put it. To me, he had the hunched,

startled look of a small owl discovered in its nest. The look of one who heard voices or consulted prophets. He certainly didn't look as though he was used to cameras.

"Who are these other people?" I said.

"Famous citizens. That's Bernalz—he gave us the first Jewish hospital here. And that's Einstein."

"Albert Einstein?"

"Yes, the space scientist."

I was quite sure it *wasn't* Einstein—the man in the photo was tall and well-groomed—but I refrained from comment.

"And that's the man who invented television," continued the man.

I was beginning to understand how the photo had acquired a reputation for depicting a legendary rabbi. This morning man seemed to see all his favorite historical figures in it.

"Come back again when Ephraim is here," said the guy. "He can tell you more."

Outside again, I stood in the suffusion of morning light, taking in the trees—the elms like elegant old stemware, the oaks calloused and iron-mettled, the pines up-spearing the sky in green-dark flames. High above, the sun had painted a jet contrail pink. Looking beyond the gates, I caught sight of a squat modern building.

"What's that?" I said.

"*Das seniorenhaus.* Sometimes they come over here to walk. And write prayers for the dead."

"And who are 'they'?"

"Old people, of course."

Das seniorenhaus . . . a seniors' home. I continued to study the building but couldn't see much through the trees.

"Does anybody ever write prayers to the rabbi in the photo?" I said.

"Sometimes. The very old people."

At that point I was steering by unexpected signs, coronas around the moon, birds out of season, light or shadow falling from nowhere, and I thought I'd take a stroll over to the seniors' home.

Thanking the morning man, I walked through overlappings and cleavings of leaf light to the gate, and then across the street to the squat building. A few elderly people sat on benches, resting in the final slack water of life, waiting to be swept out into the endless sea. A sun-hatted old woman with a trowel sat on the ground, legs outstretched in a V, tending a flower bed. She must have been about eighty, maybe older. I could never have sat like that, legs straight out, for any length of time. Maybe they all did yoga here.

A white-suited female attendant sat on a bench beside a small, wispy man in a wheelchair. He seemed to have almost no chest, and rested with his head sunk forward and his mouth—a wizened turtle's mouth—slightly open. His ash-gray pants were pulled up high on his trunk, so that a patch of scabrous skin showed between the cuffs and his drooping argyle socks. But his gaze, in contrast to the rest of him, was bright and alive.

"*Shalom,*" he called out.

The sign on the lawn said "Reuven Seniors' Home." A Jewish seniors' home. Built convivially close to a Jewish graveyard.

"*Shalom,*" I said, approaching. "Do you speak English?"

The little man chuckled. "It's my second language . . .

after American."

"Really."

"Brooklyn born and bred. Sit down, sit down. You a tourist?"

"Well . . . kind of. My name's Tavish."

"Haskell. Or Ask-Hell, as they call me here."

"I never thought I'd hear a Brooklyn accent in a Zurich neighborhood, Haskell." I took a seat on the bench between the man and the attendant. "How long have you been here, may I ask?"

"Since I got old. Ha! But here in Switzerland—let me think. Thousands of years."

The attendant, leaning forward slightly to see past me, said something in German to the little man. He paid her no attention.

"And you, Tavish?" he said. "You say you're *kind* of a tourist?"

I sensed that the attendant was not warming to me and, turning slightly, made an attempt to include her in the conversation. "I'm here on . . . personal business, but I'm also taking in some of the sights. Like your cemetery across the road."

"Great place," said Haskell. "Hey, you know who's buried there? Felix Salten."

"Who?"

"Felix Salten. The guy who wrote *Bambi.*"

"Oh . . . right. Is he in that famous photo on the wall?"

"The Bulcher photo? No, he's not there, but everybody else is."

"The caretaker said that Albert Einstein was in it."

Haskell snorted. "He doesn't know what he's talking

about. That's Erwin Schrödinger."

Now I turned toward him, ignoring the attendant. "Erwin Schrödinger? You're sure?"

"Oh, yes. He was a good friend of Bulcher."

Erwin Schrödinger, here in Zurich then? I seemed to remember that Einstein had indeed taught at the University of Zurich, but I had never known that Schrödinger had as well.

"You know the history of that cemetery very well," I said.

He waved a hand. "Well, I got some friends buried there. But I've got more buried in Brooklyn."

"Do you think you'll ever go back to America?"

"Hope to. But you never know. You never know with this world."

His eyes had grown opaque now, like a pond that has been stirred up. He gripped the armrests of his wheelchair with hands that were all bone and tendon. People show their fastenings when they get really old, as an ancient shingled roof shows its nails.

"Haskell," I said, "maybe you can help me. I'm trying to track down a Zurich family named Baruch—a mother and daughter."

"Baruch. That's not a common name here."

"They grew up in the Wiedikon neighborhood."

"I don't have much to do with them Orthodox folks. Baruch. . . . " He sat up in his wheelchair and peered at the attendant. "Wait a minute—didn't we have a Baruch here at the center?"

She gave a brittle smile. Behind her, the little gardening woman glanced up, but catching my gaze, went back to tending the flower bed.

"You know we don't give out information about our residents, Herr Levi," said the attendant.

"Oh, come on, girl," said Haskell. "Help the man out."

"You might try the ICZ office," she said to me evenly.

The ICZ—yes, the Israelitische Cultusgemeinde Zürich. Esther had mentioned it.

"Thank you, I'll do that," I said.

Haskell was unsettled to see me get up. He put his hands on the turning rims of his wheelchair, but either the brake was on or he didn't have the strength to move himself closer.

"Hey, Tavish, here's a plan," he said. "Why don't you come with me to Brooklyn?"

I glanced at the attendant for help, but she kept her gaze on the gardening woman on the ground.

"Well, I'd love to, Haskell, but . . ."

"Come up to my room. I got maps, I got photos. Some Dodgers pennants."

"Maybe another time. Right now I think I'll visit that cemetery again."

"Well, talk to Ephraim, not that other schlub. Ephraim knows the real history."

The attendant rose, stepped around me, and put her hands on Haskell's wheelchair. "Time for your medication, Herr Levi."

"Come by again, Tavish," he said faintly. "Anytime."

"I'll try, Haskell."

"You know you'll always have a place to stay in Brooklyn."

Tilting and turning Haskell in his chair, the attendant began steering him toward the building entrance. He didn't appear to have the flexibility to look back; he just kept speaking to the air in front of him. "I got all of Brooklyn in my room, and I'm *always* free."

"Right. Take care of yourself, Haskell."

"And it's Erwin Schrödinger, not Einstein!"

"Yes. Thanks for all your help."

He was still talking to the space in front of him, but I could no longer make out the words. Erwin Schrödinger—was that right? I wanted to get back to the cemetery and talk to the main caretaker, who would know. But I had gone no more than a few paces from the bench when the gardening woman looked up.

"Excuse me," she said.

"Yes?"

"Just to tell you . . . Haskell is right."

"I'm sorry?"

"We had a woman named Baruch here."

I crouched down beside her. "An older woman?"

"Not old. Younger than me. But with a stroke."

"I see. When was she here?"

"For two years or so, until . . . maybe it was last week. Then she was gone. Her daughter came to take her away. I think it was her daughter."

"A tall dark-haired woman in her twenties? Glasses?"

"Yes, that's her."

"Do you know where they went?"

She shook her head. "I don't know, but I think—why did she have to go away? Frau Baruch can't speak, can't walk, can't go to the toilet alone. This is the best place for her. Where will they go now?"

EIGHTEEN

A rotary dial phone. I'm sure it was the last in Europe. Black with white numbers arranged around the finger wheel. Each number had a set of three letters associated with it; zero was marked OPERATOR. I picked up the receiver and heard the dial tone, which prompted a rush of near forgotten sensations. I felt the resistance of the wheel as I rotated it, the press of my finger against the curved metal stop, the tensioned return of the dial into place. These old phones connected you to a system, yes, but the system was relatively unobtrusive. Now we live tethered to a net of overlapping systems, an immense Venn diagram of systems. The smallest thing, from your credit card to your dog's microchipped collar, connects you to a system. You can't escape the network of systems unless—

"Tavish!" exclaimed Zunz. "Where are you?"

—Well, *I* had escaped. It helped to be penniless.

"A Jewish thrift store in Zurich," I said.

Esther's goodwill store was a combination of the almost new and the almost antique. New Balance sneakers rested side by side with vintage high heels. Original editions of Karl May and Günter Grass sat beside bright new learn-to-read books. Cheap but ornate picture frames hung on the handlebars of an exercise bike. The bike didn't work, but it was still for sale.

"We must meet," I said.

"Of course. But what happened in Einsiedeln? I was afraid for you."

"Yes, sorry, I was . . . called away suddenly. Listen, I hope Dassvanger hasn't been harassing you."

"No. I think he gave up when he realized I couldn't tell him anything about Jaëlle."

"That's what I wanted to talk to you about. I think Jaëlle is here in Zurich."

"Zurich! Are you sure?"

"Pretty sure. At least she was here a week ago. She came to get her mother, who—"

No, save it. I didn't think there was much danger here among the anachronisms, but still. From where I sat, behind the counter, I could see a thin fiftyish woman trying on sunglasses, and a tall bearded man (he looked like Salvador Dali's *Don Quixote*) slowly turning a circular rack of suits, making it squeak. Esther was sorting clothes at the other end of the counter. Nobody was paying me any attention. But best to save it.

"I'll tell you all about it when we meet," I said. "When are you free?"

"Well, now, if you wish."

"I'm on Löwenstrasse . . ." I cupped the receiver. "Is it Löwenstrasse, Esther? Yes. There's a café here right across the street, the Minerva."

"Minerva. Give me an hour."

"And Jakob, before I forget—do you know the Unterer Friesenberg cemetery?"

"Yes, our old cemetery here."

Beside the telephone, along with a plastic bin of utensils

and a pile of electrical cords, I spotted a city map of Zurich. I plucked it out of the rack.

"There's a famous old photo there," I continued, "the Bulcher photo, that supposedly has a sixteenth-century rabbi in it. That's the rabbi I am looking for."

"He's in a *photograph?*"

"Well, everybody *thinks* it's him. And what's even more interesting is that Erwin Schrödinger is also in the photo."

"The physicist?"

"The physicist, and that's very curious because . . . anyway, I'll tell you all about it when we meet. But anything you can find out about this photo would be a big help."

"Yes, certainly, but how is this connected to Jaëlle?"

"I'm not sure, but I'm starting to think that this photo is more important than we think. I'll see you at the Minerva."

Esther looked up nervously as I put down the receiver.

"Now, Esther," I said.

She moved toward me, a garment in her hands, and I stood up to give her the chair. But she clearly wanted a view of the store and shook her head.

"I have another shirt for you," she said, holding it up.

If only I'd known last night that Esther was the key. Not Benjamin, not Tova, but Esther—the ministering angel who visited all the hospitals and seniors' centers.

"Esther, you have to tell me about the Baruchs. Mother and daughter."

She smoothed her hair nervously. I guessed she had been anticipating this; Tova must have talked to her.

"Ruth and Avi," I continued. "You knew them well."

"Of course. We were friends."

"And when they left the community, did you stop being

friends?"

She gave me a sharp glance. "People can't stop being friends, Tavish. Not if they're true friends."

"But you lost touch."

"We lost contact. We never lost touch."

She straightened the pile of papers on the counter beside the phone. I knew I couldn't push her, just gently lead her along.

"But Ruth ended up at the Reuven Seniors' Home," I said.

She stopped fidgeting. "How did you know that?"

"I was there this morning. Did you know she was there?"

She nodded. "About a year ago, I was doing my visiting at Reuven and I saw her. I was so shocked. She looked like an old woman, but she was the same age as me."

"She'd had a stroke."

"A terrible stroke; she lost her language. But at Reuven she had a speech therapist every day. They looked after her so well."

"But Jaëlle—I mean Avi—took her away last week."

"Yes, yes. I don't understand why."

"I think I do. Do you know where they went?"

Esther looked away from me unhappily.

"Esther?"

"I wish God could tell me," she said, "how we end up living the lives we do. How?"

*   *   *

I put my finger on the map and turned it around so Zunz could see. He raised his sunglasses on his forehead; I could see the tiny Versace trademark on the bridge. His phone lay beside his placemat; the screen was the same velvety midnight tint as his glasses.

"Zürcher Unterland," he said.

"Do you know it?"

"I avoid it if possible. Noisy, with the airport."

We sat among potted plants and shrubs, near a line of parked scooters. The Minerva Café. For once I was glad of the street bustle; I felt concealed, anonymous. But that didn't stop me from casing the area frequently. Across the street, a small produce market had been set up in an arcaded space, and farther up, I could see the clothing mannequins that Esther had placed in front of her store.

"And you don't have an address," said Zunz.

"No. Esther just said that the apartment is right near one of those big self-storage warehouses."

"And who is Esther?"

"From the thrift shop. See the mannequins up there?"

Zunz pushed his chair away so he could turn for a look; the one hand that remained on the table sported a gold pinky ring, octagonal, as brilliant as the sun.

"And sorry ... what kind of warehouse?" he said, turning back.

"A self-storage place. I don't know the word in German ... where you put all your extra furniture."

"Oh, *ein selbstlagerzentrum.*" He picked up his phone. "So they're living near a, Jaëlle and—what is the mother's name again?"

"Ruth. I *think* that's where they are, but I'm getting all this secondhand. Thirdhand."

"And you believe they just moved there?"

"Apparently Jaëlle took her mother out of the seniors' home last week, and then they found this place in Zürcher Unterland. That's according to the speech therapist at the seniors' home, Esther said."

Zunz swiped down his phone screen. "There are two of these . . . what did you call them? Self-storing places?—in Zürcher Unterland. No, three. One on Flughofstrasse, one on . . ."

He gave me three names, which I wrote down while darting an occasional glance at my surroundings. "We can start with these," I said, and began folding up the map.

He raised his eyebrows. "You want to go now?"

"Are you free? Sorry, I know I'm imposing again."

"No, it's fine . . . what time is it? Almost one. I must make a quick call." Phone in hand, he made as if to rise and then hesitated. "But Tavish—what are we going to do if we find them?"

He had me there. At the back of my mind I had some vague hope that, with his money and connections, he could help them.

"First I want to make sure they're safe," I said. "Then I'll figure out something. You go ahead and make your call."

He stood up, turning away from me to face the café entrance, and I took the opportunity to once more scan the square. I'm glad I did. Across the street, in the arcaded space of the farmers' market, I saw a face dart behind a pillar—a tiny face with a shapeless flat cap above it.

I half-rose in my chair, straining to see. Zarandok, skulking around. He had evidently followed me to Zurich. I went back to studying the map as if everything was normal, then raised my eyes again. No sign of him. Maybe he guessed I'd seen him.

"We can go," said Zunz, turning back to me.

"Sorry, Jakob, I'm thinking . . . maybe I should return the map to Esther. I see she's got things marked on it—maybe collection points or something."

He sat down and put his sunglasses on. "Very well."

"I'll only be a minute."

I crossed the street and made my way toward Esther's shop. As I came abreast of the arcaded market, I threw a glance back at the café. Zunz, his back to me, had gotten his cell phone out again. I dipped into the arcade and spotted Zarandok at the far back.

"What are you doing here?" I hissed.

He just darted across the aisle to a pillar and stood peering down the street at the café. I came up behind him.

"Listen to me," I said. "You need to stop following me and get the hell out of Zurich. I ran into those neo-Nazis from Bern, and—"

"I know that man," said Zarandok, eyes narrowed.

"You know Zunz? So you *do* have a history with him."

He grimaced. "His name is not Zunz."

"What?"

"You fool. His name is Rozach." He clutched my arm. "Get away from him. He is a killer."

"Hold on, for God's sake. Who's Rozach?"

"He betrayed János. To the Russians."

"*What?*"

He moved closer to me, and I could smell the tobacco on his breath. "Maybe he tell you he is a good citizen Jew? He fake you, Tavish. He is a *shvindler*."

Shvindler. A Jew who was no Jew. Zarandok twitched,

and I pre-emptively grabbed the lapel of his suit jacket.

"You're not going anywhere until you tell me the whole story," I said.

"No! We must get away."

'Tell me."

Zarandok put his gnarled little hand on my own, kneading my knuckles. "He wanted the vision of János."

"I have no idea what you're—his *vision?*"

In my bewilderment, I must have loosened my hand on his coat, because at that moment he tore himself away and bolted.

His cap came off in mid-flight, and he knocked over a whole crate of apples as he disappeared. Everybody in the place looked up. The proprietor must have thought I was responsible, because he came around from the cash to block my escape. Idiotically, I bent down to pick up an apple. What now? I made a decision in the time it took me to retrieve the crate, replace it on the table, and put the apple in it. I'd catch Zarandok if I had to chase him all the way to Hungary.

Then a patient voice spoke from the edge of the arcade. "Tavish?"

Zunz in his sunglasses and neatly pleated slacks stood beside a pillar. Slowly I bent down to pick up another apple and put it in the crate.

"Just a little accident," I said.

I couldn't see Zunz's eyes because of his sunglasses, but I had the strong feeling he was casing the place.

"Are you all right?" he said.

"I thought I saw someone. I keep thinking I'm being followed."

I put two more apples into the crate. The proprietor now stood beside me; he plucked out the apple I'd just put in and held it under my nose, barking German. Yes, okay, pal, it wasn't me who bruised your apples. How much money did I have? Not enough to pay for the apples. Another fine mess, Zarandok.

"We should go," said Zunz.

Moving close to a display of freshly cut flowers, he unexpectedly reached over for a bouquet. At the cash register, he put the flowers on the table and withdrew a bill from his wallet—fifty Swiss francs, it looked like. He did all this while barely changing the orientation of his body; I could tell he was keeping me in sight. The woman at the cash proffered the change, but he waved it away.

"*Für die äpfel,*" he said, loud enough for me to hear.

For the apples.

*   *   *

I remembered very little of the drive afterward, except tunnels: clean, uniform, sepulchral. Each one had narrow sidewalks on either side and, at intervals, orange service doors below butter-yellow security lamps. I wondered where the doors led and if they were locked.

Zunz's car was a luxury SUV—keyless entry, push-button ignition, surround-view camera. It gave off scents of nappa leather and air-freshener wintergreen. He had keyed in the first of the three self-storage locations on his dashboard GPS, and, as we drove, I numbly watched the blinking dot trace our progress. I didn't trust myself to make conversation. Zarandok was crazy—no, he *wasn't* crazy—

yes, crazy, but *this crazy*? I watched the orange service doors flash by, trying to stay lucid.

"I found out more about that famous cemetery photo," he remarked. "As you asked."

"And?"

"It *is* Erwin Schrödinger. He was at the University of Zurich then." He gave a faint smile. "And yes, there is supposed to be a legendary rabbi with him."

When I said nothing, he drummed his fingers on the wheel. "But Tavish. Tavish. Do you believe that a rabbi can travel through time and space like the angels?"

"I am not sure what I believe, now."

He gave me a quick glance. "You are like me. I was brought up to believe rabbis could do miracles, but . . . " He shook his head. "We grow out of our lives, yes?"

On my lap I held the flowers, their blossoms beaded with moisture; in the artificial light of the tunnel they were wan and lifeless. Why had he bought them?

We came out of the last tunnel and, instead of following the the sign of the plane to *flughafen*, Zunz turned off onto a boulevard and drove past electrical transmission towers, a shooting range and several ragged fields before reaching the first of the self-storage places, a nondescript cube building surrounded by a vast parking lot. He brought the car to a stop in the parking lot and sat tapping the steering wheel.

"I do not think they're living in a storage cubicle." He began keying in the second destination on his GPS.

I put my finger on the window control button and pressed. Nothing happened.

"Problem?" he said.

"I'd like some air."

He pressed the master control, and my window hummed down a foot.

"I'll open the sunroof too," he added solicitously, flicking the switch. Blue sky unfurled above me, and I tried to hold on to it, hold onto the vast rinsed calm as we drove to the second storage place. It was housed in a mini mall, surrounded by a pizza place, a vaping store, a bakery, and a pharmacy. We could have been anywhere in any featureless Western suburb. The only distinctive Swiss element was the brass fire hydrant, done in filigree and faces—gnomes and trolls, it seemed. There was no apartment building in sight. Again Zunz brought the car to a stop, frowning.

"We need better information," I said. "Let's go back."

He nodded slowly. "Yes . . . yes. But since we are here now, let us look at the last place."

The last place was five minutes away, past a construction site, a towering crane, and a few distinctive Swiss chalet-style houses. This time there was something near it that caught Zunz's eye—an unweathered apartment building with a checkerboard of new turf as a lawn. Zunz drove in and parked, looking the building up and down.

"The mother of Jaëlle," he said. "Her name is Ruth, you said?"

I sat staring straight in front of me. I was trying to feel my way into his being—killer or just *shvindler*? One thing I knew for sure: I wasn't leading any more. He had been planning ahead when he picked up those flowers.

He didn't seem to notice my silence. "Well, we will try," he said, taking the flowers from me.

Inside the lobby, we stood under a discreet CCTV camera and scanned the tenant directory. Zunz pressed "Reception" and an intercom voice clicked on.

"*Bitte?*"

Leaning forward, Zunz asked politely about Ruth Baruch. There followed a brief exchange during which Zunz held up the flowers to the CCTV camera. I stood looking into the empty lobby, wondering if I should challenge him or just get away when I saw my chance. The exchange came to an end, and Zunz shrugged, pushed the door open and waved me out with the bouquet. On the steps of the building, he surveyed the surroundings and then examined the bouquet critically, as if the flowers had failed him.

"We are not lucky today, Tavish," he said.

"As I say, we need better information. Let's go back."

He was staring across the road to a stately chateau-style building with a broad driveway that curled around a lavish stone fountain. The house looked completely out of place in the neighborhood, whose architecture was Industrial Sterile.

"Is that a hotel?" he said.

He began walking toward the car, and when I didn't move, he turned.

"Just a quick look, Tavish," he said.

He put the flowers in the back seat, and we drove out of the parking lot and down the road to the chateau. Classic gray stone, gabled roof, arched windows, and a pediment over the entrance. The sign on the front lawn said Chez Eve: Ein Spa für Frauen.

"A spa," he said, amused.

The lobby, all glass and honeyed light, held a slender sapling in a pot and a slender woman behind the reception desk. On the wall hung a giant gilt-framed print of Botticelli's Venus on the half shell. *Für Frauen*—for women. I could see through a courtyard to an elegantly landscaped waterfall that flowed past a spacious terrace. Zunz began the conversation in German, but I stepped forward.

"Do you speak English?" I said.

Zunz gave me a bland smile. "Forgive me, Tavish. Yes, English." He spread his hands on the reception desk. "My wife is looking for a place where she can take her mother for a week."

"We have a hotel spa at Rigi Kaltbad." The receptionist plucked out a pamphlet from the rack and handed it to Zunz.

"She wouldn't be able to stay here?" he said.

"No, sorry, this is a day spa."

My eye took in the inevitable CCTV camera, discreetly mounted high in a corner, and a floor plan on the wall—wellness room, sauna, massage room, mindfulness garden. Beside the floor plan was a placard with a picture of a silver-haired woman and text in English and German. "Welcome to Eve's Place! I started this spa because I desired a place of escape and healing for women. . . . "

"Very nice," said Zunz, looking up from the pamphlet. "But I should tell you that the mother of my wife is very frail."

"Our spas specialize in elder care and wellness. When would your wife want to visit?"

"I will ask her," said Zunz, getting out his phone.

He moved toward the entrance, out of earshot, and again I wondered if I should make a break for it. He stood facing the desk—and me—as he talked. I caught the words *spa* and *für frauen.*

I noticed another pamphlet in the rack: Reuven Seniors' Home. Where I had met Haskell the Brooklynite.

"I know this place," I said, plucking out the brochure.

"Oh, yes," said the woman. "They're among our best customers."

"They come here for spa treatments?"

She nodded. "We run a shuttle for the women twice a week. Eve—our owner—worked at Reuven before." She glanced through the windows at the back, where I could see a handful of elderly women in white bathrobes. One woman stood curved over a walker, and another was in a wheelchair, but they were all talking animatedly.

"They're here today, in fact," she said.

Zunz had finished his conversation and now moved toward the reception desk, smiling his bland smile.

"And so?" said the receptionist.

"She thinks her mother will love it," said Zunz. "I will give her this information. Tavish, do you have any more questions?"

Once we were outside, he turned and gazed at the chateau, raising his eyes to the top story.

"Did you see the floor plan?" he said.

"What about it?"

"Two storeys of facilities. But look—the building has three storeys."

"So?"

"It just makes me think."

He unlocked the car with the touch of his right hand. Once we were both inside, he laid his hand on something else, and all the door locks clicked.

"You can't really think that Jaëlle and her mother are in there," I said.

"Well, consider. It's well protected. It's in the middle of nowhere. It's close to the airport. And most importantly, men can't enter." He put his brochure down on the console and removed a packet of cigarillos from this shirt pocket. "Do you mind if I smoke?"

When he got no response, he tapped out a cigarillo from the pack and reached for a gold-plated lighter on the dashboard. "What we need is a woman." He flipped open the lighter and lit the cigarillo.

"What about your ex-wife?" he added, closing the lighter with a metallic snap.

Had I mentioned Julie to him? He pressed a button to lower his window and exhaled outside.

"Let's go back to town," I said.

He sighed and, resting the cigarillo in the ashtray on the console, turned to face me. "What is it, Tavish?" he said earnestly.

"What is what?"

"What is the problem? You are edgy."

"I'll tell you what the problem is. Zarandok is the problem. Though I don't think that's his real name any more than yours is Jakob Zunz."

He took off his sunglasses and, closing his eyes, put two fingers on the bridge of his nose. He didn't look surprised or angry, just deeply fatigued.

"You found him," he said.

"No, he found me. We had an interesting conversation. Short but illuminating."

Sunglasses now in his shirt pocket, he put this head

back against the headrest and straightened his arms on the steering wheel. "I don't have to ask what he said about me. He hates me."

"He said you knew János Kodaly."

"I did. At one time we were all friends together."

"He doesn't regard you as his friend now."

"I should have said, János and I were friends. Zarandok was the third wheel, as you say in English." He retrieved his cigarillo from the ashtray and drew on it hungrily. "We all met twice a week to talk about the things that mattered to us."

"Such as?"

"Chess, physics . . . rebellion. In Hungary, János and Zarandok had started a chess club that was also a club for ideas. They brought it to Zurich when they escaped. I became part of it."

"And Zarandok didn't like that."

Zunz shrugged. "Kodaly was a genius, Zarandok was a clerk. At my firm I hired only geniuses."

"Your firm?"

"I had my own cybersecurity firm back then. I hired János to explore some . . . speculative topics with me."

"What topics?"

He leaned against the seat and inhaled, narrowing his eyes against the smoke. If he was a false Jew, what *kind* of false Jew? A gentile pretending to be a Jew? A gentile who prized Jewish books?

"There is an old Kabbalistic idea," he said, "that when God first made Adam, He made him as big as the universe. And although Adam was later shrunk to the smallness of a man, his soul kept its cosmic proportions. János had that kind of soul. He had this incredible idea of—"

He suddenly sat up, staring straight ahead. I followed his gaze: a tall silver-haired woman was standing beside a car, studying her phone.

"Look," he said. "That's her."

"Who?"

He scooped up the spa brochure and handed it to me. Inside was the same paragraph I had seen framed on the wall—"Welcome to Eve's!"—with the same photo of a silver-haired woman.

"The owner," he said.

He pressed a button, and my door unlocked. "Talk to her, Tavish. Ask her about Jaëlle and Ruth."

"Why me?"

"You have a better face than me. No attempted poisonings in your life."

Ignoring my startled look, he reached behind him for the bouquet. "Don't forget these," he said.

Flowers in hand, I got dazedly out of the car. Attempted poisonings? I could have gotten free of him at that moment; I could make a run for it; but part of me wanted to hear his story. At least I could breathe a bit easier, outside that space shuttle of a car.

By then, after everything that I'd been through, I was starting to notice small akimbo things in my surroundings. As I was walking toward the woman, I glanced across the lawn to the far side of the parking lot. A gray sedan sat in the corner space, parked diagonally from us. Not big, not compact, not low-slung, not souped up, not anything but a washed-out gray. Nondescript even for a nondescript suburb. And yet its tinted windscreen seemed unusually dark.

Dark as in—you couldn't see inside even if you pressed your nose up against the glass. Was it just due to the contrast with the brilliant day, the startle of blue sky around it?

Now I was close to the woman: early forties, *blond cendré*, high boots glossed by the sun.

"Ah, excuse me, Madame . . . Are you Eve, the owner?"

She glanced up from her phone screen, taking in both me and the flowers. Tight, cautious smile. "May I help you?"

"My name is Tavish." I resisted the temptation to look back at Zunz's car. "I'm here because . . . well, I am looking for an old friend of mine, Ruth Baruch."

She stood straight now, slipping the phone into her handbag; I was sure I had seen a flicker of disquietude in her eyes.

"I am wondering if she is staying here at your spa," I continued.

"No. We don't take overnight guests."

"She might be with her daughter, Avi."

"As I say, they're not here."

She looked me straight in the eye, but I sensed she was standing *too* tall, harnessing her poise to deflect questions.

"May I ask who gave you this information?" she said pleasantly.

"Oh, I just . . . I can't remember who exactly, but I know you offer elder care here, and . . . "

"During the day only. For overnight stays, our guests go to Rigi Kaltbad."

"Rigi Kaltbad. I wonder if you could spell that for me?"

I tucked the bouquet under my arm to get out my crumpled paper and my druid's pen, and as I did so, I again caught sight of the gray sedan with the tinted windscreen.

The side windows were tinted as well—back and front.

I took a step toward the woman, and she stood even straighter. We locked eyes for a second. Her body language told everything I needed to know.

"Please listen to me," I said in a low voice. "Avi and Ruth must leave."

She drew back, eyes narrowed, and I winced inwardly: anybody who was watching would have seen her reaction.

"They're here, right?" I said in a low voice. "They must get away. *Discreetly.*"

A surveillance car, that's what it was. The gray sedan was watching the place. I should have twigged to it earlier.

"Who are you?" she whispered angrily.

I refrained from moving any closer to her; I knew it would look conspiratorial. I kept my eyes on the paper and nodded, pen raised. Discreetly, but *how?* In the midst of my panic, a bright seed from an earlier conversation entered my mind; at that moment, it seemed to have blown in from heaven.

"Get them to leave with the Reuven women," I whispered.

"What?"

"In the shuttle from the seniors' home. They'll be less conspicuous."

"The people you want are *not* here," she said coldly. "Please excuse me."

In a loud voice I said: "Ri . . . gi . . . kalt . . . bad. Yes, got it. Thank you."

I didn't look at her, nor at Zunz, nor at the gray sedan. I just kept my eyes on my scrap of paper as I walked back to the SUV. I wasn't sure if I was dealing with one enemy here or two.

"They're at the other spa in Rigi Kaltbad," I said to Zunz, opening the door.

He leaned toward me. "You're sure?"

I tossed the bouquet into the back seat. "It's only forty minutes away. Let's go."

He pressed a button beside him, and the two rearview mirrors whirred into place. Another touch, and all the locks clicked shut. But then he just sat with his hands on the wheel, watching the owner disappear into the spa.

"You know," he said conversationally, "I really think your ex-wife would like this place."

"Why do you keep harping on her?"

He was looking beyond the spa entrance now, to the gray sedan that sat parked in the corner.

"She still cares for you, doesn't she?" he said.

I sat perfectly still, wondering if I'd fucked up or *really* fucked up.

"I'm sure," continued Zunz, "that she would fly here at once if . . . let's suppose, she thought you'd been shot. In fact, I *know* she would." He took off his sunglasses, and now his face was hard. "So tell me again, Tavish. Are Jaëlle and Ruth inside?"

"I already told you—they're at Rigi Kaltbad. Are we going there or not?"

At that moment, I heard a car door slam. I looked across the parking lot to the gray sedan. A tall, slope-shouldered man had gotten out—sunglasses, jeans, bulky windbreaker. He tucked his phone into his back pocket, waved his key lazily at the sedan, and began crossing the lawn. I recognized the gait before I recognized the face: Dassvanger.

NINETEEN

May the angels with their radiant strides keep pace with you. I knew then that Zunz was the chief Friend, the voice from beyond Pluto, the guy who'd recited the pilgrim's prayer to me that first time he'd called. And I also knew that he wasn't all a lie. Something he had told me about himself, some intimate fact, was true. He wouldn't have been able to dupe me so completely otherwise. He was no alien, the prick.

He rolled down his window, and Dassvanger bent to give me a long glance intended to flay me alive. The two of them exchanged a few words in German; the only things I caught were *flug* and *flughafen*. A flight, an airport. What was that all about? Dassvanger stood straight again, checked his phone and then walked back to the sedan.

"So what happens now?" I said.

Zunz got out another cigarillo. "We wait." He put the carton on the dashboard, snapped open his gold-plated lighter and touched the flame to the end of the cigarillo.

"What did you mean about Julie?" I said.

He exhaled and leaned forward to place the lighter on the dashboard. "You'll be glad to hear, Tavish, that she is about to become part of your life again." He glanced at his Rolex. "In about an hour, in fact."

I closed my eyes. He could have been bluffing, but they'd

been talking about a flight.

"Why, for God's sake?" I said.

He shrugged. "To be sure of your cooperation."

"You *can* be sure of it. I've practically handed you everything on a plate so far. Why do you want that book so badly, anyway?"

"For the same reason you do."

"I *don't* want it. It's made my life hell."

"No, you want it, deep down. That book is a miracle."

"I thought you said you didn't believe in miracles."

"Some I do. As when, for example, a leper is made whole again."

For a moment, he seemed to disappear inside himself. I remembered Julie's description of a patient who had undergone the amytal test—where one brain hemisphere is put to sleep in order to test the capacity of the other. A hand drops; an eyelid flutters. Language is gone. The patient is trying to hold on to reality with literally half a brain. Zunz was that patient for a second, staring out from the straitjacket of his being; then, becoming aware of the ash on his cigarillo, he flicked it into the ashtray.

"János Kodaly always said he had never come across such visions in a book," he continued. "Not in Dante, not in Einstein, not in the Bhagavad-Gita. For János, the visions were just as important as the mathematics. He needed both for his incredible idea."

"His incredible idea. To make a universe."

"To make a universe."

"And let me guess: he was murdered before he could do it."

I wanted him to come clean about his involvement in

Kodaly's death, but he just lowered his window to exhale outside.

"No, he created his universe," he said.

"What?"

"Well, an embryo one."

This guy was completely certifiable. Just go along with him. Keep him talking.

"You know the Large Hadron Collider?" he said. "I'm sure you do, since you live in Geneva. The biggest particle accelerator in the world. It sends two beams of protons spinning at near light speed around a ring of twenty-seven kilometers."

"Listen, you don't need Julie for all this. Let me call her."

"You asked me about Kodaly's universe. I'm telling you." He drew unhurriedly on his cigarillo. "When the proton beams smash together, the collisions produce fireworks of other elementary particles. Such a collision happened on April 4th, 2013, while János was running experiments there. And something came out of that collision. It only lasted a quadrillionth of a second, so people couldn't really say what it was. Some thought it was a new elementary particle. But it was actually a tiny black hole, about a billion times smaller than an elementary particle. And inside that black hole was a tiny universe."

I was racking my brain to think of a way out of this while also—I couldn't help myself—trying to take in what he was saying. A *universe* inside a black hole?

"So János always claimed," continued Zunz. "And I believed him. I believed him because he described it for me. He had set up the experiment so that his tiny universe would annihilate itself immediately, but had it survived, it would have expanded in a different space-time from ours. It would have gone through cosmic inflation and developed chemical elements and galaxies and eventually life. He had all these wild ideas of what intelligent life could have been like. It might have taken the form of music, or dark matter, or vast mobile bags of ocean. He drew pictures and scribbled equations and talked with his hands. He could see it all in his head."

"So that's why you want the book—to create your own universe?"

He took the cigarillo out of his mouth. A thought seemed to have ambushed him, a regret or loss, sudden and sharp; but he stubbed out the cigarillo and his eyes went dead again. "No," he said. "I want to see what János saw."

At that moment, a shuttle bus turned in from the main road and came to a stop in front of the spa, flashers blinking. It had *Reuven Seniorenzentrum* written on the side.

"What's this?" said Zunz.

The shuttle van filled the space in front of the spa, obscuring our view of the gray sedan. We watched the shuttle driver get out, walk around the vehicle and open the side door. He pressed a button, and we heard a mechanical sound—presumably a wheelchair platform being lowered. We could see the driver's head through the windows, watching the descent of the platform. Then the mechanical noise stopped, and the driver went inside the spa.

I shrank lower in my seat. Yell, punch, honk the horn . . . *now*. Opening his door, Zunz stood up, elbow atop the door and eyes on the spa entrance. I surreptitiously tried my own door—still locked.

That's when I caught a movement behind Zunz—a blue

T-shirt and a hand flashing upwards.

"Don't move," said Jaëlle.

I craned my neck. She stood directly behind him, holding a pistol—Dassvanger's, it looked like. I couldn't see their faces, only their torsos; Jaëlle was breathing visibly. I could make out a tan line on her raised arm, just below the edge of the blue sleeve. I lowered my head even more: she held the pistol against the back of Zunz's head.

"The keys," she said. "Slowly."

The moment seemed held fast inside my lungs. I heard women's voices from the spa entrance; they'd begun to board the shuttle.

"You wouldn't shoot me in the parking lot," I heard Zunz say.

"Try me."

I looked around in a panic. The shuttle van still blocked the view of the gray sedan, and hopefully Dassvanger couldn't see what was happening. Through the windscreen of the shuttle, I saw several elderly women waiting their turn to board.

"If you're going to kill me," said Zunz, "do it now."

Jaëlle lowered the gun barrel so that it was resting against the base of his neck. "I'm not going to kill you, I'm going to cripple you for life. Give me the keys."

Zunz just stood there. Jesus, he *was* crazy.

I was so sure that she would shoot him that I blurted out, "Right-hand pocket."

Nobody moved. From behind me came the voices of the women, chatting as they boarded the shuttle. I leaned far over, so I could see Jaëlle's face; she was gritting her teeth, as if bracing herself to pull the trigger. In a moment the shuttle bus would move, and Dassvanger would see us.

"Start the car, Tavish," said Jaëlle.

Altering the angle of the gun, she pressed it hard against Zunz's head, trying to move him away from the open door. He canted his head forward in response to the pressure but didn't budge. *Start the car.* I leaned across to the driver's seat and put my finger on the ignition button. Nothing happened.

"The brake!" hissed Jaëlle.

Clumsily, wildly, I reached one hand down to depress the pedal while scrabbling for the ignition button. The next moments were both dreamlike and fast: I might have been inside a time-lapse video with clouds and their shadows zooming over an unchanging landscape. Zunz must have twisted and lashed out. Jaëlle must have fought back. I heard somebody go *hunhh.*

The next thing I knew, Jaëlle was in the driver's seat, the gun on her lap, and the car was running. She slammed it into reverse. The open door caught Zunz with a concussive *thunk* and he disappeared from view.

The car screeched to a halt, and Zunz's lighter and cigarillos flew past me. Then I was pressed against the seat by a burst of acceleration. I remember the open mouths of the old women as we roared past them.

Turning in my seat, I caught a glimpse of Zunz motionless on the ground.

"Jesus Christ," I said.

We sped along the boulevard toward the highway. Her car door was rattling loosely and a beeping came from the dashboard.

"God, did you run him over?" I said.

She just slammed her door and took a fresh grip on the wheel. The beeping had stopped, but a message in German was flashing on the dashboard . . . something about *Schlüssel*. No, she hadn't run him over; we would have felt it.

"*Je pensais en avoir fini avec toi,* Tavish," she said savagely. *I thought I had finished with you.*

"Yeah, well, sorry to disappoint you."

We were back to speaking our own languages.

The car was remarkably quiet; the only sound beside the beeping was a faint humming. I looked into the rearview mirror but saw only empty road.

"Is your mother still back there?" I said.

She ignored me, intent as she was on taking the highway ramp at a hundred kilometers an hour. The dashboard was still flashing. *Der Schlüssel befindet sich nicht im Fahrzeug* . . . What was *Schlüssel*? Something wasn't in the car. . . . The key, yes. It was still in Zunz's pocket. How long could we keep driving without the key? Jaëlle must have been going a hundred and fifty now.

"Listen to me," she said. "We're coming to Oerlikon station. We leave the car there and get a taxi, train, whatever. And we go *separately.*"

My head had cleared to the point where I was again taking in things again. I felt grit on my palm from the brake pedal and my heart scrabbling inside my chest. Something nagged in my mind. . . . Then I had it.

"No," I said.

"What?"

"We have to go to the airport. Julie will be arriving in less than an hour."

"Forget it, Tavish."

"I'm pretty sure Zunz fed her a story about me getting shot. They'll be waiting for her."

"You'll have to go back on your own."

"Goddamn it, Jaëlle—"

Then it occurred to me that her mother might still be waiting for her at the spa. She was passing cars aggressively, glancing in both mirrors, taking in the whole streaming world around her. If the police caught us, that would be a good thing, wouldn't it? They'd pull us over and we could tell them everything. How we'd stolen Zunz's car. How Jaëlle had taken a police officer's weapon. How we nearly ran over a man. Still, why didn't the police come?

"You were friends with Saoirse," I said.

"Shut up, Tavish."

"You didn't have to double-cross me, for God's sake. I would have helped you."

"*Shut up.*"

She glanced in the mirror and swore under her breath. I looked back: the gray sedan was visible maybe a hundred and fifty meters behind us.

"Jesus, how did they find us so fast?" I said.

She just gripped the wheel with both hands and sped up. I clutched the handle above my window.

"He's waiting for the right time to cut our engine," she said.

"He can *do* that?"

Reaching inside her jacket, she withdrew something and tossed it to me.

"Change of plans," she said tightly.

I knew what it was as soon as it touched my hands. She must have had it somewhere under her shirt, because it was warm from her body. It lay battered and soft in my hand—a piece of old time like a fleck of amber, with an entire vanished world inside it.

"What . . . *why?*" I said.

She just glanced in the mirror and, letting go of the steering wheel with one hand, retrieved the pistol and put it on the console.

"The next exit I'm pulling off," she said. "I'll slow down for a second. You take the book and get out."

"I'm not leaving you to face them alone."

"You want to help me, Tavish?" she snapped. "Do what I tell you. Take the book and *run.*"

She slowed for the exit and then went into a turn, and the centrifugal force pressed me against the door. I didn't have time to think; I stuffed the book inside my windbreaker pocket.

"Listen," I said. "Go to Maiensäss Ana."

Maiensäss Ana—our little alpine hut in the north. From her look, I guessed that Saoirse had told her about it.

"It's north, near a place called Renz," I continued. "You can hide there—your mother, too."

She ran a red light, turned down a street and slowed the car.

"Maiensäss Ana!" I said, opening the door.

I stumbled onto the pavement, barely avoiding the swinging door as she sped off. With one hand on the jacket pocket that held the book, I sprinted through the parking area of a gas station, past a McDonalds, up a grassy hill and across another road. I'm sure people were staring at me, but I just kept pounding along with my head down.

A garden center loomed ahead: I went through the gates

and past rows of potted flowers, bags of soil and peat moss, wooden trellises, garden windmills, a backhoe. The place was big enough so that the employees had walkie-talkies on their shoulders, like cops. Keep going, keep going. . . . I came to rows of saplings supported by wire racks, their root balls wrapped in burlap, and there I had to stop. For the second time in four days, I thought my heart was going to give out. I shrank to the ground, hand on my side, my core palpitating, and risked a glance back.

Nobody was following me.

I stumbled further along the path to an area of larger trees and crouched again, still breathing hard. The leaves around me rustled comfortingly. What had happened? They must have gone after Jaëlle. A passing employee, seeing me crouched beside the saplings, asked me in German if I'd lost something. I just smiled weakly. Just enjoying the trees, *danke*. He nodded uncertainly and passed on. I studied the little tag on the sapling in front of me: *Ulmus laevis*. White elm. I'd had one of those in my yard in Geneva. Yes, I was getting my breath back. After a moment I was conscious of the weight in my windbreaker pocket. I slipped the book out.

A miracle, Zunz had said. I turned the pages gingerly. Jesus, it was real. I really shouldn't have been handling it without gloves, but I couldn't help myself. The ink—iron gall, I guessed—was a faded purple-black, but in general the Hebrew letters were still distinct, each one cut and tapered, the way pioneers made nails. I saw the spectral crown watermark, felt the soft, grainy handmade paper. Here and there, the pages held mold or water damage, and the ink had occasionally corroded into clouds of liver brown, but most of the text was readable.

And now I saw that the spaces I'd seen on Zarandok's transcribed sheet were an integral feature of the book. Every few pages, there would be a gap in the text. Strange. Paper was so valuable back then that writers tended to use every inch of it. Were these spaces akin to the textual pauses in Torah scrolls? Or had the author intended to come back and fill them in later?

I turned a page and saw a line I remembered: *Cosmic dust comes together and starts remembering.* Aaron had quoted it to me: the resurrection of the universe—of *every* universe. Below the line was a water stain covering a third of the page. So the numbers of reawakening lived on only in the minds of the Talmeeds—and presumably in Benesh's notes.

*   *   *

Zurich Airport, ZRH, Flughafen Zürich. Heaven designed by cryogenicists. Bright sanitized colors, hyper-efficient escalators, high-definition TV screens, and all the merchants of the heavenly life—Gucci, Tiffany's, Rolex, Swatch, Victoria's Secret, Toblerone, Versace, Nina Ricci. It could have been any high-end airport anywhere in the world, except that it had the Edelweiss Shop. Heaven with a touch of Helvetia.

Getting off the tram, I followed the crowd warily to the escalator. Thank you, Zurich Public Transit. The friend of pilgrims and fare jumpers. In Switzerland, most systems are predicated on the law-abiding behavior of the users, and no human or machine had demanded to see my ticket. Riding the escalator, I grasped the moving handrail to calm my nerves. I could only hope that Jaëlle had led Zunz and Dassvanger away. I was sure now that she had *wanted* them to chase her; maybe she'd arranged for the spa owner Eve to spirit her mother away once the coast was clear. She could think on her feet, no argument there.

Where are you, Julie? And where are *you*, Jaëlle?

I was glad of all the people, all the lives swirling around, intent on their paths into the sky. Under the Arrivals sign, I stood with other harried patrons to scan the display screens. *Abflugort. Fluggesellschaft, Flugnummer:* originating city, airline, flight number. A flight from Geneva would be arriving in sixteen minutes. I headed over to the information desk which held a thin clerkly woman—severe glasses, sharp profile, hair in a bun. If Julie was on that flight, her cell would be in airplane mode. . . . But maybe she wasn't on the flight, maybe—

"*Guten tag*," I said pleasantly. "I don't suppose I can use the phone here? I've misplaced my cell."

"Very sorry," said the information woman. "This phone is for internal communication."

"It's just that I really need to find out if somebody is on Flight 541 from Geneva."

"You will have to ask the airline desk, sir. But I should tell you airlines generally don't provide this information."

"This is an emergency."

She swept off her glasses with a dip of her head. "What is the emergency, precisely?"

"The emergency is—could you just do me this favor, for God's sake?"

She didn't blink. "Is it a health emergency, sir?"

I didn't want to be in one place for long, and I certainly

didn't want to be standing at the information booth, the locus of the terminal. I just walked away, across the vast floor to the Migros food mart, where I turned to scan my surroundings. No sign of Zunz or Dassvanger. I had to locate the Swissair desk and find out if Julie was on the flight. I moved out of the food mart into the flow of people, feeling the weight of the book in my jacket pocket. The public address system was saying something in German. I got to the top of the escalator and the Swissair booth; there was a line of twenty people in front of it. I had to get to somebody in authority, fast. The public address system was now speaking English. Wait. . . . What was that?

"Herr Ein Sof, please come to the information desk."

Herr Ein Sof? I moved to the railing and looked down to the floor below. I could just make out the figure of the information woman, with her bun and glasses. *Ein Sof:* the Kabbalistic term for the Infinite, the primal Godhead. The airport was paging the Godhead.

I moved behind a pillar. One of Zunz's tricks? Very likely . . . but I'd better find out, *carefully*. I darted down the escalator, going around people, and then passed two police officers to get to the information desk. The clerkly woman gave me a *You again* look.

"I'm Ein Sof," I said.

She looked me up and down. "Can I see some identification?"

"Look, I lost my wallet along with my cell phone. Can you give me a break?"

She sighed. "You are supposed to go to the Hertz Car Rental Office immediately."

"Hertz?"

"They said it's urgent." She looked beyond me as if I was holding up the line, though there wasn't one. "Maybe they found your wallet and cell phone."

"Where is Hertz?"

She pointed. "Parking lot, ground level."

I stood there at a loss, wondering if I should risk it. Just then the announcement came on over the public address system, announcing the arrival of flight 541 from Geneva. Urgent, the woman said. Who wanted me so urgently at the Hertz office?

I don't know how long I would have stood there vacillating, but the decision was made for me.

Zunz and Dassvanger were suddenly there at the entrance. I backed away and they followed, spacing themselves out, walking unconcernedly. I had the odd feeling that we were following some choreographed routine, as slow and meditative as tai chi. I stopped and they stopped. We faced each other, the airport crowds streaming around us. The arrivals gate was behind me and the baggage carousel to my right; it was only then that I noticed the absence of the airport police officers.

Zunz had a bandage on his forehead. I tried to guess from his face what had happened in the last hour, but he was impassive. Dassvanger was the one I was really worried about. He had only to flash his police credentials to the authorities here, and . . . I took the book out of my jacket pocket and stepped closer to them.

"Jaëlle gave me the book," I said, holding it up.

I saw Dassvanger glance at Zunz, whose eyes flickered lazily over me and then ranged beyond, to take in the surroundings.

"I'll give it to you when I see Julie come through the gates safe and sound," I said. "Deal?"

They made no response. Again I edged backward, toward the arrivals gate, and when I reached it I stood in such a way that I could keep an eye on them while watching the arrivals. They came closer and spread themselves out even more. To my right, the luggage carousel started up, and the first bags came down the inclined ramp from the baggage bay.

Two streams of activity divided my attention: the moving baggage carousel on my right and the flow of arriving passengers behind me. Dassvanger and Zunz stayed where they were.

"What happened to Jaëlle?" I said.

Zunz shrugged. "I don't care about her, Tavish. I'll get what I want eventually."

"She worked for you, didn't she? At your cybersecurity firm?"

"Let us not speak of her."

I turned fractionally to scan the arrivals and then faced Zunz again. I *couldn't* give them the book—it was Jaëlle's. But what choice did I have? Around me, the arriving passengers streamed toward the baggage carousel. Families, couples, children. . . .

"You never really answered my question," I said to Zunz.

"Your question?"

"Why you want the book so badly."

We didn't need to raise our voices to be heard; the baggage carousel—a belt of angled black plates inching around a loop conveyor—was amazingly quiet. The plates overlapped as they came to a corner, and then spread out to become uniform on the straightaway. At any other time, watching it would have been oddly meditative.

"I did answer it, Tavish," he said.

"You want to create your own universe? You want to be God?"

"No, I want to be a righteous man. Far more difficult."

Dassvanger was frowning, as if this exchange interrupted the choreographed routine that had been so carefully set up. Zunz was looking past me to the doors of the arrival gate.

"János Kodaly talked so much about that book," he continued, "that one day I asked him to write out a page for me. It was the passage about the cosmic resurrection."

I glanced at the people coming out of the arrivals gate: all shapes and sizes, like old apothecary bottles—squat, tall, narrow, stubby-necked, slender-necked, tinted, clear, decorated, plain. Julie, where are you?

"I started working away at the text with a German-Aramaic dictionary," Zunz continued. "Translating word by word. I broke my mind on it. But after a week, something strange happened."

"What?"

"I already told you about this, Tavish. Have you not been listening to me at all?"

Certainly I was only half-listening to him now, agonizing over Julie's whereabouts He suddenly looked as though he regretted this interlude of self-revelation.

"Give me the book," he said harshly.

"No, we had a deal."

"Last chance," interjected Dassvanger, who had his cell phone out. "You have no way out of here."

Once again I glanced toward the arrivals gate. "Where's Julie?"

Zunz turned to cast a dark look at Dassvanger, whose eyes flickered to the arrivals gate. Something was wrong. Only a few stragglers were coming in now through the gate. Was Julie even on that flight? Where *was* she?

Dassvanger was giving orders on his cell phone.

I acted without thinking. Darting across the floor to the carousel, I shouldered my way between the passengers to jump up on the moving surface. Dassvanger reacted fast, but he was impeded by passengers and their luggage carts. Hunched over, trying to keep my footing on the inclined surface, I scrambled over a bag of golf clubs and onto a suitcase. My destination was the feeder ramp, which led to the upper level.

I shot a glance over my shoulder: Dassvanger was on the carousel himself, standing precariously like a lumberjack on a floating log, arms out and knees bent. Zunz was just staring at me. I reached the ramp and went up it crab-like, scrabbling on the rollers, ignoring the yells, clambering over baggage as it slid toward me. At the top, I pushed aside the curtain of plastic strips that covered the opening.

Two baggage handlers in overalls froze, one with a bag in his hands. I was lucky they were so astonished. I blew past them to the open door and raced down the hallway. Pain in my chest . . . keep going. I clattered down an iron staircase and through one door, then another. I had reached the luggage loading bay: a guy in overalls had just deposited a bag on a conveyor belt. He stared at me.

"Sorry, lost!" I said, and darted away again.

I'm sure the airport security had been alerted by now. I

didn't know if that was good or bad. I crouched in a corner, wheezing, and then continued, convinced I would meet Zunz and Dassvanger around the next corner. By sheer chance, I went through a door that opened onto the ground floor of the main parking lot. Across the road, tucked in the corner of the parking lot, was the Hertz rental office.

As I stood there, completely at a loss, a Hertz rental car came out of the lot fast—way too fast. It screeched to a halt beside me.

"Get in, Tavish!" said Julie, leaning across the front seat.

TWENTY

Maiensäss Ana went from my life when Julie left, taking all its gifts—the pour of the mountain stars, the garrulous frogs, the pines with their calling owls, the bluebells, the squelchy wetland, the warm parley of cabin smells—old oakum, larch logs, burning applewood, lamp oil, fresh-picked mushrooms frying in butter—all of it gone and I barely survived its going. Built by Julie's great-grandfather, the cabin had been both summer and winter retreat for us. No plumbing, no electricity, and a privy out back. Saoirse had loved the place. We had spent many sunlit hours sitting on the bank of the brook, all three of us, our toes in the bracing alpine water, watching the minnows drag their tiny shadows across the sun-pebbled bottom.

"We're going to the police?" said Julie, hands tight on the wheel.

"No, first we need to get to Maiensäss Ana."

She detached a hand to sweep off her sunglasses, and I could see the burnishing of the years around her eyes, the high cheekbones, the small cleft in mid-brow, the exasperated glance—all the things I knew so well.

"I told Jaëlle to meet me there," I said.

"For God's sake, Tavish."

"I know, sorry. But she gave me the book—"

"She *gave* you the book?"

"Long story."

Maiensäss Ana: another casualty of our shipwrecked marriage. I knew that Julie hadn't been to the place in several years; she and Pierre used his family's chalet in the Bernese Alps.

"You saved my life, Julie," I said. "Again."

"You can thank Cléance, again."

"Cléance?"

"I was in such a state after that man . . . what is his name?"

"Zunz."

"I was in such a state after he called me that I immediately called Cléance. I told her you'd been shot and that I was taking the next flight to Zurich. She was suspicious."

"Cléance is one of the most clearheaded people I know."

"She told me *not* to take the next flight to Zurich until she found out more. But I couldn't just sit around, so I took the train to Lausanne and rented a car."

"And you paged me when you got to the airport."

"I couldn't remember if it was Ein Sof or *Ein Sock*."

"You got it right. The Primal Godhead rather than a sock."

"Shut up, Tavish." She drove in tight-lipped silence for a minute. "Maiensäss Ana doesn't even belong to you."

"It was all I could think of, sorry."

We were going northeast on the A1, into Lake Constance country. The moon over the mountains was a translucent shard, a shaving from the horn of some extinct beast.

"And what did you tell Pierre?" I said tentatively.

She kept her eyes on the road. "I told him that you were shot and that I had to go to Zurich."

"What did he say?"

"He said to call him as soon as I could. He knows you

don't have anybody in your life, Tavish."

I didn't ask her if any other discussion had gone on—I was too grateful.

"And if this Jaëlle is not at Ana," said Julie, "what will you do?"

"I'll wait. But I don't expect you to, Julie. You didn't ask for any of this."

"You're right. But I'm in the middle of it now. This man Zunz probably knows about Pierre and the kids." She gave me a flinty glance. "That's why you need to give up the book."

"What?"

"Call him. Tell him you'll give him the book."

"You don't know what you're saying."

"I'm sure Cléance would agree with me. You must call her, by the way."

"Cléance would *not* agree with you. I'm not surrendering to that prick."

Jaëlle must have worked for him at his cybersecurity firm. And that time in Lausanne, when she claimed to be checking my phone for a bug—she was actually *installing* it. But how much had she told him about Saoirse? Maybe not much . . . initially. That part of her life might have been too precious. She would have told him about the Interstellar Academy, very likely, and Zunz would have seen that she knew enough about János Kodaly to pull off a con. (I wouldn't have been surprised if Kodaly sometimes talked to the camp kids about his adventures in physics.) But had Zunz discovered more about her on his own? Or had she told him everything from the start?

"Anyway," said, Julie, "call Cléance tomorrow."

I watched the Swiss countryside flash by: the orderly flow of hayricks, the meticulously constructed white fences, the cows with their cowbells sounding drowsy and bronze-soft in the dusk. The last of the day was shoaling red beyond the mountains. I thought again of Maiensäss Ana, of the blue vitreous evenings we'd spent in the yard of our neighbor Herman, listening to the stars.

"I wonder how Herman is doing," I said.

"He's got a new telescope, he said in his Christmas card."

"Benesh would be interested. He knows the guy."

"Which one is Benesh?"

"The blind Talmeed. He listens to the stars, too."

In another reality, a different ordering of time, I would be reminiscing with a grown-up Saoirse about how we used to walk over to Herman's place, and he would be in his front yard, a thin friendly man with a face of old scrimshaw, listening to the stars through headphones. He would put them on Saoirse's head, and she would sit fascinated, listening with all her being. I tried the headphones myself once or twice, but all I heard was static.

Julie glanced in the mirror. "Will they follow us, Tavish?"

"I hope not. They don't know where we're going. God, I hope not. Did you bring your cell phone?"

"Of course."

"Please, please don't use it unless you absolutely have to."

"I *know* that, Tavish."

Ahead was Lake Constance, which formed a rough triangle between Switzerland, Germany, and Austria. The lake town of Bregenz was the last waypoint—or the first, if you were walking in the right direction—on the Swiss section of the Jakobsweg.

*   *   *

Lacking lamp oil, we had to clean out the *maiensäss* by candlelight. We opened the shutters, brought in firewood, disposed of mouse nests, and swept out the acorn pieces, cedar seeds, and other unidentifiable debris brought in by squirrels. Fortunately we discovered some vinegar, and so were able to clean tables and dishes. After the cleaning, I took a quick late-night dip in the freezing brook. It shocked the dirt off me like a sandblasting, and I came back feeling much more civilized. Pausing at the chopping block, I took in the familiar profile of the cabin by moonlight: the steep asphalt-shingled roof with its projecting eaves; the stone chimney with its quaint wrought-iron roof; the picture window rosy with candle glow; the tiny crooked space under the front porch for storing firewood. A *maiensäss*, the traditional cabin of the alpine pastures. A place of birdsong and owl light and endless, unsoundable darkness. Ours, once.

Inside, Julie was taking it all in, as I had been outside—the old picnic table by the window, the cracked St. Moritz beer steins on the kitchen shelf, the candleholders made out of old ski tips, the vintage 1930s *alpinisme* poster that showed a ruddy-faced female alpinist leaping lightly over an ice crevice, above the caption, "Over the glacier!"

"I can't stay long, Tavish," she said.

"But you'll stay tonight?"

She looked around, biting her lip. I suspected she had called Pierre when I was at the brook and told him—what, exactly? That it had all been a false alarm?

"But you decide," I said.

She brushed a strand of hair out of her eyes. "Are the mattresses okay?"

"Let's find out."

Luckily, along with the vinegar, we'd discovered a bit of scotch. Later, after we'd got out the inflatable mattresses (perfectly sound, it turned out), we sat at the table in the moonlight, sipping the scotch and sharing a stale sandwich that Julie had bought in Lausanne. Nothing around us suggested that we were in the twenty-first century. Stone fireplace, wooden snowshoes on the wall, a coat rack with antler ends for pegs. . . . We could have been in Plato's cave, the subalpine version.

"This is what it's all about," I said, taking out the book and placing it on a clean sheet of paper towel.

She opened it gingerly in the lamplight. The pages were almost transparent in places, like the skin of a baby bird; the grained and rippled covers suggested the scratched surfaces left by retreating glaciers. The very stains and blots seemed to have a hieroglyphic quality. I recalled something the medieval alchemists had said: if you were to split a unicorn's horn lengthwise, you would find strange marblings inside, the faint images of fabulous animals. . . .

"Why does Zunz want it so badly?" she said.

"He seems to think that it will tell him how to create a universe. But I don't think that's all of it."

Not even part of it, I suspected. What had he said at the airport? He'd broken his mind on the book, trying to understand it. . . . Now I remembered: the rabbi's work had unlocked his mind, given him the gift of dreams. Yes, he'd even told me about it: he called it a scientific book, a work of natural philosophy. A museum, like Galileo's book. It had apparently given him something he had always craved: the taste of an eidetic imagination. And the equations were somehow part of it, as they had been for János. Zunz had said that János possessed a cosmic soul, one as big as the universe; maybe, for Zunz, that kind of soul needed both equations and vision—the numbers along with the "inflaming."

Bringing the book close, Julie breathed in, eyelids fluttering. "It smells like . . ."

"Yes, vanilla. It's the degraded lignin in the paper."

"So the book *is* very old."

"Seems so. The problem is, it's got Schrödinger's equation, which is not that old."

"Then it was written in later. I don't see what the fuss is about." She began turning the pages carefully, curiously. "You can't really believe that a book can tell you how to create a universe?"

"Well, the Talmeeds think so."

"And this Jaëlle—does she think so?"

"Maybe. I just know she wants the book badly. There's a story there."

"A story," echoed Julie. "And what was the story between Jaëlle and Saoirse?"

"No idea, but I'm quite sure they were close. Very close."

Julie brushed some crumbs off the table. "Tavish, you said that Jaëlle had the *aura* of Saoirse."

"I meant that she *was* Saoirse, but in a different body. I know you think that's crazy."

"I did, until . . . I remembered a case."

"A case?"

She studied the scotch inside her chipped mug. "It was

before I met Pierre. I knew about it because I was working on the hospital floor where it happened. A fourteen-year-old girl had been in a car accident and was in a vegetative state. She had a sister, Rosa, two years older. Rosa was totally *accablée*—how is that in English?"

"Devastated."

"*Worse* than devastated. And Rosa started to do the things that her sister had done—things of habitude. Swimming, for example. She wasn't a swimmer, really, but her sister loved it, and Rosa started going to the pool every day. And after some time, she even started to wear her hair like her sister, and speak the same way, and such things. And when her sister died. . . ."

I wanted to tell her that I knew all about this phenomenon: the Kabbalists had spoken of an *ibbur*, a benign spirit that takes possession of a living person because it misses life so much, because it has so much left to accomplish . . . and the two souls become one, an interblent being, heartwood and sapwood of a single tree.

"When Rosa went to the pool," Julie continued, "she wouldn't wear *les lunettes* . . . the swimming glasses. She would come home with eyes red from the chlorine, and her mother would say, *chérie*, please wear the swimming glasses, but she wouldn't—because her sister never—"

Closing her eyes, she suddenly withdrew her hands from the table just as I reached for them. Her face was set against the onslaught of tears. Looking at her, I relived the emptiness for a moment, the killing nullity, that had engulfed us when Saoirse died. Like a bloody pulp, it settled into our bones, became the marrow of our days. Maybe Jaëlle had felt it as deeply as us, except that she—or her unconscious—couldn't let Saoirse go. *Alive*, said her tattoo.

We sipped our scotch and the silence overtook us again. The wind moved, a grieving emptiness, in the pines. We'd been happy here, years ago. And then something slipped out of me, called forth by the wind.

"You know, I always wondered. . . . "

Julie put the book down, wary. Over her shoulder, I saw my own reflection in the picture window, hunched and bearded with week-old stubble.

"I always wondered if . . . you forgave me for the accident."

She shut her eyes briefly, and the candles flickered with her exhalation.

"I mean, if you *really* forgave me," I added.

She was looking severely at the mug of scotch in her hand, as if it had made the remark. "I can't believe you have to ask that, Tavish."

"Sorry."

"It was not a matter of forgiving you because—I want you to put that right out your mind."

"Yes. The question is . . . "

She sighed. "What? There's always a question with you."

"I just sometimes wonder—I know it's crazy—if Saoirse forgives me."

The candle flickered again.

"And even crazier," I continued, "I've been thinking that maybe Jaëlle can tell me. I think she can."

Julie got up, swept our mugs off the table and went to the kitchen counter. I heard the clink of the dishes against the enamel dish tub. Then she came back and stood behind me, her hands resting lightly on my shoulders, and we both looked at our faces nested in the reflected candle glow.

"Nobody needs to forgive you for anything, Tavish," she said. "Saoirse would tell you that if she were here. She would keep telling you that for the rest of your life, if necessary. But maybe you can listen to her now."

"Yes."

I felt one hand leave my shoulder; she turned to nod toward the entrance. "You take the bedroom. I'll sleep there."

She was pointing to the narrow bunk beside the door—Saoirse's bed. I got to my feet.

"No, the mattress in the bedroom is in better shape," I said. "I'll be fine in Saoirse's bunk."

*   *   *

I *wasn't* fine. But I think I'd been under duress for so long that eventually my body succumbed to sleep, taking my overwrought mind with it. And at one point I found myself again inside the great house of Rabbi Emeth, the book transformed into a mansion, with ornate shadows and oaken doors and lighted menorahs sunk in the walls. I could see echoes of Hebrew letters everywhere, in the cornices above the windows, in the panels of the doors, in the upswept forms of the menorahs. I was trying a locked door, rattling the handle, when I saw at the end of the corridor something glimmering. I began running toward it, my footsteps echoing in the gloom. But it wasn't Saoirse; it was Hans Kovag, the street sweeper.

I stopped short, bewildered. He was strangely translucent, like one of those filmy deep sea creatures with their brightly colored internal organs. What are *you* doing here? I said irritably. Saoirse is here, somewhere. Help me find her. But he didn't seem to hear; as usual, he was wearing his headphones.

I woke up still angry, still seeing Kovag's squat, diaphanous form in my head. A sliver of morning showed on the floor, shining through a gap in the curtains. Julie, dressed, was sitting at the table, her face still. Before her was a book—*On a marché sur la Lune.* One of Saoirse's Tin-Tin books. I sat down opposite Julie while she turned the pages mechanically.

"I have to go, Tavish," she said, looking up. "Are you coming or staying?"

"I told Jaëlle I'd be here and . . . I just have to be here. Listen, Julie . . ."

I knew it wasn't the best time, with Saoirse's book lying dusty and mildewed on the table, but it was now or never.

"I look around here," I said, "and I think about what's happened to me in the last twelve years."

"Tavish—"

"Please just listen. My horizons have shrunk to nothing. Just imagining the big things has been totally beyond me. But since all this craziness began, I've started thinking about the big things again."

I could see the tiny lower lashes of her eyes, as sparse and delicate as the hairs on arctic flowers.

"What big things?" she said.

"The big-horizon things, the . . . really big things." I hoped she would know what I was talking about. "In the Islamic tradition, they talk about an angel so big that it takes a bird seven hundred years to fly between his earlobe and shoulder. *That's* how big I'm thinking."

"This pilgrimage did that for you?"

No, *you* did that for me. I didn't say it because of the turmoil in her eyes, but I think she got the message because she stood up.

"Please stay," I said. "Just for coffee."

"We don't have any, Tavish."

"We'll go over to Herman's. I have to call Cléance anyway."

When she looked away, I added, "He'll want to see you."

"All right," she said unhappily, "but I want *you* to tell him that I can't stay. Otherwise he'll want to talk all morning. Yes?"

"Okay."

"And let's take the car. I'll leave from Herman's place."

* * *

"Cléance."

"Tavish, our long-lost pilgrim! Are you all right?"

"Yes, yes. That story about me getting shot was just a story. As you suspected."

"Where are you now? No, don't tell me. I hope you're using old technology for this call."

"*Very* old," I said, looking around Herman's kitchen. I was pretty sure he saved any new technology for his star-listening rig.

"Listen, Cléance," I said, "I have the book."

In the silence I could hear Julie and Herman talking on the veranda. The old guy was still with it. Still tending his garden, still making cassis from black currants and honey, still listening to the stars. I could see his rig from where I sat: cables, amplifiers, and an array of photoelectric cells, all sitting on a small trailer inside his garage. On clear nights, he would wheel it out onto his lawn, set up his telescope ,and plug in all the extension cords. And yes, he had a bigger, shinier telescope. In his old age, he was reaching out farther into the universe.

"I'm keeping the book for Jaëlle," I continued.

I heard her say something to somebody, presumably Aaron or Benesh.

"I know she caused us a lot of trouble," I continued, "but I found out that she is a descendant of Rabbi Emeth. Actually, it was Zarandok who—"

"Tavish," said Cléance, "Jaëlle is *not* a descendant of Rabbi Emeth."

"What?"

"Yes. Aaron can tell you all about it."

"But that can't be. Zarandok told me—"

"Zarandok rarely knows what he's talking about. You should know that by now. Yes, there were probably descendants of the rabbi in the Bern and Zurich cantons, but they couldn't have been Jaëlle's family. Let me pass you over to Aaron."

I was staring at the only picture in Herman's kitchen— of an old ski jump that they'd torn down years ago. Jaëlle *wasn't* a descendant of the rabbi? So what was her claim to the book?

Aaron said, "*Shalom*, Tavish!"

"Aaron, my friend. So glad to hear your voice. Tell me about your genealogical research."

"Glad to hear your voice, too, Tavish. It seems that Jaëlle and her mother come from a rabbinical family—but not from Spain. From Ukraine."

"You're sure of this?"

"Pretty sure. Orthodox communities keep surprisingly good genealogical records—it's part of their identity."

"But is there a descendant of the rabbi in the area?"

"Well, there are references to descendants, yes. We need to do more research."

"We sure do. I heard a crazy story that only descendants of the rabbi can understand his book."

"Where did you get this crazy story?"

"From Zarandok . . . who says he got it out of Paracelsus."

"I think he got it from his own wobbly brain."

"But do we know *anything* of the rabbi's family history?"

"Well, it's mainly . . . crazy stories. But we don't have time to look into that now, Tavish. Listen, what happened to you in Bern?"

I tried to free myself, not for the first time, from my entangling doubts about Jaëlle.

"A lot of stuff I'd rather forget," I said. "I can tell you one thing: Zunz is a madman."

"A madman with money. He bought Dassvanger."

I was wondering if Jaëlle had originally been among the people he'd bought. Somehow I doubted it. But he had some hold on her; he had forced her to go along with the kidnapping scheme.

"Zunz told me he'd survived several poisoning attempts," I said. "Was that just another invention?"

"Who knows? But we learned that he ran a cybersecurity firm—he had contracts in some important places. It could be that he, not Kodaly, was the first target of the Russians."

"Who then found out about the book."

"Maybe."

Phone in hand, I got to my feet to look out the window. According to Zarandok, Zunz had betrayed Kodaly to the Russians. Was that true? If so, had he done it just to save his own life, or—

"Anyway, you have the book now," said Aaron.

I hesitated. "Yes."

"We'd really like to see it, Tavish." When nothing was forthcoming from me, he said easily, "But all in good time. The place where you're at now—you're sure it's safe?"

"For a while, anyway."

I heard Julie laugh from the veranda. So many things I still wanted to say to her—would I get the chance?

"Listen, Aaron," I said, "did we ever hear what happened to Kovag?"

"He disappeared after Dassvanger arrested him."

"Ludi thinks he's dead. Remember Ludi, his half-brother? He tracked me down in Zurich."

"Hmm . . . Maybe Ludi knows something we don't. All we know is that Kovag disappeared after the police took him."

"We absolutely have to find out more about him, Aaron."

"Well, Benesh is the one who knows the most, but he has gone off on his own somewhere."

"What? This is no time to do that."

"I agree, but that's Benesh. He's done it before." I heard him exchange words with Cléance. "Listen, we don't want to talk too long," he continued. "Can we contact you at this number again?"

"Yes, Herman can get a message to me."

"Good. Because we've decided to go to the police."

"I can definitely get behind you on that one."

"The Swiss Intelligence Service. No cantonal police—
we've learned our lesson." There was a pause. "Hold on for
a bit longer, Tavish. I think you will have help very soon—
maybe tomorrow. And we'd really like to see that book before we have to give it to the government."

*   *   *

Julie was as good as her word. I had the second part of my
"thinking big" speech ready, but I never got the chance to
deliver it. While Herman was in his kitchen making more
toast, I told her what Aaron had said about the police; she
nodded, kissed me on each cheek, and called out to Herman that she really had to get going. When he came out,
looking bereft, she kissed him, too. From the kitchen window, we watched her drive down his little dirt lane which,
after two kilometers of bumps and the swishing of long
grass on the undercarriage, would take her to the main road.

That's how big I'm thinking now, Julie.

But there was nothing to do except borrow Herman's
splitting maul (I knew I'd need to keep busy) and go back
to the *maiensäss*, where I chopped some wood and made a
fire. It was when I sat down to clean one of the lamp globes
that I noticed the Tin-Tin book that Julie had found. On
the cover, Tin-Tin and Captain Haddock, in orange space
suits and bubble helmets, stood in the middle of a moon-
scape, gazing in wonder at a 1950s-style rocket ship. Even
the dog, what's his name, wore a bubble helmet. Milou:
that was it. In Saoirse's English Tin-Tin books, the dog
was Snowy; in the French ones, Milou. And when she got
a dog on her tenth birthday—

No. Go outside.

Down at the brook, I washed my hands and face and stood looking out at the mountains, letting the breeze dry my skin. Would Jaëlle even come? What if the police came before her? And what if I had to spend another night here, my mind alive as a cave of bats? I just had to keep busy. Starting now. The book . . . with full sunlight outside, I wanted to take a *very* good look at it.

Behind the *maiensäss*, in a swath of brocaded green light under a big oak, I took a seat at our weathered picnic table and began carefully turning the pages. First, the ink. It looked to be the same earth-dark shade everywhere, but iron gall ink is deceptive: without experts and their instruments, I had no way of determining if it was the same age throughout. Next, the equations. They didn't look as though they'd been scribbled in centuries after the text had been composed. Each occupied its own space on the page. None had been squeezed in between lines of Aramaic. The ink was the same purple-dark color as the text. The equations actually seemed to be in slightly worse shape than the writing, with more haloing and discoloration, and I couldn't tell if numbers and text had been written by the same hand.

And yes, the blank spaces were a puzzle. Some of them were quite large, almost half a page. The traditional breaks in Torah scrolls were nothing like this. Had the author intended to come back to fill in the spaces? He might have roughed out his thoughts and equations elsewhere and only put them in when complete. Didn't Michelangelo or somebody do that?

I had gone through every page of the book and was working my way backward when a line caught my eye.

I labor with the generations past and to come, with the seers of all ages. . . .

"Tavish," called a voice.

Benesh in his sunglasses was standing twenty meters away at the top of the rise, beside the *maiensäss.*

"Benesh! For God's sake."

He had already begun walking toward me down the incline, tapping the pebbly trail with his cane.

"Where on earth did *you* come from?" I said.

"Herman Vonn's place. I followed the smell of your woodsmoke."

I guided him around the chopping block to the picnic table. He set his daypack down and got out a water bottle.

"Nice," he said, as if he could take in the view.

"Please don't tell me you drove to Herman's in your car."

"No, I left the car for Aaron. I came by tractor."

"*Tractor?*"

"I got a bus to Renz, and then a local farmer gave me a ride from there. He didn't let me sit up front with him, though. I had to stay in the wagon."

"People are always spoiling your fun, Benesh. But how did you know I'd be here?"

"You told me about this place."

"I did?"

"In Bern, remember? You said Herman Vonn was your neighbor. I called him last night." Maybe he picked up on my dismay, for he added, "He didn't tell me anything I didn't already know. But I thought there was a good chance you might be here."

"But if you can find us, then Zunz can."

"Zunz is not part of the star-listening brotherhood." He

took a sip from his water bottle. "Are you here alone?"

"I am now."

Even with Julie gone, I was still trying to think big—I knew it meant my survival. Looking at Benesh, I remembered our conversation at the Zytglogge: here was a guy who'd fought hard to keep thinking big. And I figured I'd need his help, because now I had to think big enough to accommodate Julie—her world, her life, her decisions.

"Benesh," I said, "you need to call Aaron and Cléance. They're worried about you."

"They worry about me and I worry about them. And we *all* worry about you, Tavish."

"Well, I've survived so far. And I have something to show for all my trouble."

I touched his left hand with the book, and he opened his palm. Once he had it in both hands he turned it over, tracing a finger down the back cover and then lightly feeling his way down the spine. Finally, he held it to his nose.

"I never thought I'd actually have it in my hands," he said with a smile.

"I'm just going to move your water bottle away from it."

He laid the book on his open palm, to keep it off the surface of the picnic table, and put his other hand on it— like a witness about to swear on the Bible. "I wish I could see the equations," he said.

"I'll describe them for you and we'll write them out. We'll figure it out together, Benesh."

"Does it look genuine to you, Tavish?"

"Well, it's definitely old. And all of a piece—no quires added later."

"And the equations?"

"They don't look interpolated in. But there *is* something strange about the book itself."

"Yes?"

"Every few pages, there is a blank space after a section of text. At first I thought the spaces might be something like the traditional breaks in Torah scrolls, but these are much bigger. You could fit ten lines into some of them. I'm wondering if the author deliberately left spaces so he could come back and fill them in later."

"Fill them in with equations?"

"Maybe. Maybe he had other notebooks where he roughed out stuff. Like Michelangelo."

Benesh removed his hand from the book but kept his fingers close, as if he could feel its presence. "You know, both Aaron and Cléance think this book is a holy miracle. What if it's not?"

"But how can you explain it?" I said. "I mean, it's strange enough to find a twentieth-century equation in a sixteenth-century book, but you said that at least one of these equations describes *unknown* physics. How on earth could—"

Just then, he held up a hand and turned toward the cabin.

"What is it?" I said in a low voice.

"I heard something," he whispered.

He picked up his cane and turned around on his seat, and we both sat motionless for a full minute. Behind us came the sound of the brook, still vehement with meltwater. I got to my feet.

"Stay here," I whispered.

"I better come with you."

"*No*, Benesh."

On my way toward the cabin, I paused to pick up the splitting maul from beside the chopping block.

I went around to the front door and up the steps, and paused to listen for another full minute. Nothing. Maybe Benesh had heard a squirrel—they still considered the cabin their home. I stepped onto the porch, trying to avoid the plank that squeaked, and nudged open the door.

Jaëlle was sitting at the table, the Tin-Tin book open in front of her, her eyes red from crying.

TWENTY-ONE

I got the impression that a whole lifetime had gone by since we'd parted. Her face could have been dead tissue, her eyes seemed to have ash suspended in them. Once she had looked as if she could handle fire or flood or any kind of transformation; now, wan and puffy-eyed, she was a woman made relic by loss.

"You must be more careful, Tavish," she said dully. "Zunz could have just walked up and shot you."

I saw her knapsack in the corner and presumed that she still had Dassvanger's pistol somewhere. She closed the book and sat looking around the room.

"So this is the *maiensäss*," she said.

I put the splitting maul down beside the door. Behind me I heard Benesh's cane on the porch; not surprisingly, he hadn't stayed put. I opened the door for him, and Jaëlle looked up listlessly.

"I know you," she said.

He stood at the threshold, familiarizing himself with the contours of the room and of her voice. "I know *you*," he said.

"This is Benesh," I said. "You stole his life's work from him, remember?"

Having apparently lost interest in the conversation, she turned around on the bench, so she could look out the picture window.

"Saoirse told me about listening to the stars here," she said. "I found that so strange—the stars had voices."

"They *do* have voices," said Benesh.

Taking up her knapsack, she withdrew a well-stuffed file folder tied with an elastic band. "Here," she said, putting it on the table. "The work of your life."

I handed the folder to Benesh, who slipped it protectively under one arm.

"I figured it out," said Jaëlle, indicating the folder. "Most of it, anyway."

"Figured *what* out?" I said.

"The book. The equations." She waved a hand and returned her gaze to the room. "Listening to the stars. That's when she decided to be an astrophysicist."

A binary star system—looking at it from Earth, you saw only one star, and yet it was actually two stars held together by gravity. Two bodies, one self . . . astrophysically speaking. I was feeling my way with great trepidation into Saoirse's *actual* life.

"Why didn't you tell me you two had been friends?" I said. "I would have helped you."

She avoided my eyes. "Saoirse would never have approved of what I was doing, Tavish. Anyway, Zunz was listening all the time, and—"

"But why did you go along with him? You basically did everything he asked."

She turned her desiccated gaze on me. "He knew where my mother was. He said he could either help her, or . . ."

"You *used* me, Jaëlle." I glanced at Benesh for support, but he just stood silent near the door. "You pretended to be Saoirse."

"I didn't *have* to pretend, Tavish. Don't you understand?" She took off her glasses and, eyes closed, touched one lid lightly, as if the images in her head were too fragile to be disturbed. "The first time you and I talked on the street," she continued. "You were looking at my books—remember? And you said I reminded you of your daughter. That's when I *understood*." She wiped her eyes. "And Zunz learned about it later because he was recording our conversations. The kidnapping was *his* idea, Tavish."

A long silence followed. Still holding the folder, Benesh took a few steps forward. In my distraction I forgot to warn him about the table; he bumped against it lightly and, setting down the folder, took a seat.

"What did you mean, Jaëlle," he said, "that you've figured it all out?"

She turned to look out the window again. "It doesn't matter now."

"It does to me." Benesh tapped the folder. "You know where the equations came from?"

She shifted, restless, her eyes fluid-dark and sad. *I didn't have to pretend.* But she sure had pretended to be Kodaly's daughter. A bit of minor universe building on Zunz's part, maybe. But she probably hadn't had to pretend much there, either: the book had drawn them both like a magnet.

She reached over to her knapsack and, removing a photo, laid it on the table.

"There," she said.

I peered over Benesh's shoulder at the photo. I knew it at once: the Bulcher photo from the Unterer Friesenberg cemetery, which showed Erwin Schrödinger and (supposedly) the Rabbi of the Twelve Winds.

"What are we looking at?" said Benesh.

"It's a famous photo from the old Jewish graveyard in Zurich," I said. "Erwin Schrödinger is in it, and someone who—okay, so this guy is *not* the Rabbi of the Twelve Winds. Who is it?"

"My great-grandfather," said Jaëlle.

The remains of the fire shifted in the grate, and we heard the wind spiriting in the pines outside.

"An Orthodox Jew named Edvard Lem," she continued. "A rabbinical student, but also a student of Erwin Schrödinger."

"You're kidding."

"Schrödinger said once that if Edvard Lem had lived, he would have been one of the greatest physicists in history. But he died of typhoid in 1929."

"And what was his connection to the Rabbi of the Twelve Winds?" said Benesh.

"Intergenerational collaborator, you could say."

"I don't understand," I said.

She hunched over the photo. "I think Edvard Lem believed that he and the rabbi were spiritually connected, that they shared the same . . . *racine de l'âme*, what is that? Soul root, yes. He wanted to find out everything he could about his soul root, Rabbi Emeth. His researches took him to the Zurich printshop of the man Lavichet."

"*Our* Lavichet," said Benesh.

"The righteous gentile, yes. He had employed Rabbi Emeth as a scribe and probably sheltered him at his printshop for years. The shop, it was destroyed in 1924. But Edvard Lem found a coffer with objects that once belonged to the rabbi—a prayer shawl, phylacteries, a quill pen, and ink . . . and a bound handwritten book."

"*The Celestial Gate*," said Benesh.

"The only version existing," said Jaëlle.

"I think I'm beginning to understand," said Benesh.

"You are?" I said.

"My mother knew the whole story, once," put in Jaëlle. "But now . . ."

"Wait a minute," I said. "You're saying this guy Lem *added* those equations?"

"He was completing the vision of the book," said Jaëlle. "As Rabbi Emeth wanted."

I labor with the generations past and to come, with the seers of all ages. . . . I remembered the line from the book, and the blank spaces. The rabbi had deliberately left them for the illuminations of a distant age?

"But the numbers of reawakening," said Benesh. "They describe a physics that is completely unfamiliar to us."

Jaëlle nodded. "Yes, that's the part I can't figure out. But I will." She looked up at me. "Saoirse and I."

I stared at her. "What?"

She just swung her long legs over the seat of the table and got to her feet. When I moved close, she reached for her knapsack and set it defensively in front of her. Benesh, sensing her movement, had taken a firm hold of his life's work.

"Where is the book?" she said.

"Forget the book," I said heatedly. "You're not leaving until you tell me everything."

She hesitated. "Julie can tell you everything, Tavish."

Benesh had turned his body slightly toward me, listening for the way I took this in.

"What are you talking about?" I said.

"I spoke to her."

"You *spoke* to her?"

Something seemed to have changed in Jaëlle; her face seemed to hold small sanctuaries of light and shadow. "I have been watching the lane all day," she said, "and I saw her drive away. I waved her down at the little bridge, and . . ."

"And what?"

"We talked."

I stood still, marooned in the sunlight.

"Talked about what?" I said.

"About everything. About Saoirse, mainly. Julie will tell you." She looked away. "I must go; my mother needs me."

Benesh got to his feet. "Tavish, let's go to Herman's and call Aaron."

"Sit down, both of you," I said. "Nobody's going anywhere until—"

At that moment, from the direction of Herman's house, we heard gunshots. A flurry of them.

I was out the door before either of them moved. Down the steps, around the cabin, along the brookside trail. Glitter of water beside me, the soft earth under my feet. I was pretty sure Jaëlle was at my heels initially, but then I left her behind. I knew this country well, knew where the trail disappeared, knew where you had to enter the thick stand of spruce to pick it up again. I made my way through tree shadows that thickened as I moved. All I could think of was Julie. Had she gotten away safely? What if Zunz had been here all the time, *waiting*? The gunshots had come from beyond Herman's place, where the ground rose into the foothills. I tried to orient myself as I went, but I was fighting a haze of panic like charged plasma in my head.

I scurried along keeping low until, feeling I was going to be sick, I stopped beside a big pine tree. At first I crouched down, but that made my windedness worse, so I half-straightened, bent like an old man, one hand on the tree. The forest was absolutely silent. I panted at the ground, trying to modulate each breath. Now, finally, I was able to orient myself. I remembered an outcrop farther up that would give me a good view of the countryside. No—go straight to Herman's. Call the police. But could the shots have been a farmer hunting? I breathed laboriously for a full minute. The outcrop, okay. I could see everything from there.

With my eyes on the rising ground ahead, I almost stumbled over something on the trail. A log—no—

A man lay on his back, looking at the sky with eyes ice-clear and abyssal. A big man, bearded. . . . It took me several seconds to recognize Ludi, the neo-Nazi doorman.

He seemed frozen in the act of drawing a breath, lips parted, eyes staring. I felt the carotid artery: nothing. A length of his jacket zipper had been split open, and the area underneath was dark with blood. I felt his wrist—again, nothing. I didn't want to look inside his jacket so I pointlessly felt his bull neck once more.

Stillness. Everywhere stillness.

I stayed in a crouch, listening. Was Jaëlle still behind me somewhere? I couldn't hear any sounds of pursuit. Realizing I was vulnerable where I was, I darted off the trail into the trees. Julie was gone, right? I saw her drive off. . . . I moved further away from the trail, trying not to rustle the leaves and bracken. And Herman . . . had he heard the shots and gone outside to investigate? Was he also now lying on the ground, staring at the sky?

I moved down a rise: there was no trail, just roots, and bracken, and rock shelves. Herman's place was off to the left somewhere. At the bottom of the rise I'd be able to find the trail. I slid into a gully and then pulled myself up by the thick, prehensile roots of a hemlock. A trail opened up under my feet. I had no idea where I was. Okay, yes, Herman's house was over there, a few hundred meters away.

I hadn't gone more than twenty paces when I instinctively left the trail once more. The trees thinned out but still provided cover. I got close enough to Herman's place to see his old split-rail fence and his front yard lean-to, where he parked his stargazing rig before setting it up on the lawn. Very faintly I could hear the clucking of his chickens from the backyard. Nothing seemed amiss.

I stole up to his house in two frenetic sorties—first to his pickup, then to the kitchen window. Standing flat against the stuccoed side of the house, I scanned the yard. Stillness again. I ducked under the window and got up onto the front porch to look in. The kitchen was empty. I felt exposed there, so I nudged open the front door as quietly as I could.

Silence met me, an uneasy silence. I could hear the sound of a clock from deeper in the house. Herman had only one phone, in his living room. I moved across the kitchen to the threshold and there stood still.

Herman sat rigid in an armchair, his bony hands gripping the chair arms. Across from him, Zunz slumped on the sofa, a pistol resting in his lap. His half-lidded eyes took me in, blinked, struggled to focus. I could see blood on his polo shirt, blood on his shoes, blood on his hands and forearms where I guessed he'd been holding his stomach.

"What happened?" I said.

Herman looked too terrified to speak. Zunz moved his lips, and his gun hand twitched. The phone was on the table at the other end of the sofa; to get to it, I had to go past him.

"Tavish," he breathed.

"Who shot you?"

"There's someone out there," whispered Herman, his eyes darting to the window.

"You need an ambulance," I said to Zunz, and moved into the room. Gritting his teeth, he willed himself to sit up; the pistol had shifted so that it was pointing more or less at me.

"The book," he said.

"I don't have it."

"Where . . . ?"

"The *maiensäss*."

He took this in with difficulty and blinked. "Let's go."

"No. You need an ambulance."

He raised the pistol so that it pointed at Herman. The old man closed his eyes.

"I'll kill him first," said Zunz laboriously. "Then . . ."

"All right," I said. "Yes. I'll take you to the maiensäss."

Zunz closed his eyes again. Someone out there. . . . Did Herman mean Ludi? With great difficulty Zunz sat up and looked curiously at the pistol in his lap, as if seeing it for the first time. I wondered if he and Ludi, both armed, had come across one another in the forest. Now one was dead, the other clearly near death. And where was Dassvanger?

Herman watched Zunz with his face slightly averted, as if expecting a blow.

"You can't walk, Jakob," I said.

He half stood up, slowly, and then sat down again. His body mimicked a weak cough—eyes closing, chest caving, torso hunching forward—but no sound came from his open lips. Then something in him rallied, and he pulled himself to his feet, swayed, and stumbled toward me. I put out my hands, but he stopped three feet away and raised the pistol.

"Go," he said.

At the front door, he tottered closer to me, and I felt the gun in the small of my back. We moved out onto the front porch, and he put a hand on my shoulder to go down the steps. He sagged like a man re-experiencing gravity after a long absence. Everything about him—an undone shoelace, a drooping eyelid, a spiderweb of spittle on his lower lip— seemed to press him to the earth. I'm sure I could have grabbed the gun then, but I just kept going with his hand on my shoulder.

We got barely halfway across the lawn, to the lean-to that housed Herman's star-listening rig. It was all set up—with clear skies forecast, I guess he'd been planning to spend the evening there. I felt the gun leave my back, and turned to see Zunz lower himself heavily into one of the lawn chairs near the lean-to. I thought for a moment that he'd knocked himself unconscious. He lay with his eyes closed, head lolling. I cast my eye around the woods. *Someone else out there.* Did Herman mean Ludi, or—?

Zunz opened his eyes and tried to say something. I came closer.

"I can see. . . . " he whispered.

"What do you see, Jakob?"

He closed his eyes again. Coming close, I smelled something wet and dark—like rotting leaves, except putrid—and I involuntarily backed away, my gorge rising. He opened his eyes.

"The book," he breathed.

"Yes. We'll get it."

I knelt down beside him. His pockmarked face was badly mottled. I vaguely remembered the Ukrainian leader who had been poisoned—dioxin, was it? Though he had survived, his face was scarred for life. . . .

Zunz suddenly opened his eyes wide. "János!"

He said the name desperately, plaintively, as if calling out to his brother.

That's when I heard a noise from the bushes. As I turned, a spark went through my body, something like a spark, shattering and fast. It entered my lower back and then opened up inside me, a dark moth spreading its lacerating wings. Everything around me slowed, becoming gray and blurred, like images in an ultrasound. I heard the horn of the semi, very close, and I spun the steering wheel desperately, because the blare of the horn came from Saoirse's side; but I couldn't avoid the propulsive smash, the rending of metal, the flying glass. . . .

Lying on the lawn, I climbed high into the sky and back in time, back to when we were a family.

TWENTY-TWO

The world changed around me, becoming white and sterile. I drifted awake, and slept, and drifted awake again. At one point I noticed people sitting beside my bed. A tall dark-skinned man, a tiny bright-eyed woman and a red-haired man in a wheelchair.

We were wrong, Tavish.

A soft light overhead. White ceiling tiles with orderly rows of tiny dots. I tried to focus on the people, their faces. Was it the small woman who had spoken?

The miracle was not the book.

Where was Julie? I wanted to ask them, but my tongue felt old. Swallow. The words were in there somewhere. Swallow again. What miracle?

. . . Kovag . . .

Everything was white, white tiles and white sheets. I was still looking at the orderly rows of dots overhead, but the pattern had shifted, like sand grains rearranged by the wind. It was a different ceiling. I'd changed rooms . . . or hospitals.

"Tavish, are you awake?" said Julie.

Yes.

"Don't sit up," she said.

Yes, I'm awake. I realized the words were still in my head and made an effort to get them out.

"Julie."

"How are you feeling?" she said.

I closed my eyes. I had been lying on the lawn and then I was climbing high in the sky, above the jet stream—I had felt the wind as I passed through it—and I was going *back*—

"You've had many visitors," she said. Her blouse was sun-foliate, a collage of bright colors against the white, but I could see the strain, the rawness, around her eyes.

"Cléance. . . ." I said.

"Yes, they were all here—even Zarandok, briefly. But now they're on the pilgrimage route."

"What?"

"They're trying to find this man Kovag."

It took a moment for this to register. "Kovag? He's dead."

"That's what everybody thought, but I guess he didn't die. He's on the pilgrimage route, walking . . . slowly. To the end of the world, Cléance says."

Alive. *Alive?* And Ludi . . . he never knew it. I'm sure he went to Maiensäss Ana to find Dassvanger, seeking revenge, but then ran into Zunz. And the only one who survived it all was Dassvanger, that prick.

I must have said it aloud because Julie said, "Jaëlle shot him right after he shot you."

"Is she . . . ?"

"She was gone when the police arrived. As for Dassvanger—he will probably recover for his trial, sadly." After a pause she added, "Zunz never recovered."

I could see him clearly, his gaze an emulsion of pain. He had craved Kodaly's vision, yes, but was it out of ambition, or guilt? Did he want it for himself, or to realize it for the friend he had betrayed?

"And . . . the book?" I said.

"Gone, too. Benesh doesn't know what happened to it."

Jaëlle. Something told me I'd never see her again. I wanted to climb into the sky again and follow the jet stream back, but Julie was leaning forward, her face anxious.

"Tavish, do you remember that the doctors asked if you have feeling below your injury?"

"Did they?"

"You said yes." Her eyes searched my face. "Do you still have feeling?"

I was looking out the window by my bedside—it must have been another day—and I saw something fluttering. A winged seed, 'coptering down from the heights, falling helically, undoing an invisible braid in the air. Set adrift by a fluke of wind . . . or maybe it had just happened in space, the way elementary particles happen. Or drifted in from another solar system, floating through interplanetary darkness like a snowflake. Odysseus in from the infernal regions. Indomitable, unyielding. *From baffling maladies he hath devised escapes. . . .*

Feeling. Does pain count as feeling?

"Listen to me, Tavish," Julie was saying. "Dassvanger put a bullet in your lower back, but to the side, away from—

From baffling maladies he hath devised escapes.

"Maybe he was rushed with the shot," she continued, "because he knew Jaëlle was there, and. . . . Anyway, you're going to be in a wheelchair for—"

"I'll join them," I said.

"What?"

"Cléance, and Benesh, and Aaron. I'll join them on the pilgrimage."

"Yes, but not now. You need to rest. Look, I have something for you."

What do you find on a pilgrimage? Angels, prophets . . . *ancestors.* That's why Kovag was on the pilgrimage route— to learn where his visions had come from.

"I found this on Saoirse's grave this morning," Julie said, reaching into her handbag.

She put something in my open palm, and my fingers closed around a worn, frayed edge. I brought it close to my nose and caught a faint note of vanilla.

"It was all wrapped up. . . ." Her voice caught.

Right where we'd find it.

The pages were as soft as a moth's wing, and my dream came back to me: the Hebrew letters fluttering off the page to become a great mansion, and I was walking through the empty corridors again, trying all the locked doors. . . . And then, unexpectedly, a door opened. She was there. From the threshold I could see her sitting at a desk, pencil in hand—sitting in the pose I know so well, hunched over, one forearm laid diagonally across her chest. Sunlight was streaming in through the window. Directly in front of her was a page bearing a single equation. No, not an equation . . . *the* equation. The numbers of reawakening. She sat very still, absorbed, universes billowing in her head—an explorer, a haunter of remote shores, a pilgrim of the upper world.

*   *   *

I was still climbing high into the sky and back in time—I felt as though I had been doing it forever, all my life and all my afterlife—but now I'm coming down among the late-evening stars, to grass and lawn chairs and lemonade, to a summer's night in Herman's front yard. Saoirse is sitting in one of the lawn chairs, wearing the big headphones, looking up at the sky. Herman is watching his monitor, alert to the green flickers and pulses, the aural signatures of stars and planets. Julie is sitting across from me drinking lemonade. Saoirse takes off the headphones.

They all have different voices, she says.

That's right, says Herman, pleased. Different intensities of light, different distances.

Venus sounds like a rustling wind, continues Saoirse. Or wind blowing through old cornfields when they're all papery and withered.

Really? I say. (I tried the headphones earlier in the evening, but all I heard was static.)

And Alpha Centauri, Saoirse continues. . . . It's a hum, but a friendly hum. Like a bunch of people just standing around humming.

She looks into the sky for a moment and says: Does the whole universe make a sound, Herman?

Hmm, says Herman. I think you need a really big pair of headphones to answer that.

After a silence, Saoirse says: I'm going to ask the meteorite man. He'll know.

The meteorite man? says Julie.

The man at the camp. He helps us find micrometeorites.

Have we met this meteorite man? Julie asks.

No. He's shy. But he knows a lot.

As much as your old dad? I say.

More, Dad. Do you know an equation about the end of the universe?

Well, I did, but I've forgotten it.

An equation about the end of the universe? interjects Herman.

Yes. *And* the beginning.

The end and the beginning—in one equation?

It's that kind of equation.

Saoirse takes a sip of her lemonade and adds: But the meteorite man hasn't figured it out yet. He says some parts are . . . muddy.

Well, *chérie*, says Julie, maybe you can help him make it clear. You're good at equations.

Saoirse gazes up at the stars for a long moment and then puts the headphones back on.

Yes, she says, someday I will make it clear.

Acknowledgments

Aramaic seems like a beautiful and concise language, but I think I would have needed several lifetimes to learn it thoroughly. I therefore had to depend on the expertise of Judy Barrett, an independent Aramaic scholar and student of the Zohar. Sadly, Judy passed away before this novel was completed, but her help and enthusiasm in the early stages of the project meant a great deal to me. Of course, she cannot be held responsible for any errors in the book.

I've tried generally to respect the geography of the Swiss pilgrimage routes, though I did make up a few things. (For example, Baulmes Monastery no longer exists.) Thanks to Lisa Medd for walking part of the Jakobsweg with me in central Switzerland. Lisa also read and commented on the manuscript, as did Rell DeShaw, Jennifer Watson, and Patrick Dumais. Maeve Findlay-Shields did a superb job of editing and fact-checking. Penny Williams and Dianne Perrier did yeoman's service in the proofreading department.

The book that Saoirse reads from in chapter fourteen is Terence Dickinson's classic guide to stargazing, *NightWatch*. Saoirse is riffing on a passage in Dickinson's work that describes the expansion of the universe in terms of the time it takes to read a single sentence.

Finally, I am grateful to the folks at the University of New Orleans Press and Publishing Lab for helping make this novel the best it could possibly be.